EUROPE

Other books in the Current Controversies Series:

The AIDS Crisis
Drug Trafficking
Energy Alternatives
Gun Control
Iraq
Police Brutality
Sexual Harassment
Women in the Military
Youth Violence

EUROPE

David L. Bender, *Publisher*
Bruno Leone, *Executive Editor*

Bonnie Szumski, *Managing Editor*
Carol Wekesser, *Senior Editor*

Michael D. Biskup, *Book Editor*

RILEY-HICKINGBOTHAM LIBRARY
OUACHITA BAPTIST UNIVERSITY

No part of this book may be reproduced or used in any form or by any means, electrical, mechanical, or otherwise, including, but not limited to, photocopy, recording, or any information storage and retrieval system, without prior written permission from the publisher.

Cover photo by Impact Visuals.

Library of Congress Cataloging-in-Publication Data

Europe / Michael D. Biskup, Carol Wekesser, book editors.
   p. cm. — (Current controversies)
  Includes bibliographical references and index.
  Summary: Includes articles debating topics related to the current political and economic situation in Europe.
    ISBN 1-56510-024-7 (lib. : alk. paper) : — ISBN 1-56510-023-9 (pbk. : alk. paper):
  1. Europe—Politics and government—1989- —Juvenile literature.
2. Europe—Economic integration—Juvenile literature. 3. Europe—Foreign relations—1989- —Juvenile literature. [1. Europe—Politics and government—1989-   2. Europe—Economic integration.
3. Europe—Foreign relations—1989-]   I. Biskup, Michael D., 1956-
II. Wekesser, Carol, 1963-   III. Series
D2009.E853   1992
940.55'9—dc20   92-23066
                                                                   CIP
                                                                    AC

© Copyright 1992 by Greenhaven Press, Inc., PO Box 289009, San Diego, CA 92198-9009

Contents

Foreword   11

Introduction   13

Chapter 1: How Will European Unification Affect the World?

European Unification: An Overview *by Spyros G. Makridakis and Michelle Bainbridge*   17
> Efforts to unite Europe have been made for decades. Now, as this unification is finally beginning to take place, Europeans must weigh the costs of unification against the benefits.

European Unification Will Be Beneficial

European Unification Will Help Unify the World   24
by Giovanni Agnelli
> Europe has been torn by nationalism and ethnic strife for hundreds of years. European unification will bring an end to this conflict and will make Europe a world leader for peace.

European Unification Will Strengthen Europe   28
by Hans-Dietrich Genscher
> Although European economic, political, and military unification will not be easy to achieve, it will strengthen Europe by promoting economic progress and peace.

European Unification Can Provide Opportunities for American Business *by Daniel Burstein*   37
> The economic unification of Europe offers many American business opportunities. An increased involvement in Europe could strengthen the U.S. economy and improve America's competitiveness in the world market.

European Unification Can Serve as a Model for the Former Soviet Union *by Desmond Dinan*   46
> The Commonwealth of Independent States (CIS), once known as the Soviet Union, needs economic assistance and political guidance. The European Community, with its strong economy and successful unification, can act as a role model for the CIS.

Contents

European Unification Will Be Harmful

European Unification Will Weaken Europe *by Angelo Codevilla*   52
> European economic unification will simply result in increased government bureaucratization, which will prevent Europe's economies from thriving. European nations would be much stronger if they remained separate and free from excess government regulation.

European Unification Will Increase Regional Conflicts   57
by Thomas Molnar
> Europe has a history of national and ethnic conflicts. European unification is both unnecessary and harmful and will only exacerbate these regional conflicts.

European Unification Threatens U.S.-European Relations   63
by Robin Knight
> Now that the United States and Europe are no longer united by the common threat of a strong Soviet Union, their relationship is increasingly strained. European unification will only increase Europe's independence from the United States and exacerbate trade and security disputes between nations.

Chapter 2: How Is German Unification Affecting the World?

German Unification: An Overview *by Henrik Bering-Jensen*   69
> Unification has increased Germany's influence in Europe. Some believe that Germany's stronger economic and political clout will result in dominance of the European Community. Others, including many in the United States, see Germany's new assertiveness as beneficial to the EC.

German Unification Is Beneficial

German Unification Strengthens the European Community   77
by Peter Hort
> Germany has consistently taken the lead in helping establish the European Community. Unification made Germany larger and stronger and gave the EC an automatic link to Eastern Europe. In this way, German unification has helped strengthen the EC.

A United Germany Will Benefit Both Europe and the United States   82
by Robert Gerald Livingston
> German unification has allowed Germany to take on more of a leadership role in Europe. Poised between Eastern and Western Europe, Germany has become a powerful ally to both. Germany's spirit of cooperation with Europe also enhances its relationship with the United States and relieves the United States of some of the financial burden of strengthening Eastern Europe's economy.

German Unity Will Benefit the United States *by Elizabeth Pond*   90
> A united Germany's economic and political power can help the United States reduce its military expenses and enable it to work on its

own domestic problems. In addition, strong U.S.-German ties ensure
that the United States will continue to have political and economic influence in Europe.

Unification Will Strengthen Germany's Economy 96
by Jeffrey T. Bergner
Unification has positioned Germany to become one of the world's
greatest economic powers. With the labor force of the East and the
capital of the West, Germany will develop a strong economy.

German Unification Is Harmful

Unification Has Harmed Germany *by Amos Perlmutter* 102
German unification was premature. Rather than emanating from the
people, it was instigated by two overly ambitious men, the past German foreign minister, Hans-Dietrich Genscher and the present chancellor of Germany, Helmut Kohl. Unification has led to the political
and economic downfall of Western Germany by enabling Eastern
Germany's morally corrupt neo-Nazis to hold positions of power and
by forcing West Germany to take responsibility for the East's crumbling economy.

Unification Has Strained Relations Between East and West Germany 106
by Tyler Marshall
The economic, social, and political disparities between East and West
Germany have created a psychological barrier between these two regions. Unification has exacerbated tensions between them.

German Unification Has Harmed Women's Rights 115
by Women and Revolution
When Germany united, the western half imposed its laws and ideology on the eastern half. As a result, women in the former East Germany may lose the right to abortion and have their jobs and daycare
benefits threatened.

Chapter 3: Would Western Policies Benefit Eastern Europe?

Western Policies in Eastern Europe: An Overview 123
by Joel Havemann
The nations of Eastern Europe have attempted to establish Western
economic and political policies in the past few years. While some of
these policies have been successful, others have failed or have not
been fully implemented.

Yes: Western Policies Would Benefit Eastern Europe

Western Nations Can Help Eastern Europe Prosper 131
by Zbigniew Brzezinski
Eastern Europe will not be able to prosper without economic assistance from Western nations. Among other measures, the West should
relieve these nations of some of their foreign debt and should promote
economic cooperation in the region.

Contents

The West Can Help Strengthen Democracy in Eastern Europe   135
by Jan Zielonka
    After years of totalitarian rule, Eastern European nations are attempting to establish democracies. These nations need Western economic aid and political support if they are to succeed. Strong democracies in Eastern Europe will benefit the region and the West.

Capitalism Would Benefit Eastern Europe *by A.W. Clausen*   143
    Establishing capitalist market economies is essential if Eastern European nations are to thrive. These nations must immediately establish privatization and other free market reforms.

U.S. Aid Would Benefit Eastern Europe   152
by Lawrence S. Eagleburger
    Eastern European nations are struggling to establish democracies and strong economies. The United States can help by providing technical assistance, by expanding trade with the region, and by encouraging American companies to invest in Eastern Europe.

No: Western Policies Would Harm Eastern Europe

Western Policies Will Fail in Eastern Europe   160
by Thomas E. Weisskopf
    The West is encouraging Eastern European nations to rapidly establish privatization and other Western policies. These policies, however, will only create inequality in Eastern Europe and will fail to help the region prosper.

U.S. Aid Could Harm Eastern Europe *by Nicholas Eberstadt*   167
    Many analysts have argued that U.S. economic aid is essential for Eastern Europe to prosper. A close examination of U.S. aid to other nations, however, reveals that American assistance is often harmful and prevents nations from gaining economic independence.

Capitalism Will Harm Eastern Europe *by Cornelius Lehane*   176
    Capitalism is based upon greed and oppression. Forcing Eastern Europeans to accept capitalism will only increase inequality and economic hardship in the region.

Chapter 4: What Measures Would Strengthen Eastern European Economies?

Eastern European Economies: An Overview *by Carol J. Williams*   185
    Eastern European nations are in the midst of the difficult process of transforming their economies from communism to capitalism. The extent and success of the region's economic reforms vary from country to country.

Socialism Would Strengthen Eastern European Economies   190
by Tim Wohlforth
    Because many Eastern Europeans mistakenly confuse their discarded communist economies as socialist, they are rejecting all forms of socialism. Many socialist institutions, however—such as worker-owned factories—could benefit Eastern Europe's economies.

Privatization Would Strengthen Eastern European Economies 194
by Anne Applebaum
    To become prosperous, Eastern European nations must privatize their economies. This requires turning state-run companies over to private investors, a process that may be difficult but necessary.

Stable Currencies Would Improve Eastern European Economies 201
by Steve H. Hanke and Kurt Schuler
    Before Eastern Europe can thrive economically and become an integral part of world trade, its nations must establish stable, convertible currencies. Without such currencies, Eastern European nations will have no efficient way of trading their goods and services on the world market.

Joint Ventures with Western Businesses Would Improve Eastern Europe's Economies *by Eberhard von Koerber* 207
    Creating business ties between firms in the West and factories in the East will enable Eastern European nations to reform their economies more easily and more successfully. Such ties will also benefit Western businesses.

Helping Eastern Europeans Adopt Free Market Policies Would Improve Their Economies *by John Brademas* 212
    Eastern European nations were ruled by totalitarian governments for more than forty years. Consequently, most Eastern Europeans have little or no knowledge of how capitalism works. Americans must help educate and train Eastern Europeans in economics and free market policies.

Free Trade Unions Would Strengthen Eastern Europe's Economies 218
by Adrian Karatnycky
    Eastern Europeans are unaccustomed to free trade unions whose members can strike and make demands from the government and from companies. To thrive economically, Eastern European nations must establish such trade unions to provide workers with more of a voice in making economic and political policies.

Tax Reform Would Strengthen Eastern Europe's Economies 225
by William D. Eggers
    While income taxes in Eastern Europe have been low or nonexistent, taxes on private companies have been extremely high. These high corporate taxes and other taxes impede economic progress. Eastern European nations should reform their tax systems to spur economic growth.

Chapter 5: What Role Will International Organizations Play in Europe's Future?

Chapter Preface 234

International Organizations Will Benefit Europe

International Organizations Can Help Maintain Peace in Europe 236
by Uffe Ellemann-Jensen

Contents

The breakdown of communism in Eastern Europe and economic unification in Western Europe challenges Europeans to develop economic prosperity and political security for all of Europe. The North Atlantic Treaty Organization (NATO) and other organizations can work to unify and strengthen Europe, promote peace, and help integrate Eastern Europe into the European Community.

NATO Will Play an Essential Role in European Peace 242
by Richard Nixon
Although some analysts believe NATO is obsolete, the organization continues to play an important role in maintaining stability in Europe. NATO can help secure peace in Eastern Europe and protect Europe from aggression.

The Western European Union (WEU) Could Provide European Security *by Hugh De Santis* 249
As Europe grows in economic and political power, it will depend less and less on NATO for protection. The Western European Union (WEU), an alliance of European nations, can effectively replace NATO and protect Europe.

International Organizations Will Harm Europe

International Monetary Fund Policies Harm Eastern Europe 257
by Paul Hockenos
The International Monetary Fund, which has loaned money to Eastern European countries, has dictated that these countries adopt economic and political policies that have created unnecessary austerity. These IMF loans have created a form of oppression by driving the Eastern European countries into debts they cannot pay back.

The World Bank Encourages Regressive Socialist Economic Policies *by Melanie S. Tammen* 264
World Bank loans to Eastern Europe have been ineffective in establishing capitalism. Instead, the loans provide socialist governments with money to implement their own programs. Consequently, without private enterprises, Eastern European nations are unable to make enough money to pay off their debts.

NATO Is Unnecessary *by Doug Bandow* 268
NATO was created forty years ago to halt Soviet aggression. Once the Soviet Union initiated democratic reforms, this threat toward Western Europe disappeared. NATO has effectively completed its job. Now, it is an obsolete institution that no longer serves a vital purpose and that should be abolished.

Glossary of Acronyms 272
Bibliography 274
Organizations to Contact 277
Index 280

Foreword

By definition, controversies are "discussions of questions in which opposing opinions clash" (Webster's Twentieth Century Dictionary Unabridged). Few would deny that controversies are a pervasive part of the human condition and exist on virtually every level of human enterprise. Controversies transpire between individuals and among groups, within nations and between nations. Controversies supply the grist necessary for progress by providing challenges and challengers to the status quo. They also create atmospheres where strife and warfare can flourish. A world without controversies would be a peaceful world; but it also would be, by and large, static and prosaic.

The Series' Purpose

The purpose of the Current Controversies series is to explore many of the social, political, and economic controversies dominating the national and international scenes today. Titles selected for inclusion in the series are highly focused and specific. For example, from the larger category of criminal justice, Current Controversies deals with specific topics such as police brutality, gun control, white collar crime, and others. The debates in Current Controversies also are presented in a useful, timeless fashion. Articles and book excerpts included in each title are selected if they contribute valuable, long-range ideas to the overall debate. And wherever possible, current information is enhanced with historical documents and other relevant materials. Thus, while individual titles are current in focus, every effort is made to ensure that they will not become quickly outdated. Books in the Current Controversies series will remain important resources for librarians, teachers, and students for many years.

In addition to keeping the titles focused and specific, great care is taken in the editorial format of each book in the series. Book introductions and chapter prefaces are offered to provide background material for readers. Chapters are organized around several key questions that are answered with diverse opinions representing all points on the political spectrum. Materials in each chapter include opinions in which authors clearly disagree as well as alternative opinions in which authors may agree on a broader issue but disagree on the possible solutions. In this way, the content of each volume in Current Controversies mirrors the mosaic of opinions encountered in society. Readers will quickly realize that there are many viable answers to these complex issues. By questioning each author's conclusions, students and casual readers can begin to develop the critical thinking skills so important to evaluating opinionated material.

Current Controversies is also ideal for controlled research. Each anthology in the series is composed of primary sources taken from a wide gamut of informational categories including periodicals, newspapers, books, United States and foreign government documents, and the publications of private and public organizations. Readers will find factual support for reports, debates, and research papers covering all areas of important issues. In addition, an annotated table of contents, an index, a book and periodical bibliography, and a list of organizations to contact are included in each book to expedite further research.

Perhaps more than ever before in history, people are confronted with diverse and contradictory information. During the Persian Gulf War, for example, the public was not only treated to minute-to-minute coverage of the war, it was also inundated with critiques of the coverage and countless analyses of the factors motivating U.S. involvement. Being able to sort through the plethora of opinions accompanying today's major issues, and to draw one's own conclusions, can be a complicated and frustrating struggle. It is the editors' hope that Current Controversies will help readers with this struggle.

Introduction

For most of the five decades following World War II, Europe was distinctly divided into east and west. Eastern Europe, dominated by the Soviet Union, remained economically depressed, while Western Europe prospered. Although the Soviet Union had been allied with many of the countries of Western Europe as well as the United States during the war, the West remained suspicious of the intentions of the communists. This suspicion, coupled with the Soviet intervention and military takeover in Eastern Europe, encouraged Western Europe to band together to ensure the West's continuing political and economic independence and growth.

At first, several Western European countries formed a military alliance for joint security with the United States. They helped create and participated in such organizations as the United Nations and the North Atlantic Treaty Organization. Then some of the Western European nations began to see the advantages of working together economically as well. By pooling industrial resources and instituting mutually advantageous import and export regulations, they found they were better able to compete with larger economic powers such as the United States. To further these ends, six countries—West Germany, France, Italy, Belgium, the Netherlands, and

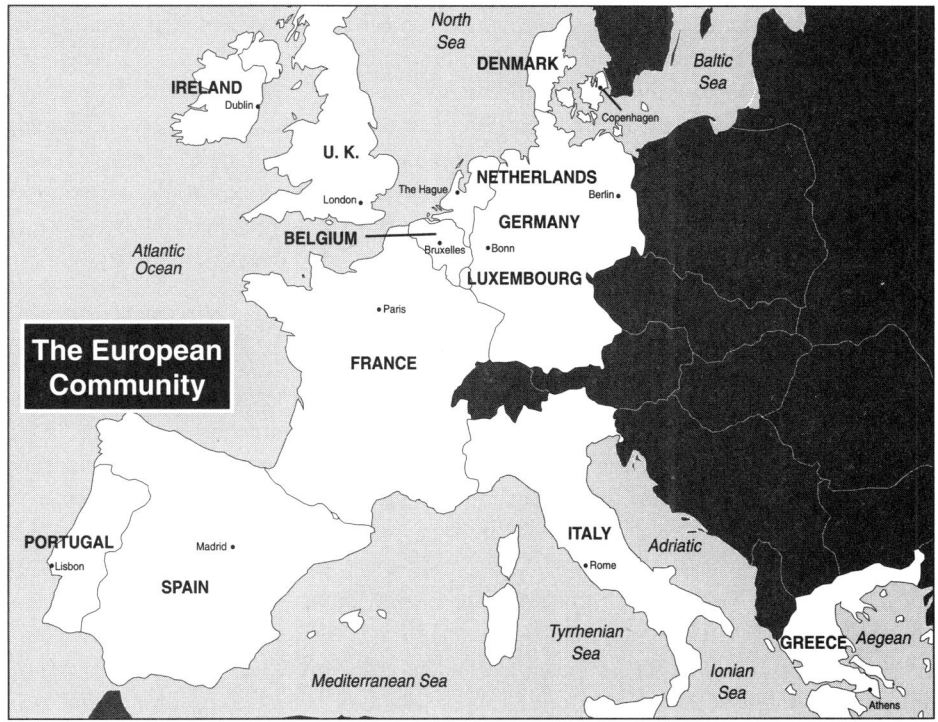

Introduction

Luxembourg—formed the European Coal and Steel Community (ECSC) in 1951. In 1958, these same six nations formed the European Economic Community (EEC), also known as the Common Market, to promote the gradual integration and growth of the Western European economies. By the mid-1980s six more nations—the United Kingdom, Ireland, Denmark, Greece, Spain, and Portugal—had joined the EEC.

Pleased for the most part with the success of their economic cooperation, the EEC members began work in the 1980s toward a fuller union of Western Europe. They began forming the European Community (EC), whose eventual goals would include a common language, currency, and economic and political systems. In effect, the planners wished to create a United States of Europe, wherein each presently autonomous nation would become a member state of the larger union, governing itself in much the same way Idaho or California or New York governs itself in relation to the United States federal government. The EC would be different in that, unlike the United States of America, each EC nation would be responsible for its own defense.

At the present time the EC has a government structure in place and has some limited powers. The seat of government is located in Brussels, Belgium. Its organization consists of five institutional systems: An Executive Commission, a Council of Ministers, a European Parliament, a Court of Justice, and a Court of Auditors. The EC is headed by a president who is appointed by the Executive Commission. Proponents of the plan wish to see the gradual enlargement of this body's powers and gradual reduction of individual nations' autonomous powers. Opponents fear the results of such a plan.

Besides language barriers and differences in economic prosperity (which could lead to some members taking on a larger share of the economic burdens of the organization), a major impediment to full implementation of the EC is nationalism. Many opponents to the EC have strong fears that such a union would destroy the rich cultural traditions and individual identities of the member nations. If all converted to the same language, for example, some fear what would happen to the precious literary heritage of the individual nations.

Just as worrisome as the insidious deterioration of national personalities and heritages is the fear that the EC would become an overweening bureaucracy that would impose inappropriate rules on all members regardless of their individual situations. *New York Times* reporter Alan Riding says, "In many countries there remains a strong perception that faceless unelected bureaucrats in Brussels are busily writing rules aimed at making uniform a region that has always prided itself on its diversity."

For example, the EC was concerned that the process involved in making certain European cheeses was unsanitary and a possible health hazard. It passed a health code that would have banned cheeses made with unpasteurized milk. One of the cheeses directly affected by the code would have been the immensely popular French cheese, Camembert. Cheese producers in Camembert, France, were outraged at the thought that this product, which they had been making in a traditional way for many decades, would be arbitrarily banned by the EC bureaucracy. They argued that the health code endangered their livelihoods and that changing the cheese would endanger sales.

Advocates of the EC insist that such fears are groundless. Peter Ludlow, director of the Center for European Policy Studies in Brussels, states, "A united Europe will not be based on the American principle of the melting pot." Despite the institution of an official language, for example, individual nations would retain their own language for daily and cultural use and use the EC language (English) for political and economic interactions. The primary legislation of the EC would be directly related to common political and economic goals and would be subject to the approval of the Council of Ministers representing all member nations. There would be no arbitrary rule-making by the EC governing bodies. Instead, EC rules would work toward making Europe a strong, competitive force on the world market. Proponents claim that a federation of European nations would increase the European gross domestic product between 4.5 and 7.0 percent, create 1.8 to 5 million new jobs, and lower consumer prices by 6 percent.

The success or failure of the EC is just one of the issues that faces the continent of Europe today. Others considered in *Europe: Current Controversies* are German unification, Western policies in Eastern Europe, the strengthening of Eastern Europe's economy, and the role of international organizations in Europe's future. The editors have selected the viewpoints with the aim of enlarging the reader's knowledge of today's Europe, America's long-standing neighbor, ally, and trading partner.

Chapter 1

How Will European Unification Affect the World?

European Unification: An Overview

by Spyros G. Makridakis and Michelle Bainbridge

About the authors: *Spyros G. Makridakis is a research professor at INSEAD, a leading European business school in Fontainebleau, France. He is the author of numerous articles and books, including* Forecasting Methods for Management. *Michelle Bainbridge is a research assistant at INSEAD.*

> *A day will come when you, France; you, Russia; you, Italy; you, Britain; and you, Germany—all of you, all nations of the Continent will merge tightly, without losing your identities and your remarkable originality, into some higher society and form a European fraternity. . . . A day will come when markets, open to trade, and minds, open to ideas, will become the sole battlefields.*
>
> Mikhail Gorbachev, quoting Victor Hugo, in a speech delivered to the Council of Europe in Strasbourg

At the Yalta Conference in 1945 the world was divided into political spheres of influence to be shared by the superpowers. Just as the Yalta discussions were kept secret at the time, so were those of another meeting held a little more than thirty years later in Tokyo between Japan's major industrialists and Ministry of International Trade and Industry (MITI) officials. The Tokyo conference visualized a division of the world into three major areas, each specializing in its own field of competence. North America, with its vast agricultural plains, was to become the breadbasket of the world, supplying cheap and abundant food. Europe, rich in culture and haute couture, was to become the cultural museum and high-life entertainment playground for the rich and successful. Finally, Japan was envisioned as the manufacturer and supplier of conventional and high-technology products for the entire world. Financial and other services were not included in the division preparing the ground for competition among North American, European, and Japanese firms.

There is little doubt about Japan's increasing dominance in manufacturing, particularly in computer- and information-related industries, its willingness to spend huge sums to become a primary player in the area of biotechnology, and

---

From Spyros G. Makridakis and Michelle Bainbridge, *Single Market Europe: Opportunities and Challenges for Business*. San Francisco: Jossey-Bass, 1991. Copyright 1991 by Jossey-Bass Inc., Publishers. Reprinted with permission.

its heavy investment on a worldwide basis in the service sector in an attempt to achieve equal status with American and European giants. Japanese companies have set ambitious, long-term objectives (usually in terms of 20 to 30 percent market share) and then slowly and patiently developed and implemented strategies to achieve these objectives. The Japanese have shown little or no concern for financial outlays or for the short-term losses they might incur in order to achieve their long-term market share objectives. The acquisition of CBS Records and Columbia Pictures by Sony illustrated once again the Japanese attitude toward long-term investment and determination to dominate high value-added sectors no matter what the initial costs were. Moreover, Japanese acquisition of huge chunks of real estate in various Western countries (for example, the Rockefeller Center in New York City and the Forum Des Halles in Paris) and their worldwide expansion policies have raised many critical questions about their long-term goals and willingness to play by accepted rules. What remains to be seen is the possible response of European and North American countries to the Japanese challenge. There is no doubt that the speed-up in the creation of a single market throughout the twelve EC countries and the United States-Canada trade agreement have been direct responses to the Japanese threat.

> *"Some argue that a common European market is merely a grand illusion."*

The Single European Market: Expectations and Reality

What have been the effects of the creation of the European Community (EC)? What about the outcome of further attempts at European integration? As with all such important questions, there is a wide divergence of views. Some argue that a common European market is merely a grand illusion, that nothing much has changed or will change, and that the unification of Europe is a well-orchestrated advertising campaign resembling an empty balloon, having no substantial value beyond its large volume. Experts on the European Community claim that though in theory its objectives might seem great, in fact, bureaucracy, national scrambling, and contradictory practices have reduced its effectiveness and produced a different reality from that envisioned by the creating fathers of a unified Europe.

Those on the opposite end of the spectrum view the EC as creating a "Fortress Europe," using a central legislative and executive body to protect Europe from outside competition. More and more Europeans believe in a united Europe that goes beyond an economic community or single market, looking for a political, not just an economic, union. The desire to be European, rather than a specific nationality, is increasingly voiced within Europe, particularly by young Europeans who do not understand or identify with the nationalistic chauvinism of their parents and grandparents.

Although there may be elements of truth in these opposing views, the reality lies somewhere in between. As is often the case, the goal of the common market is to facilitate the achievement of economic objectives and permit European firms to compete on equal terms at a global level with North American, Japanese, and other national firms. If short-term action is needed to achieve such objectives, there is little doubt that certain measures will be employed, much as the American Congress or the Japanese Diet do not hesitate to pass legislation with which to protect—or even help—their national companies or interests. European leaders and prominent businessmen have been against protectionism, being suspicious of reciprocity and wanting to be treated as the negotiating equals of the Americans and Japanese in regard to trade issues and other disputes. Although many idealists believe in a "federal state of Europe," such a dream, if it can indeed become a reality, will take a long time to come to pass. . . .

Background of the Single Market Movement

The European Coal and Steel Community (ECSC), established in 1951 in Paris, was the first attempt at European cooperation. Its goal was to pool and better manage the coal and steel production of the six signing countries. The Treaty of Rome was a natural extension of the ECSC (signed in 1957, effective from January 1, 1958), creating both the European Economic Community, or Common Market, and the European Atomic Energy Community (Euratom). The Treaty of Rome is heralded as the birth of the movement toward a common European market. Its purpose was to achieve not only economic and monetary union but eventually also political union of the European states.

> *"More and more Europeans believe in a united Europe that goes beyond an economic community or single market."*

The progress between 1958 and the end of 1985 was slow and uneven. This period was primarily marked by legislative efforts aimed at reducing tariff and customs barriers in order to create a freer flow of goods and people. However, myriads of nontariff obstacles existed to bar foreign rivals and, by so doing, to offer protection to national firms from competitors both inside and outside Europe. Moreover, most services were excluded from the reduction of tariff and customs barriers. In addition, preferential treatment of national suppliers for government procurements in defense and other sensitive or critical areas was common practice: such contracts were not open to competition from firms of other EC countries.

During the "golden sixties," when most European countries experienced smooth and strong growth rates, there was little motivation for European unity. Following the 1973 energy crisis, Europe experienced a slowdown in economic growth, high inflation, and double-digit unemployment. During the early eighties, the economic scene had gone from bad to worse so that debates about "Eurosclerosis" had become commonplace (referring to the fact that Europe's institutions and firms had become unable to adapt to the economic difficulties and rise to the competitive challenges facing them). By the middle of the 1980s, it was clear that no single European country could achieve competitive parity with North America and Japan. Initially, leading European businessmen (both from within the EC and outside it), became convinced of the necessity for a single market if Europe was to survive the global competitive game. Later on, political leaders joined them.

> *"The ultimate objective is to achieve an economic integration among the member states that will eventually lead to some form of political unity."*

In December 1985, the European leaders adopted the White Paper, which contained 279 proposals aimed at achieving a single market by December 31, 1992. Less than two years later, the Single European Act (SEA) came into force, amending the treaties of Rome and Paris. Among the stipulations included in this act, one of the most important was that a qualified majority voting rule for most (although not all) proposals should supersede the unanimity previously needed by the Council of Ministers to adopt proposals. The majority rule unblocked the decision-making process at the community level, as individual countries or a minority of countries could no longer veto measures that they disagreed with. Consequently, more progress has been achieved in those few years than in the thirty-odd years since the signing of the Treaty of Rome.

The Ultimate Objective

The purpose of the European Community extends well beyond simply creating a free-trade zone. The ultimate objective is to achieve an economic integration among the member states that will eventually lead to some form of political unity. To this end the following goals have been articulated:

1. Complete elimination of customs duties among member states.
2. Unqualified restriction of obstacles to the free flow of import and/or export of goods and services among member states.
3. Common customs duties and unified industrial/commercial policies regarding countries outside the community.
4. Free movement of persons and capital.
5. Common agricultural and transport policies.
6. Common technical standards as well as health and safety regulations.
7. Common measures for consumer protection.
8. Common laws to maintain competition throughout the community and fight monopolies or illegal cartels.
9. Regional funds to encourage the economic development of certain countries/regions.

10. Greater monetary and fiscal coordination among member states and certain common monetary/fiscal policies.

Major issues remaining are the harmonization of value-added tax (VAT) and excise duties, the adoption of a unified monetary system and common economic policies, and the achievement of political integration of the twelve EC states....

The Benefits and Costs of a Single Market

Much of the progress toward economic integration and the creation of a single European market will depend on the perceived benefits that such a market will bring to each of the twelve EC members and the costs that it will involve. The predominant feeling is that the creation of a single economic market will lead to higher growth and lower prices. Although precise figures cannot be presented, several estimates of the effect of the single market exist. Prominent among such estimates are those included in the Cecchini reports, sixteen hefty volumes of sector-by-sector analysis of the costs of not having a single market. Sponsored by the commission, these reports are considered to be optimistic and should therefore be taken to denote the upper limit of the expected benefits.

The Cecchini reports estimate that overall growth in GNP will be accelerated by about 6.5 percent because of the single market. Of this, 2.4 percent will be due to the adoption of common technical, safety/health, and other standards; 2.1 percent will come from the exploitation of economies of scale; and the remaining 2 percent will come from other sources such as elimination of border formalities and decreases in current inefficiencies that hamper competition. In addition, Cecchini envisions a 6 percent price reduction as a result of freer competition, a 5 percent increase in demand, and correspondingly higher profits for businesses. Even though the selling price of goods and services will be reduced, effectively shrinking their revenues, businesses will still be able to achieve higher profits because of lower costs of capital, greater demand, increased efficiency, and a host of other factors. The reports see no obvious costs and conclude that the opportunity costs of non-Europe are too large (more than 250 billion ECUs) to let the opening of a single market pass unexploited.

"The predominant feeling is that the creation of a single economic market will lead to higher growth and lower prices."

Critics of the Cecchini reports have pointed out that they were not objective since they were financed by the commission itself. Even the staunchest critics have agreed, however, that the single market will provide significant benefits to both businesses and consumers, the level of which benefits they foresee as about half of that predicted in the Cecchini reports. From the two estimates one could conclude that the benefits from the single market would be around 4 percent of GNP—although here it is important to stress that

Chapter 1

this middle-of-the-road figure is being challenged by new studies.

An area that the Cecchini reports did not touch on is the long-term effects of a single market. As prices drop and consumers are provided with a wider choice, demand will undoubtedly increase, as will investments. Moreover, if European firms become more competitive worldwide there is little doubt that their riches will be ploughed back into Europe, increasing the standard of living and further stimulating demand. Uniform product and safety standards as well as greater economic and political stability will decrease the potential risks as they are perceived by firms and contribute to higher levels of investment in all EC countries. Finally, the substantial help offered to the less developed countries (such as Portugal, Greece, and Ireland) and the impoverished regions of the community (such as Southern Italy and Northern Ireland), in the form of regional or structural funds, will stimulate higher growth rates in these countries or areas, further adding to overall demand. For these reasons it might be possible to envision long-term growth rates and other benefits well above those announced in the Cecchini reports. In a study, for instance, an American researcher concluded that long-term benefits might be as high as one-third of the total GNP of all twelve countries, revealing huge opportunities for Europe and perhaps even a cure for the Eurosclerosis responsible for the fact that per capita GNP of the twelve ($11,600) represents only 60 percent of the per capita GNP of the United States ($19,800).

> *"Europe could . . . become the economic superpower of the 1990s."*

Intangible Benefits

In addition to those mentioned above, the single market will bring another critical benefit that is essentially intangible and bound to the long term and thus much more difficult to quantify. A single market of 325 million consumers fostering very close links with the 33 million EFTA consumers is approximately the size of the U.S. and Japanese markets combined. In addition, if the four Eastern European countries likely to develop strong trading links with the EC (Czechoslovakia, Hungary, Poland, and Yugoslavia) are added to the total European market, this figure rises to close to half a billion consumers. Europe could therefore become *the* economic superpower of the 1990s. More important, however, such a huge market and economic strength will put the Europeans in a very strong bargaining position on political—and especially commercial or economic—issues. Whereas individual European countries have been ignored or pushed around, as part of a real European union they will necessarily be taken seriously. Europeans will be in a position to demand parity with, and impose reciprocity on, the United States and Japan. If they are ignored they can threaten to retaliate, and their market is too large for anyone to take their retaliation lightly. In addition, although European technical standards were ignored prior to 1984, they are now considered world standards, thus providing European firms with a definite competitive advantage. It will be interesting to see which standards are adopted with regard to high definition television (HDTV), although at present Europe would seem to have an edge. . . .

The costs of the single market are frequently borne by those countries that pay more to the EC budget than they get from it. Since 1979 the United Kingdom and West Germany have tended to be the only net contributors to the community budget (mainly because of the large proportion of the EC budget accounted for by agriculture), while all the other countries have generally received more from the budget than they pay to it. Apart from actual financial outlays, however, there are other costs that may well concern some of the less economically developed countries more than their industrial neighbors (for example, Greece, Portugal, and Ireland). We feel that the less economically developed countries may see their industries dominated by powerful competition from firms from the large EC nations. As the companies that are less able to compete (for example, those currently protected by favorable national legislation and regulations or who hold monopolistic positions in their home country) are frequently to be found in the less economically developed countries, further internal costs are expected. There is little doubt that the majority of weaker and less efficient firms will have to find specialized niches, become more competitive, sell out to larger firms, or go bankrupt. But this is seen as a price worth paying in order to achieve higher competitiveness at the overall EC level.

For the less developed EC members, there are possible long-term benefits as well as the costs mentioned above. The regional and structural funds available, if combined with specialization (to help them carve out market niches), should help the less developed countries accelerate economic growth by concentrating their efforts. At the same time, leaving the door open to outside competition could wipe out local industries or reduce them to a position where they are no longer able to fend off foreign predators. In the long run, the most likely scenario is that the benefits will compensate for the costs involved; but there are no guarantees that some of the national economies will not suffer, at least in the short term. The same is true for less developed regions of richer countries or the smaller and medium-sized firms that pepper the European corporate map. If they are unable to adapt quickly enough to the new realities of the integrated business environment, they will be gobbled up by other EC-based corporations hungry for efficiency.

There is no doubt that there will be a great deal of very significant change during the period of transition leading up to and following the creation of a single market Europe. However, it must be accepted that the forces leading to a single market are now irreversible (as was unanimously agreed by the European leaders in Hanover in 1988). What remain to be seen are the speed of economic integration and the extent of the benefits and costs that it will bring to the various EC economies. The alacrity with which the single market is achieved will prepare the ground for the eventual political unification of Europe.

European Unification Will Help Unify the World

by Giovanni Agnelli

About the author: *Giovanni Agnelli is the chairman of the Fiat Group, an Italian industry.*

In 1946, Winston Churchill spoke in Zurich of the need to build a "United States of Europe," and on the fifth of May 1949 the Statute of Europe was signed by ten European countries, expressing the will to create a European Assembly.

The rest is recent history.

It was still a history of division and political and ideological antagonism. Europe was not the principal player in that ideological juxtaposition—but it was nevertheless European territory which until 1989 was divided between the two leading world powers.

But it was a history of Western Europe which grew and developed with the principles of peace, democracy and economic development to the forefront. It was a Europe which shared the road to liberty with the United States.

Today it is a Europe which, following the symbolic and physical dismantling of the Berlin Wall and the end of the Cold War, can think about gathering together in one cultural and philosophical identity all those peoples who have shared its long history even before considering the political dimension.

So, now let me try to pull together the threads of this complicated passage of events which have led to present-day Europe.

Europe Leads the World

We know that in its basic features and elements, this part of the world has been and still is the model for the world at large.

We know that the concept of the nation state, scientific method, and the notion of liberty have been transmitted from Europe to the world community.

And we know that European culture, in its widest sense, has been adopted by all the developed countries of the world.

From "Europe: Many Legacies, One Future," a speech by Giovanni Agnelli, delivered at the 1991 Romanes Lectures, Oxford University, May 9, 1991.

Certainly the countries showing new development, such as Japan and those of southeast Asia, tend to conform to this culture.

To a great extent it is true that this cultural supremacy has been achieved through colonization and oppression—a serious historical flaw which we now acknowledge, but which still does not cancel out the important role Europe has played in world development.

Today we are free of the notions of racial supremacy which were rife in our continent until fifty years ago.

We have been freed—both by necessity and by belief—from the hegemonic ambitions which previously set one European state against another.

> *"We have to confront the problem of finding a new balance which will see Europe assuming the responsibilities which she is duty-bound to take on."*

And we are also free of both the responsibility and the conceit involved in being the political and cultural centre of the world.

These freedoms, which we hope are permanently ours, allow us to think more clearly about the future role of Europe in the light of our past experience.

Faced with a world that is moving towards global dimensions, divided into large continental regions, Europe has to be united. This is an absolute necessity for our political and historical survival.

So our most important objective must be the unity of Europe. This does not mean rushing blindly into the future, nor does it mean renouncing the differences which are part of our ideal heritage.

Many of us hope that the new century—less than ten years away now—will bring together and unify the destiny of all the peoples and nations which see themselves reflected in our common history and ideals.

The huge task of carrying out this process rests with the European Community.

Balancing the East, West, and South

We are at the centre of three problematical areas.

To the west, we already have a strong relationship with the greatest political and economic power in the world.

The historical and cultural ties which bind us are clear, but we have to confront the problem of finding a new balance which will see Europe assuming the responsibilities which she is duty-bound to take on in the future new world order.

To the east we have a world in a state of renewal which is looking to the West with hope and with practical expectations. The problem here is how do we speed up this process of recovering, for the West, nations and cultures long frozen in a system which went against our own traditions of freedom and pluralism?

To the south we have the pressures of the Islamic world and Africa which

Chapter 1

look at Europe from positions of ideological opposition and economic confrontation.

Finding the balance will not be easy, yet this is one of the most serious problems facing us in the next century.

In the confrontations between Europe and the world, one answer might be for Europe's regions to take on vocational roles.

So, for example, Europe's Mediterranean countries, particularly France, Spain and Italy, have front-line responsibilities towards the Islamic world and the growing migratory pressures.

And because of her history, language and culture, Britain should take on the foremost role in relations with the United States.

The same goes for Germany with regard to negotiations with the East: because of its geographically central position, it makes sense for it to take primary responsibility for relations with the Eastern Bloc.

However, differing priorities of roles and political commitment can only be fully accomplished if their roots are firmly bedded in European unity.

How we achieve this unity is still open for discussion. In particular, there are differing views about how we should achieve political, monetary and military unification.

But, on the other hand, we are already part of an entity which is neither state nor nation but which nevertheless expresses a collective and common understanding in which different languages, traditions and cultures are united.

> *"As Europeans, we are therefore on the threshold of a historic occasion."*

We cannot take the necessary further steps towards unification without a determined act of will on everybody's part.

Despite what has been said, the story is not over—though it has once more changed its historical course.

The traditional destiny of nation states is coming to an end in these last years of the twentieth century, however vital the role they have played in the progress of the world.

Global Problems Demand Attention

Not even the most powerful European state is today capable of having a significant influence within the world community.

On the other hand, past problems such as poverty, new ones such as the protection of the environment, and age-old ones such as the preservation of world peace are now present on a global scale.

These problems require an increasingly urgent political and economic solution from industrialised countries.

Within the world pattern of large regional areas, only a united Europe will be able to make an effective contribution to solving the imbalances between North and South, to making the world fit to live in, to reducing and eliminating armed conflict.

As Europeans, we are therefore on the threshold of a historic occasion: we are, that is, again an essential point of reference for the world, no longer now based on conquest and political and military hegemony but on the values of our tradition and culture.

So that is why it is now time to salvage our ancient heritage, and rediscover the strong threads which unite us and which define our common identity.

If we can do that, then it will be easier for us to bring to this concept of a new Europe a form which is truly relevant to the modern world. Let us place in the scales of the new century the full weight of our history and civilization.

European Unification Will Strengthen Europe

by Hans-Dietrich Genscher

About the author: *Hans-Dietrich Genscher was the German minister for foreign affairs from 1974 to April 27, 1992.*

Five hundred years ago, the great Portuguese seafarers swept Europe out of its medieval straits and boldly extended its horizons. They were thus the initiators of the European age. Europe ruled and shaped the world—with all that this entailed, for good and ill.

The European age was also an age of constant wars among the nations of Europe, wars which we now recognize as European civil wars. At the end—in 1945—Europe had destroyed itself; it seemed to have no future.

Today, five hundred years after the beginning of the European age and five decades after the catastrophe of 1945, we Europeans are being given a historic new opportunity.

A New Vision of Europe

The peaceful revolutions for freedom in the nations of Central, Eastern and Southeastern Europe have radically altered Europe. In this process Germany regained its national unity.

The vision of a Europe whole and free, united by the great European concept of freedom and democracy, of the dignity and uniqueness of each individual, rises before us.

We are experiencing a new domino effect of freedom. Old structures and ideologies collapse as a result of their inability to meet the challenges of modern society, the challenges of the present. Collectivism has failed; the future belongs to individuality.

We have the opportunity to make the 21st century a truly "European century": no longer by means of war and conquering, but through a new culture of the coexistence of nations.

However, the European century of peace, freedom and prosperity will not fall

From "The Future of Europe," a speech by Hans-Dietrich Genscher, delivered at the Palacio das Necessidades, Lisbon, Portugal, July 12, 1991.

into our lap. The crisis in Yugoslavia, whose significance extends far beyond that country's borders, is at the forefront of our minds at present.

No other state, no European institution—neither the EC nor the CSCE—can, or must, tell the peoples of Yugoslavia how to organize their future. Only they themselves can decide their future.

> "We have the opportunity to make the 21st century a truly 'European century.'"

But what the new Europe of the Charter of Paris can, and must, demand is that this decision be made through a process of dialogue and negotiation, without coercion or force, in which human rights and minority rights, democracy and the right of self-determination must be respected and realized.

The EC and the CSCE have no magic wand with which to solve the centuries-old problems of the Yugoslavian peoples overnight—problems which are exacerbated by ideological antagonisms between old power structures and the new democratic forces in the republics.

The path to the single, free Europe is still fraught with danger:

• the danger that the old demon of violent nationalism and nationality conflicts in Europe will re-emerge,

• the danger that we are underestimating the major challenge posed by the economic development in Central and Eastern Europe and in the Soviet Union, and that for a long time Europe will remain divided into rich and poor countries,

• the danger that old modes of thinking seek to solve the problems by power politics, thus running counter to human rights, minority rights and self-determination, and finally

• the danger that an inward-looking Europe will no longer have the energy to help shape the new, multipolar world.

These dangers, however, must not blind us to the opportunities. Pessimism, faintheartedness and despondency are incompatible with a good, future-oriented policy eager to seize opportunities.

A Vision of the Future

No one can say for sure what Europe will look like in the first decade of the new millennium. But we must illustrate the prospects.

1. *The United States of Europe will be completed.*

The European Community is politically and economically on the way towards European Union, and thence to the United States of Europe. Our guiding principle is a Europe with a common constitution, a single economy and currency, and a common foreign, security and defense policy....

The large European single market, open to the outside world, is on the point of being completed. Many essential elements of our program for a Europe without borders have already been realized. The citizens of the Community will measure the success of the internal market program first and foremost by the degree of free movement achieved for the individual. I am particularly gratified, therefore, that Portugal, too, has now acceded to the Schengen Convention. The creation of economic and monetary union is the logical extension of the single market. It will be a big step along Europe's path toward unity.

We are creating political union parallel to economic and monetary union. There are two prime objectives to be attained first and foremost:

Firstly, we must clear the way for a truly common foreign, security and defense policy. Only thus will the Community be able to shoulder the political responsibility appropriate to its economic weight and contribute to stability and peace in the world in this time of upheaval.

Secondly, we must strengthen the role of the European Parliament in the European decision-making process and thus give European union greater democratic legitimacy.

Our affirmation of a democratic Europe also means that we will preserve the equilibrium between the institutions and states within the Community. The rights of smaller member states must be observed and institutionally safeguarded. There must and will be no "directorate", no dominance on the part of the larger member states.

> *"Franco-German cooperation, which is so important for the future of Europe, acts as a driving force behind European integration."*

Franco-German cooperation, which is so important for the future of Europe, acts as a driving force behind European integration. I support the French proposal that national parliaments be more closely involved in the Community decision-making process.

A Federal Europe

The United States of Europe will be a federal Europe. As we understand it, federal means the rejection of a centralist Europe.

We promote the concept of a federal Europe of subsidiarity, a Europe of regions and a myriad of national and regional traditions. We want to exploit the creativity afforded by this European diversity, because it is a prerequisite for Europe's vitality, now as in the past.

In the discussion about political union, therefore, we Germans are calling for the establishment of a regional committee, in which the regions can have their say in shaping Europe.

The nation-state alone is no longer able to meet the challenges posed today by the global tasks and problems affecting all of us across boundaries.

This is true in the spheres of economics, environment, technology, infrastructure, energy, internal and external security, migratory flows, the fight against international crime, and many others.

This is the deeper reason underlying the need to create the United States of

Europe.

2. *The United States of Europe will reach from the North Cape to Sicily, and from the Atlantic to the East of our continent.*

The European Community does not yet have a common foreign policy. But nonetheless it already plays the central role in shaping the new Europe, thanks to the ever-closer dovetailing of the external policy formulated in the EPC with the policy of the Community.

It shapes the face of the new Europe in the European economic area being sought together with the EFTA states through its forward-looking association agreements with the countries of Central and Eastern Europe; through its cooperation with the Soviet Union and its role as the driving force behind Western support for these countries, including the Soviet Union; as an active partner in the creation of the pan-European peace order, the pan-European energy area, the pan-European infrastructure area, the pan-European economic area and the pan-European environmental area within the CSCE framework; and, in relation to its southern neighbors, by reviewing its common policy on the Mediterranean.

A Growing EC

The ever-increasing association of the EFTA states and the countries of Central and Eastern Europe with the Community points beyond the goal of a large, pan-European economic area. In the longer term, most if not all of the EFTA states will join the Community. The prospect of accession must also be open to the countries of Central and Eastern Europe.

The present Community of Twelve will thus grow into a federation of some twenty states, closely linked with the United States of America and, in an ever-closer relationship, with a Soviet Union united by voluntary cooperation.

For the Community, this is only the logical follow-up to the end of the division of Europe. It has never considered itself to be a Western European organization or a closed society.

There is no political discussion in Poland, Hungary or Czechoslovakia today in which the magic word "Europe" does not occur. The Community is the source of hope which gives the people there the energy to see through these difficult times.

> *"There is no political discussion in Poland, Hungary or Czechoslovakia today in which the magic word 'Europe' does not occur."*

We take the fears that have been expressed by a few of our partner countries seriously, namely, that accession of new members would burden the old ones, and that the Community's efficiency could suffer. These fears will prove to be unfounded:

Firstly, any country wishing to join the Community must meet the political and, especially, the economic conditions for entry. For this reason alone there will be no over-hasty accessions.

Secondly, in strengthening the Community on its way to European Union, we will also create the necessary instruments and decision-making structures. This is another reason for making every possible effort to bring the inter-governmental conference to a successful conclusion.

Thirdly, we will increase economic and social cohesion within the Community.

> *"By enlarging the Community we are also achieving European unification, the United States of Europe, for the benefit of all."*

And fourthly, the Community's extension southwards through the accession of Portugal and Spain showed once again what positive, dynamic effects new accessions can have for the further development of the Community.

In the end, we will realize that by enlarging the Community we are also achieving European unification, the United States of Europe, for the benefit of all.

3. *Eastern Europe will have succeeded in the transition to democracy, economic progress and an environment worth living in.*

This vision is implicit in the forecast of an extended Community, the larger United States of Europe. I am aware that it will endure only if we all act resolutely now.

Support for the East Is Vital

After the fall of the Iron Curtain, Europe must not become a society of new divisions: it cannot allow a further, lasting division along what would now be economic, social and ecological borders.

The people in the east of our continent need our firm support. They need the undivided, pan-European perspective. They need it as backing for their domestic and foreign policy and as a guideline for establishing their democratic structures. They need it for the necessary restructuring of their economy and for the rehabilitation of their environment. And, not least of all, they need the know-how and financial assistance of all Western democracies to correct the effects of decades of error. And we, the European West, must take an interest in the success of the reform policy in Central and Eastern Europe, including the Soviet Union, because in the long run in the single Europe things cannot go well for the West if things go badly for the East on a long-term basis.

No one should underestimate the magnitude of the tasks ahead. They can only be resolved if Western Europe, North America and Japan act together in solidarity and if each side makes its full contribution. In this respect Germany expects increased commitment from its partners. We neither can, nor want, to bear the burden of development in Eastern Europe alone. We do not want to monopolize relations with the countries of Central and Eastern Europe, including the Soviet Union.

United Germany will bear its increased responsibility not in yesterday's nation-state sense, but in the European spirit of tomorrow.

We are offering our partners in the European Community our solidarity in a determined policy of European unification towards European Union. No one should mistake the historic opportunity emerging from the unification of Germany: to create European Union and eventually the United States of Europe, and at the same time to shape a Europe whole and free. . . .

Aid to East Will Help West

The assistance we give to the Soviet Union and to Eastern Europe is not a sacrifice, but an investment in our own European future and in the future of a peaceful world. It is also an investment in our common ecological future.

And finally: if Eastern Europe and the Soviet Union succeed in becoming flourishing market economies, they will provide huge markets for tomorrow, where potential demand will give our national economies a tremendous additional boost for decades.

Europe can once again become the heart of the world's economy.

4. *The CSCE will be the solid framework for the whole of Europe.*

In his speech on June 18, 1991, on the eve of the first meeting of the CSCE Council of Foreign Ministers in Berlin, Secretary of State James Baker recalled the shared values of the West and the transatlantic community that is based on them, and issued the bold challenge to extend this community to Central and Eastern Europe and the Soviet Union.

> *"Europe can once again become the heart of the world's economy."*

The framework for this blueprint for the future, becoming more and more solid, will be the CSCE. Its foundation will be the "Charter of Paris for a New Europe" drawn up in November 1990.

What would have been regarded even recently as utopia has become reality: all CSCE participating states, the united Germany at their center, have committed themselves to human rights, minority rights, self-determination, democracy and the rule of law, and to economic freedom and responsibility. They have thus laid the foundation for the community of values of the Euro-Atlantic area. Our task now is to shape this area in accordance with the spirit of the Charter of Paris.

Europe is taking on a definite form. With the Council, the CSCE now has at its disposal an efficient organ, the nucleus of a political and security steering body. This also opens up the prospect of a kind of European security council for the forthcoming 21st century.

With the expanded responsibilities of the conflict prevention center in Vienna and the emergency mechanism decided upon in Berlin, we have taken the first steps in this direction, first and foremost to make Europe capable of action, even in worsening crisis situations. We should consider creating European "blue-helmet" units and we should set up European "green-helmet" units to protect our natural environment. In this age, we can only create security together.

From this mode of thinking there emerge new structures for cooperative security in Europe, a new pan-European security structure which must afford all members protection against force and the threat of force. After the dissolution of the Warsaw Pact, the countries of Central and Eastern Europe must be able to take their place safely and with equal rights in such a pan-European security structure.

This security structure can build on the progress made thus far in the disarmament process. The CFE Treaty on conventional disarmament in Europe is a sound basis for a stable, lasting peaceful order on our continent. . . .

A New Type of Security

The Atlantic alliance takes on a completely new character in the new cooperative security structure.

Cooperative security, i.e., security with one another, will grow and will reduce the need for security against one another, but not altogether remove it. The alliance will retain essential importance as an anchor of stability for the whole of Europe and as a transatlantic forum for consultations.

Our alliance has extended the hand of friendship and partnership to all European states to the East of us, including the Soviet Union. It has already expanded its contacts with the countries of Central and Eastern Europe, including the Soviet Union, considerably, and has promised a broad range of initiatives for the future. These initiatives will further strengthen the security of all concerned.

Our alliance also welcomes the formation of an independent European security and defense identity such as we are seeking in the European Union, first of all on the basis of the WEU. A strong European pillar in the alliance will increase its integrity and efficiency.

The days in which security and stability were defined purely in military terms are gone. These terms are being understood more and more in a political, economic, social and ecological sense.

> *"The Europe of peace, freedom and prosperity will not fall into our lap. But never have we been in a better starting position."*

In the creation of a pan-European peaceful order understood in this way, all existing institutions and associations will have important tasks which complement one another.

The alliance and the WEU, and above all the European Community, will play pivotal roles. The EC is the core and driving force of Europe as a whole. The Council of Europe will have a decisive part in shaping the pan-European legislative and cultural area. The ECE, OECD and the European Bank for Reconstruction and Development are important components of the pan-European architecture overarched by the CSCE.

The weighting of the individual institutions will be a dynamic process whose contours will be apparent only in the 21st century. I am convinced that the CSCE will evolve into an ever more solid framework, the bracket for the emerging pan-European order in all spheres.

> *"Europe will help shape the new multipolar world."*

The Charter of Paris has committed Europe to common values. At the same time it opens the door for more and more pan-European institutions. The whole of Europe is beginning to organize itself.

A European Answer to Every Problem

The more we shape the pan-European area, with a common security area, a common economic, ecological, technological, transport and communications area, the stronger will be the framework for the resolution of the major problems in Central and Eastern Europe, including the Soviet Union.

In the whole of Europe pan-European confederal structures will emerge. Within this pan-European area there will be federations, such as the European Community and other associations, but also individual states.

The great blueprint for Europe offered by the Charter of Paris gives a European answer to every question in Europe. Now we must aim to seek similar European answers in all spheres.

The road points not backward to the nation-state of the past, but forward to the anchoring of all developments in Europe.

Here, too, we need a new way of thinking on all sides which must not be bogged down in the power-politics attitudes of the past and which must take our shared values seriously. The new Europe must be founded on these values.

5. *Europe will help shape the new multipolar world.*

The end of the bipolar confrontation in Europe and in the world and the emergence of a new, multipolar world order have heightened awareness of the global challenges facing us today everywhere.

Basically, it is a matter of constructing a world order of peace in which the United Nations must at last play the central role assigned it in its Charter. This new world peace can only become reality if we meet five major challenges.

We must commit ourselves to human rights and the right to self-determination throughout the world; to cooperative security in all regions of the world; we must make significant progress on the way to a strict policy of nonproliferation of weapons of mass destruction and the control of arms exports—if any proof was required of the need for this, then the Gulf war provided it; we must quickly overcome the economic division between North and South; we must help to end mankind's war against nature.

Chapter 1

Europe must set an example regarding the guiding principles of the future world peace order: the peaceful settlement of conflicts, harmonization of interests, cooperation in the spirit of mutual dependence and equal rights instead of hegemony.

I am certain that a Europe that, as President François Mitterrand said, has returned to its geography and history, our common Europe, will face up to its responsibility in the world and be instrumental in forming this new, multipolar world of the future.

As far as the future is concerned, however, we must be clear in our minds that the image Asia, Africa and Latin America in particular have of Europe is marked in part by negative impressions as a result of their products' failure to find access to our markets. Only our contribution to the further consistent liberalization of world trade within the GATT framework can help here.

Today, and in the coming years, our special attention must be focused on our neighbors, the Mediterranean countries and the Arab world. Throughout its history this region has been inextricably linked with Europe, for better and for worse.

Thus we share Portugal's view that the Community's policy on the Mediterranean is an essential instrument of EC foreign relations. We particularly welcome the emerging closer cooperation between Portugal, France, Italy and Spain and the Maghreb countries, which aim to increase stability in the region.

Progress in the Middle East peace process is the basis for durable peace and stability in the region as a whole. Europe must, and will, make its contribution and bring its experience to bear in this regard. The CSCM proposed by Portugal, France, Italy and Spain could provide a stability framework for the entire region.

The Gulf war made it drastically clear: the political, economic and ecological situation throughout the Mediterranean region directly affects not only the southern Europeans, but also us. This will remain the case and must be the factor determining our thinking and our actions.

Realizing the Vision

Let me repeat: the Europe of peace, freedom and prosperity will not fall into our lap. But never have we been in a better starting position.

Together we have the material prerequisites. We also have a number of well-proven institutions which we can jointly adapt and extend to meet the requirements and challenges. We have the ideas. And above all, we share the common values on which to base our policies, and we have the high motivation and the technical and scientific know-how of our citizens. This is our most valuable asset. Every individual is called upon to play his part so that the great project of a peaceful and prosperous Europe can be realized.

European Unification Can Provide Opportunities for American Business

by Daniel Burstein

About the author: *Daniel Burstein is a journalist and author of* YEN! Japan's New Financial Empire and Its Threat to America *and* Euroquake: Europe's Explosive Economic Challenge Will Change the World, *from which this viewpoint is excerpted.*

Quick—which nation has made the greatest cumulative investment in Europe outside its own borders? Which nation made more cross-border acquisitions in Europe during 1989 than any other? Which nation's corporate subsidiaries employ the greatest number of Europeans outside the parent company's home country?

The nation that fits this description is *not* the powerful Germany—at least not yet. The answer to all the above questions is: The United States of America, in its role as a great European power.

America's Biggest Trading Partner

American companies have made over $180 billion worth of direct investments in Europe. For some perspective on that eye-popping number, it might be useful to think of it as *three times* more than all the Japanese direct investment in the United States, which has rightly attracted so much attention in recent years.

One of the big American investors in Europe is IBM. Massive as IBM's business is in the American marketplace ($25.7 billion in 1989), its revenues in Europe are almost as large ($23.2 billion). And its European business is growing nearly five times faster.

Another big investor is the Ford Motor Co. Its 12 percent market share makes it as integral a player as any in Western Europe, the world's largest automobile market. "We have historically approached Europe as a single market," says An-

From Daniel Burstein, *Euroquake: Europe's Explosive Economic Challenge Will Change the World.* Copyright © 1991 by Burstein & O'Connor, Inc. Reprinted by permission of Simon & Schuster.

Chapter 1

drew Napier, the British-based director of Ford's 1992 task force. "Nineteen-ninety-two implies many challenges for us, but becoming pan-European is not really one of them. I think it is fair to say we are the most pan-European of all the automobile companies in Europe."

The European Community is America's biggest trading partner, accounting for roughly one-fifth of all foreign trade in which the U.S. is involved. Most important, it is the biggest buyer of American goods, absorbing 23.3 percent of all U.S. exports in 1988, compared with Canada, which took 21.5 percent, and Japan, which took only 11.7 percent.

> "The 'American' sector may account for as much as one-tenth of the entire EC economy."

Subsidiaries of American manufacturing firms in EC countries are estimated to do over $375 billion worth of sales annually. Adding the revenues of service firms, the "American" sector may account for as much as one-tenth of the entire EC economy. Beyond the enormous scope of this transatlantic economic relationship, of course, are thousands of political, cultural, and military-strategic ties which bind the United States and its European partners.

Until recently, American power, leadership, and vested interests in Europe were so obvious that they scarcely merited discussion. It was shocking *news* when Toyota captured 10 percent of the American automobile market. But the fact that General Motors has long enjoyed more than a 10 percent share of the European market (chiefly through its Opel division) is deemed "natural."

Changes Will Deeply Affect the United States

The United States, then, is a major European power. What happens in Europe, both positive and negative, will have deep repercussions on the U.S. domestic economy and on the business plans of American companies. These will be felt with a special intensity because Americans have become so accustomed to the status quo of the U.S.-Europe relationship that they have forgotten or ignored the possibility of dramatic change. . . .

Two vital competitive issues are at stake in Europe today. In the first place, the U.S. must adequately defend its powerful remaining economic interests against what now will be ferocious German, pan-European, and Japanese competition. Second, if American companies and Washington decision-makers play their cards right, they may be able to take advantage of the real strengths Americans still have in Europe to gain back some of the competitive ground they have lost. The European economy has become so big and so dynamic that even a modest improvement in the U.S. position there could have a substantial impact. If pursued properly, the new opportunities in Europe could be exploited to forestall an otherwise likely implosion of the U.S. domestic economy and to buy some time for the long-term program of American renewal. . . .

Enormous opportunities lie ahead in Europe for American business and

American national interests. The savviest companies and the shrewdest investors are sure to find plenty of profit in the New Europe. A larger and more open question is whether the United States will manage to turn the many tactically advantageous circumstances into strategic gains for the next century's global competitiveness race. Let us outline some of these opportunities and look at what Americans are doing to capitalize on them:

1. American companies are already pan-European in their thinking and management. The large American multinational companies operating in Europe today are following the pan-European trail blazed by American managers in the 1960s. Four or five managerial generations ago, as Jean-Jacques Servan-Schreiber pointed out, Americans were building Continent-wide corporate structures while Europeans were sticking to the narrow comforts of their own national markets. This American corporate network is not as powerful or dominant as it once was, and many key American players have lost their footing along the way. But the most excellent American companies are today more sophisticated at playing the pan-European game than many of their European competitors.

A good example is American Express. No European company can begin to compete with its product mix and expertise in both travel and financial services. "We've been in Europe for a hundred years," says CEO James Robinson III. "Tourism is already the world's biggest industry, and it's growing in Europe. The European financial-services market will now become much more integrated. I would venture to say that few developments could play better to our unique corporate strengths than 1992."

> *"Enormous opportunities lie ahead in Europe for American business and American national interests."*

A Europe-Wide Strategy

Adds Joan Spero, an Amex vice president who put together a veritable "diplomatic corps" inside the company to deal with issues relating to EC-92, "American businesses are used to dealing with many different European markets at once and operating across borders. The 1992 program will make it that much easier for them to access an even larger European market. More European consumers are going to have more money to spend on exactly the kinds of products and services American Express offers." All over Europe, financial institutions are trying to find ways to build a pan-European customer base. American Express already has one in place.

"American companies have always had a *Europe-wide* strategy which gives them common management methods, budgeting, accounting, and information systems right across Europe," says Eric Friberg, managing director of McKinsey & Co.'s Brussels office. Even more important than this valuable pan-European infrastructure, he believes, is the human dimension: "American companies have spent twenty to thirty years creating a cadre of multilingual, multicultural managers. This is the greatest strength of American business. Sometimes it scares Europeans."

U.S. Firms Employ Talented Europeans

Friberg's point is well illustrated by the case of Transmanche Link, the British-French construction consortium building the tunnel under the English Channel. As Transmanche grew increasingly desperate about cost overruns, delays, and engineering problems involved with the $12 billion project, it sent out an SOS to Egon Zehnder International, the Zurich-based international headhunting firm, to find the world's best project manager to bring in as chief executive. The man they got was Jack Lemley, an American, who has done a stunning job of getting the project back on track.

Friberg's view is no mere self-congratulatory celebration of the virtues of American managers. Most of the human resources he speaks of are not Americans at all, but European nationals working for American firms. Big U.S. multinational firms, in fact, have been the chief consumers of talented Europeans with multicultural management abilities—or those on a track too fast for some of continental Europe's staid business communities. A typical example is Eckhard Pfeiffer, the German manager of Compaq Computer's European operations. When Wall Street analysts want to know about Compaq's future prospects, they trek to an industrial park on Munich's Elektrastrasse. There, Pfeiffer plots the pan-European strategy responsible for over a billion dollars' worth of Compaq's annual sales—almost half of all Compaq's revenues. Pfeiffer's operation, says *Business Week*, is "Compaq's engine of growth."

As for Hewlett-Packard, its personal-computer business is so much stronger in Europe than in the United States that it took the unprecedented step in 1990 of moving its worldwide PC headquarters out of Sunnyvale, California, to Grenoble, France, under the stewardship of a talented Frenchman, Jacques Clay.

All of this is to say that in terms of their operations as well as their management, many American companies are already well positioned in Europe. While growth in the Japanese market remains difficult for Americans to convert into opportunities, European growth is playing to American strengths. Barring management missteps and corporate crises at home, most of the big U.S.-based multinationals already present in Europe should do very well there in the 1990s.

> *"Most of the big U.S.-based multinationals already present in Europe should do very well there in the 1990s."*

2. Business alliances are the way of the future. New conditions in Europe are prompting once self-sufficient American companies to seek joint ventures, marketing agreements, and strategic alliances with European partners. At one end of the spectrum there are big, visionary pacts such as the IBM-Siemens joint quest for next-generation technology, or AT&T's equity stake in the Italian phone company Italtel, which facilitates joint pursuit of Italian and European telecommunications opportunities. Ford and Fiat are cementing a $5 billion partnership in farm equipment that basically lets Ford get out of a business in which it was doing poorly, while keeping a finger in it for the future.

> *"English . . . is indisputably the way of the future."*

At the other end are more-focused and lower-profile collaborations. For example, Chrysler plans to reenter the European market by producing minivans at the facilities of Austrian specialty vehicle-maker Steyr-Daimler-Puch Fahrzeugtechnik, and Scott Paper (the U.S. company which is Europe's leading tissue manufacturer) is creating a joint venture with the German-Swedish paper group Feldmühle to gain better access to the German and Dutch markets. American Airlines has taken on a European collaborator, too, establishing a marketing agreement with the French railway system to link air reservations in and out of Paris with rail travel to other parts of France.

Failed Corporate Marriages

Faddishness helps to explain some of this recent spate of cross-border alliances, and not surprisingly, a few of these marriages have already begun to unravel. A much-touted strategic alliance between AT&T and Olivetti ended in high-profile friction, Daimler-Benz had a falling-out with General Electric which almost led to an international lawsuit, and a joint venture between Chrysler and Renault to build four-wheel-drive vehicles in France was jointly terminated.

But the principle of global partnerships will endure. American companies have powerful assets to bring to the bargaining table in forming such alliances, not the least of which is the access they can provide to the U.S. domestic market. Given the erosion of manufacturing competitiveness at home, developing a system of alliances with other global leaders may be the most appropriate and advantageous course for many U.S. firms.

3. American companies speak English! A considerable competitive advantage resides in the fact that managers of U.S. companies—whether American or European by birth—speak English, since this has emerged as the common language of European business. Local languages may remain extremely important within individual countries, and German may be gaining some popularity. But as far as pan-European business is concerned, English—the medium for conducting 50 percent of the world's business deals and storing 80 percent of its computer-based information—is indisputably the way of the future. With native speakers of English in the U.K. and Ireland, and a vast number of Continentals who speak it as a second language, English has emerged as the single most

Chapter 1

widely spoken European language.

Even the French, who are notoriously chauvinistic about their language, have begun to recognize this fact of life. "French is dead as a world language," concedes Yves Sabouret, a top executive with the giant French publisher Hachette. "If you are in the media, information, and entertainment businesses, you cannot doubt that English is the language that will experience the most future growth."

4. European profits can be reinvested to enhance the overall global competitiveness of American business. Increased revenues and profits from the European market can be plowed back into improving the general competitiveness of American companies. Digital Equipment has survived rough weather in its domestic U.S. business by riding the back of a huge boom in Europe—now the company's fastest-growing region and the source of 45 percent of total corporate revenues. The biggest U.S. company of all, General Motors, has adopted a similar strategy. GM now sells 30 percent of its total auto production in Europe and earns 50 percent of its worldwide profits there. The European operations are doing so well that GM plans to expand production by 25 percent, even as it closes U.S. facilities.

"I don't think one can overestimate the importance of GM Europe to the entire GM organization," says Maryann Keller, the world's leading GM watcher. Europe, she explains, "is where the cash is coming from for investment in GM North America."

> *"The European market could serve to carry many American companies through what would otherwise be a traumatic contraction at home."*

In other words, despite woeful management mistakes and a precipitous loss of market share to Japanese rivals at home in the U.S., the European business is healthy enough to provide GM the reinvestment cash it needs to attempt a domestic turnaround.

5. Europe may help the American growth businesses of the 1980s to continue growing in the 1990s. As a result of the unusually long period of sustained U.S. economic expansion in the 1980s, many American companies have been left with the capacity and staff necessary to satisfy a continuously growing market, at a time when many sectors are facing saturation and even contraction. The U.S. computer business is one of the best examples, and as we have noted, companies such as IBM, DEC, and Compaq are easing the transition by turning to Europe for revenues and profits.

European Opportunities

Real estate developers and construction companies, facing the aftermath of American overexpansion, plummeting real estate values, and the collapse of the S&Ls, are looking to Europe for opportunities. While office space is oversupplied in many major U.S. cities, it is desperately short in much of Europe. "There is more economic activity now than I've ever seen in Europe," says Donald Williams, CEO of the Trammell Crow. "The 1992 unification is a reality.". . .

Investment bankers also smell money in Europe, although none of the smart ones expect Europe's deal-making ever to match that seen on Wall Street in the 1980s. While the art of the deal is slowing down in the U.S., it is heating up in London and European points beyond. Jeffrey Rosen, of the New York investment-banking firm Wasserstein, Perella & Co., complains that striking up conversations with potential clients on the Concorde's swift ride across the Atlantic has become tougher recently. It seems too many rival American bankers are trying to do the same thing. "They race to either end of the aisles," says Rosen. "Nobody gets to eat anymore, because everyone's so busy trying to do business.". . .

European Markets

The danger exists, of course, that U.S. strategic planners may overestimate Europe's potential or attempt to move too quickly without establishing sufficiently deep local roots. But if exploited judiciously, the European market could serve to carry many American companies through what would otherwise be a traumatic contraction at home.

6. American businesses lead the world in sectors likely to experience robust European growth. Although U.S.-based companies have lost global leadership in manufacturing, they are far out in front in many areas of the emerging service economy, such as finance, software development, information-systems management, communications, entertainment, leisure time, and franchising, among others. In all these sectors, the outlook for Europe in the '90s is bullish.

A number of excellent services originally developed for American domestic consumption are now finding new markets in Europe. Ted Turner's Cable News Network has won a loyal audience in several European countries, and the *CBS Evening News with Dan Rather* has become popular in France. More American films and television programs are now being developed with the European market in mind than ever before. The quirky *Twin Peaks* TV series was as popular on videocassette in Europe as it was in the U.S. on network TV. The European video even had its own ending that answered the question "Who killed Laura Palmer?" long before American audiences would find out.

> *"A number of excellent services originally developed for American domestic consumption are now finding new markets in Europe."*

The enthusiasm that greeted the Euro Disneyland project has led other American companies into developing theme parks and new entertainment ventures all across a continent that, from an American viewpoint, is seriously underserved when it comes to leisure-time facilities. Toys "R" Us stores are sprouting up at prime locations off the German autobahn as America's master toy marketers cash in on the European baby boom. Even something as uniquely

Chapter 1

American as the National Football League is cultivating a European market. NFL exhibition games are now played annually in cities such as London, Paris, and Berlin, while domestic games are regularly televised in the U.K.

U.S.-based accounting firms are already the leaders in cross-border accounting worldwide and are now experiencing rapid European growth as the EC moves toward standardizing its financial rules and procedures, as well as certain taxes. For American international-law firms, advertising agencies, public-relations companies, and executive recruiters, Europe is now perceived as a new frontier.

> *"The best tactic for American companies worried about the Japanese is to make alliances with European partners."*

7. *Europe offers American businesses new strategies for dealing with Japanese competitors.* From the standpoint of business strategy, one of the most promising aspects of Europe's new economic vitality is the potential trump card it offers Americans doing battle with Japanese competitors. Whether American companies will choose to play this card remains to be seen, but a few are already trying.

A U.S.-European Alliance Against Japan

IBM and Siemens, as noted earlier, have teamed up to try to catch Japanese leaders in the race for mass production of the next generation of computer memory chips. On another front, Philips and Thomson, already allies in European HDTV ventures, have formed a special U.S. consortium with NBC to try to outflank Japanese efforts to capture the American HDTV market.

"The best tactic for American companies worried about the Japanese is to make alliances with European partners," says Edith Cresson, France's minister of European affairs. "Americans and Europeans complement each other's strengths and weaknesses very nicely. We both face the same problem with the Japanese. Why not solve it together?" It is a tempting offer, although the simplicity of the idea belies the complex mechanics and conflicting interests involved in putting such deals together. Nevertheless, the European "trump card" holds a great deal of promise as a much-needed new strategy for countering Japanese competition.

8. *Americans can be leaders in creatively developing the Eastern European and Soviet markets.* Although Germany may be inclined to regard all of Eastern Europe as its natural home market, there is no fundamental reason why Americans can't be very successful between the Elbe and Urals. So far, certain American companies are showing a healthy interest in Eastern Europe, and even seem willing to take big risks for the sake of getting in on the ground floor of this complicated but exciting market. PepsiCo exhibited daring as well as a flair for creative bartering when it entered into a $3 billion deal to provide the Soviets with bottling plants that can churn out as much as 75 million cases of Pepsi

a year. In return for all those soft drinks, PepsiCo will get Stolichnaya vodka and Soviet-built oceangoing freighters and tankers. Philip Morris, meanwhile, is finalizing a barter venture that may net it up to one-fifth of the Soviet cigarette market in a country which has twenty million more smokers than the United States. . . .

A Need for Technology

The Soviet Union desperately needs American technology, although it generally has little hard currency with which to buy it. But the Soviets also have some technology of their own that may prove to be marketable. The Bechtel Group has undertaken a feasibility study for converting a government research center outside Moscow into a prototype American-style cluster of high-tech enterprises. Arthur D. Little, Inc. has entered into a joint venture with the prestigious Soviet Academy of Sciences to commercialize technology developed by leading Soviet scientists.

"It costs $250,000 to $300,000 a year to support a top-level scientist at major American corporations," says Barney O'Meara, a consultant on East-West technology trade. "You can have the same caliber of talent, complete with overhead, lab space, and graduate students in the East for $25,000 to $30,000.". . .

In a 1990 survey, 70 percent of American senior managers said they were preparing new business strategies based on the revolutions in Eastern Europe and were developing plans to enter those markets. OPIC, the U.S. government agency that provides political risk insurance to U.S. companies abroad, reports American investments in Eastern Europe rising from a base of zero in 1988 to $500 million in 1989 and $1.5 billion in 1990. . . .

> *"A sense of the possible, a belief in the future, a vision—these are unquantifiable yet essential forces in the global competitiveness battle."*

A sense of the possible, a belief in the future, a vision—these are unquantifiable yet essential forces in the global competitiveness battle. Indeed, these forces drove the American economy for two hundred years, as the nation advanced from the frontiers of the West to the New Frontier of the space program. . . .

Perhaps Western Europe's economic success, coupled with the de-communization of Eastern Europe, will simply contribute to the expanding global economic pie, with American business getting its share.

European Unification Can Serve as a Model for the Former Soviet Union

by Desmond Dinan

About the author: *Desmond Dinan is the director of George Mason University's Center for European Community Studies in Fairfax, Virginia.*

The year 1992 is synonymous with the European Community's single-market program and, more generally, with the revitalization of Western Europe. But the year 1992 will most likely be remembered for epic events in the East, as the former Soviet republics assert their autonomy, search for stability, and, in many cases, struggle for survival. The "acceleration of history" in 1988 and 1989, culminating in the Soviet Union's collapse in 1991, threatened to throw 1992 off course. In the late 1980s the Community pursued the complementary objectives of deeper integration and an imaginative *Ostpolitik*. On the one hand, the Community advanced its internal market agenda, embarked on economic and monetary union, launched a common foreign and security policy, and strengthened its institutional structure. On the other, the Community concluded commercial and cooperative agreements with the former Soviet-bloc countries, coordinated Western aid to Eastern Europe, absorbed the German Democratic Republic, took the initiative in establishing the European Bank for Reconstruction and Development, helped to negotiate the European Energy Charter, and signed far-reaching association agreements with Czechoslovakia, Hungary, and Poland.

Aid to Russia Is Essential

From the outset, the European Community and its twelve member states had been strong supporters of *glasnost* and *perestroika*. In effect, that meant supporting Mikhail Gorbachev. But it was only in late 1989 that Moscow was ready to conclude a commercial and cooperative agreement with the Community, a "modest and prudent first step" in developing an economic and political

Desmond Dinan, "The European Community and the Collapse of the Soviet Union," *National Forum/Phi Kappa Phi Journal*, Spring 1992. Reprinted with permission.

relationship (according to John Pinder, *The European Community and Eastern Europe*). Apart from trying to encourage trade between the Community and the Soviet Union, Brussels sought by signing a formal accord to reassure Moscow that the Soviet Union would not be excluded from Gorbachev's metaphorical European house. In the following year, with German unification a reality and the Soviet Union descending into disorder, it was more important than ever for the Community to involve the U.S.S.R. in the new European architecture. As a grudging host to several hundred thousand Soviet troops, Germany especially urged the Community to pursue a positive, constructive policy in the East. In December 1990 the Community approved emergency food aid and an ambitious technical assistance program for the Soviet Union.

> "On the day of his departure, the Community paid genuine tribute to Gorbachev's 'great vision of a new Europe and a safer world.'"

Events in 1991 severely strained the Community's newly established relations with Moscow. Brussels protested against repression in the Baltic States and fretted about the apparent ascendancy of conservative communists in the Kremlin. Yet the Commission opened an office in Moscow, in time to observe at close quarters the failed military coup, Boris Yeltsin's triumph over Gorbachev, and the rapid dissolution of the U.S.S.R. With great regret, the Community watched Gorbachev go. On the day of his departure, the Community paid genuine tribute to Gorbachev's "great vision of a new Europe and a safer world," a vision that helped to "end the partition of Europe and to bring down the German wall."

EC-CIS Collaboration

The Community responded to the sensational circumstances of late 1991 and early 1992 by sending emergency food aid to Moscow and St. Petersburg and by immediately exploring options for longer-term economic assistance. A Commission report in January 1992 proposed accords between the Community and the U.S.S.R. successor states that would not go as far as the recently signed "European Agreements" with Czechoslovakia, Hungary, and Poland but would nonetheless promote economic reform and political stability in the former Soviet Union. Moreover, the Community wants to encourage collaboration between the components of the newly established Commonwealth of Independent States (CIS). Commission vice-president Frans H.J.J. Andriessen remarked that "the degree to which we are willing to help [the Soviet successor states] may be determined by their willingness to cooperate with each other."

As it was, the Community concluded its European Agreements after arduous negotiations that pitted the member states' protectionist proclivities against their political rhetoric. When it came to granting the Eastern European countries liberal market access, especially for steel, agriculture, and textiles, a number of member states succumbed to domestic protectionist pressure and blocked generous terms. Only when Hungary and Poland embarrassed the Community by threatening to walk out of the talks, and Vaclav Havel warned that "right-wing authoritarian and nationalist forces would exploit a failure to reach agreement," did the recalcitrant member states—notably France and Spain—come to their senses.

Eastern Europe's Advantages

The Community's efforts to assist the former Soviet republics are likely to engender an even stronger protectionist reaction in the member states. Although the proposed EC-CIS accords do not entail the same degree of market access as the Community conceded in its European Agreements, they doubtless involve an element of openness unacceptable to many member states. Nor will the Independent States' arguments be as persuasive as those of the Eastern European countries. For one thing, the Independent States are physically more remote from Western Europe than the Community's immediate neighbors to the east. For another, the plight of the Independent States has far less emotional appeal in Western Europe than has the fate of the recently liberated countries of Eastern Europe. Moreover, precisely because the Community has just granted liberal commercial concessions to Czechoslovakia, Hungary, and Poland, and is ready to negotiate similar arrangements with Bulgaria and Romania, member states are bound to feel that they have little left to offer without "giving away the family store."

> "The plight of the Independent States has far less emotional appeal in Western Europe than has the fate of the recently liberated countries of Eastern Europe."

In December 1991, the issue of diplomatic recognition posed an immediate political problem for the Community. The contemporaneous Yugoslav crisis also obliged the Community to come up with acceptable criteria. Hence, on 16 December 1991, the foreign ministers of the twelve states adopted the "Guidelines on the Recognition of New States in Eastern Europe and the Soviet Union." Demonstrating a commitment to the Conference on Security and Cooperation in Europe (CSCE), a process in which the Community and its member states have always played a prominent part, and a desire for a pan-European approach to the emergence of new international entities in the East, the Community's criteria drew heavily on the CSCE's Helsinki Final Act (1975) and the Charter of Paris (1991). Thus the Community stressed the principle of self-determination, together with respect for human rights and the rule of law. In general, the Community promised recognition to "those new States which . . . have accepted the appropriate international obligations and have committed themselves in good faith to a peaceful process and to negotiations."

The question of relations with the Soviet republics and the practical problems of promoting economic and political reform in the CIS reinforced the Community's need to develop a common foreign and security policy. Already, the requirement to respond rapidly and coherently to events in Eastern Europe in 1988 and 1989 had helped to close the gap between the Community's external economic relations and its member states' foreign policies. Hitherto, Community competence had not covered foreign or security policy, although since 1970 the member states had coordinated their separate foreign policies by participating in a process called European Political Cooperation (EPC). The success of the single-market program, revolution in Eastern Europe, and the Community's inability to realize its full potential in the Gulf Crisis combined to convince the twelve members to strengthen EPC and to develop a "security identity" for the Community. Consequently, as part of the proposed Act of European Union agreed to at the Maastricht Summit in December 1991, the member states decided to launch a common foreign and security policy (CFSP). Although the Act of Union has yet to be ratified in the member states' parliaments, the situation in the CIS presents an opportunity to implement immediately certain elements of a CFSP. Thus, on 10 January 1992, the twelve foreign ministers discussed the possibility of opening combined diplomatic missions of the Commission and the member states in some capitals of the former Soviet republics.

American Concerns

Discussions in the Community in 1991 about acquiring a security dimension and, ultimately, a military potential had provoked an intemperate American response, with warnings from Washington about the dangers of undermining NATO. Apart from particular concerns about the Alliance, the United States seemed slightly alarmed, or at least discomfited, by the Community's rising political profile and forceful policy toward the East. Despite a deepening United States-EC political relationship, culminating in the Transatlantic Declaration of November 1990, strains between an increasingly insecure America and an increasingly assertive Community are more and more apparent in the foreign policy field. They came to a head in December 1991 when U.S. secretary of state James Baker surprised his European allies by unexpectedly announcing, in a speech at Princeton University, that the United States would host an international conference in Washington the following month to coordinate aid to the former Soviet republics.

> *"The United States grew more and more concerned about losing leadership in Eastern Europe to the Community."*

In classic Gallic, indeed Gaullist style, President François Mitterrand articulated the extreme European reaction by pointing out that the EC member states are providing the bulk of assistance to the CIS and that the United States should instead come to Europe to coordinate the aid effort. Mitterrand's unrestrained response went to the core of the "burden sharing" debate between Washington and Brussels over assistance to Eastern Europe and the disintegrating U.S.S.R. By endorsing Commission President Jacques Delors' proposal at the summit of major industrialized countries in Paris in July 1989 that the Commission coordinate the Western aid effort for Hungary and Poland, President George Bush gave concrete expression to his previously stated goal of boosting the Community's political persona. Subsequently, the so-called "G24" group of donor countries decided to extend Community-coordinated assistance to all Eastern European countries, including the Baltic states. At the same time, despite a resounding victory in the Gulf War and the arrival of what commentator Charles Krauthammer has called the "unipolar moment," the United States grew more and more concerned about losing leadership in Eastern Europe to the Community, an international parvenu.

> *"The European Community is a striking example of reconciliation and successful integration for the countries of the former Soviet Union to emulate."*

Washington's sometimes churlish role in the Community-sponsored negotiations for a European Energy Charter demonstrated U.S. concern about losing the Eastern European initiative to the EC. Baker's Princeton University speech similarly smacked of an ill-prepared attempt to assert America's role in the international effort to assist the crumbling Soviet Union. Notwithstanding Mitterrand's initial hostility, the EC Council of Ministers endorsed the Community's participation in the Washington conference but took great care to coordinate its position beforehand and to affirm the Community's leading role in assisting the East. "The Community and its member states," the Council of Ministers concluded, "will participate in the conference on the basis of a common position to be closely coordinated beforehand. . . . The [conference's] four working party co-chairmanships assigned to Member States or the Community will be held under a dual arrangement involving Member States concerned and the Community."

A Model of Peace

The Community's geopolitical proximity to the CIS, its economic well-being as compared with that of the United States, and the Act of European Union ensure that Brussels will be a key player in the former U.S.S.R.'s future. Moreover, the European Community is a striking example of reconciliation and successful integration for the countries of the former Soviet Union to emulate. Despite their vastly different political cultures and levels of economic development, at least these countries can look to the postwar integration of their Western European counterparts as a model of peace, progress, and prosperity. The lesson has not been lost on some Eastern European statesmen. Commenting on the fate of the former Soviet bloc, Jiri Dienstbier, foreign minister of Czechoslovakia, remarked that "we will be secure only if the relations among all European countries are, let's say, like the relations between Belgium and the Netherlands." If only by proffering examples of that kind, the European Community and its member states will continue to be positive forces for change in the erstwhile U.S.S.R.

European Unification Will Weaken Europe

by Angelo Codevilla

About the author: *Angelo Codevilla is a fellow at the Hoover Institution, a political think tank affiliated with Stanford University in Stanford, California.*

Should Americans be delighted that, as the State Department believes, Europe is uniting into a powerful partner for peace, prosperity, and civilization? Should we join in the fashionable fears of those who see the Maastricht Treaty of December 1991 endowing 350 million Europeans with a Japanese-style industrial policy that will relegate the U.S. to third place in a global economic competition? Or will we look on with dismay as European governments, under leaders largely lacking in aptitude, legitimacy, and vision, buck the healthiest trends in the modern world?

The Vision of de Gaulle and Adenauer

The first postwar wave of European leaders were conservative Catholics from the border areas of France, Germany, and Italy. No one could think of Charles de Gaulle as slack in patriotism or unmindful that executive authority is important. Nevertheless, he shared his conservative family's premodern vision of the good life—abhorring regimentation as well as looking back to centuries when localities and regions had managed their own affairs without much interference from the central government. Konrad Adenauer, an old-fashioned Rhenish Catholic, shared this vision.

Their vision, "the Europe of the Fatherlands," was shared by Italy's postwar re-founder, Alcide de Gasperi, and was embodied in the founding document of the Common Market in 1957: Governments, while giving up none of their responsibilities, would free their societies and economies to grow together. Not least of the reasons why these conservatives wanted to draw their peoples together was to safeguard European civilization against Communist barbarians. Thus the guiding vision, the source of legitimacy for the early vision of Europe, was a combination of decentralized government, liberal economics, free trade,

Angelo Codevilla, "The Coming Euromess," *National Review*, June 8, 1992. Copyright 1992 by National Review, Inc., 150 E. 35th St., New York, NY 10016. Reprinted with permission.

and Christian culture.

Until the mid-1960s, European leftists fought against European unity. The socialists saw the Communist regimes not as barbarians but as brothers. They wanted rapprochement or even unity *with* Communists, not against them. They also regarded the Common Market's commitment to free trade, and to diminishing the powers of national governments to grant privileges, as an attack on the practical basis of socialism—patronage. As socialists took power within European countries, they naturally transformed the pan-European enterprise according to their vision.

EC Became a Tool for Socialists

During the 1980s, as socialism became less and less acceptable *within* each of the countries of Europe, socialists sought to move more and more regulatory and taxing powers to the European Commission in Brussels. Because the EC Commission is not directly accountable to any set of voters, and because to challenge any of its acts is to challenge the whole construct of "Europe"—and implicitly to challenge intra-European peace as well—the EC Commission was the ideal tool for super-centralist socialist management.

As internal tariff barriers fell, the Commissioners balanced their obligations to expand intra-European trade with protectionism via "antidumping" measures, wielded in particular against Japanese exports, and regulations to "harmonize" standards across the Community. The EC Commission brings together various producers of any given item, say a lawnmower or a condom, and negotiates agreement on a single standard for its production (yes, there is a Eurocondom, precisely 15.2 cm long). The Commission is even restricting to some half-dozen the varieties of apples allowed to be sold in the Community.

> *"Eurosocialism will produce stagflation, not wealth."*

Such Eurosocialism will produce stagflation, not wealth. No one should have been surprised that the mighty German economy choked in its attempt to assimilate the former East Germany. The Germans proceeded according to socialist, not capitalist, principles. Not only did they exchange the near worthless Ostmark for real Deutschmarks, but they immediately extended the West's social-welfare system to the East, enabling most Easterners to live far better than they ever had, without working. Moreover, instead of letting Eastern companies fail and giving each worker a share of the assets to be sold off, they began an open-ended restructuring process that is dragging the rest of the country down. And the ensuing systemic, long-term recession is dragging down the rest of Europe. The Germans were following the sad example of Italy, which has spent perhaps a trillion dollars on a forty-year attempt to bring its Southern regions up to Northern standards. Alas, distributing money to the indolent, corrupt South corrupted the North more than it helped the South.

Chapter 1

Yet this is precisely the approach that the EC as a whole is taking with regard to its poorer members—Spain, Portugal, Greece, Ireland, etc. Nine out of the EC twelve are net recipients of subsidies. The bargain is straightforward: the poorer members take welfare in exchange for raising the cost of doing business to match that in high-cost countries. The adoption of a single Eurocurrency would lock in the high costs and hence the respective roles of rich and poor. In the long run, this is a bad bargain for both sides.

Failed Industrial Policy

Another rationale for the EC's subsidies is that they allow governments to pick and foster "champions" which will then conquer global markets. Although agriculture is the field in which this is applied on the largest scale, this is "industrial policy"—the governmental tool that American policy intellectuals now almost unanimously agree is the key to prosperity. Well, its record in Europe is dismal. The latest "champion," Groupe Bull computers, absorbed about a billion dollars and then flopped on world markets. (The EC Commission uses them.)

It is unlikely that the EC twelve will generate enough income, and enough discipline, to "harmonize" labor costs and social policy from Crete to Scotland. It is even less likely that they will be able to deal with the post-Communist economies on their doorstep. The EC is in the process of closing, not opening, its doors to the rest of the industrialized world because it is driven both by rising German labor costs and by a neo-mercantilist mentality: export more than you import, while keeping domestic prices and wages high. This mentality, which earlier in this century lowered Argentina from the First World to the Third, is unlikely ever to help the former Second World to climb into the ranks of the First. Indeed at this rate the EC will be characterized by labor costs on the level of Germany, trade-union activity on the level of 1970s Britain, bureaucracy as punctilious as in France and as honest as in Greece, and citizens who, to get along, will have to learn to act like Italians.

Eurosocialists are destroying one of the last habitats of that rarest of European creatures—political legitimacy. In 1992 record numbers of Frenchmen, Italians, and Germans are voting against their traditional political parties. Italy has begun a revolution against its entire political class. Positive enthusiasm is limited to Lombard separatism and to a movement

> *"As Europe's economic slump deepens and as a host of problems arise, European politicians will regret having built the EC."*

for direct election and deposition of office-holders. In Germany massive resentment of Easterners, immigrants, and taxes is mixed with near reverence for the Bundesbank and Deutschmark as the repositories of Teutonic virtue. In Spain the age-old pattern seems to have re-asserted itself: Madrid is respected insofar as it leaves the regions alone (and when you go to the Barcelona Olympics, please don't call Catalan a dialect of Spanish). In Britain the widespread pattern of regional reassertion breaks down—Scottish separatism subsided in the recent election—and the government's legitimacy rests on its promise not to return to socialism as well as to maintain a separate British identity. In France, where the ruling party gets under 20 per cent of the vote—neck and neck with the extremist National Front—legitimacy will belong to whoever best ends Arab immigration. The consent of the governed rests on bases that differ greatly from place to place, but which are none too solid anywhere.

> *"Today's EC represents bureaucrats, not people."*

In our civilization, political authority is ultimately moral and can only come from the voters. Europeans are barely obeying their national governments. Why should they obey Brussels? Why should a Portuguese sardine cannery and its workers accept being forced out of business because of regulations they feel they had no say in? Why should Spaniards pay high interest rates because Germans chose to handle reunification in a particular way? Why should Englishmen be forced to give labor unions privileges that they democratically revoked? It is a safe bet that, as Europe's economic slump deepens and as a host of problems arise, European politicians will regret having built the EC edifice without a thought about how the privilege of governing was to be earned.

Of, by, and for Bureaucrats

European unity *could* be built on political decentralization and democratic diversity within a free-trade area rather than on a foredoomed attempt at *Gleichschaltung*. Why, for example, prevent the Danes from experimenting with legalization of drugs? Why threaten the Lombards' or the Catalans' precious dreams of autonomy? Why try to force the Irish to tolerate abortion? Left to themselves, all parts of Europe will satisfy themselves. The role of pan-European institutions should be to mediate between rich forms of life, and to draw out common sentiment. But today's EC represents bureaucrats, not people.

What then will come of the Single European Act of 1986? Maybe very little. Consider: as 1992 began, all 12 states had passed a grand total of 43 out of the 282 laws which they had committed themselves to passing by the end of 1992. No state had passed more than 190. Note also that of the 12 states that approved standards for admission to the "Single European Currency" (low rates of inflation and budget deficits, etc.) only two met those standards. Consider also that similarly grandiose plans had been formulated twenty years ago; then the price of oil rose—and European governments forgot their commitments.

The new Europe showed its impotence as Serbia wrecked Dubrovnik, one of Europe's treasures, and later Sarajevo. Serbia could only have retreated before any sort of European expeditionary force. Yet no politician in the EC could

Chapter 1

bring himself to argue for force. Thus the EC let Serbia establish an evil little empire next door. Discussion of procedures for formulating a common foreign policy substituted for such a policy.

What would the EC countries do if the next coup in Moscow brought a regime intent on using guns to compel butter? Or what if a Riyadh-Baghdad-Damascus axis threatened another oil embargo? Within the EC countries there are more than enough people, Marks, francs, microchips, and guns. But there is no Churchill, no de Gaulle, not even a George Bush to call right and wrong by name. The EC would probably pay ransom and ask for American help while decrying America's shortcomings.

While Europeans are demanding a lightening of taxation and regulation, they are getting a heavier dose of both. While Europeans are feeling less and less comfortable with rule from faraway national capitals and are demanding power for local and regional governments, they are becoming subject to the whims of a single set of unelected Eurocrats in Brussels. While Europeans are rejoicing at the end of the cold war, while they are looking forward to reabsorbing Eastern Europe and to greater partnership with America and Japan, the Eurocrats' trade barriers are helping to keep Eastern Europe a welfare case and are driving the industrial world toward increased protectionism.

Alas, it looks as if, once again, Europe will be a source of cautionary lessons—and of trouble.

European Unification Will Increase Regional Conflicts

by Thomas Molnar

About the author: *Thomas Molnar is a scholar and the author of numerous books, including* The Pagan Temptation, Authority and Its Enemies, *and* The Church, Pilgrim of Centuries.

It would be logical for me to say that, returning to the United States after another four months in various countries of Europe, east and west, I found a great many misconceptions about the continent in American media and public opinion. Yet it would not be fair to limit myself to such a remark, because in Europe too such misconceptions are staggering; at least those which are engendered in the east about the west and in the west about the east. This is the more astonishing as these two halves are scheduled to be gradually working out their rapprochement, in order finally to unite. The truth is, however, that such a "unity" is nothing more than a slogan, a magic word that carries two different meanings: the east of Europe regards unity as a method of receiving vast sums from the west, in the form of gifts, investments, joint ventures, and tourism (myriad hotels are being built to receive visitors); the west of Europe regards unity as a means of flooding the east with needed and unneeded merchandise, as a means of making instant and huge profits through investment (there are already guidebooks to this effect).

Mutual Suspicions

The negative aspect of these sharp ambitions on both sides is the fear of the other's Machiavellianism, or, more plainly, its tricks. The west, including even Austria, is worried about the new migrants from the impoverished lands: Gypsies from Rumania, black-marketeering Poles, masses of Russians; the east is even more worried that the respective national resources and patrimonies will be bought up by foreign capital under the pretext of "privatization," and that "western culture" will invade minds and tastes that have successfully resisted forty years of communism and brainwashing.

Thomas Molnar, "Europe Is Not What It Seems," *Chronicles*, vol. 15, no. 4, April 1991. Reprinted with permission.

Chapter 1

This is, then, the rather desolate truth in place of the illusion that East and West Europe wish nothing better than to cooperate and unite. Underneath the politicians' official embraces, old and new fears surface, national jealousies thrive, and among western investors themselves a kind of shark-morality prevails: who can cut a larger slice from the soon-to-be neocolonized east? About 40 percent of Hungary's newspapers are already in the hands of western press-lords: Maxwell, Murdoch and the French Hersant. With only 30 percent of the take, the German *Springer Verlag* (Hamburg) is already in the position of vetoing the arrival of French newspapers—or at least delaying them for days (and who wants yesterday's papers?).

A Distaste for Unification

These are more than just glimpses of the supposedly happy east/west relations. In Western Europe proper the idea of unity is regressing, although the cause has become so sacred that all lips pay service to the wonderful prospects coming in 1993. Yet the Germans want none of the "union," none of the common currency, and if you look at France or Spain, you readily understand why the Germans are so reluctant and why they will end up dictating the future. France is full of striking workers, students, public employees—and every month a huge foreign trade deficit. Spain is increasingly desolate, its industry retrogressing, its (socialist) government supported by only 29 percent of the population. The Germans, with their skill and know-how, penetrate Spanish economic life like a knife into butter, and they are also mightily present in Eastern Europe (and Russia), where France is virtually absent.

The long and short of it is that hegemonic Germany does not need a united Europe, and, together with England although for different reasons, Helmut Kohl or his successors will systematically torpedo such a construct. Why England, after Margaret Thatcher? Because no matter what Englishman becomes prime minister—tomorrow even Neil Kinnock—he will return to the Thatcherite line. England is not part of the Continent, the Heseltine claim was a political gimmick; truth is, Englishmen detest the Continent, and the opening of the tunnel may even exacerbate this feeling. What we may expect is that the January 1, 1993, deadline for unity will be put off to later, then again and again, until such time that the whole unmanageable mess will be dropped and forgotten.

> *"The long and short of it is that hegemonic Germany does not need a united Europe."*

For the past three or four years the notion of unity was a strategy of France to a) prevent German unification, b) prevent Russo-German rapprochement (a new and dreaded Rapallo), and c) tie a relatively weak West Germany to a permanently lame France. This strategy failed at every point, although François Mitterrand now puts on a good face—hiding his fury.

Yet, the clowning goes on, and Kohl, Giulio Andreotti, and John Major keep smiling at the prospect of unity, hiding their second thoughts, at least as long as Jacques Delors lords it over in Brussels as high commissar of unity. Delors, a cold technocrat and a Christian Democrat to boot (a good mask for deeper layers of Jacobinism, thus ultra-centralization of all powers), is a typical Frenchman in the sense of "either I lead you, or I prevent you from playing the game." All groups that include the French end up succumbing to this sense of superiority—except the Germans who, when powerful, display a different but just as devastating arrogance. Delors' mandate as Brussels' superstar will soon end, and chances are that Belgian Prime Minister Wilfried Martens will succeed him. This means, since Martens is a Fleming and not a Walloon, that British interests will be better safeguarded than the French, and we may then see an ephemeral alliance between London and Berlin—against Paris. At any rate, the triangular situation does not promise much "unity" but a lot of haggling, which will also be to the detriment of the "small" ones, from Lisbon to Oslo to Athens—not to speak of Eastern Europe, still only interested in getting funds.

> *"Among the citizens there is absolutely no enthusiasm for the 'commonly shared' Europe."*

Attitudes of Common Europeans

This is the happy harmony at the top; among the citizens there is absolutely no enthusiasm for the "commonly shared" Europe. Juan Goytisolo asks in the leading Spanish paper, *El Pais*, just what may be the issue or the tradition on which the nations of Europe would see eye to eye? The common man's attitude is either complete indifference or indeed fear that he would lose his job to better qualified European "brothers," or that his little private sphere of life would be invaded by North Africans and Asians. European unity may be efficacious in one area, but it will also breed racial hatred, which is already growing as the laws issued from Brussels clearly advantage the "immigrant" over against the local population. The common man knows he is being sold a bill of goods; his reaction is not yet savage, but his patience is not inexhaustible. A typical reaction by a French shopkeeper: For the time being, we hardly manage to coexist with North Africans, and not at all when they approach majority in any given *arrondissement* or village; but God only knows what will happen if Germany kicks out its Turkish workers (replaced easily by ex-East Germans), who then merely cross our borders—without a passport.

Although "European unity" is becoming a swear word, the Strasbourg "parliament," blissfully ignoring popular wishes, has just now voted a resolution turning the future Europe into a "federation." Federation, confederation, total unity—whatever the label—all people expect the consumer society to continue and even to be further "Americanized." I said "all expect," but this is not quite true. In the West, consumerist habits are by now so ingrained that not even confiscatory taxes prevent the citizen from living a life of mindless purchase. In the East, things have not gone that far, because a perhaps majority of citizens value their regained homeland and want to continue their national existence, interrupted for half a century. But inside every East European country there is also a vocal minority—technocrats, liberals, agnostics, pro-capitalists—who want an instant consumer society, to hell with the nation's past and communal interests. These people publish most of the newspapers and magazines, shape the TV programs, teach at the universities. Many young priests have joined their ranks. Facing this strong minority, there is the usual silent majority, reluctant to disperse the national patrimony in the name of "privatization," and insistent on, for example, religious instruction in schools. You find the split between Lech Walesa and Adam Michnik, or between Jozsef Antall and Janos Kiss. For the time being, the forces of tradition are strong enough to win elections for top posts; the zealous brothers from among western bankers and speculators have, however, mounted their financial offensive to put the local liberal Democrats in power. Walesa is the target of scurrilous attacks—and his name stands here as a collective phenomenon.

Few Commonalities

At any rate, it is hard to imagine that the cause of European unity would resist the innumerable conflicts that are quite natural for Europe, although baffling to Americans. How do you achieve union when, on the one hand, Germany is strong and vital enough to reabsorb in a matter of a few months her eastern provinces, while France is so weak as to want to grant independence to Corsica? How do you achieve union when all the nationality conflicts are ablaze in Eastern Europe, and Russia herself becomes fragmented, each fragment entertaining hostile intentions? No wonder that under the circumstances those who begin to doubt the magic January 1, 1993, are proposing new configurations, not as artificial as Jacobin Jacques Delors' Robespierrian abstraction. If not pan-European unity, they say, why not regional groupings, as suggested by Italy's foreign minister, Gianni De Michelis, who foresees German hegemony and proposes as a counterweight a line reaching from Barcelona to Trieste, and farther up to Slovenia and Hungary. Others have a Baltic-to-the-Mediterranean axis in mind, reaching as far as Morocco. Skeptics say that one look at the map demonstrates that the northern capitals (and industrial areas) are nearer each other, such as London to Stockholm, than the southern capitals, say from Madrid to Ankara, a line that passes through vast underdeveloped regions. In other words, it seems that a united Europe would still offer unbeatable advan-

> *"Unity would . . . mean exploitation not only of Eastern Europe by Western Europe, but of the soft southern underbelly by northern industry."*

tages to the northern countries over those of the south. Unity would thus mean exploitation not only of Eastern Europe by Western Europe, but of the soft southern underbelly by northern industry.

Mme. Marie-France Garaud, who used to be Georges Pompidou's and Jacques Chirac's chief advisor, now admits in *Géopolitique* that unity remains an empty slogan when reality is preparing a continental shift from west to east (including Russia), whether fragmented or unified. There may be in this a historic justice. A united Europe did exist, under the Church's aegis, in the Middle Ages; it was the *christiana respublica*. It broke up around 1500 A.D., when the Turkish invasion detached east from west. During the subsequent centuries the west profited by the Renaissance, the age of discoveries, science and industry, while the east fell into stagnation, devastations, wars, and poverty. "Unity" under these conditions has been a historical misnomer, a mere geographical fact. It appears now that the east is taking its revenge: while Western Europe has nothing to offer except more consumer goods, Eastern Europe reenters history, thanks partly to the recapture of the national idea and to the historical imperative of Russo-German cooperation. Many, mostly outside, fear a recrudescence of national feelings and other strong emotions, eventually ideologies. If so, this cannot be helped; it is primarily the fault of the Western Allies after the Second World War, which instead of integrating the "two Europes" pushed one into the crushing arms of the Soviet Union. Resistance and accumulated suffering created new national energies that will be difficult to channel because the only alternative channel is a democratic-liberal model unsuitable for Eastern Europe.

> *"Conflicts would still remain, except that they would not be called 'foreign wars' but 'civil wars.'"*

A Soulless Supermarket

In this perspective—which is not that of the eternal illusionists and late-regretters—the "unity" of Europe is a last-minute trick to pour the east in the mold of the west. The goal is a continent-wide supermarket, without a soul, without an identity, without the lessons of the past, and above all without protection from future dangers. East European populations aspire understandably to all those things from which they were deprived for five decades, whether it be easy travel abroad or imported luxuries, or even (why not at this stage) pornographic literature. Thus they give the impression of being as frivolous as their counterparts in the west. But, do not underestimate the will to national sovereignty and the power of symbols and traditions. This is the reason (which we in the west try not to see) why German unification is regarded by Eastern Europe as a positive thing. Over against a vaporous "united Europe" a German hegemony is not really feared, particularly if Russia also envisages her own modernization through German know-how. Contrary to recent history, Eastern

Chapter 1

Europe sees in the cooperation of Berlin and Moscow a potent factor for peace in the area, or at least a period in which the small countries will not have to take sides between the two continental "superpowers," and will not have to suffer devastation by one, then another, army. In this light, a "united Europe" seems like a paltry, technocratic dream, an unnecessary complication. Conflicts would still remain, except that they would not be called "foreign wars" but "civil wars." What is the advantage, except, as Talleyrand said after the Vienna Congress (which also gave birth to a "united Europe"), a new but just as hypocritical verbiage?

European Unification Threatens U.S.-European Relations

by Robin Knight

About the author: *Robin Knight is a writer for* U.S. News & World Report, *a weekly newsmagazine.*

Twenty-five years ago, Europeans were preoccupied with *le défi américain*, the American challenge described by French author Jean-Jacques Servan-Schreiber. Today, the talk is of *le défaut américain*. From challenge to weakness in a single generation. Levi's and Harley-Davidsons may remain fashionable in Europe. But the balance between the Old World and the New is shifting, and with it many of the assumptions on which an era of unprecedented partnership, prosperity and stability has been based.

Divorce, or even a trial separation, is impossible; in 1991, U.S.-European Community trade totaled $190 billion, with a $17 billion surplus in America's favor. More than half of America's overseas investments are in Europe, and nearly 2 million Americans live there. Moreover, much of Europe's new assertiveness stems from developments that may not endure—the cohesion of the coalescing EC, steady economic growth, the absence of external threats and Germany's willingness to subordinate its own interests to those of other nations. Nor is Europe, with a few exceptions, gearing up for a battle with America for supremacy or seeking to exclude the United States from its decisions.

United States Balances German Power

Instead, from Russia to Britain, Europeans want the United States to maintain its military, economic and personal ties to Europe. Some European states, especially small countries such as Denmark and the Netherlands, even look to the United States as an antidote to increasing German power. That feeling may even grow if security risks proliferate and Germany builds up its military and economic muscle. And on a range of issues, from terrorism and drugs to human

---

Robin Knight, "Breaking Away," *U.S. News & World Report*, April 6, 1992. Copyright, April 6, 1992, U.S. News & World Report. Reprinted with permission.

Chapter 1

rights, Europe's interests and values coincide with America's. "The relationship will never be as competitive as the U.S.-Japanese one because U.S.-European cultures have far more in common," says British historian William Wallace.

Yet some parting of the ways seems inevitable. The United States is preoccupied with domestic issues, its population is becoming less Eurocentric and its government is hamstrung by budget deficits. Trans-Atlantic trade disputes are escalating. Europe is robustly competitive and increasingly ready to take the lead in addressing contentious regional problems such as Yugoslavia's civil war and aid to the former Soviet republics. Slow growth on both sides of the Atlantic and elections in 1992 in the United States, Britain and Italy, in 1993 in France, and in Germany in 1994 could further strain trans-Atlantic tensions. As *The Guardian*, a London newspaper, put it recently: "The tension lines are clear and potentially menacing."

> "The U.S. has become less important to Europe, and Europe has become less important to America."

The tension was evident in Helsinki, at a meeting of the 51-member Conference on Security and Cooperation in Europe. The French proposed turning the CSCE into the dominant security and peacekeeping body between the Atlantic and the Urals and leaving the North Atlantic Treaty Organization as little more than a nuclear alliance of last resort. The Spanish and the Belgians said they hoped to join France and Germany in creating a new European defense force. The Germans suggested giving the CSCE some teeth and pushed through a plan to use the CSCE to mediate the bloody dispute between Armenia and Azerbaijan over Nagorno-Karabakh. American influence was marginal.

European Home

Ironically, while a succession of Soviet leaders up to and including Mikhail Gorbachev (whose "common European home" had room for Moscow but not Washington) struggled in vain to "decouple" Western Europe and America, the demise of the Soviet Union has done more to promote that goal than four decades of Soviet missiles, tanks, blockades, blandishments and threats. "The U.S. has become less important to Europe, and Europe has become less important to America," says Richard Gardner, a former U.S. ambassador to Italy and now professor of law at Columbia University. "We've waked up to find that having won the cold war, we have a devastated domestic scene. There's been a real political sea change."

NATO has long been the strongest link between Europe and the United States, which otherwise has little leverage over European decision making. To quote Vice President Dan Quayle, the alliance may still be "sustained by trust, tested by time, built on principle." But absent a credible external threat, it is losing its cohesion.

American troops are going home in growing numbers, and the significance of this withdrawal is hard to overstate. In 1989, there were more than 320,000 U.S. troops in Europe. Today, there are some 220,000. Officially, the number will level out at 150,000 in 1995. But pressures are building in Congress for even deeper cutbacks. Sen. John McCain, a member of the Armed Services Committee, predicts the level could be as low as 75,000 in 1995—at least 15 percent below what the Germans regard as the acceptable minimum. Should the U.S. deployment slip below 90,000, the American commitment could lose its credibility—and with it the crucial support of the German government.

Trading Blows

Threats from either side are likely only to widen the trans-Atlantic rift. "The stronger the anti-European line in Washington, the sooner the U.S. will be forced to take all its troops home," says a German diplomat. "No one wants that—at least, not yet." But acrimony is already a fact of life: At a conference in Munich that was attended by Vice President Quayle and other top European and American leaders, American and European participants swapped barely veiled threats over troop withdrawals and trade.

The French belief that Europe can advance only by distancing itself from America poses a second challenge to the alliance. Indeed, it is the French who have aroused the most concern in Washington. Many of the constraints on French policy have disappeared with the end of the cold war: Paris is now openly promoting its vision of a Europe free of American troops. France and Germany will soon announce an agreement on the mission of their joint military corps, and that could further undercut NATO's role as Europe's principal defense alliance.

> *"The type of European Community that now exists is not necessarily the one American officials wanted."*

"The French may have turned a corner," says Hans Binnendijk, director of Georgetown University's Institute for the Study of Diplomacy. "They are prepared to take positions they know will irritate the U.S. because they believe the U.S. will eventually pull out anyhow. If they have to choose between the U.S. in Europe and an independent defense identity, they would choose an independent defense identity."

The trade friction between the growing European Community and the United States sounds even more explosive. President Bush has accused the EC of hiding behind a protectionist "iron curtain." The EC has responded by listing all the allegedly discriminatory practices of the United States.

A six-year drive by the General Agreement on Tariffs and Trade to liberalize world trade rules is faltering, thanks mainly to a French-led refusal to cut EC farm subsidies significantly. In retaliation, the United States plans to boost payments for farm exports, and Congress has voted a $1 billion war chest for use in combatting "unfair" foreign agricultural practices. "We're in a very dangerous

Chapter 1

period," says William Brock, a former U.S. special trade representative. "If the GATT talks collapse over European intransigence, the sense of frustration and disappointment could boil over and cause some very real damage in the Atlantic alliance."

The tug of war is another reflection of the changing balance of American and European power: Washington no longer can set the terms of world trade as it did for the past 40 years. The 12-nation EC, which accounts for one third of global commerce, has become too big and powerful to push around, and the type of European Community that now exists is not necessarily the one American officials wanted. Notes British historian Wallace: "Things will be different. The U.S. has to adjust to being, at most, a first among equals."

More trade clashes lie ahead—over steel products, military sales, telecommunications and support for the aircraft industry. Still, U.S. companies continue to invest heavily in Europe and to find the increasingly integrated European market a congenial one. U.S. investment in Britain doubled between 1985 and 1990 and now totals $65 billion. "They [U.S. firms] don't accept the idea of European borders," says Carl Wilhelm Ros, executive vice president of L.M. Ericsson, a Swedish telecommunications firm. "They act as if it's a common world, and they're successful."

Success Story

None has been more successful than that most American of companies, Levi Strauss. The leading jeans manufacturer in each of the 12 EC nations, its only real competitor is the American VF Corp., maker of Lee jeans. One fourth of Levi Strauss's worldwide sales come from Europe, and the firm now regards itself as "a European company with American roots," says Carl Von Buskirk, vice president for Europe.

Scores of other successful U.S. corporations in Europe think and act similarly, but the competition is likely to get tougher. "A European renaissance is taking place. That is a real challenge," says Jean-Pierre Rosso, worldwide president of Honeywell's home and building materials operations. "It used to be accepted that American companies were the best managed. It's not true anymore." Smaller U.S. firms new to the European market, and those trying to compete with European technologies, sometimes sound apprehensive about Europe's new competitiveness. Still, American businessmen regard the European playing field, unlike Japan's, as more or less level.

> *"It used to be accepted that American companies were the best managed. It's not true anymore."*

In the new markets of Central and Eastern Europe, American firms often have distinct advantages, including a vibrant, diverse culture; modern technology; immigrant communities that bridge the old East-West gap, and the aura of success that comes from having won the cold war and faced down a despotism that many Eastern Europeans never expected to outlive. Finally, the United States stirs up none of the ambivalence touched off by Germany, its only true competitor in the race to develop the eastern half of the continent.

So far, however, the American performance in Eastern Europe has been disappointing. Only 1 percent of the 500 privatization deals in Czechoslovakia involve U.S. firms. Germany claims to be providing half of the support for reform in the former Soviet Union, compared with 6 percent from the United States. America is exporting its culture as books, films and television series flood the East, but at a time of wrenching change and deep recession in Eastern Europe, it is jobs and investment that count.

> *"It will be a tragedy, and probably a costly one, if the United States and Europe ... are allowed to drift farther apart."*

All kinds of explanations for the reluctance of the United States to get more deeply involved in Eastern Europe are offered, including American impatience, a dearth of resources, local xenophobia and doubts over property and tax laws.

Isolationism Unchecked

But a better explanation for America's hesitancy in Eastern Europe, and for some of the tensions in relations with Western Europe, can be found much closer to home. Officially, the Bush administration's goal was mapped out by Secretary of State James Baker in a 1989 speech in which he called for "a true partnership" between Europe and America.

In reality, election-year opposition to overseas investments and entanglements, the swollen federal budget deficit and lackluster leadership from the White House have allowed the rift between the United States and its oldest, closest and most important allies to grow. "Bush and his aides have simply failed to explain convincingly how the forces of the new isolationism threaten to weaken America and its allies alike," says Richard Burt, assistant secretary of state for European affairs in the Reagan administration and a former U.S. ambassador to Germany.

"We are in agreement perhaps 95 percent of the time," the U.S. ambassador to Germany, Robert Kimmit, claimed in January. That is why it will be a tragedy, and probably a costly one, if the United States and Europe, with so much in common, are allowed to drift farther apart.

Chapter 2

How Is German Unification Affecting the World?

German Unification: An Overview

by Henrik Bering-Jensen

About the author: *Henrik Bering-Jensen is a reporter for* Insight *magazine.*

When Germany reunified in 1990, Chancellor Helmut Kohl went to exceptional lengths not to show any emotion. "This is a historic day for Germany" was about as far as he would go. In those early days of reunification, the prudent thing was clearly to say as little as possible as blandly as possible, and Kohl became the butt of jokes in Bonn for his woodenness.

In a marked departure from this low profile, Kohl went on the television show *Farbe Bekennen* (*Show Your True Colors*) and behaved like a heavyweight champion. He delightedly told German reporters who had been the main player at the European Community summit in December 1991, whose views had carried the day. "It was always me. This is what they all said."

Defining a New Role

Criticized for this new directness, Kohl later shrugged his shoulders and said: "If you always want to be liked, you can neither shape nor move anything." He went on to stress the need for Germany to take on "a bigger role" and "new responsibilities in the community of nations."

Since 1990, Germany has clearly been struggling to define a new role for itself. This has chiefly gone on within the two structures that have underpinned Western Europe since the start of the Cold War: NATO in the military realm and the European Community in the areas of politics and economics.

The original purpose of the North Atlantic Treaty Organization, as was bluntly stated by its first general secretary, Lord Hastings Ismay, was to keep the Americans in, the Russians out and the Germans down. As the years passed and Germany became a more mature democracy, this was no longer stated in such harsh terms, but the fact remained that for its security, Germany was totally dependent on its allies, chiefly the United States.

The same subordination held true in the EC, where West Germany had to sub-

Henrik Bering-Jensen, "Germany Resurgent," *Insight*, March 23, 1992. Reprinted with permission.

mit itself to French political leadership. The existence of a rival German state and the threat from the Soviet Union assured that Bonn always had to follow the lead of France because if it did not, France might consider direct negotiations with the Russians or might recognize East Germany. The division of labor in the EC left the politics to France while Germany supplied the economic power; France was the driver, Germany was the train.

> *"Germany has clearly been struggling to define a new role for itself."*

With the collapse of the Soviet Union and its empire, the logic behind Germany's subordinate role in these organizations has also collapsed, and the postwar balance of power on the European continent has been upset. Germany no longer needs to reflexively defer to the wishes of its allies, giving it a lot more room to maneuver, to shape and move things, in Kohl's phrase. In a forthcoming book, *America, Germany and the Future of Europe,* Gregory F. Treverton of the Council on Foreign Relations argues that, like it or not, the center of gravity in Europe has moved east, from Paris to Berlin.

Says Treverton, "We were used to a very unusual kind of Germany, one that was very unassertive, one that did not have a sense of national interest or nation. That is over now. We have a Germany which is back again, united, that has less necessity to constantly subsume its national interest to larger groupings, a Germany that is bound to be more assertive, bound to say from time to time this is what our national interest requires, and we want this to be done."

Indeed, people these days speak of a new German pushiness, manifesting itself in a broad range of issues. To some ears, when former Foreign Minister Hans-Dietrich Genscher talks of a new security system for all of Europe, it sounds like a German-dominated continent, where German policies are masked as European. The Poles complain that Germans are buying up huge amounts of former German territory and exploiting cheap Polish labor.

From diplomats both in France and Britain, one hears mutterings and complaints of being "bullied by Bonn"; terms like "strong-arming," "throwing its weight about," "a German Europe" suddenly have become common. The German newsweekly *Der Spiegel* ran a cover story on the international uneasiness about Germany. The cover carried the image of a strapping, blue-eyed youth with the world on his shoulder and the headline, "Admired, Feared, Envied . . . the Unloved Germans."

Going on Its Own

More specifically, the complaints of Germany's allies focus on three areas. First, Germany went its own way on the question of the civil war in Yugoslavia. Against the strong opposition of the U.S. State Department, the U.N. Security Council, and its main EC allies, Germany announced that it would recognize the republics of Croatia and Slovenia as independent states. In doing so, it dragged along the entire European Community, which voted unanimously to grant formal recognition to the republics, a 180-degree reversal of EC policy. It was the first time Germany had publicly broken with the position of fellow EC members, forcing them to follow its lead.

Germany's forcefulness in reversing the community's policy on Yugoslavia was accompanied by a similar independence in economic policy that may be even more distressing to its European partners. Fearing inflation due to the massive government expenditures to rebuild the eastern part of the country and absorb it into the welfare state, the German Bundesbank has raised interest rates, a step that clearly did not go down well in some of the other capitals of Europe, whose currencies are linked to that of Germany.

With the Bundesbank increasingly playing the role of central bank for the EC, any moves it makes have a ripple effect throughout the Continent, as the other national banks are forced to follow suit. In some cases, notably that of British Prime Minister John Major, the higher interest rates will be an electoral problem of the first magnitude. The same people who mutter about Germany throwing its weight around note pointedly that the Bundesbank unilaterally raised interest rates only 10 days after the summit, which had emphasized the need for a common European monetary policy.

> *"The division of labor in the EC left the politics to France while Germany supplied the economic power; France was the driver, Germany was the train."*

Finally, some Europeans are annoyed by what could be termed Germany's Rodney Dangerfield complaint: It gets no respect. On this front, the Germans have been pushing for more members in the European Parliament. And—the horror—they have also asked that German be made one of the official languages of the European Community, together with English and French, forcing Eurocrats to bone up on their schoolboy German. Similarly, German diplomats in the United States have been instructed to conduct key business in their native tongue; in the past, they mostly spoke English. Though Kohl and his government have not been pushing the idea, some German politicians are arguing that Germany (along with Japan) should be made one of the permanent members of the U.N. Security Council.

Two Separate Perceptions

The British papers have been the most resentful of Germany's new power, harking back to the days of Margaret Thatcher, when the EC was described by one of her ministers as "a German racket to take over Europe." In those days, Foreign Secretary Douglas Hurd would emerge from meetings with Thatcher warning his Cabinet colleagues that they had better not mention the Germans, like Basil Fawlty warning his hotel staff not to mention the war.

The difference now is that the Brits are not alone. After the EC summit in

Chapter 2

Maastricht, Netherlands, the French daily *Le Figaro* wrote, "Just a few days ago, Helmut Kohl was presenting himself as a convinced European. Since then Germany has increased its interest rates, forcing France to follow, and decided to recognize the Yugoslav republics of Slovenia and Croatia. What is left of the Maastricht idea of joint economic and foreign policies?" The paper added plaintively: "The Europe designed at Maastricht was not supposed to be a German Europe."

Predictably, all this griping has exasperated the Germans themselves. After all, only a year ago they were being labeled wimps for not sending troops to participate in the Persian Gulf war. The accusation then was that Germany was "a checkbook power"—in the phrase of *New York Times* columnist William Safire—which paid others to do the dirty work. Now they are suddenly the horrible Hun again, the bully on the block, ready to force their European partners into submission on the question of Yugoslavia.

Risk Adverse Population

The irony is that many Germans see the government's passive Persian Gulf stance more as the model of what they want the new Germany to be. Kohl, for his part, has insisted that "no one really needs to be afraid of the Germans. No one is running around with jackboots wanting to mug someone. . . . I don't believe we've earned the mistrust. No one can wish more than that the Germans agree with the words of Thomas Mann that we are German Europeans and not European Germans."

Kurt Biedenkopf, minister-president of Saxony, allows that "it is obvious that there is a new assertiveness if a country is united." However, he adds, "the conclusion that is drawn from this new assertiveness, that Germany is going to start dominating Europe again, is ridiculous."

According to Biedenkopf, there is one clear and simple difference between the past and today. In 1900, the average age of the population was 25, and the vast majority of the country was poor. By the end of this century, the population will have an average age of 50, and most will be well-off. They can travel anywhere they want to; they can work wherever they want to in Europe. "If you have a wealthy, aging population," says Biedenkopf, "chances are that it will be very risk averse, careful not to endanger what has been achieved."

> *"The irony is that many Germans see the government's passive Persian Gulf stance more as the model of what they want the new Germany to be."*

Just how far Germany is from being able to assume a real leadership role was proved by the Gulf war, according to Thomas Kielinger, editor of the Bonn weekly *Rheinischer Merkur*. A narrow interpretation of the constitution, which forbids sending German troops outside the NATO area, carried the day. For a while, Germany was even reluctant to send planes to help protect Turkey, a NATO member, from the Iraqi Scud missile threat.

Indeed, Germans tend to interpret their Yugoslavia policy, which may have looked bullying to outsiders, as being very similar, springing from a German abhorrence of armed conflict and a desire for the parties in Yugoslavia to reach a negotiated settlement. In the German view, which many analysts now subscribe to, such negotiations could only begin if the right to self-determination was assured. But from the start, Kohl ruled out as unseemly participation in U.N. peacekeeping forces in the Balkans.

> *"Germans ... reject any new role for the country. ... 40 percent would prefer to be like the Swiss—fat, happy and neutral."*

What those fearful of a powerful Germany fail to take into account, says Kielinger, is the lack of a national consensus about Germany's role in the world, as well as the absence of a strong political elite that knows where it wants to go. In fact, opinion polls show that an overwhelming majority of Germans (75 percent) reject any new role for the country. And 40 percent would prefer to be like the Swiss—fat, happy and neutral. These days, the famous German penchant for order and organization, which has had murderous consequences in the past, seems focused more on the environment than on politics. Citizens carefully sort their trash in bins of different colors, green for recyclable items such as paper and cartons, black for household refuse and yellow for plastic; bottles are taken to a bottle bank.

Indeed, some observers believe that a moralistic and self-righteous Germany, given to a Wilsonian "too proud to fight" foreign policy, is far more likely to emerge than a Fourth Reich. So strong is the tug of German pacifism, in this view, that a common European foreign policy might not be such a hot idea after all. If Europe had a political union at the time of the Gulf war, Kielinger notes, a majority vote would have gone against involvement, and Britain and France would have been unable to participate. Therefore, a looser and more flexible approach that would allow individual nations to form ad hoc alliances might be preferable.

The Influx of Refugees

According to Treverton, rather than a classic case of *Drang nach Osten*, a push toward the East, Germany's current preoccupation with Eastern Europe can be better described as *Zwang nach Osten*, being pulled eastward out of necessity. In the German view, the potential for escalating chaos looms just beyond its eastern borders, and its allies have failed to fully appreciate the seriousness of the dangers it faces.

The German nightmare scenario is the arrival of hundreds of thousands of refugees at its borders, fleeing the conflicts in their own countries and dreaming of streets paved with marks. Unlike Britain, points out German historian Jochen Thies, Germany does not have a channel to isolate it from its neighbors. In some places, the Oder and Neisse rivers that separate Germany from Poland can be waded by a small child.

While attention at the moment centers on Yugoslavia, developments in Poland give just as much cause for concern. Officials in Kohl's office take a dim view of Poland's stability, pointing to 1990's presidential elections, in which Stanislaw Tyminski, an unknown Polish-Canadian businessman married to a mystic from Peru, flew home and promised to make every Pole a millionaire.

Lech Walesa eventually defeated him, but not before Tyminski managed to beat former Prime Minister Tadeusz Mazowiecki in the first round, thereby demonstrating the volatility of Poland's politics. German officials emphasize the magnitude of Poland's problems by comparing it to post-Franco Spain, which had a much healthier economy yet needed 10 years to enter the EC.

Disorder in the East

Add to that events in the former Soviet Union. There is still a ragtag army of 270,000 Soviet soldiers on German soil, and their withdrawal will not be complete until 1994. The Germans were severely shaken by the coup in Moscow in August 1991, which threatened to put on hold the Russian retreat. And they shudder when they hear Lech Walesa admitting to a German magazine that in the case of a

> *"In the German view, the potential for escalating chaos looms just beyond its eastern borders."*

civil war in the former Soviet Union, the Polish army could not stem the tide but would allow refugees passage to Germany.

Besides fearing a deluge of refugees, the Germans also worry about other fallout from disorder to the east—literally, in the case of Soviet-designed nuclear plants throughout Eastern Europe, whose safety record is grim. Chernobyl-type accidents do not respect borders. Says Kielinger: "I fail to see why the fact that Germany keeps a very attentive eye to events east of her in any way reveals a central European power that wants to cast its shadow over the area."

In one sphere, undeniably, the Germans can be said to be active rather than reactive, and that is in economics, which in the long run will translate into political power. By virtue of its location in Europe, Germany is perfectly situated to invest in Poland, Czechoslovakia and the Baltic states, where German industry already is rushing to fill the vacuum left by the retreating Russians. Goethe Institutes, quasi-governmental establishments dedicated to the understanding of German language, thought and history, seem to be cropping up throughout Eastern Europe. Germany accounts for one-third of the trade between Eastern and Western Europe. In Poland and Czechoslovakia, it is responsible for about 60 percent of foreign investment. Polish complaints about imperialism are brushed aside by German officials, who say investors will go elsewhere if their money isn't wanted.

Becoming a Normal Nation

Filling this vacuum is made much easier because the United States is not seriously involved in the reconstruction of Eastern Europe. Apart from a few giants like Philip Morris and Coca-Cola, few U.S. businesses seem able or willing to make the long-term investments such a move would require. As things stand now, it is Germany that will run the greatest risks in Eastern Europe, and it is Germany that therefore stands to benefit most. Indeed, given the stakes involved, it is something of a mystery to German observers why the U.S. government is devoting so much of its diplomatic and political efforts to solving intractable crises in the Middle East at the expense of trying to shape events in Eastern Europe.

The U.S. government still sees a need for a presence in Europe, both to protect its interests and to calm nervous allies. But it has not reacted to the new power of Germany with anything like the emotion of France or Britain. Indeed, American observers tend to see developments in Germany as a sign that the country is becoming a normal nation. Today's federal Germany, with much power given to the states and securely integrated in Europe, bears little resemblance to the aggressive juggernaut that Bismarck launched in 1871.

For that matter, successive American administrations have long wanted Germany to take a more active political role, commensurate with its economic stature. "Let me state, clearly and unequivocally, that we welcome and value this German assertiveness in collective actions to achieve common goals," U.S. Ambassador Robert Kimmitt has stated.

Indeed, it is the American view that this participation should be on a world level, not only a European one, and that Germany should be an active member in multinational military coalitions and U.N. peacekeeping forces. From this perspective, the key test of Germany's ability to play a constructive role in the broader world is going to be whether Helmut Kohl can get a constitutional amendment through the Bundestag allowing the use of troops outside Europe.

> *"The Germans can be said to be active rather than reactive, and that is in economics, which in the long run will translate into political power."*

Though the British have been more peevish about growing German power, the real loser appears to be France. According to Thies, the French are losing a centuries-long philosophical argument about the essence of Europe: Notwithstanding Charles de Gaulle's famous phrase, the French, when they say Europe, have tended to mean Roman Catholic Europe, essentially Western Europe, a view that excludes the areas where Eastern Orthodoxy holds sway and that, incidentally, tends to make Paris the center of the continent. Thus, over the past decade, France has been pressing for a "deepening" of the community—more integration of present members—which in the mouth of EC-President Jacques Delors sometimes sounds as if the EC is a straitjacket, designed to restrain Germany.

For their part, the Germans have favored a much broader view of Europe—a continent and a community stretching from the Atlantic all the way to the Urals, and one in which Germany will have a pivotal role as the bridge between East and West. This is the view said to be close to Genscher's heart and the one that events seem to favor. With new states applying for membership, Germany's influence will grow, while the ability of France to use the EC as an adjunct to its statecraft and grandeur will wane. "This accounts for a lot of grumpiness on the French side," says Treverton. For those favoring a less centralized, less Delorsian EC, this may not be such bad news.

German Unification Strengthens the European Community

by Peter Hort

About the author: *Peter Hort is a correspondent for a German newspaper, Frankfurter Allgemeine Zeitung. A Brussels correspondent, he reports on European Community affairs.*

No other member country of the European Community is more strongly bound to the idea of European unity than is Germany—and in the context of the bellicose history of this century, this is hardly surprising. It was indeed a Frenchman, Jean Monnet, who after the Second World War initiated the move towards uniting the old sovereign nations of Europe; but it was in the ruins of Germany that support for his proposals was most resonant. Half a century previously, a year before the start of the First World War, Walter Rathenau had, in a speech in Berlin, pronounced the prophetic words: "The European economies must sooner or later merge to form a community; this will lead to the alleviation of conflicts, to the saving of energy and to a civilization based on solidarity." Not until the early Fifties, however, did Konrad Adenauer commit himself "wholeheartedly", as Monnet writes in his memoirs, to the French Schuman Plan, which led to the European Coal and Steel Community. This organization was the seed of the European Community.

Developing the EC

The creation of the European Coal and Steel Community, the European Economic Community and the political cooperation which followed is closely associated with German names: Walter Hallstein, Carl Friedrich Ophüls, Heinrich von Brentano, Hans von Boeckh, Hans von der Groeben and many others made a substantial contribution to the establishment of the Community. Their reports from the Fifties and Sixties bear witness to the wholehearted enthusiasm which went into the crafting of both the concept of One Europe and the institutions

From Peter Hort, "Germany and the European Community," in *Meet United Germany*, Susan Stern, ed. Frankfurt am Main: Frankfurter Allgemeine Zeitung GmbH Informationdienste, 1991. Copyright 1991 by the Frankfurter Allgemeine Zeitung GmbH Informationdienste. Reprinted with permission.

which realized the idea. It is no exaggeration to say that, after the lost war, many Germans saw Europe as an *Ersatzheimat* (substitute for their native country), and they were willing to make a commitment to it. . . .

Resolving Financial Problems

In the Federal Republic in the early Eighties, there was a more immense gap than in any other country between the expectations of the population and the ability of EC institutions to make things happen. Notwithstanding all its successes, the Community could simply not keep pace with what the Germans wanted. As the magnetism of the European idea faded and solidarity among member countries dwindled, appeals from Germans became ever more frequent and more vocal for a clear limit to be placed on their country's payments to the EC. The *Bundesbank* calculated in January 1982 that the German share of the EC budget had climbed from DM7 billion (Deutsche mark) in 1975 to DM 14 billion in 1981. According to these calculations, the over-expensive Community was consuming six per cent of all federal expenditure. The government was warned not to allow payments to the EC to grow too high, because this would make the task of squaring the federal budget more difficult. Even though such asset-transfer calculations completely ignore the benefits of EC membership, they played a dominant role in the ever-more complicated relationship between the Germans and EC institutions. The call for far-reaching reforms became increasingly vocal. But the more obvious it became that clear-cut reform of the budget, of Community structure, and of agricultural policy was necessary, the less willing the relevant EC institutions were to set about this task. The question of financing was sidelined for a long time; consensus on further development of the Community among heads of governments and states seemed extremely limited. In the midst of this growing inaction and lack of direction, West German Foreign Minister Hans-Dietrich Genscher took a fanciful initiative: by adopting a European Act aimed specifically at implementing the old idea of European union, the Community should drag itself out of the prevailing torpor. European Union had never been closely defined, but Genscher hoped to give the Community a new goal and a new lease of life by binding the EC and European political cooperation more closely under the umbrella of the European Council. The Council should be endowed with better decision-making processes, the European Parliament should be invested with more authority, and security policy should be incorporated into European political cooperation as envisioned by Jean Monnet. The Italian government acted on the proposal; the Genscher-Colombo Initiative finally led, in late 1985, to the festive adoption of the Single European Act, the first fundamental reform since the

> *"No other member country of the European Community is more strongly bound to the idea of European unity than is Germany."*

Treaty of Rome in 1957.

With Jacques Delors' assumption of office as president of the European Commission in spring 1985, financial reform was finally brought onto the agenda. After painstaking internal coordination, early in 1987 the Commission presented a comprehensive reform package containing three main components: the introduction of a fourth source of funding—a share of each country's GNP—whereby the EC's own revenue would be raised and, at the same time, distributed more fairly; stabilizers to reduce the disproportionately swollen agricultural expenditure to 50 per cent of the total budget; and the doubling of the structural fund to substantially increase the transfer of resources to the poorer countries. The Commission hoped that this 3-pronged package would enable the Community, chronically in the red, to solve its financing problems once and for all. When the package first came up for debate in 1987, it became apparent that the difficult reform could not be readied for adoption at the first attempt. In particular, UK Prime Minister Margaret Thatcher opposed the call for higher Community revenue as long as there was no radical savings plan for agricultural expenditure. After the Belgian and Danish governments had failed to reconcile differences of opinion on the Delors Package sufficiently for a compromise to be reached, the German government—not totally unprepared—took on the role of chief mediator early in 1988. Chancellor Helmut Kohl and Foreign Minister Hans-Dietrich Genscher brought all their prestige to bear and set themselves the goal of ensuring that the long-overdue reform was adopted under their aegis.

> *"Many Germans saw Europe as an **Ersatzheimat** (substitute for their native country), and they were willing to make a commitment to it."*

A Special Challenge

It is undoubtedly one of the EC's moments of glory that, at the memorable Brussels "crisis summit" in February 1988, the German government managed to cut through the Gordian knot of the reform package in a 38-hour negotiating marathon, and to push through Delors' proposals for a better-functioning Community without major amendment. At one stroke, a way had been found to resolve the crippling wrangling that had been going on for years over the restructuring of the budget, what to do about the depressing mountains of surplus butter and other foodstuffs, and the lack of solidarity between poor and rich member countries. At least until 1992, the Twelve would not be continually faced with new deficits; the worst was over. Chairman of the Council Helmut Kohl received much well-deserved praise; one somewhat fulsome compliment from the European Parliament, which for years had been calling for reform, was that he had "brought about a miracle". The German government drew resounding acclaim for not merely resting on its laurels but vigorously pursuing the next stage of integration: the completion of the single market planned for 1992....

The view ahead was obstructed by the upheavel in Eastern Europe. This became a special challenge: the democratization and opening up of Poland, Hungary, Czechoslovakia and other former East Bloc states eliminated the division of Europe into a prosperous Western sphere and a poor Eastern sphere. Now that the neighbouring Eastern European countries, once almost given up for lost, were suddenly drawing closer, the Western Europeans were strengthened in their conviction that they should accelerate and extend the restructuring of the Community which had begun in 1990 with German economic and monetary union. The unification of Germany, exalted by many as the high point of the peaceful revolution in Eastern Europe, acted as a catalyst in discussions on the extension of the Community. By attempting to define a common foreign and security policy for the Community of Twelve, the EC saw a way to live up to its aspirations to become the political nucleus of Europe. It was also necessary to lay down a basis for the subsequent admission of new EC members from among the Eastern European countries. Austria, which applied in 1989 for full membership of the EC, was not alone in seeking to join the Community: Poland, Hungary and Czechoslovakia all wish to join at some point.

> *"The unification of Germany ... acted as a catalyst in discussions on the extension of the [European] Community."*

Germany as a Model

Thus, Germany's role in the EC seems to be growing in two ways: for one, the country's influence has increased noticeably since unification and the surprisingly smooth incorporation of the former German Democratic Republic (GDR) into the EC; for another, Germany is a bridge and mediator with the East. The irritation, and occasionally even resentment, this has aroused in France and the UK is understandable; but the worries of Germany's neighbours about its dominating an ever-larger European Community are largely unfounded. Since 9 November 1989, when the Berlin Wall was breached, the political parties in Germany have never left a shadow of a doubt that "German unification and European unity are two sides of the same coin" (Hans-Dietrich Genscher). In other words: the great majority of Germans can only picture "Germany, one fatherland" as a country firmly anchored in the European Community and the North Atlantic Alliance. A relapse into the bygone days of nationalism or even a "Fourth Reich"—to name the bogey conjured up by the British press—is inconceivable. It is thus entirely understandable that the government in Bonn should endeavour to join other countries in the vanguard of the move towards union and to refute the latent fears voiced by some partners.

Even though the political centre of the Community has shifted to the East and the dominance of French ideas and the French language is becoming weaker, there is no need to fear "Germanization". The Germans may have gained in influence but there is little risk of other countries being stifled. The extension of the majority principle in political union and the growing legislatory influence of the European Parliament are two pillars of a new balance of power which guarantees smaller partners a voice. With economic and monetary union, as well as with political union, the onus is once again (as it was in the infancy of the Community almost 40 years ago) on the Germans to put forward and see through liberal ideas. Undoubtedly it will be beneficial to all if the *Bundesbank* acts as a model for the European central bank and if—as the tenor of government negotiations suggests likely—its political independence and commitment to price stability become precepts of the European central bank. The majority of member countries appear willing to emulate the obvious success of the German system and transfer the *Bundesbank* model to Europe.

A Second Chance

On the road to political union, Germany can also be a model for the Community. The only blueprint acceptable for an ever-larger and more closely bound Europe is a federal system, which will assure the individual members sufficient influence and will keep the responsibilities of central government to a minimum. The key word here is "subsidiarity", a concept which is also gaining importance in such highly centralized countries as France, Italy and Spain. In this light, nobody need fear the Germans: they have more to offer the Europeans than they seek to gain. They remain, not only in financial terms, the net paymasters of the Community. There is no wavering from their loyalty to the Community, as they have proved consistently since the days of **Konrad Adenauer** and **Robert Schuman**. And they have realized that they must use their "second chance" (Fritz Stern) at the end of this warlike century to the benefit and not to the detriment of their neighbours.

A United Germany Will Benefit Both Europe and the United States

by Robert Gerald Livingston

About the author: *Robert Gerald Livingston directs the American Institute for Contemporary German Studies at Johns Hopkins University in Baltimore and was president of the German Marshall Fund of the United States from 1977-1981.*

When communist East Germany vanished in October 1990, the old West Germany, America's familiar and comfortable ally, disappeared too. It is clear that the new, united Federal Republic is bound to be powerful, but it is not yet clear how it will employ its power. Some critics point warily to German history, to neo-Nazi violence in its troubled East, or to the growth of right-wing parties in the West. Others see a new foreign policy "assertiveness" in Germany's early recognition of Croatia and Slovenia, its refusal to send Turkey more German weapons after Turkey's attacks on Kurdish rebels, or Chancellor Helmut Kohl's visit with the outgoing Austrian president, Kurt Waldheim.

Unfounded Fears

Pentagon planners have even been formulating future policies to prevent Germany's emergence, possibly nuclear-armed, as a rival to America's solitary superpower status. The Germans are nowadays routinely bracketed with the Japanese as competitors, rivals, and an economic "superpower" about whom Americans should worry.

Europeans are more anxious than Americans about the new power at Germany's disposal. By every standard except size of territory and ownership of nuclear weapons, Germany is indeed once again the ascendant state in Europe—and the only one to emerge from the Cold War clearly much stronger. Had Germany's chief European allies, France and Great Britain, been able to win Washington's support, they might well have made an all-out effort to pre-

From Robert Gerald Livingston, "United Germany: Bigger and Better," *Foreign Policy* 87 (Summer 1991). Copyright 1991 by the Carnegie Endowment for International Peace. Reprinted with permission.

vent or at least delay German unification.

Yet most fears about Germany are unfounded. They misunderstand—or underestimate—the profound changes that transformed Germany in the postwar decades. What is more disturbing, such fears can blind policymakers to the real forces shaping an increasingly powerful Germany. . . .

United German Strategy

Negotiations over unification have brought Germany to a more fortunate position than it has ever had in modern history. With its frontiers settled and without any territorial claims of its own, for the first time in centuries it faces no military threats from any direction. Its economy is well positioned to exploit the coming expansion of the EC, new investment needs and trading opportunities in Eastern Europe and in the former Soviet Union, and the enhanced technological competitiveness that will result from modernizing industries in its own eastern states. Germany's corporatist approach enables it, like Japan, to marshall its economic power and, more consciously than Japan so far, to deploy it for political purposes abroad.

What those purposes will be—with Europe (and Germany) no longer divided and with Soviet communism dead—is what many analysts, both inside and outside of Germany, are now debating. Commentators in Germany have called for a great domestic debate on the future of united Germany's foreign policy, similar to the debate that took place over integration into NATO in the 1950s or over Chancellor Willy Brandt's *Ostpolitik* in the early 1970s. Kohl has been urging a constitutional amendment that would allow German military forces to participate in actions outside the NATO treaty area. Yet the public seems to have little interest in such a debate. That relative lack of interest in foreign policy is partly a result of the tumultuous process of unification; but many Germans also feel that the united Germany's strategies will grow naturally from approaches employed by the former West Germany—adjusted, of course, to take advantage of the new openings in the East.

> *"Pentagon planners have even been formulating future policies to prevent Germany's emergence, possibly nuclear-armed, as a rival to America's solitary superpower status."*

United Germany is not likely to revert to old-fashioned nation-state maneuvering. Hans-Dietrich Genscher regarded his "policy of responsibility" as a practice beyond traditional balance-of-power politics. That is not to say that Germany does not pursue "national interests," only that it prefers pursuing them through multilateral structures like the EC or the Conference on Security and Cooperation in Europe (CSCE). That is also not to say, as Germany's early recognition of Croatia demonstrates clearly, that it will not act on its own when the multilateral organizations fail, particularly in the East.

Chapter 2

Like the old Federal Republic, Germany sees itself as a resolutely "civilian" power, whose strongest suit is its powerful economy. Germans do not discount the occasional utility of military force, but the vast majority would strongly oppose the acquisition of nuclear weapons or, with very few exceptions, the deployment of *Bundeswehr* units in any country conquered by Hitler or anywhere outside of Europe, except on the rarest of occasions.

Eastern European Strategy

In Eastern Europe and the EC, the two areas that will be of primary interest, Germany's policies will reflect two powerful domestic forces: They will seek stability, and they will prefer a consensual approach. With unification, Germany resumes its historical role as a Central European power, whose interests in the East are every bit as important as those in the West. The Atlantic-oriented West Germany that we knew from 1949 to 1990 was an abnormality in German history. Russian power has now receded once again from Eastern Europe. And as has so often happened in the past, German power is replacing it there.

Germany feels highly vulnerable to the current instability in the East. In Kohl's words, "What will be needed more than anything else is to stabilize the political, economic, and social conditions in Central and southeastern Europe as well as in the successor states of the Soviet Union." Small states like Croatia or Hungary already look to Bonn for detailed guidance. If Slovakia breaks out of its federation with the Czech lands, it too will look to Germany. Czechoslovakia and Poland are coming under Germany's economic sway. And Ukraine and Russia curry German favor for their hard-pressed economies.

> *"Most fears about Germany are unfounded."*

German policy in the region will have multiple aims: promoting democratic political parties, advocating human rights, supporting environmental cleanup, urging the shutdown of antique nuclear reactors, and, of course, advancing German economic and financial interests. Germans resist calling the East a "sphere of German influence," fearing that the phrase conjures up old balance-of-power concepts of military and political domination that they have rejected. Yet it is becoming a sphere of influence nonetheless, if one designed mainly to promote a zone of stability. And it will be a German zone because the United States and other Western countries lack Germany's strong interests, motivations, and capabilities.

Many factors draw Germany's attention eastward. There are large ethnic German minorities (about 2 million) in the former Soviet Union, a sizable number (probably about 400,000 but the figures are disputed) in Poland, and 70,000 to 100,000 in Romania. Their rights are guaranteed by Germany's treaties with the former Soviet Union, Poland, and Romania. Also, more than 227,000 Soviet soldiers and 153,000 civilians and family members still live in eastern Germany. They are supposed to be gone by 1994, and Germany has paid out or pledged more than DM 15 billion to build housing for them at home, to transport them back, to retrain some of them in civilian skills, and to pay them while they remain in Germany.

Area of Influence

Germany has far outstripped all other Western countries combined, extending grants, credits, or credit guarantees totaling more than DM 75 billion to the former Soviet Union, a substantial portion of it in connection with the withdrawal of the Soviet troops from the eastern part of Germany, and another DM 30 billion or so to the East and Central European countries. In trade and private investment in most of the region as well, the Germans are well ahead of other countries.

Germany champions EC membership soon for at least Czechoslovakia, Hungary, Poland, and the Baltic states. Those countries in turn recognize that their access to Community and particularly German markets is crucial to their livelihood. Without much investment (except in Hungary) from American, British, French, or Japanese firms, "the only thing worse than being dominated by the German economy," as the dry Czech joke has it, "is not being dominated by it."

Not only is Eastern Europe historically German foreign policy turf, but today it is also an arena where international institutional constraints on German action are fewer than in the West. As a result, the Federal Republic has a far freer hand in Eastern Europe and the former Soviet republics than it does in Western Europe, where institutionally—and instinctively—it has felt compelled to act in tandem with France in the EC and the United States in NATO.

Germany's other priority arena continues to be the EC. Until the mid-1980s, the EC served as a club where membership allowed West Germany to work toward regaining respectability. Not only did the EC come to represent an *ersatz* (substitute) for a lost Fatherland, it quickly became immensely beneficial economically. In 1991 the EC's common market took almost 53 per cent of Germany's exports (as compared with about 6 per cent going to the United States).

> *"Negotiations over unification have brought Germany to a more fortunate position than it has ever had in modern history."*

While united Germany will give priority in the West to acting within and through the EC, it no longer sees the EC as an institution in which to sublimate national aspirations but rather as an instrument to lend the German voice greater force. The economic and monetary union that is scheduled to emerge during this decade will be one in which Germany's economy will be preponderant. Unification also increases German weight within the Community at a time when the EC finally seems to be moving toward political union. Now about half again as populous as any of the three other principal EC members—Britain, France, and Italy—Germany is much better able to shape Community policies to suit German aims. Emblematic of Germany's recognition that its EC voice is stronger was Kohl's recent decision to seek equal status for German with French and English as an EC working language.

Maintaining Stability

As the world's second-largest exporter, Germany has every interest in keeping the EC's trading practices open and in pressing the EC to accept former neutrals like Austria, Finland, and Sweden as well as the six close East European countries—Czechoslovakia, Hungary, Poland, and the three Baltics. All those countries have been economically and politically closer to Germany than they have to other EC members. Championing their entry thus works reciprocally to Germany's advantage: It increases Bonn's influence in capitals like Prague, and once those countries are associated or included it adds to the number of Germany's friends in EC institutions.

The old Federal Republic's EC policy focused on the core relationship with France, to which Bonn customarily deferred. The habits of 35 years are not lightly cast aside by a German government steeped in continuity. Its leaders will continue to take new initiatives with France, like the mainly symbolic proposal for a German-French army corps. However, on essentials such as deference to French *dirigiste* (state-directed) ideas on trade or agricultural policy, the united Germany is likely to become somewhat more independent.

The United States and the Atlantic Alliance, essential for an exposed and vulnerable West Germany that stood on the front line of the Cold War, will slip to second or third rank for Germany. The Soviet military threat has vanished. NATO's organizing principle, anticommunism, has become irrelevant. Consequently, united Germany can soon dispense with what the United States and the Atlantic Alliance principally had to offer: military security. In Bonn, deference to the relationship with Washington will continue for a long time to come. Germany's leaders realize full well that an American presence in Europe allows its neighbors to feel far more comfortable with the new and larger Germany. If gratitude plays any role in international affairs, moreover, German leaders of Kohl's generation—who recall the Marshall Plan, the Berlin blockade, and America's full support for German unification—will not turn away from the Americans. Kohl has always stood on the U.S. side, he told the *Wall Street Journal* and *Handelsbatt*, because that has been his life experience.

> *"With unification, Germany resumes its historical role as a Central European power."*

In all those relationships—with the East, with France and the EC, and with the United States and NATO—West Germany developed a distinctive foreign policy approach that the united Germany seems likely to continue in its basic forms: It will adhere to multilateralism, devote itself to stability, and apply the lessons and techniques learned in the West over 40 years to diplomacy with the postcommunist East.

In the 1950s, West Germany found its way back to acceptance by integrating itself into multinational organizations like NATO and the EC, willingly playing a subordinate role in them for many years, exercising prudence in tactics, and cherishing a low national profile. Under Helmut Schmidt's chancellorship in the 1970s, Germany's profile began to rise as it joined the big industrial countries at the G-7 summits. At the same time, it began to promote in the East that same multilateralism that it practiced in the West. Genscher developed and systematically extended the CSCE in ways that drew in outsiders from the East and from as far away as Central Asia, much as West Germany, once itself an outsider to the West, had been brought into Western multilateral organizations three decades earlier.

Since the end of Europe's division, Germany has been infusing Western organizations with a pan-European character. That approach is visible, for example, in Germany's support for the creation of NATO's North Atlantic Cooperation Council that includes the states of the former Warsaw Pact, and in its support for the inclusion of Czechoslovakia, Hungary, and Poland in the EC. Germany has even taken multilateralism so far as to encourage Japan to associate itself with the CSCE.

> *"Germany feels highly vulnerable to the current instability in the East."*

Given its devotion to multilateralism, Germany's readiness to recognize Croatia and Slovenia in 1991 was startling. It was a demonstration of Germany's freer hand in the East. Genscher applied maximum pressure to bring all EC members into line, so that German unilateralism was superficially (and grudgingly) endorsed. In fact, by the late summer of 1991, Genscher faced heavy pressure from the Bavarian Christian Social Union, the Social Democrats, and parts of the Christian Democratic Party (CDU) to recognize Croatia and Slovenia. Catholic Bavaria had for some time been expanding ties with Catholic Croatia, and many of the 400,000 Croats working in Germany live in that state. In the summer of 1991 the Social Democrats and parts of the CDU began responding to nightly televised scenes of carnage in Croatia by demanding government action to stop the killing. The political parties reflected public sensitivity to previous foreign criticism of German passivity during the Persian Gulf war. Genscher came under wide attack for continuing to back the territorial integrity of Yugoslavia and felt he had to change course decisively or lose his leadership in foreign policy making.

A European Power

Germany brings many advantages to its new international role. It is a homogeneous, cohesive country, without politically troublesome minorities like the Corsicans, Basques, or Scots. Its large foreign population enjoys almost no political rights, such as voting, and is fragmented among many nationalities. Its political system produces a higher degree of consensus on most foreign policy issues than is customarily appreciated abroad. Its corporatist approach works well for it in foreign economic policy.

Prudence, restraint, and a willingness to face up to its Nazi past have also finally enabled Germany to regain the moral high ground Hitler abandoned so willfully and self-destructively. And with unification, that strain of self-pity so common to political statements has mercifully vanished. A comfortable self-confidence and a bit of legitimate pride characterize Germany's approach now. . . .

> *"The Federal Republic has a far freer hand in Eastern Europe and the former Soviet republics than it does in Western Europe."*

United Germany may yet develop global interests but, other than commercial ones, those are not likely to be significant for decades to come. Europe to the Urals is world enough for a time. Bonn's reluctance to join the American-led coalition during the Gulf war will typify its approach outside Europe for the foreseeable future: pay, if it must, but not play. Only rarely will it pursue assertive policies outside of Europe, as it did in condemning its old friend Turkey recently. The action against Turkey stemmed primarily from sensitivities about Germany's failure to act in the Gulf.

Stung by foreign criticism of its alleged spinelessness during the Gulf war, German public opinion seems to be shifting also in other areas—to the point where it could permit Germany to join in U.N. peacekeeping (but not peacemaking) missions outside Europe.

A Better Germany

Drawing on 40 years of very close cooperation with the old Federal Republic, the United States should not have much of a problem with united Germany's enhanced roles in Eastern and Western Europe or with whatever modest ones it might eventually assume outside Europe as well. Unlike France, Germany openly wants the United States to remain in Europe. That gives Americans good leverage over its policies. Its general aim to keep the EC open and liberal is clearly in the U.S. interest. Its willingness to take up the many responsibilities in the East at a time when resource constraints keep Americans from shouldering many burdens there constitutes a logical division of labor that will permit the United States to concentrate on other regions where it, rather than the Germans, holds the strong cards: the Middle East, Central and Latin America, and to some extent the Pacific Rim.

What will perhaps be hardest for the United States to accept will be the German intention to reshape institutions like NATO to the realities of a new Europe. The Germans well recognize that NATO provides a tried and true basis for American involvement in Europe. Rather than challenging U.S. alliance leadership, they are likely to do everything they reasonably can to enhance it. A more sensitive issue is the use of NATO bases within Germany for U.S.-led expeditions in the Near East, such as the Gulf war. It is probably best not to seek explicit clarification of this issue now, until a firmer public consensus for German missions outside Europe has developed.

The United States should not push united Germany to go beyond its two chosen arenas. That would risk splintering the domestic political consensus upon which its enhanced involvement rests and could revive apprehensions on the part of other countries. Its historical experience, its multilateralist inclinations, and its present economic reconstruction burdens will keep it from overreaching. This united Germany is bigger. It is also a far better Germany for the United States than any it has seen this century, the hesitant and guilt-ridden Federal Republic of 1949–90 included.

German Unity Will Benefit the United States

by Elizabeth Pond

About the author: *Elizabeth Pond is a John D. and Catherine T. MacArthur Fellow and is doing research in Germany. She is the author of a forthcoming book on German unification for the Twentieth Century Fund, a New York City organization that sponsors and supervises research on economic, social, and political issues.*

Yes, Germany is becoming more assertive in foreign policy. This is all to the good for the United States.

It is not that German instincts will prove any more infallible than American instincts. Bonn will be right in some cases, such as pressing for destruction of all battlefield nuclear weapons and recognizing Slovenia and Croatia as a means to help end the fighting in Yugoslavia. It will be wrong or irritating in other cases, such as raising German interest rates to record heights at a time of world recession.

Germany's Security Function

More important than the compatibility of specific German judgments—and the interests of the world's two largest exporters should, in fact, often coincide—is the general German assumption of some of the American burden of leadership in Europe. This, as much as declining military expenditures, should free Washington to get on with its own post-Cold War domestic agenda. . . .

It makes sense for the United States to continue to give priority to its bilateral relationship with the Germans whom President Bush had in mind in early 1989 when he anointed them "partners in leadership." Events in the train of unification are, in any case, creating their own enormous pressures on Bonn to exert leadership in Europe. And while conventional wisdom presumed that the new fully sovereign Germany must necessarily flex its new leadership in "renationalization" of defense—and in rebellion against its encumbering European partners and erstwhile American patron—a strong case can now be made for a con-

From Elizabeth Pond, 'Germany in the New Europe." Reprinted by permission of *Foreign Affairs* (Spring 1992). Copyright 1992 by the Council on Foreign Relations, Inc.

trary thesis of intensified cooperation among the allies.

Chancellor Helmut Kohl and other older Germans in high office feel an urgent need to knit their country into an interwoven Europe before ceding their posts to a generation they fear might be less inhibited by German history and therefore less European. And many Germans, who in the past enjoyed invisible American security but felt morally superior because they did not have to dirty their own hands with fighting, may well gain more appreciation for the United States as they themselves inherit part of the old American security function.

> *"Germany is becoming more assertive in foreign policy."*

Conversely many Americans who previously deemed Germans pusillanimous may, in the post-Cold War era, gain an appreciation of the German art of cooperative, ambiguous solutions. The United States may come to see differences with Germany and with Europe less as zero-sum clashes of interest (the view that prevailed during the Reagan administration) than as joint searches for the maximum common good (the view that has generally prevailed in the Bush administration).

Maintaining U.S. Connections

Certainly the Germans have demonstrated this spirit in promoting European integration. The French and all other *realpolitiker* assumed that the Federal Republic, having achieved its desired unification, would have less need for allies and would demote them—unless Paris bound it firmly to European Monetary Union before unity occurred. Yet the Germans have so internalized positive interdependence and the negative risks of solo operations that they themselves are seeking not only monetary union but also a political union that would go far beyond any pooling of sovereignty the French or British are prepared to accept.

Similarly German habituation to the stability provided by NATO's collective defense disposes Bonn to perpetuate NATO so long as there is any risk of unpredictable events in the neighborhood. Every Bonn government has explicitly acknowledged this advantage; Yugoslavia's irrational civil war and the messy breakup of the Soviet Union have now spread recognition of this advantage more broadly among the general public. Moreover President Bush's unstinting support for unification in 1989–90 showed the Germans the benefits of maintaining an alliance with a large, distant friend who is not as burdened by European history as are Germany's neighbors. The French-German relationship will always form the core of the European Community, but the Germans will also need, for a long time to come, a less parochial counterweight to Paris and London. . . .

A new Germany and a more cohesive, more powerful democratic Europe that can take over some of America's security burden on the old continent is all to its advantage, whatever the short-term frustrations in facing a more-or-less single ally that is suddenly bigger and richer than the United States. The United

Chapter 2

States should therefore support European evolution and increase its direct dealings with the EC in line with progress toward political unity in the region. President Bush made the correct decisions in 1989 and 1990 in opening full diplomatic relations with the EC and in deferring to the EC the lead in dealing with the economic development of eastern Europe and the Yugoslav civil war. Washington should trust this instinct and not go back to the resistance of previous American administrations to letting Europe mature into an equal ally.

Unitary diplomacy with the EC will, of course, never fully supplant bilateral diplomacy with individual European countries, any more than bilateral diplomacy displaces direct contacts, say, between the U.S. Department of Commerce and economics ministries in European lands. Bilateral contacts will continue, not least with Germany, to be the driving force of European integration. But Washington should no longer insist that European national governments negotiate everything bilaterally and severally with Washington, no longer protest that any coordination of a single European policy prior to U.S.-European talks would constitute ganging up on the United States. . . .

Germany and NATO

Before the opening of the Berlin Wall the consensus seemed to be that NATO was suffering from congenital and perhaps terminal crisis; that American and German interests in particular were bound to clash as postwar Germany and its "successor generation" came of age; that only Moscow could offer reunification to the Germans, for a price; that (in the right's formulation) Gorbachev was playing the peace and disarmament theme so cleverly that Western publics, swept up in "Gorbymania" and the fading Soviet threat, would outrace themselves to disarm and leave Moscow to dominate Europe; that (in the left's formulation) the United States could no longer impose bipolar confrontation on Europe; that the Americans would or should tire of paying for European defense and American hegemony and go home; that the Europeans would or should respond by accommodating themselves to the Soviet Union. Implicit in much of this analysis was fear that the weakness of open Western societies would prove vulnerable to the strengths of the Soviet command society.

> *"It makes sense for the United States to continue to give priority to its bilateral relationship with the Germans."*

After the opening of the Berlin Wall in November 1989, the consensual worry still maintained a kind of half-life among certain analysts. Even if NATO survived, it was thought, a newly sovereign Germany no longer dependent on American security would deem NATO a shackle "keeping the Germans down." Surely the united Germans would, in another widely used image, "hollow out" their commitment to the alliance and expel Western allied troops from their territory. Or Germany might revert to aggressive behavior and become the "Fourth

Reich.". . . .

The center-right government in Bonn not only did not regard a continued stay in Germany by American and other allied troops as onerous, but actively desired it. So did German voters, who reelected the government two months after unification with a decisive majority and totally forgot their previous war angst.

To be sure, West German enthusiasm for America and NATO could be abnormally colored at this point by gratitude for Washington's stalwart support for unification against the French and British (and Soviets). But there probably will continue to be numerous issues in which German stakes will coincide more closely with American than with French or British interests, and Germany will value its augmented influence in European councils arising from its American connection in NATO. Indeed it is natural for Germany to want to retain NATO's military prowess and practiced political crisis management. The Atlantic alliance is the sole international organization with an integrated military command adaptable to a variety of situations. It is an existing institution that can perpetuate the American habit of political engagement in Europe—so long as the numbers of GIs in Europe decline substantially—without requiring generation of impossible new popular American support for this involvement. It is a forum the Europeans trust and understand. The Germans and the British—as well as the former Soviet republics—realize that maintaining NATO is the only way to keep the Americans in Germany, as all wish to do. . . .

Germany Takes the Lead

Germany will clearly be the leader, both financially and intellectually, both unilaterally and through the EC. Bonn is contributing half of all the international aid to the former Soviet Union and eastern Europe. Economic development of Saxony is designed to help stimulate next-door Silesia and Bohemia in a regional cooperation effort that deliberately reverses the German contempt for Slavs of a half-century ago. German investment and trade in eastern Europe and its hiring of cross-border Polish and Czech labor far exceed the economic involvement of any other Western country.

In addition German jurists are already helping the Estonians write a constitution, aiding the Hungarians in adopting the entire German civil code and sponsoring meetings of justice ministers from east European and Soviet successor states. The German Social Democratic, Christian Democratic and Liberal think tanks are sharing the techniques of political and social organization in eastern Europe as they did 15 years ago in Spain and Portugal. The more liberal German Catholic Church has some impact on the more medieval Polish and Lithuanian Catholic hierarchies—as do the German Protestants on the Latvian and Estonian Protestants. There are scores of bilateral stu-

> *"Germans . . . are seeking not only monetary union but also a political union."*

dent and teacher exchanges; training programs for business managers and local administrators; workshops for parliamentarians, legislative staff and librarians; joint history and textbook-writing projects; and city partnerships. Grass-roots Polish-German and Czech-German environmental, "friendship" and other societies are mushrooming. Riga is awash in German delegations. The Goethe Institute outposts are facilitating the flow by spreading knowledge of German language, politics, culture and counterculture. The Germans are particularly suited to help nurture democracy in eastern Europe because of their own relatively egalitarian society (by contrast to the French and British) and by their own postwar experience in turning an authoritarian into a democratic mentality.

> "President Bush's unstinting support for unification in 1989–90 showed the Germans the benefits of maintaining an alliance with a large, distant friend."

There is no cause for alarm here, as the French in particular have expressed it, about German cultivation of a special sphere of influence in the region. On the contrary, the United States should welcome the burst of German activity and try to match it with its own exuberant grass-roots exchanges among the Polish, Lithuanian and Ukrainian émigré communities in the United States. . . .

Shifting Burdens of Leadership

Managing Soviet collapse, German ascent and east European transition will not be easy. Preserving the congruence between democracy, prosperity and peace east of Germany will not be easy either, especially in the midst of rising expectations, world recession and pent-up nationalist animosities in the erstwhile Soviet empire. Yet the means of maintaining essential European security are at hand—those that will give positive political and economic evolution the best chance, much as America's improvised trans-Atlantic security guarantee of the late 1940s gave West Europeans the space to construct their economic and political miracles.

In this developing system of the 1990s, the two critical powers on the continent are now the United States and the German-driven European Community. They are linked in a four-decade-old Euro-Atlantic enterprise that the participants are discovering, to their surprise, is a real community and not just a frontier alliance against the wolves. The trans-Atlantic community is in its own way already post-national—not to the same degree as the EC, to be sure, but with that mutually perceived interdependence that has made NATO the longest-lived alliance in history.

Within this community the time has come to shift some of the burden of leadership, both in funding and in initiatives, to the Europeans in general and Germany-in-Europe in particular. The time has come to acknowledge that trans-Atlantic policy debates have long since gone beyond traditional clashes of monolithic national interest to become, in effect, exercises in domestic coalition-building between ever-shifting constituencies that now span the Atlantic.

In this community the Germans are being forced by circumstance to abandon their dream of remaining an apolitical Switzerland writ large. They will increasingly exercise leadership in the EC, eastern Europe, the Euro-Atlantic community and the Group of Seven.

Surely the Americans should welcome such positive assertiveness by their "partners in leadership."

Unification Will Strengthen Germany's Economy

by Jeffrey T. Bergner

About the author: *Jeffrey T. Bergner is the director and founder of a consulting firm in Washington, DC that advises the government on foreign policy issues. He is also an adjunct professor of National Security Studies at Georgetown University in Washington, D.C. Bergner has written numerous articles and book reviews in the area of international affairs.*

The simple addition of the two German economies late in 1990 produced a total gross national product in excess of $1.4 trillion. This was not only the largest GNP of any West European country (a designation the West German economy held in its own right), it was almost the size of the next two West European economies *combined.* . . . If the currency reform of 1948 produced an "economic miracle" in the western portion of Germany, the integration of the two parts of Germany will almost certainly produce a second.

The Cost of Unification

This is not to say that the process of economic integration will be easy or without cost. Clearly, initial estimates of how much West German tax revenue will be required to cover the transitional losses were low. These were amended upward twice in 1990 alone, and Chancellor Helmut Kohl has had to backtrack on his "no new taxes" pledge and propose a $31 billion tax increase. Also, it is fair to say that the magnitude of the task of modernizing the former East German economy was also underestimated. Lacking firsthand experience of the actual condition of the East German infrastructure and the East German industrial base, West Germans could not have guessed the full extent of the problem.

It is also not to say that reunification will proceed without other economic and social difficulties. There remains always a possibility of inflation, although the addition of so many unemployed workers to the economy will likely restrain inflationary pressures. Massive—though temporary—unemployment will itself constitute a wrenching political problem. Estimates are that 3.7 million

From Jeffrey T. Bergner, *The New Superpowers.* Copyright © 1991 by Jeffrey T. Bergner. All rights reserved. Reprinted with permission of St. Martin's Press, Inc., New York.

old jobs in the former G.D.R. will disappear (nearly 40 percent of the former employment base). At the beginning of 1991, 600,000 former G.D.R. workers were unemployed, and nearly three times that number were working reduced hours. A difficult transition is clearly underway.

But it is critical to distinguish between transitory problems and fundamental structural problems. It is all the more important to do so because not every political party in Germany and not every journalist has an incentive to do this. In this regard, it is well to recall some of the realities of the rosy days of the first economic miracle.

> *"The magnitude of the task of modernizing the former East German economy was also underestimated."*

As Ludwig Erhard, Konrad Adenauer's economics minister, learned from personal experience, the German boom of the late 1940s and early 1950s did not occur without serious birth pains. Inflation began nearly as soon as currency reform was put into place. Unemployment rose rapidly. The opposition Social Democratic Party called for the reintroduction of rationing and for an across-the-board freeze on prices. A general strike was called in November of 1948. Erhard tried to explain again and again—not always to receptive ears—the difference between short-term and long-term problems. He argued that patience was required and that temporarily high prices would bring forth a profusion of new goods that in turn would moderate price levels. To secure his policies he agreed to additional governmental regulations, thus creating the social market economy.

Suitable Marriage Partners

Such an outcome is not at all difficult to envision at the current time. Faced with substantial unemployment, the German government has found that it must adopt certain special policies for eastern Germany in order to weather the transition to a market economy in that part of the country. But for purposes of understanding the deeper possibilities for the German economy, we must focus not on temporary difficulties and expedients, but upon structural realities. And in this regard, one must simply say that East and West Germany could not possibly have been more suitable partners for marriage.

West Germany required a solid location for investing its cash surplus. This investment could have occurred to some extent in the western German economy itself, and indeed it will do so. But the massive surplus could not have been productively invested in this economy by itself. The East provides a ready-made location for this investment. It has a base of educated workers and consumers who speak German. It offers a reservoir for potential investment in which the West Germans have a natural competitive advantage over their industrialized competitors. And finally, just about the only difficulty that any observer could identify for West Germany in the years before reunification was

Chapter 2

the internal decline of the ethnic German population. This problem is resolved, at least for the time being, by the addition of 25 percent more ethnic Germans to its population.

From the standpoint of the East, reunification works equally well. It is clear from the long-term decline in growth rates that the East Germans had taken their economy as far as it could go without structural reorganization. The East German economy was simply not replenishing itself with adequate investment. Neither was it replenishing itself with productive workers, and of the available work force, many were underutilized and undermotivated. The East German economy needed a major infusion of new capital, of incentives, and of productive labor. All of this will be achieved by reunification.

Estimates for growth in the eastern portion of Germany vary, but are uniformly optimistic. Some former West German officials speculate that yearly growth could be about 10 percent a year. This estimate is seconded by Axel Siedenberg of Deutsche Bank, who sees growth in the 8 to 10 percent yearly range. The Industrial Bank of Japan suggests a growth rate of nearly 10 percent per year. One thoughtful observer expects a growth of productivity in the eastern portion of Germany in the range of 20 percent per year for the next several years. In short, prospects for rapid growth should be very good over a multiyear period until eastern Germany reaches the level of the western portion of the country.

Modernizing the East

Can the western portion provide help for the East without damage to its own economic standing? Some critics have said that a unified Germany will be economically weaker than West Germany alone. But the experience of recent years, in which the West German economy grew rapidly even as it assimilated many new refugees, suggests that the former West Germany will strongly benefit from unification. Indeed, economic results to date suggest that unification has been a powerful economic stimulus for growth in the former West Germany. In the third quarter of 1990 economic growth raced along at 8 percent, helping to put overall real growth for 1990 at 4.6 percent. Employment in the western part of Germany rose 775,000, the largest increase in more than thirty years.

"The German boom of the late 1940s and early 1950s did not occur without serious birth pains."

But who will pay the costs of modernizing the East? First, many of the costs of modernizing the East's industry will be borne by private firms in the West. These are the very firms that are flush with financial reserves. To the extent that additional borrowing is required, in many cases it will be backed by new assets of land (or, less likely, useful industrial plants) in the East. It seems well within the capacity of West germany industry to provide the necessary capital for modernization over a period of five to ten years. To the extent that foreign investors participate, this process will be speeded up.

Funds for the modernization of infrastructure may be somewhat more difficult to attain in sufficient quantities to make the kind of progress that Germans in both the East and West desire. One source of funding will be the sale of former G.D.R-owned enterprises. How much money this will raise is uncertain at this time. More likely will be direct German federal funding for the cost of environmental and other infrastructure problems, supplemented in turn by growing revenues from the five federal states in the East. But infrastructure modernization is by its very nature a time-consuming process that cannot be completed all at once. It requires substantial planning to make major changes in local transportation systems, utilities, sewer systems, and communications systems. These are long-term projects that do not always require substantial funds up front. Often, these monies are expended more slowly than either planned or hoped, and it is likely that the German government will find that these funds will spend out more slowly than anticipated.

Reasons for Optimism

The German government will be required to assume the direct costs of reunification. These will not be insignificant; health insurance and unemployment compensation for formerly employed workers in the East will be costly. But there are several reasons for optimism. First, the former West German government all along allocated funds within its budget that were associated directly or indirectly with the existence of two German states. In 1989, for example, direct subsidies from West to East Germany totaled about DM (deutsche mark) 2.5 billion. Of these funds, nearly DM1.4 billion was paid directly to the G.D.R. for postal and communications facilities, for transit fees, and for the release of political prisoners. Additional funds were expended on resettlers and immigrants from the East, as well as for "welcome money." The former West German government offered subsidies for home loans and furnishing to resettlers, as well as unemployment compensation for those unable to find work. In addition to these payments, the West German government forgave duties and value-added taxes on intra-German trade. In all, these costs ran to perhaps DM5 billion. The German Unity Fund of DM115 billion will be funded by DM20 billion from government revenues and DM95 billion borrowing. The DM20 billion will be composed of the above-mentioned funds the former West German government would have spent between 1991 and 1994 on subsidies that are no longer needed.

More significant, however, is the projected growth of German tax revenues from reunification. For 1990, the increase of one percentage point of economic growth in West Germany (from 3 to 4 percent) resulted in increased tax revenues

> *"East and West Germany could not possibly have been more suitable partners for marriage."*

of DM12 billion over initial projections. Over the next four years, increased tax revenues are now estimated at DM115 billion more than initially forecast.

These numbers should not be surprising. What they reflect is that the entire German budget will be far larger in coming years, both on the expenditure side and on the revenue side. Those analysts who focus exclusively on the costs of reunification (which have been estimated to be variously between DM500 billion and DM1.1 trillion) are bound to produce a pessimistic picture. The fact is, however, that although German government borrowing will rise, the growth of revenues in both the western and eastern portions of Germany will over time offset a great share of the federal costs associated with reunification. One should note that in addition to the large West German firms going into the East, many small new businesses are springing up there. In the first half of 1990 alone, 100,482 applications to begin new businesses were registered in the East. Some of these businesses will not succeed, but many others will, providing both additional employment and state and federal tax revenues in the eastern portion of Germany.

	German GNP (in billions of dollars)		
	West	East	Total
1990	1,290	216	1,506
1991	1,341	237	1,578
1992	1,395	260	1,655
1993	1,451	286	1,737
1994	1,509	315	1,824
1995	1,569	346	1,915
1996			1,992
1997			2,071
1998			2,154
1999			2,240
2000			2,330

None of this is intended to minimize the pain of transition which will be experienced by many Germans who are unemployed or working reduced hours. Clearly, the hope that reunification could be financed without a tax increase has disappeared: new taxes on income, gasoline, cigarettes, and consumption will be in effect over the next several years.

But when looked at in the large, the outcome will inevitably be highly positive. Reunification puts an end to a great many structural inefficiencies and irrationalities that limited the economies of both former Germanies. A skilled, labor-short West has joined a capital-short, structurally deficient East. The result has provided a new internal market 25 percent larger than the previous F.R.G.

market. It has almost overnight reduced the structural inefficiencies of combined German agriculture by half. It has matched pent-up consumer demand with high-quality products. And it will allow a nearly 50 percent reduction in German armed forces from a combined East and West total of 670,000 to 370,000, at the same time resulting in greater security.

Let us consider a combined German economy in which the eastern portion grows rapidly, say at 10 percent annually, and the western portion grows at 4 percent. After five years the eastern and western portions of Germany grow at an average combined overall rate of 4 percent. The chart reflects these assumptions. As the chart shows, the German economy would reach nearly $2.5 trillion by the turn of the century. If, in response to strong growth the value of the mark should increase against the dollar by even 1 or 2 percent a year, the relative value of the German economy could approach $3 trillion by the year 2000. It is perhaps worth noting that these assumed overall German growth rates are *less* than those actually registered in the West German economy in the years 1948-1953....

Today's Europe has not only its geographical center but also its economic center in Germany. Europe as a whole will become stronger and richer vis-a-vis other regions, particularly the already poor ones; but Germany will become stronger and richer than the rest of Europe. Whether, how, and in what degree Germany can exercise this strength depends upon how much independence of action it retains as a nation within Europe.

Unification Has Harmed Germany

by Amos Perlmutter

About the author: *Amos Perlmutter is a professor of political science and sociology at American University in Washington, D.C., and editor of the Journal of Strategic Studies.*

The 1990 political reunification of the two Germanies was celebrated with heartfelt euphoria as one of the greatest and most immediately apparent triumphs in the West's Cold War victory. It meant that after four decades Germany and Europe were no longer divided, for that's what German unity represented to Western Europe.

Unsettling Signs

Two years later, some dubious, ominous and unsettling signs are appearing that the consequences of unification may threaten the very goals it meant to bring about, which is to say the stability of a more united Europe. The hurried and emotional rush to unification may have undermined the prospect of stability for both Germany and Europe for some time to come.

There were voices at the time that argued against the unseemly rush to unification, most notably that of Henry Kissinger, who argued that the time was not ripe, that it would take in rational terms at least 10 years for unification to evolve without pain, strain and unforeseen consequences and problems. But voices like that of Mr. Kissinger were lost in the euphoria over unification that had seemed as such a distant and perhaps even formal reality prompted by irrational factors which were political, economic and psychological in nature.

Chancellor Helmut Kohl, for one, saw the opportunity to create for himself the image of a modern Bismarck, unifier of the two Germanies, making the most politically powerful and stable state in Europe.

The real and perhaps the present motor behind the drive to unification was not Mr. Kohl, but his foreign minister, Hans-Dietrich Genscher, better known as one of the three saxons "guards," author and father of Genscherism, the policy

---

Amos Perlmutter, "Unsettling Fallout from Unification," *The Washington Times*, May 20, 1992. Reprinted with permission.

of appeasement and rapprochement with Moscow, neo-Stalinist dominated East Germany, Czechoslovakia and Hungary and military dominated Poland.

Mr. Genscher, the longest-lasting foreign minister in Western Europe, followed in the tradition of Ostpolitik, pioneered and invented by the Social Democrats Kurt Schumacher, the founder of the German Social Democratic Party, who was followed by the highly visible Willy Brandt, Herbert Wehner ("uncle Herbert"), the party's chief strategist, and Egon Bahr, a Social Democrat head of Policy Planning in the 1960s and Mr. Genscher's most trusted ally.

> "The consequences of unification may threaten the very goals it meant to bring about, which is to say the stability of a more united Europe."

As foreign minister, Mr. Genscher was a constant thorn in the U.S.-NATO Cold War policy. Mr. Genscher sought a tacit alliance with Leonid Brezhnev, persistently fought modernization of NATO in the mid-1980s while pursuing a policy that all but legitimized the neo-Stalinist, Brezhnevite domination of East and East Central Europe by recognizing Eastern European communist regimes.

Mr. Genscher's Deutschland-politik was a foreign policy in which Germany was in its own way the spearhead of East-West rapprochement. By 1989, his policy had borne fruit, but ironically, it was being conducted in the East by those who had opposed communist rule of Eastern Europe, which Foreign Minister Genscher legitimized, shored up and strengthened. In 1992, with the ship of state steering for potential trouble, Mr. Genscher opted to resign and jump ship, leaving Mr. Kohl, who had opposed Genscherism but could not resist the siren call of his own ego and Bismarckian ambitions of a greater Germany, to deal with the consequences of reunification.

Those consequences, a direct result of unplanned unification, are serious, and appear to bode nothing but difficulties for German and European stability.

Mean-Spirited Strangers

If the citizens of the two Germanies seemed strangers to each other before unification, they are even more estranged now that they are formally unified into one nation. Mean-spiritedly, they ridicule each other with the impolite terms of Wessies and Ossies. To paraphrase an old description of Americans and the English, they are strangers divided by the same language, both calling themselves German, now living under one flag, one government, one territory and one Kohl.

By yanking East Germany into its embrace, the German Federal government brought into its fold a state and people who constitute an inherently sick society, politically, economically and above all morally. These are a people who have endured, and lived under totalitarian rule for 60 years, under the Nazis,

Chapter 2

and then under the Stalinist rule of Walter Ulbricht, and Erich Honeker-Erich Mielke, people inured and used to the political culture of a police state, which has brutalized and demoralized them. It is the kind of state in which half the people spied on the other half, and vice versa, in which ministers, teachers, educators, professors and intellectuals engaged in a dizzying orgy of spying for Stasi. Fathers spied on sons, husbands on wives, children spied on their parents, in such relentless and continuous fashion that it almost makes the efforts of the Gestapo, the NKVD and the KGB seem halfhearted by comparison.

East Germany emerged dazed from the collapse of its Stalinist government like survivors of a moral, political and intellectual holocaust. It remains a morally devastated society, without memory or experience of democratic institutions.

The process of rebuilding East Germany and its intellectual and spiritual morale will take longer than integrating its homespun and ineffectual economy into Germany, a process that has already burdened the state to the tune of some $50 billion, with the price tag getting ever larger. The rush to unification has forced East Germans to confront the dark lessons of their own self-inflicted wounds suffered under the oppressive Stasi regime.

Reviving Old Hatreds

The rush to unification has had another unintended and ominous result. It has brought to the surface and strengthened the semi-dormant forces of neo-Nazism and anti-immigrant racism that had hitherto been effectively stifled. The Nazi skinheads from the East have bolstered the neo-Nazi forces in the country as a whole, to the point that they have finally won political representation in the state legislatures of some regions where they managed to get 5 percent of the vote.

In the international arena, German arrogance is resurfacing with unfortunate result. It was Mr. Genscher who led the way to recognizing and therefore legitimizing the Yugoslavian Serb-Croat divide that exacerbated the ensuing Bosnian-Herzogovinian-Muslim-Christian-Slavic massacres. Here, no one is in control, not the Serbian military or police that instigated the civil war, not the United Nations or EEC force and certainly not the German government whose policy legitimized the Yugoslavian civil war.

> *"As foreign minister, Mr. Genscher was a constant thorn in the U.S.-NATO Cold War policy."*

Unification, hurried or otherwise, is nevertheless, here to stay. It is a done deed impossible to undo. It will exact its price. That is the end of Mr. Kohl's dominance, if not that of his party. It has meant the rise of racist forces in Germany, it has led to the end of the economic miracle state.

Germany's integration of its morally brutalized East German brethren does not auger well for the future. If anything, it has the potential to destabilize Germany, weaken its economy and engage all of its attention, which in turn does not bode well for European stability.

German unification may have been a symbolic and even euphoric triumph, but its consequences on a healthy, stable and politically model state and society were disregarded by the now out-of-office Mr. Genscher, whose policies led to early unification and by a chancellor too enamored of becoming a new Bismarck.

Unification Has Strained Relations Between East and West Germany

by Tyler Marshall

About the author: *Tyler Marshall is a staff writer for the* Los Angeles Times.

> *"Once, we swore to the nation's unity despite its division; today, despite unity, we have to realize that the nation remains divided."*
>
> —Egon Bahr
> Former West German Cabinet minister

It took several months for the architects of German unity to grasp the extent of economic devastation left by four decades of communism in the east and the difficulties it presented in rebuilding a unified nation. Then they ran into another problem, far more alarming and infinitely more intractable than an economic crisis.

The Wall Within

The terrible truth: Germans are still divided, not by the physical and ideological barriers that kept them apart for 40 years, but by experience, emotion, psychology, expectation—their very approaches to daily life.

Collectively, these differences produce an invisible but formidable "wall within" that threatens both the eastern region's short-term economic recovery as well as the whole nation's longer-term social cohesion and political stability.

The growing awareness of this inner wall has deadened the joy so openly shared among Germans during their initial months of mixing together, replacing it with a sobering, hard reality.

"A unified state has been created, but the split between the two halves is so deep in economic, social and human terms that we could not have imagined it in our worst nightmares," Parliament member Wolfgang Thierse told the congress of his Social Democratic Party.

From Tyler Marshall, "New Wall Divides Germany," *Los Angeles Times*, June 16, 1991. Copyright, 1991, Los Angeles Times. Reprinted with permission.

For many, it was a headline writer for the Frankfurter Rundschau who best captured the import of this inner wall; summing up a trip by two of Chancellor Helmut Kohl's Cabinet ministers to the east, he wrote: "Chancellor's Vanguard Travels Through a Foreign Land."

More worrisome for national planners is evidence that after the collapse of the Berlin Wall brought the two Germanys together, the gap separating them seems to be widening.

In a powerful historic irony, this gap has generated a sense of separate identity among eastern Germans that decades of Communist propaganda failed to achieve. Those who talk of the east achieving economic equality with the west in several years predict that a unity of spirit will take generations.

> *"Germans are still divided, not by the physical and ideological barriers that kept them apart for 40 years, but by experience, emotion, psychology, [and] expectation."*

The very words *ossie* and *wessie*, for example, used to differentiate eastern from western Germans, emerged only after the fall of the physical German frontier. They have since entered the nation's slang as verbal shorthand for the two stereotypes: the naive, confused, inexperienced *ossie* and the slick, arrogant, know-it-all *wessie*.

In the months since East and West Germans danced together atop the Berlin Wall, these stereotypes have become the daily fare of tabloid headline writers, barroom jokes and mutual insults.

New newspapers and magazines have sprouted in the east, appealing mainly to a steadily strengthening separate *ossie* identity, often playing on the east-west differences with such headlines as "Western Woman Laughs at Naked *Ossie*" and "*Wessies* Demand 80% of All [Eastern] Property Back."

Raised in Different Worlds

An east-west cleft is certainly not new in Germany. Since the country was first unified in the last century, wine-sipping Roman Catholic Rhinelanders reared along Germany's western frontier have considered themselves lighter, more spiritual souls than the heavier, earthier, Protestant beer drinkers of the Prussian east.

But Germany's "inner wall" is far higher than history.

In part, it is simply a product of time: the near half-century the two Germanys spent apart, effectively as enemies. But it also stems from the total contrast between these separate postwar experiences.

Out of the wreckage of the Third Reich, western Germans filled a cultural vacuum and built their famous *wirtschaftswunder*, or economic miracle, as much with free-wheeling, American-style "go-go" as with Marshall Plan aid.

But as western Germans listened to Elvis Presley, watched Marilyn Monroe strut her stuff in "How to Marry a Millionaire" and learned the value of the

Chapter 2

high-powered sales pitch, their eastern cousins were slipping under the shadow of a neo-Stalinism that stifled personal initiative, scorned self-promotion and suppressed individual thinking.

As a result, with only a little exaggeration, German unification has been depicted as a collision between confident, open, upfront westerners born into the cut-and-thrust of free market competition, and uncertain, bewildered, eastern Germans bred with an introverted, passive nature, group loyalty, an instinct to keep one's true thoughts for a select few, to avoid conflict and to withdraw when challenged.

One Nation, Two Worlds

Easterners "came to unity with all the skills you don't need to get ahead in a market economy," said Manfred Stolpe, the state premier (governor) of the eastern state of Brandenburg. "They developed a special knack for keeping a low profile and were creative only if asked to be."

Although planners were aware that the east's weak, obsolete economy would likely buckle under the full weight of western competition, few understood that there would be a second, equally devastating juggernaut from the west—one of brimming confidence, innovative ideas and flashy style that has overwhelmed and demoralized many easterners.

> *"This gap has generated a sense of separate identity among eastern Germans that decades of Communist propaganda failed to achieve."*

"I stay quiet around *wessies*," admitted an eastern Berlin office worker, "because I'm afraid I'll be used, laughed at or make some terrible mistake."

Commented an 18-year-old western Berliner, "If you just want to bum around, then it's OK 'over there,' but if you really want to do something at night, then you stay here in the west."

"One nation, two different worlds," summed up Wolfgang Roth, deputy parliamentary floor leader for the opposition Social Democrats. . . .

Difference in Communication

Differences in body language occasionally generate misunderstandings. One woman brought in from the west to help restructure eastern Berlin's Humboldt University instantly alienated her eastern colleagues by entering an office unannounced, confidently flopping into a chair and launching into light chit-chat. Although she almost certainly meant no offense, the easterners with whom she would have to work said they considered her demeanor presumptuous and arrogant.

Wolfgang Engel, resident director of the Dresden State Playhouse, who has served as a guest director at theaters in Vienna and Zurich, says there are differences between western and eastern German performers and their abilities to express emotion.

"Because he's accustomed to it, an actor from the west [can] . . . turn his soul inside out," Engel said in an interview. "A GDR [eastern] actor can do that, too, but it takes longer. Maybe he has an internal barrier that questions whether it's right to reveal too much of himself or whether it might somehow be used against him."

Eastern and western audiences react differently too.

To a considerable extent, the skill of the East German stage was to communicate subtly with an audience, passing hidden meanings or truths that the public could savor but the censor could not challenge.

For easterners, this was all part of a schizophrenic life, in which daily newspapers dealt in fairy tales and truth was carefully concealed in novels and the theater. Westerners found this theater of the metaphor, as Engel called it, obtuse, intellectual and cold.

One result of the east's old Communist "work collective" was that it frequently spilled into free time, with office or factory colleagues grouping together for the theater, sporting events or to help in apartment renovations or in case of illness. That contrasts sharply with the more individual lifestyle of the west. Easterners continue to rely more on the home as the principal place to meet and entertain friends, while westerners, at least in urban areas, prefer to meet outside the home.

However, with unification, many of the factories and offices have closed; as easterners compete for the first time in their lives in an open job market, they fret that they no longer have time to keep up their friendships.

Lack of Understanding

All these differences, so evident when eastern and western Germans are compared, defy the conventional wisdom that in the East European nations, the people had so totally rejected the Communist systems swept away by the 1989 revolutions that no emotional legacy was left at all.

"Nothing disappears without a trace," says author and political commentator Guenter Gaus, who served for seven years as West Germany's permanent representative in East Berlin. "Everyone—those who weren't part of the system, those who rejected it and had nothing at all to do with it—they were all shaped by its demands far more than they themselves realized."

> *"Many believe that the internal wall separating the Germans also divides other east and west Europeans."*

Many believe that the internal wall separating the Germans also divides other east and west Europeans, complicating the cohesion of a free and open Europe as it searches for its own unity.

"Those in Eastern Europe share a common heritage," said medical scientist and political activist Jens Reich. "If I'm in Prague or Moscow and speak with a stranger, I understand immediately why the market system can't function there. We have all traveled on the same ship, had the same experience."

Gaus says he believes a crucial problem in the German unity process has been an inability on the part of the western-dominated German government to acknowledge these differences—differences that, on a purely personal level, make it far more difficult for easterners to find their way in a rough-and-tumble, free-market society.

> *"Eight months after unification, there remains no powerful, influential, eastern voice."*

"We've had misunderstandings because western Germans have yet to realize that for 40 years, they have lived under a false assumption—namely the assumption that once the [Communist] system disappeared, [eastern Germans] would be the same as we are," he said.

"Because so many believed the system had disappeared without a trace, the majority in the west placed their belief in the power of the market," Gaus added. "We have fallen victim to that idea."

Kohl's Response

Among the believers was Chancellor Kohl.

Initially convinced that only opportunity separated the two German peoples, he repeatedly rejected calls for special parliamentary committees or a ministry for eastern affairs during the run-up to unification.

Kohl admitted, "We have drifted much further apart than we thought."

One result of Germany's psychological mismatch is that the eastern region, with 20% of the country's population and about 43% of its land area, is virtually without voice or influence in Germany's first united government.

In Kohl's government of 52 Cabinet ministers and ministerial state secretaries, seven are easterners. In the Bundestag's 23 influential permanent committees, where key legislation is shaped for presentation to the full Parliament, eastern members hold one chairmanship, the Committee for Family and Senior Citizens Affairs.

In the country's two largest political parties, Kohl's Christian Democrats and the main opposition Social Democrats, not a single eastern member of Parliament serves as chief party spokesman on a key issue.

Although the Bundestag's seniority system and an unfamiliarity with the rules of Western-style parliamentary democracy certainly play a role in dampening the voice of eastern members—they are defined as freshmen—the "inner wall" adds to the problem.

"When an issue comes up in [a parliamentary party meeting], my tendency—the tendency of most of my western colleagues—is to jump at it, you know, and run with it, really attack it," said deputy Social Democratic floor leader Roth. "Meanwhile, the eastern MP [member of Parliament] sits there and asks if he might be permitted to ask a question. He's completely out of the discussion. It's a mentality problem that's the result of 57 years of dictatorship."

Politicians in Bonn still refer to the east as "over there" and in informal conversations, the personal pronouns "we" and "they" now divide a people verbally almost as efficiently as the barbed wire that kept them physically apart for 40 years.

Sometimes they don't talk at all. When asked how eastern members of the Christian Democrats view German security policy, the party's chief parliamentary spokesman on the issue, Karl Lamers, hesitated briefly before replying: "I've got no idea how they relate to it. It's a vacuum."

Eastern members of Parliament share the sense of estrangement.

"We have a totally different way of thinking," noted Werner Schulz, an activist who helped overthrow East German communism in 1989 and now serves in the Bundestag as a member of the Alliance '90 Party, a coalition of eastern organizations. "It's still a foreign society to me."

There's a similar western dominance in the media.

Eight months after unification, there remains no powerful, influential, eastern voice—neither institutionally, as in a newspaper or magazine, nor individually, as in a television commentator or newspaper columnist.

Those voices that do speak aggressively for the east often are from the west.

> *"For the westerner, unity has disturbed virtually nothing in daily life."*

The eastern Berlin magazine, "*extra*," launched four months ago to capitalize on the emerging *ossie* identity, carried an inaugural editorial urging its readers to have the courage to stand up and resist "economic colonists from the west, for whom the east has become such a fantastic buy."

The magazine neglected to say the group that owned it had itself just been bought by western German publisher Gruener und Jahr and Britain's Robert Maxwell and that the editor who signed the editorial was from the west.

Less Than 3 Percent

The growing *ossie-wessie* identity only strengthens the inner wall that continues to separate Germans.

One tourist industry survey showed that during the first full year of an open inner-German frontier, less than 3% of western Germans crossed into the eastern region for more than a couple of days.

Michael Kruse, who is researching youth attitudes across the east-west divide as part of a doctoral thesis at Bielefeld University, said that young east and west Berliners, who mixed quickly and enthusiastically in the initial months after the

Wall came down, have gradually retreated to their own sides.

"When I ask why, they always say, 'I was over there and it was all really nice, but somehow they're just different than we are,'" Kruse said. "Western youths characterize their eastern counterparts as boring, obsequious and as people who avoid direct eye contact. Young easterners complain that western acquaintances are aggressive people, whose direct eye contact in the subways is irritating and who come on with power enough for three people."

Kruse noted that in one neighborhood along the old Berlin Wall, teen-agers easily crossed through the newly opened barrier in the first months of 1990 to swap records, experiences and to party.

An Invisible Wall

"Now the Wall has disappeared, but you get the feeling there's another, invisible wall there that's getting higher every day," he said. "The Westerners would rather travel [12 miles] to the Ku'damm [the Kurfuerstendamm, western Berlin's main drag] than 500 yards to the youth club in Baumschulweg [a street in the east], while the easterner who lived directly on the Wall would rather go to Rostock or Dresden or Leipzig than into the west."

The divergent experiences in the months since unification—the west booming as the east sinks into a morass of unemployment and industrial decay—have only underscored and intensified the differences.

For the westerner, unity has disturbed virtually nothing in daily life. The 30% unemployment, the dying industries, the polluted rivers, the job-retraining programs and agonizing adjustments are all "over there."

But the easterners' different experience affects even what they read and talk about.

Magazines and newspapers carry "how-to" articles on obtaining work, on self-salesmanship and fighting depression, all non-issues in the larger, mainstream western media. Gaus' book, "Wendewut," about a middle-age eastern woman's problems in adjusting to her changed life, is a best-seller in the east, but it has been largely ignored in the west.

Conversation in an eastern German living room invariably starts with a list of who has work and who doesn't, how to pay the new-style phone bill or when the rents will rise—topics all but irrelevant at western cocktail parties.

> *"In eastern Berlin... marriages are down by 40%, births are off by a third and divorces and alcohol consumption are up."*

Eastern Germany is probably the only region in the industrialized world where detergent commercials on television trumpeting how one brand outperforms another are the subject of so many prolonged, sometimes intense, dinner conversations.

Suddenly, choices are required for everything from life insurance to body deodorant.

"There are 72 different kinds of toilet brushes on the market," noted Ingrid Koeppe, an eastern member of Parliament who said she counted them. "I'm astonished how much time people set aside just to pick one out."

Under the Communists, East Germans had just two types—one round, one square.

A Lost Generation

In peacetime, few peoples have experienced a more complete transformation.

Guaranteed jobs and fixed rents are gone. Crime has mushroomed; schools are being reorganized in size as well as curricula; the banking, health and legal systems have all been transformed; income tax rules have changed; utility bills are new and confusing; newspapers carry "real" news.

For some, the changes have become too much.

Joerg Richter, a psychologist who helps staff the phone lines at a small crisis center called Telephone of Trust in cramped quarters just off eastern Berlin's main Alexanderplatz, said one-third of the callers find life "so complicated that they can't see their way through it."

"A backlash in the east has spawned T-shirts emblazoned with the words, 'I Want My Wall Back.'"

A generation of over-45s, too old to retrain, too young to retire, often seem incapable of seeing beyond the unemployment line that later could contain half of the eastern German working population. Many political observers now believe they are part of a "lost generation" who will be permanently jobless or underemployed during the years when they should be most productive.

"They are passive, they feel helpless," Richter said.

The calls represent the tip of an iceberg of anxiety that has begun to show up in statistics.

Two Stereotypes

In eastern Berlin, for example, marriages are down by 40%, births are off by a third and divorces and alcohol consumption are up.

The region's suicide rate, traditionally twice that in the west, remains high, but the predominant reasons have changed—from domestic unhappiness to social uncertainty—giving rise to what one social psychiatrist called "a second suicide wave."

"What we experienced in 1945 was a total, violent, bloody and visible destruction," said the respected eastern writer and essayist Friedrich Dieckmann. "But this has been a remarkably soundless collapse, and that makes it harder psychologically, not easier."

Friedrich Schorlemmer, a politically active Protestant pastor from the east, put it this way: "Many people in the east now live in a mood of depression: We've done nothing, we're not needed, we live mainly from handouts. . . . It can't go on like this."

When asked how he believed eastern Germans would eventually adjust to the challenge of life in a free-market economy, Dresden theater director Engel quoted fellow director Benjamin Korn: "Half of the east Germans need a psychiatrist; the other half will become wolves."

Indeed, the initial euphoria of Germany's national reconciliation has been replaced by a sense of disappointment and disillusionment. The hugs, the excited waves and honking of horns that greeted easterners coming west for the first time in November, 1989, have dissolved into a low-grade grumbling among westerners about having to pay higher taxes to lift people whom they increasingly look on as "dumb, lazy easterners" out of economic squalor.

"After the honeymoon, we have reality again," said Reich, the scientist. "It's not a hostile relationship, but a very alienated, frustrating one."

Social observers fear resentment and anger could follow. A backlash in the east has spawned T-shirts emblazoned with the words, "I Want My Wall Back."

And the full brunt of eastern exposure to the west has generated the very sense of East German identity that the Communists failed to instill.

"I never loved my GDR identity and acquired it seriously only after 1989," Reich said. "To survive as a person, you can't reject all that has happened over the decades."

In the course of an hourlong interview, Reich spoke of apolitical benchmarks of life that characterized the German Democratic Republic, such as a quality of life in the polluted southern industrial towns where thankless conditions welded people together in much the same way as they have in the coal-mining regions of South Wales or West Virginia.

"It was polluted and it wasn't healthy, but it was home and it was their life," said Reich. "Now they're frustrated with an invasion of people [from the west] with well-tied neckties, flashy suits and smart behavior."

New East German Identity

A revival of interest in former GDR products, rejected by easterners only a year ago as second-class junk, is another indicator of the appeal to this new eastern identity. In recent weeks, papers circulating in the east have carried advertisements for "low-cost, fresh, new GDR products."

And the Berlin district council of Mitte, which formerly comprised downtown East Berlin, recently surprised westerners by refusing to rename Wilhelm Pieck Street, retaining the name of the first East German president.

How long it will take to overcome these differences is far from clear, but the answer carries implications for the longer-term social and political stability of Central Europe's biggest, richest nation—a nation that in the course of history has survived instability badly.

German Unification Has Harmed Women's Rights

by *Women and Revolution*

About the author: Women and Revolution *is a journal printed by the Spartacist League Central Committee Commission for Work Among Women, located in New York City. The Spartacist League is an international, revolutionary socialist organization that advocates the political theories of Marx, Engels, Lenin, and Trotsky.*

Five months after the July 1, 1990, economic annexation of the former East German deformed workers state (DDR) by capitalist West Germany, anxiety and anger have replaced D-mark intoxication. To strip the East of any remnants of its planned economy as quickly as possible in order to reap maximum profits, the Frankfurt and Wall Street bankers are instituting a program of mass pauperization. And as plants are privatized or closed altogether, it is the most vulnerable who get the ax first. Already the capitalist rulers have packed planes full of Mozambican, Cuban and Vietnamese workers and sent them back home. Working women, too, are being laid off by the hundreds of thousands, while the social programs for childcare, maternity leave and free abortion and contraception are being massively dismantled. Workers make bitter remarks about Hitler's "Kinder, Küche, Kirche" (children, kitchen, church), knowing this is the "new" future for women planned by their arrogant imperialist rulers, and they don't like it one bit.

Two Laws in One Country

On October 3, 1990, the capitalist exploiters and their political spokesmen celebrated the formal political reunification of East and West Germany with choruses of the *Deutschlandlied* and church bells ringing "für Volk und Vaterland" (for people and fatherland). But four days earlier women and their allies took the lead in fighting against the socially reactionary consequences of reunification when a protest march of 20,000 people greeted the new "Fourth Reich." Called by feminist and abortion rights activists, the "Demonstration Against the

From "German 'Fatherland' Against Women," *Women and Revolution*, Winter 1990/1991. Reprinted with permission.

Incorporation of the DDR, for a Self-Determined Life" denounced West Germany's notorious "Paragraph 218" anti-abortion law, one of the most restrictive in Europe, and its imposition on the former DDR where abortion has been not only legal but *free* since 1972. Banners spoke out against *Grossdeutschland* (Greater Germany) as well as Paragraph 218; one read "A woman who doesn't break the law will be broken by the law!"

> *"The Frankfurt and Wall Street bankers are instituting a program of mass pauperization."*

Although devoid of immigrant presence and with only token speakers from the powerful unions, the September 29, 1990, demonstration significantly linked demands for women's rights with resistance to reunification. Anti-woman repression is a spearhead of the all-sided social reaction which the triumphant German capitalist regime has in store for all working people in the ex-DDR. Now the extension of the capitalist system of impoverishment and oppression brings the deadly threat of illegal abortion to women in the East.

There have been continuing protests, East *and* West, against the universally hated Paragraphs 218 and 219, which allow abortion only in a "social emergency." Kafkaesque "counseling" requirements humiliate women. Draconian prosecutions of doctors and their patients under Paragraph 218 have been the central concern of women's rights activists in the West in recent years. In 1988 in an unprecedented show trial the state of Bavaria tried and convicted the heroic Dr. Horst Theissen, a Memmingen gynecologist, for performing "illegal" outpatient abortions. The case is currently on appeal.

East German mothers and striking West Berlin day-care workers were among the first to march in the streets against the threatened extension of Paragraph 218 to the East. Opposition later grew so widespread that Bonn had to agree to a "compromise" for reunification. To dampen protest and buy time, the ruling coalition has temporarily delayed slashing abortion rights East of the Elbe. Thus two laws are now in effect in one country—and the *doctor* is supposed to check a woman's postal code to see which law she is subject to!

Mobilizing Efforts

Chancellor Helmut Kohl's Christian Democratic Union (CDU), screaming about "abortion tourism," longs to prosecute West German women seeking abortions in the ex-DDR. To sidestep the furor over this absurd proposal, the government is concentrating on mandatory pre-abortion "counseling" for *all* women. This means monstrous encroachments into women's private lives, in a health system where intervention in private matters by the state is already Orwellian and in a country where there is no separation of church and state. In an effort to secure a clerical monopoly of Inquisition-like "counseling" boards, the Catholic church has pulled out all the stops against the civil-libertarian "ProFamilia" family planning centers as too "pro-woman"! The demands of the Spartakist Workers Party, German section of the International Communist League (Fourth Internationalist), "Priests, cops and judges out of the bedrooms!" and "Abolish the church tax!" speak to the hearts of working women and men in Germany.

Pushing its "right-to-life" bombardment Goebbels-style, the CDU has the Social Democrats (SPD) and the "liberal" FDP (the coalitionist party with the CDU) singing in chorus about "protecting unborn life." The idea is to pass a law against abortion for the whole *Reich* in two years. The pious calls of "down with Paragraph 218," on the lips of all but the CDU when the courageous Dr. Theissen was on trial, have now died away with barely an echo.

Women Lose Influence

In Poland, the capitalist-restorationist government run by Solidarność and dominated by the Roman Catholic church has submitted a law to the Sejm (parliament) outlawing *all* abortions and criminalizing the doctors. But Polish women too are hitting the streets and demonstrating for abortion rights. The struggles of German and Polish working women and men must be linked. The key is to mobilize the powerful union movement through the large, ex-Stalinist OPZZ in Poland and the social-democratic DGB, now the labor federation for all of Germany.

> *"The extension of the capitalist system of impoverishment and oppression brings the deadly threat of illegal abortion to women in the East."*

At the demonstration in Berlin, the SpAD submitted greetings, which read in part:

> Capitalist *Anschluss* means slavery for women. Down with Paragraphs 218 and 219! For the unlimited right to free, safe abortion! Down with the reactionary Paragraph 175 threatening homosexuals! . . .
>
> The struggle for the defense of women's rights is inseparably bound up with the struggle against an imperialist *Grossdeutschland*. The power of the working class must be unleashed to defend women and immigrant workers, Roma and Sinti. And the working class has the power to fight against capitalist counterrevolution!

The DDR guaranteed full employment and subsidized housing. Single women with children under three years old could not be fired, and single parents could take up to eight weeks a year paid leave to care for sick children. Assured of re-employment at an equivalent job, all women could choose to take the "baby year"—paid leave for up to 18 months after giving birth.

Based on working-class property forms and a planned economy, the former

DDR provided a secure and relatively egalitarian existence for all working people. But the East German revolution had not been achieved by a proletariat mobilized to fight for its class power under the leadership of a Leninist vanguard party. Social revolution had been imposed by the Kremlin from above in the wake of the Red Army victory against the Nazis in 1945. The result was a society qualitatively similar to the bureaucratically degenerated Soviet Union. With its anti-internationalist dogma of "socialism in one country," the Stalinist bureaucracy undermined the tremendous gains of the collectivized economy and denied political power to the militant working class, imperiling the very survival of the deformed workers states.

This fundamental contradiction surfaced in every aspect of East German life, not least in the treatment of women. The bureaucracy, upholding the traditional bourgeois values of woman as childbearer and homemaker, sees the family as "a fighting unit for socialism." Thus DDR law required state-run enterprises to have full day-care facilities; they were subsidized for all working parents, allowing women to participate fully in the economy. But the facilities closed in the evening, creating a "second shift" of childcare and household drudgery for working women.

According to a dispatch by Associated Press, a survey by the Inter-Parliamentary Council in Geneva shows that there are significantly fewer women in the present governments of East Europe than under the Stalinist regimes. In Bulgaria and Hungary, previously 21 percent of the parliamentary seats had gone to women; the figures are now 3.5 and 7 percent respectively. Of course these bodies were mere showpieces for the Stalinist bureaucracies; in no way did they embody the political power of the working class. But the "free" elections have uprooted even this tenuous integration of women into political life. As the bourgeois press agency admitted, "Little sensitivity to women's equality is evident in the new democracies" (17 November 1990).

Lowest in Western Europe

The status of women in the DDR deformed workers state compared very favorably to their status in the capitalist Federal Republic of Germany. Percentages of working women and access to day-care facilities in West Germany are among the lowest in Western Europe, far behind countries like Belgium and France with considerably lower per capita income. Only 57 percent of West German women work and only *three percent* of all children have places in day care. Even Bonn's official figures speak of over half a million too few places in day-care centers.

> "'Priests, cops and judges out of the bedrooms!' and 'Abolish the church tax!' speak to the hearts of working women and men in Germany."

The qualitatively better provisions for women's participation in economic life in the deformed workers states underscores the Trotskyist position of unconditional defense of these states against imperialist attack and domestic counterrevolution. When the East German Stalinist regime began to crumble in the fall of 1989, the ICL intervened to call for workers and soldiers councils to oust the bureaucrats in a political revolution that would establish the rule of the working class, spread the struggle for socialist revolution to the West and lay the basis for a socialist society based on an internationally planned economy. As the Stalinist ruling party in the DDR, the SED/PDS, began to disintegrate and the rapacious German bourgeoisie moved in to grab the DDR for exploitation, the SpAD fought as the only hard, unambiguous opposition to a capitalist reunification of Germany.

> *"Only 57 percent of West German women work and only three percent of all children have places in day care."*

First Fired: Capitalist Shock Treatment

The day after official political reunification, German newspapers ran headlines announcing 2.2 million unemployed in the former DDR, where there are just over 16 million people. Another 1.7 million were working short weeks (often no hours at all), the preferred scheme of the Social Democrats (SPD) for disguised dissolution of the workforce. Now metalworkers union tops speak of achieving *60-65 percent* of West German wages by 1992. And beginning 1 January 1991, when rents are allowed to float to "free market" levels, there will be massive homelessness as single parents (95 percent women) and families find they just can't pay.

The proportion of women among the total unemployed has risen from month to month; currently it is 55 percent in the East as a whole and over 10 percent higher in the industrial south of the ex-DDR. Today a common sight at rush hour in Halle, Leipzig and other industrial cities is women crying in the streetcars on their way to work—they know it is the last time. As the West German *Frankfurter Rundschau* headlined, it is "Women and Children First." The restoration of capitalism in the DDR means a social counterrevolution in which working women have been forcibly removed from active participation in economic life and driven back to "home and hearth."

Under the old DDR labor laws, plants could lay off only workers who were given another job. Factory managers all over East Germany have already thrown this on the scrap heap; for months they have been firing pregnant women, women on maternity leave and those who had been sick "too often." Other protective measures, from childcare and maternity provisions to the monthly housework day off, are supposed to continue until January 1, 1991, when West German regulations will come into effect.

"Protective" legislation (from the days of the Kaiser) banning women from the night shift also goes into effect on January 1, and then tens of thousands of women in industry, or one-quarter of the night shift, will lose their jobs. In the chemical industry alone, 24,000 women workers are threatened with mass layoffs and plant closures. The capitalists are deliberately destroying the East German textile industry, where some 93,000 women work. And the Social Democratic union tops have been in the forefront of setting up class-collaborationist "plant councils" to throw the onus on the workers to decide whom to ax first. While mouthing off about extending protection to men, they want to retain DDR laws only a little longer—until the plants are shut altogether! Meanwhile, surviving plants, like parts of Berlin's Stern Radio, are working around-the-clock speedup and overtime, including 12-hour shifts on weekends.

In the service sector, traditionally "women's work" in the former DDR, "pioneering" fly-by-night "entrepreneurs" are setting up shop and imposing starvation wages and unlimited, unpaid overtime. The new labor exchanges report that in commerce, banking and insurance establishments "now they only want men." If a woman is single, childless and in her 20s, maybe; but for a woman over 45 the answer is "no way" (*tageszeitung*, 31 July 1990). Anti-discrimination laws prohibiting invasive inquiries into family status never fettered the West German bosses, and now bosses in the East have caught on. As a mother of two children (eleven and three years old) heard at a job interview: "Your qualifications are right, your age is fine, but your little son is ten years too young" (*Frankfurter Rundschau*, 12 June 1990).

The "New Germany"—Catch 22 for Women

East German women are trapped in a vicious circle. They must earn more to support themselves and their families—but they are losing their jobs altogether. If they do have jobs, those jobs are threatened because there is little affordable childcare available for the kids. A woman can even lose unemployment benefits if she can't prove her children have access to day care! And many don't qualify for unemployment benefits in the first place. A mother of six, for example, who was supported in the DDR in "baby years" and now must find a job to feed her children, cannot get unemployment—she hasn't "worked" long enough in the last five years!

Workplace kindergartens and crèches, previously required by law, are now "voluntary." Although still subsidized, these facilities are being shut down; "nonproductive" real estate—including the land set aside for playgrounds!—is being sold off to Western industrialists. Faced with growing protests, local governments are running a shell game, claiming they will assume responsibility for a few day-care centers; but Bonn intends to cut 35 billion D-marks in funding for social programs in the East. In the month of July alone the price of existing day care in-

> *"Fly-by-night 'entrepreneurs' are setting up shop and imposing starvation wages and unlimited, unpaid overtime."*

creased fivefold.

The louder the clerical reactionaries scream about "protection for the unborn," the less protection there is for children *after* they're born. However outmoded, the ex-DDR's socialized medical system of polyclinics provided comprehensive, free medical care and was renowned for its obstetric and pediatric medicine. Now it too is being destroyed by massive layoffs and funding cuts. West Germany's bureaucratic, "cost effective" system of state-insured assembly-line health care is supposed to go East.

Tied to this wholesale loss of health benefits is loss of access to contraceptives. While not universally available, the pill had been dispensed free of charge in the DDR. It will cost 40-80 D-marks per quarter, more than in West Germany. This is prohibitive—most women factory workers earn less than 900 D-marks a month! With health care slashed, no jobs, no day care available, it's no wonder many East German women are deciding not to have children. The number of abortions in the East has indeed risen dramatically this year.

German Labor Must Defend Women's Rights

Working East German women and men have remained leaderless before advancing capitalist misery. Protests against the effects of *Anschluss* have been consistently *demobilized* by the labor misleaders, from the strikebreaking SPD leaderships now policing the unions to the fast self-destructing ex-Stalinist SED/PDS. But the present ferment over abortion could help galvanize the workers of East and West Germany for a political struggle against the "reunified" capitalist onslaught. The fight for *free, legal abortion* is a struggle which must be taken up by the whole German labor movement and linked to the demand for *free, quality medical care for all.*

Sporadic, isolated resistance to the Fourth Reich has begun, but it must be broadened and extended to the powerful West German working class. On 25 November 1990 railroad workers went out on strike, giving workers in the East a taste of their social power for the first time since the 1953 workers uprising against the Stalinist regime. The union tops quickly sold out the strike. To lead these struggles it's necessary to build a revolutionary, internationalist workers party like Lenin and Trotsky's Bolsheviks. Today our comrades of the Spartakist Workers Party of Germany seek to build such a party. As a platform for the desperately needed program to *win*, they are waging a class-struggle campaign, calling for *workers resistance East and West* to defend the livelihoods of workers, women and men, German and immigrant.

The plight of East German women starkly reveals that defense of women's rights is part of the struggle against the oppressive capitalist system. For in that system, to paraphrase the Stalinists, the anachronistic institution of the family is nothing less than the "fighting unit of capitalism." Only socialist revolution can achieve the liberation of women from drudgery and oppression by laying the material basis for true social equality. Some hard class struggle lies before us.

Chapter 3

Would Western Policies Benefit Eastern Europe?

Western Policies in Eastern Europe: An Overview

by Joel Havemann

About the author: *Joel Havemann is a staff writer for the* Los Angeles Times *newspaper.*

Ryszard Puchala is camping out in a mile-long line at the government-owned cement factory, waiting three days to buy raw materials for his construction business.

It may not be worth the trouble. So sour is the economy of Poland's countryside that most of the local farmers cannot afford Puchala's services anyway.

Times are tougher still at the other end of Eastern Europe, where Romania is trying desperately to inject Western investment into its foundering economy. A sign of its difficulty: On a list of foreign countries whose businesses have invested in Romania, the United States ranks sixth, just below Libya.

Capitalism, the prescribed antidote to four decades of repressive communism in Eastern Europe, has paradoxically made the patient sicker, at least for the short term. The lifting of government controls has sent prices soaring far faster than wages. Antiquated factories, operating for the first time without government subsidies, are closing for lack of customers, leaving countless workers without jobs for the first time in their lives.

Even in Hungary and Czechoslovakia, the region's two most vibrant nations, 1990's recession struck deeper than any in the United States since the Great Depression.

For most countries, conditions will get worse before they get better.

The free-market medicine, however, may be beginning to take effect. The most obvious evidence can be found in the big cities, where private shops are blossoming to meet long pent-up consumer demand.

Deeper Changes Evident

Some of the signs point to more fundamental change. Jarek Astramowicz is one—a new breed of Eastern European businessmen who want to make capital-

Joel Havemann, "A Rocky Switch to Capitalism," *Los Angeles Times*, July 8, 1991. Copyright, 1991, Los Angeles Times. Reprinted with permission.

Chapter 3

ism work and themselves wealthy. The 33-year-old Astramowicz, who left for Merrill Lynch in Boston a decade ago, has returned, and, as a consultant for Elektrogaz Ventures, is working on a plan to extract methane from the Silesian coal fields.

"The amount of work there is to do here is overwhelming," Astramowicz says. "I work 14 to 16 hours a day, six or seven days a week."

> *"Capitalism, the prescribed antidote to four decades of repressive communism in Eastern Europe, has paradoxically made the patient sicker."*

And although much of Eastern Europe's heavy industry may be beyond salvation, some of its light industry may prove globally competitive when set free of government ownership.

A happy combination of well-trained work forces and low wages puts Romania's textile and furniture industries in this category. Bucharest's gigantic Stil Conf textile plant has split into nine autonomous parts; Aurel Filfan, the general manager of the unit specializing in menswear, says decentralization has permitted him to tailor his production to the market, not to some bureaucrat's orders. Although the government is still the owner, Filfan says: "We enjoy much more freedom to do things our own way."

Uncertainty Grows

Hanging in the balance are the new democracies established by the revolutions of 1989. Capitalism may bring prosperity tomorrow. But today's hard times have spawned political unrest everywhere, from protests by Poland's Solidarity union to strikes by Romanian doctors, teachers, factory hands and railway workers.

Some officials are beginning to wonder if Eastern Europe will be able to get there from here.

"We can't be sure that the next government will continue what we're doing," says Janusz Siwicki, Poland's vice minister for privatizing government-owned industry. He warns of politicians "who promise everything tonight or tomorrow morning at the latest."

Most Eastern Europeans, however, have greater faith. "There's no turning back," insists Romanian Finance Minister Eugen Dijmarescu. "This government might quit, but that will not change the transition under way."

The United States and other industrial nations have much at stake: the development of not only a major market for their goods and a source of cheap labor but also a powerful force for world peace. Western Europe fears a tide of immigrants if Eastern Europe fails to satisfy its citizens' pent-up demand for decent lives.

Yet support from the West—in the form of both foreign aid and private foreign investment—has left Eastern European officials shaking their heads in dismay. They find themselves competing for scarce resources not only with each other but also with the immensely larger, sicker Soviet Union.

"I'm afraid there's more political commitment than financial commitment," says Czechoslovak Finance Minister Vaclav Klaus, the dynamo behind his nation's forced march toward free markets.

In Romania, where the politics remain unstable and the commitment to free markets is uncertain, Dijmarescu raises his eyebrows at Western Governments' declared determination to help his country. "From this declaration to the deed," he says, "there is still a lot of room."

If anything is certain in Eastern Europe's caldron of capitalism, it is that each country is going its own way, propelled by its own particular history, leadership and circumstances.

A North-South Divide

Forget about the "East Block," the undifferentiated column of countries with guns pointed West. David C. Roche, a London-based economist with the Morgan Stanley investment banking firm, says Poland and Romania are as different now as, say, the United States and France.

A north-south divide is shaping up with Poland, Czechoslovakia and Hungary better positioned to succeed than their neighbors to the south.

There are sharp contrasts even within the regions.

Poland leaped first to free markets. In its "big bang" of January, 1990, it simultaneously abandoned price controls, legalized private enterprise and devalued its zloty, which is still the only Eastern European currency that can be traded on international currency markets.

> *"Support from the West—in the form of both foreign aid and private foreign investment—has left Eastern European officials shaking their heads in dismay."*

The immediate consequences were an explosion of inflation and a burst of unemployment. But Poland also turned a trade deficit in 1989 into a surplus in 1990, and Roche says "Poland has a very good chance of becoming the next Spain," the most recent economic success story in Western Europe.

Czechoslovakia held back at first but took the free-market plunge at the beginning of 1991. With its industrial tradition and highly skilled work force, Joseph Tragert of PlanEcon, a Washington consulting firm, calls Czechoslovakia the most attractive for foreign investors.

Hungary, which had dabbled in free markets for two decades, is moving toward a gentler form of capitalism as it seeks to protect its citizens from the most brutal consequences of the transition. Although it has attracted the most foreign investment to date, Thaddeus Kopinski, of the U.S. Chamber of Commerce in Washington, says it is "resting on its laurels and not providing a sufficiently liberal trade and investment climate."

To the south, the revolutions in both Romania and Bulgaria remain unfinished, with major reform laws still not in place and Communists by other names clinging to important posts.

> *"We have an enormous cadre of managers who have no experience with real markets."*

The CIA calls Romania's free-market reforms the slowest in Eastern Europe; Roche calls Romania the "least likely to succeed." Brian V. Mullaney, his Morgan Stanley colleague, says that Bulgaria, which ceased making payments on its foreign debt more than a year ago, is "essentially insolvent."

Yugoslavia, which had cast off Soviet domination years ago and developed a respectable economic system of its own, has disintegrated into warring republics, leaving the central government powerless to enforce its economic reforms.

Albania, so isolated that even its telephone system was not linked to the international network until 1990, inaugurated its first non-Communist government since World War II in June 1991.

Each country's predicament may differ in the details. But from north to south, Eastern Europe is wrestling with common problems. The economic collapse of the Soviet Union, a major market for all its former satellites, has hurt everywhere. But most of what ails Eastern Europe is home-grown.

Roads are terrible, telephone systems scarcely function. Largely still absent are the basic institutions of capitalism: stock markets where shares of companies can be bought and sold; legal systems that define private ownership rights; financial institutions where money can be borrowed. Poland turned the former Communist Party headquarters into a stock market for five of its most promising companies, but one promptly went belly up and another is gasping for breath.

Industries Needed

And these are the least of the difficulties. Even with all the free-market institutions in place, Eastern Europe will need productive industries and capable people to run them. For the most part, it now has neither.

Industry's dreary state during four decades of government ownership is almost impossible to exaggerate. In a study for London's Centre for Economic Policy Research, economists Gordon Hughes of Edinburgh University and Paul Hare of Heriot-Watt University sought to measure value added by various industries to the raw materials they took in.

To their astonishment, they found a host of industries actually subtracted value—that is, what left their doors was worth less than what entered. Such was the case for Hungary's steel industry, Poland's chemical industry and the food processing industry in Poland, Czechoslovakia and Hungary.

It's not hard to see why. Much of the gigantic Huta Warszawa steel plant, covering 75 acres on Warsaw's outskirts, now stands idle. (The work force, 11,000 before the 1989 revolution, is at 5,000 and falling.) Before the 1989 revolution, the government would have bought what the plant produced.

"If we had been idle this way under the old system, the secret police would have arrested us," says Jan Olek, Huta Warszawa's production coordinator.

The new system requires Huta Warszawa to go out and find its own buyers. But Henryk Staniszewski, a bear of a man who is Huta Warszawa's production director, says he is not looking.

"Many other countries obviously manufacture steel cheaper than we do," he says with an air of resignation.

Staniszewski's comments suggest another of Eastern Europe's great handicaps: a deficit of managers, not only in industry but also in government, who know how to make free markets work.

"Private enterprise is breeding a new generation of cold-blooded, Western-style business executives."

"Under the old way, nobody profited from being profitable," says Stanislaw Wellisz, a top advisor in Poland's finance ministry. "We have an enormous cadre of managers who have no experience with real markets."

Thomas S. Scharf, president of Lloyd Equities in New York, found that out the hard way. The Polish-born Scharf, who fled the Nazi onslaught as a boy, is preparing to build and manage multifamily housing in Warsaw.

He has every advantage. He speaks Polish. And Poland desperately needs housing: Warsaw has a waiting list of 1.5 million households looking for a place to live.

Yet it has taken Scharf a year and a half to launch his project.

"Poland may have a new government," he says, "but the Communists still are the bureaucrats. Under the old system, they had every incentive to say no, because once they said yes, there was nothing for them to do. And even if you can make a deal with one group of bureaucrats, they leave and you have to start all over again with another."

Privatization Is Slow

In Romania, Finance Minister Dijmarescu estimates an immediate need for 20,000 managers savvy in the ways of free markets. Only a few hundred are now being trained.

Privatizing state-owned industry in Eastern Europe is proceeding more slowly than had been hoped. Hungary is probably making the best progress, although it sold less than 3% of its state-run businesses to private investors in 1990.

Czechoslovakia is preparing to auction shares of 1,000 to 2,000 enterprises to the highest bidders. Poland is going to try to give shares away.

Siwicki, Poland's vice minister for privatization, acknowledges that much of his country's heavy industry will quickly collapse when subjected to free-market competition. Poland's best results so far have come from smaller firms.

Marek Ogrodzki, chairman of Omig, a Polish manufacturer of electronics components for telecommunications systems, took his company private in 1989. He promptly slashed his work force in half by firing "300 paper-pushing bureaucrats who produced nothing" and laying off 200 production workers.

Absolute Independence

The recession in Poland, where Omig makes 70% of its sales, has hurt. But Ogrodzki—unlike the management of state-owned Huta Warszawa—is looking for new products and new markets, including cable television.

Ogrodzki can hardly conceive of how the company had worked when the government owned it. "I have absolute independence," he says. "I'm not a component in a giant planning system. Nobody orders me around."

New private enterprises are being created much faster than state-run businesses are going private. Hungary is bursting with private shops, restaurants and services. In Warsaw, where food store shelves were often empty as recently as 1989, yesterday's street-corner fruit stand is growing into today's new supermarket.

"After 40 years of having nothing to buy, the customers are coming" says Tomasz Neumann, the 31-year-old president of Vicomus, a Warsaw shop that sells imported musical instruments ranging from children's toys to electronic keyboards worth several thousand dollars. "People had savings—the Communists didn't confiscate everything—and many people have relatives abroad," Neumann says.

> *"Traditional market capitalism is simply not able to cope with the problems that these countries face."*

On Nowy Swiat, Warsaw's answer to Rodeo Drive, Krystyna Pracz, a 35-year-old engineer at the state-owned pharmaceutical manufacturer, has just bought a bathing suit for 160,000 zlotys (about $15)—one-tenth of the average monthly Polish salary.

"It's expensive," she concedes, "but Polish women like to dress well, and sometimes we make sacrifices elsewhere."

Shopping is still not so much fun in the southern tier of countries. At Unirea, a Bucharest department store, Valentina Nastase, 46, has just decided not to buy a pair of blue jeans for 2,500 lei ($42 at the official exchange rate).

"It's not easy to find what you want," she says, "and when you do, it's very expensive."

Private enterprise is breeding a new generation of cold-blooded, Western-style business executives. One such is Tomasz Lukasiewicz, director of development for Universal, an export-import trading company that went private and is looking for new lines of business.

"Now is a splendid occasion to buy companies very cheaply" because many are bankrupt or cash-starved, says the 34-year-old Lukasiewicz. Universal has bought 30, including a printing company, a hotel and a condom manufacturer.

> *"Western investors have found little of value in Czechoslovakia's heavily polluting and energy-wasting factories."*

Like many an American workaholic, Lukasiewicz has little time to see his wife and two sons. "We're working 18-hour days, and we're very stressed," he says. "But there's a huge chance now—high risk and high gain."

As usual, the southern countries are lagging. In Romania, the one private entrepreneur who has made a substantial mark is Ion Tiriac, the onetime guru to tennis pros Guillermo Vilas and Bjorn Borg. Tiriac's enterprises include Romania's first private bank.

"This country needs a hundred Tiriacs," says a Western source in Bucharest.

To make up for its deficit, Eastern Europe is searching for capital from abroad. Except for Hungary, which has attracted more than half of the foreign investment in the entire region, each country has been disappointed so far.

"The figures aren't very impressive," admits Zbigniew Piotrowski, president of Poland's Foreign Investment Agency, pointing to Poland's end-of-year total of $350 million. He blames Poland's laws, which still raise bureaucratic obstacles to ventures whose foreign ownership is more than 10%, and its customs, which have left many Polish businessmen "distrustful of foreigners."

Western investors have found little of value in Czechoslovakia's heavily polluting and energy-wasting factories. Much Czechoslovak production had been geared to the low demands of Soviet and East German markets, both of which have disappeared.

Romanians Must Improve Their Image

In Romania, Westerners are still waiting for political stability and a more attractive foreign investment law. They will not soon forget that Romanian President Ion Iliescu, who had served in the regime of Nicolae Ceausescu, summoned mine workers to Bucharest in 1990 to bludgeon anti-government protesters into submission.

"We have to build our image," says Misu Negritiou, president of the Romanian Development Agency, with considerable understatement. He hopes Colgate-Palmolive will soon approve a soap and toothpaste plant in Romania.

Bulgaria destroyed whatever chance it had of doing substantial business with Western firms when it ceased payments on its foreign debt.

The northern countries are also more attractive as markets for Western products. In Romania and Bulgaria, says Dilip Chandra, general manager for IBM in Eastern and Central Europe, such necessary conditions as "the free flow of capital, access to foreign currency and repatriation of profits" are still not available.

Foreign aid has been easier to come by than private foreign investment—all told $56 billion has been pledged in grants, loans, loan guarantees and debt relief—although Eastern European officials remain unsatisfied.

On the ground in the East, Western Europe's aid program generates more praise than America's. Gregory Vaut, an American who directs the Foundation for the Development of Polish Agriculture, says bureaucrats from the 12-nation European Community "broke a lot of rules" to provide assistance when it was needed.

In contrast, Wellisz, in the Polish Finance Ministry, says: "The U.S. foreign aid program is tied in knots. Instead of support, we get a fact-finding mission once a month."

The economic revolution in Eastern Europe may well fail without foreign assistance—lots of it.

"Traditional market capitalism is simply not able to cope with the problems that these countries face," warns Roche, the Morgan Stanley economist. "A foreign investor is not going to be able to come in and earn a 15% return on his investment simply by putting padlocks on the doors of inefficient factories."

Perhaps Eastern Europe's greatest asset is the spirit of its people. Barbara Puchala, Ryszard's wife, knew only deprivation under communism. Now she does not know what to expect.

"I am afraid of the future," she says. "But I don't want to go back to the past."

Western Nations Can Help Eastern Europe Prosper

by Zbigniew Brzezinski

About the author: *Zbigniew Brzezinski was the national security adviser under former U.S. president Jimmy Carter. He is the author of* The Grand Failure: The Birth and Death of Communism in the Twentieth Century.

When historians begin to chronicle the end of the 1980s, they will be tempted to conclude that those years marked the final battle in the great contest of ideas that, beginning with the French Revolution, raged for 200 years over the nature of the individual's relationship to society and society's relationship to the state. The fall of communism in the USSR and Eastern Europe permits us to weigh the future of East-West relations from a new perspective, an emerging philosophical consensus grounded in the supremacy of the individual. The rights of the individual are on the rise, asserting their authority over the state. But, like most battles, this one is complicated and confused, and its outcome is far from certain. But that should not prevent the West from getting involved. The question is, how?

Ideologies Born in the French Revolution

The French Revolution's faith in rationality, its extraordinary optimistic utopianism, gave birth to a widely held conviction that the world was entering a new era in which deliberate social engineering based on utopian aspirations and political decisions implemented from the top down, would foster a just society. These ideas found expression not only in democratic idealism, especially socialist utopianism, but also in totalitarian ideologies—Hitlerism and Marxism-Leninism. Both branches of totalitarianism preached the possibility of a perfect society through subordination of the individual to society and the subordination of society to the state. World War II ended Hitlerism. Marxism-Leninism lasted until the 1980s, when it fell completely in Eastern Europe and began to crash—and continues to—in the Soviet Union.

The discredited faith in state domination is being replaced by a new, widely

---

Zbigniew Brzezinski, "To Strasbourg or Sarajevo?" *European Affairs*, February/March 1991. Reprinted with permission.

accepted political notion based on the supremacy of spontaneous human action. It holds that the inherent complexity of social change cannot be totally subordinated to social planning, that the conduct of human affairs requires pragmatism and experimentation, and that the guiding principle of social organization must be absolute freedom of choice to make political and social decisions.

In a speech to the United Nations, Mikhail Gorbachev said, 'Freedom of choice is a universal principle which should allow no exceptions,' a quotation that captures the essence of the change sweeping international politics. It signals Western civilization's move toward a consensus regarding the individual's relationship to society, a common commitment to make the primacy of the individual the foundation of the citizen's relationship to society. Under the new consensus, politics is a mechanism that serves collective individual aspirations arising from guaranteed freedom of choice.

Wrenching Changes

The consensus, in its particulars, may be ill-defined. While previously the Soviets automatically regarded the US as the essence of imperialism, today some idealize life in America and attempt to copy it. Soviet delegations often travel to the US in the sincere hope of absorbing the American model of social and political development and transplanting it unchanged to the Soviet Union. But the essence of freedom of choice, the supremacy of spontaneous human response, is that each society has to devise solutions to the problems it confronts. Although it may rely on certain basic principles—e.g., freedom of choice and free-market mechanisms—their application does not yield models that can be easily transplanted. It would be tragic if the Kremlin merely replaced Marxism-Leninism with Friedmanism, if it simply switched 'isms' and overlooked that every successful society is a product of its own history and must adapt its cultural experience to certain shared frameworks.

Futile attempts at political transplants aside, no one can predict with certainty that the defeat of state supremacy will mean the victory of Western-style democratic pluralism and free-market economics. Communism has been dismantled in Eastern Europe and is clearly in its death throes in the USSR, but what will follow is unclear—evolution, reform, revolution, retrogression?

> *"The essence of freedom of choice . . . is that each society has to devise solutions to the problems it confronts."*

We must distinguish between two different stages of change in East Europe. One involves early attempts at democratic construction; the other is the dismantling of totalitarianism. Poland, Czechoslovakia and Hungary are engaged in the former. If they succeed, they will serve as models for reform in the rest of Eastern Europe. But if they fail, it is very likely that prospects for constructive change in Eastern Europe and the Soviet Union will diminish. The remarkable changes in Eastern Europe have evoked much interest, enthusiasm and hope in the West. Yet it is increasingly apparent that the process of change has run into mounting difficulty.

Some of the reasons for the difficulty are rooted in the past, in the legacy of the old system. Others are newer:

• First, the prompt unification of Germany is absorbing German attention and money. And the integration of East Germany into the Federal Republic is disrupting economic relations between the former East Germany and Poland, Czechoslovakia and Hungary.

> *"Liberation from 40 years of communism . . . is producing dangerous levels of suffering, deprivation, frustration and even despair."*

• Second, the economic crisis in the Soviet Union affects the economic well-being of the countries attempting to reform, all of which have over the past several decades built up extensive trade with the USSR. Trading patterns are now under severe stress; the situation will worsen with the introduction of world prices, particularly for energy supplies. This will place serious strains on some of the economies of Eastern Europe. . . .

• And [third], foreign debt—particularly in Poland and Hungary—complicates recovery and weakens already unstable domestic financial structures.

These pressures intensify social frustrations of the kind expressed so vividly in the Polish presidential elections. The surprising results of the first round of voting were an indication of widening social protest and dissatisfaction. Indeed, it is becoming a fact in Eastern Europe that liberation from 40 years of communism—a liberation fervently hoped for by the majority in every country—is producing dangerous levels of suffering, deprivation, frustration and even despair. This is not what the masses expected; this is not a fulfillment of their (sometimes naive) hopes.

The frustrations carry over to ethnic tensions, which are flourishing in the wake of relaxed political constraints. Social-economic tensions inflame relations between Hungary and Romania, the Slovaks and Czechs, and throughout all of Yugoslavia. These tensions, which seem to sharpen daily, call into question whether democratic construction over the next few years will succeed or be diverted in directions inimical to the institutionalization of democracy. . . .

Aiding Eastern Europe

Concerning Eastern Europe, we must recognize that security and stability will arise from peaceful social and political change. Thus, it is in our interest to help democratic construction in those parts of Eastern Europe where it is under way. To spur economic development, we have to take steps to relieve the debt burden some of these countries are carrying. This increasingly urgent issue will, I believe, be addressed by the industrialized nations this spring; the Club of Paris is

Chapter 3

beginning to reassess its position and investigate solutions to the debt crisis.

The West must also do more to promote regional cooperation in East Europe, fashioning economic assistance to help it flourish. The nationalist tensions born of the compartmentalization of Eastern Europe during the years of Stalinist domination are not in the interest of Europe. East Europeans must be urged to seek cooperative solutions to problems of the environment, transportation and economic development. European recovery after World War II was the result of deliberate efforts by Americans and Europeans to promote European cooperation. So it must be for East Europe's entry into the larger community of cooperative nations.

And finally, we must recognize that the problems we confront are unprecedented, both conceptually and historically. The fact is, we have entered into the great unknown. We simply have no relevant experience to draw on in mapping the transition from communist systems to pluralistic democracies based on free markets. We have no lessons that apply. We have some general notions about ways to rebuild capitalist economies; we applied these to Europe and Japan. We also used them to help Spain and Portugal make the transition from fascism. But we have no historical lessons that are fully conceptually developed for dealing with a transition from communism to democracy.

This means there is a need for very serious conceptual as well as institutional efforts in the West and between East and West. Our approach to the problem so far has been haphazard. We have created some institutions to help, such as the European Bank for Reconstruction and Development. Individual nations have mounted initiatives. But there is no collective program involving the US, West Europe, Japan and the countries of Eastern Europe to define the broad conceptual outlines of a common effort to ease the pains of transition.

The legacy of communism is a massive social, economic reality. It is a seamless web that, if it is to be torn away, requires an intense, prolonged intellectual and financial effort. We have failed to give it adequate attention. And I fear that our increasing preoccupation with such problems as the Persian Gulf crisis will divert our attention from the central historical drama of our time—whether we can together chart a path to a constructive future for the millions now engaged in an attempt to move beyond the tragic experience of the past decades and toward a better life.

> *"The legacy of communism is a massive social, economic reality."*

The West Can Help Strengthen Democracy in Eastern Europe

by Jan Zielonka

About the author: *Jan Zielonka is an associate professor of international relations at Leiden University in The Netherlands.*

Eastern Europe is no longer good news. After a short period of euphoria evoked by the spectacular collapse of communism, concern is growing that even Poland, Czechoslovakia, and Hungary are drifting away from the intended safe harbor called democracy. As two U.S. observers put it at the end of 1990:

> The winterscape of Eastern Europe is forbiddingly dark. The fervor for freedom that spilled into the streets last year and fueled the 20th century's most remarkable round of democratic change has run low. In its place, there is a dark awareness of freedom's costs, destitution and demagoguery.

The initial warning came from Hungary in the spring of 1990. There the first free national elections after 40 years produced nasty infighting between major political contenders, the Alliance of Free Democrats (AFD) and the Hungarian Democratic Forum (HDF). The latter party won the elections and formed a new coalition government, but the infighting continued with opposition parties issuing scathing reports on the government's alleged mismanagement of the country's affairs, and the governing parties questioning the "Hungarianness" of some leading members of the opposition. In the meantime, the frustration among ordinary Hungarians grew, as demonstrated by the taxi and truck drivers' strike in October 1990, which caused nationwide chaos and greatly undermined the credibility of the new Hungarian political elites.

Polish Strife

In Poland, a major split within the Solidarity movement provoked even greater polarization than in Hungary, with the subsequent presidential elections producing packages of empty slogans, waves of ethnic hatred, and the danger-

Reprinted from Jan Zielonka, "East Central Europe: Democracy in Retreat?" *The Washington Quarterly* 14 (3) by permission of The MIT Press, Cambridge, Massachusetts, and The Center for Strategic and International Studies, © 1991 by The Center for Strategic and International Studies and The Massachusetts Institute of Technology.

ous phenomenon of Stanislaw Tyminski, the electoral dark horse who skillfully employed a combination of aggressive populism, economic demagoguery, and a charlatan-like appeal. In the end, Lech Walesa won the elections, but only at the cost of ending cohesion within the former alliance of democratic forces.

For some months, Czechoslovakia—or more properly now the Czech and Slovak Federal Republic—looked like an oasis of peace and common sense in the region. But in the fall of 1990 there was a major conflict within the new governing party, the Civic Forum, followed by a heated controversy between the Czechs and Slovaks that prompted President Václav Havel to ask for emergency authority to rule by decree. The Civic Forum subsequently split into two factions.

> *"The Hungarian electorate . . . looks for pragmatic rather than ideological solutions to the country's problems."*

In the meantime, the economic, environmental, health, and housing statistics in all three countries have been giving increasingly alarming signals. In the Soviet Union a dangerous shift toward authoritarian rule has gradually been taking place, making all east central Europeans particularly uneasy. And the war in the Gulf deprived Eastern Europe of Western attention as well as resources, dashing hopes for increased Western help for the transition effort.

Adam Michnik, editor of the Polish newspaper *Gazeta Wyborcza* and a long-time Solidarity adviser, described the current trend in extremely pessimistic terms:

> This is the ideal time for demagogy. Demagogy that aggressively attacks the government may be successful, which must lead to destabilization. Destabilization elicits chaos. Chaos generates a new poverty and a new dictatorship. All postcommunist countries will face this. Everywhere phantoms from the past awaken: movements that combine populism, xenophobia, personality cult and a vision of the world ruled by a conspiracy of Freemasons and Jews.

Does Michnik's pessimism represent a prophecy or an emotional overstatement? Will east central Europe share the fate of many Latin American nations that shed their dictators but failed to establish durable democracy? After a period of rising freedom, is the pendulum swinging back toward authoritarian resurgence?

Strengthening Democracy

The transition of east central Europe toward democracy can be neither smooth nor painless. Despite all alarming developments, however, there are few reasons to believe that the region is so to speak condemned to despotism, and that the pendulum of history is now swinging away from democracy. Arguments predicting an authoritarian future are often simplistic, and they minimize the democratic achievements so far and their durable consequences. Moreover, the West can do much more than it has so far to strengthen the course of democracy in the region.

Despite all their problems, solid foundations have already been laid for a new democratic system in all three countries under consideration. They peacefully completed free presidential, parliamentary, and local government elections, providing victories for the political forces that pushed through the democratic transformation of 1989. They prepared the ground for both a multiparty system and a system of checks and balances between the executive, the judiciary, and the legislature. They abolished state censorship and allowed various types of nongovernmental associations to flourish. Likewise they implemented important reforms in the areas of human rights, education, and culture. They reformed the army and police and reoriented their foreign policies by developing close cooperation with leading democracies. Last but not least, in all three countries economic reforms have been initiated aimed at transforming the command into a market-oriented economy and, in particular, reinstating rights to private property.

Threats to Democracy

All these achievements can hardly be undone by sheer political manipulation or by a quiet coup by any self-appointed dictator. Of course, there are still numerous threats on the road toward democracy. After all, as Ralf Dahrendorf observed: "The only common feature to all transitions is the tension arising from being threatened every single day." But the existence of threats does not presuppose an ultimate failure of democratic aspirations. In particular, one should warn against all simplistic theories about the dictatorial temptation. Democracy in east central Europe is threatened by various, often conflicting factors, and it is very difficult to say which type of scenario is truly dangerous.

> *"The West can do much more than it has so far to strengthen the course of democracy in the region."*

On the one hand, democracy could be strangled by populist mobilization of the masses fueled by the marketization of the imbalanced economy and fostered by ethnic or egalitarian hatred. On the other hand, democracy may also be threatened by the indifference and apathy of citizens who abstain from political participation and from all sorts of economic expansion.

Another possibility is that excessive governmental powers, combined with restrictions imposed on political parties, could jeopardize democratic developments. Democracy can also be killed, however, by the unrestrained partisanship of many small and largely ideological parties that, unable to form a stable coalition, would paralyze any normal functioning of the state.

There could also be a threat from old-regime supporters who maintained positions in various segments of the economy, media, security apparatus, and local administration. This old *nomenklatura* could undermine democratic efforts through instigating waves of strikes, fabricating disinformation, and utilizing authoritarian tendencies in the Soviet Union. On the other hand, democracy would also be threatened by anti-Communist purges, political witch-hunts, and all sorts of retaliation that would undermine the principles of the rule of law.

Fueling ethnic infighting is dangerous, but so is ignoring ethnic concerns and aspirations. Democrats should prevent a resurgence of chaos and anarchy, but corporate behind-doors agreements by the elites might also prove disastrous.

In short, the process of building democracy is a balancing act in which one-sided scenarios and emotional overstatements have no place. Authoritarian temptation has not one but many faces, and all existing stereotypes should, therefore, be judged with extreme caution.

Exaggerated Skepticism

Those who believe that democracy is in trouble in east central Europe refer to three major factors to justify their skepticism: (l) the alarming economic situation of the region; (2) the frightening populist rhetoric of the successive political campaigns; and (3) the lack of democratic tradition in the region, or worse, an awakening of the "phantoms of the past," as Adam Michnik put it. All three factors can indeed bring democratic dreams to an end, but not necessarily. In fact, a careful examination of the arguments of the skeptics indicates that there are far fewer reasons to be worried than might appear at first glance.

Skeptics are right in claiming that economic health is indispensable for the success of democracy: economic problems have repeatedly been exploited by various types of dictators in the Third World. Skeptics tend to forget, however, that in east central Europe dictatorial solutions for economic problems have already been tried for many years and with very discouraging effects. Not surprisingly, therefore, most Poles, Hungarians, Czechs, or Slovaks seem to identify economic welfare with the existence of stable democracies in Western Europe, the United States, and Australia rather than with the authoritarian rule in South Korea, Singapore, and Taiwan.

More important in this context is a possible misreading of some economic data. Statistics are cited to prove the depth of the misery among the population that is expected to lead to an explosion: falling real wages, unemployment, a catastrophic drop in production, and a general collapse of living standards. To a considerable extent, however, economic decline in east central European countries reflects the impact of determined efforts to speed up the pace of economic transformation and is helping to cleanse them of the distortions and inefficiencies of centrally planned economies. For instance, a fall in production in deficit facto-

> *"Failure to come up with a substantial aid package for democracy building in east central Europe may have serious negative implications for Western countries."*

ries, however painful it may be in the short term, may yet lead to longer-term benefits.

Moreover, some statistical figures are highly misleading. For instance, skeptics are fond of repeating the rapidly rising figures of unemployment in the region, but they usually fail to mention that most comparisons refer to the Communist era, when unemployment officially did not exist. When governments in east central Europe first began to register the jobless and offer unemployment money, thousands of people who had never held jobs signed up, including housewives.

> *"The process of building democracy is a balancing act in which one-sided scenarios and emotional overstatements have no place."*

Focusing on the rhetoric and language of political campaigns in east central Europe can also be misleading. Aggressive populist slogans were indeed disturbing during the successive electoral campaigns last year, especially in Poland and Hungary. However, careful postelection surveys conducted by the Hungarian Social Science Information Centre revealed that the HDF's tremendous effort to mobilize its supporters through populist appeals during the first round of local elections did not succeed. The HDF's supporters were motivated less by ideological commitment than by economic grievances. Among the opposition parties, the great winner in the local elections was not the ideologically driven AFD, but the Alliance of Young Democrats (AYD), which tried to present itself as a party of expertise and pragmatism. Populist rhetoric is always frightening, but it seems to carry little appeal for the Hungarian electorate, which looks for pragmatic rather than ideological solutions to the country's problems.

Presidential elections in Poland have also been run according to the liberal versus populist dichotomy. But the opinion polls conducted by Krzysztof Jasiewicz from the Polish Academy of Sciences revealed that only tiny minorities within Polish society may be described as "populist," with most of the people expressing moderate, centrist views.

A Tradition of Democracy Does Exist

Referring to the lack of democratic tradition in east central Europe can also be misleading. One may ask, in particular, which period of time is under consideration? We can trace the existence of the Polish and Hungarian diets back into the seventeenth century and earlier. The Czech parliament created by the constitution of 1920 reflected in part the new state's Austrian and Hungarian heritage.

If one refers to the interwar period of this century, then there were indeed examples of dictatorial rule in Hungary and Poland, but not in Czechoslovakia. Moreover, the international setting of authoritarianism in Poland and Hungary at that time differed very much from what is today, making all simple analo-

gies rather dubious. As Timothy Garton Ash put it:
> If more or less authoritarian regimes flourished in East Central Europe between the wars this was partly because there were examples of authoritarianism elsewhere in Europe, which could also somehow be associated with the dream of modernity. Today, there are no such examples, and modernity is unambiguously associated with democracy.

Referring to the lack of democratic tradition in east central Europe since World War II does not make the argument any stronger. People in that region may be unfamiliar with the procedures of democracy, but they are all too familiar with the mechanisms of authoritarianism. Will they follow a populist demagogue offering them a well-known repertoire of repression that has already brought their countries economic misery, ecological destruction, and a decline of moral standards? One should also keep in mind that postwar dictatorship in east central Europe flourished within an entirely different ideological environment. Today we experience a remarkable intellectual domination of liberalism with its praise for democracy and criticism of all dictatorial aspirations. . . .

The Need for Western Help

Foreign aid has always been crucial in fostering democratic transitions in Europe. The Marshall Plan made the German transition possible, and Greece, Portugal, and Spain have benefited from early entry into the European Community.

> "East central Europe has always displayed a mixture of hope and despair, of democratic progress and autocratic temptation."

Today, there is a general consensus among Western policymakers that democratic restructuring in east central Europe deserves to be helped as well, and by the end of October 1990 the Group of 24 industrialized nations (G-24) had committed itself to a $21 billion package of aid and credits over the next two years to the *entire* area of Eastern Europe. The problem is that even this amount of help meets only a small portion of East European needs (estimated at $270 to $370 billion over the next five years), and there are no prospects of admitting Czechoslovakia, Poland, and Hungary to the European Community.

The amount of aid offered so far contrasts sharply with the relative scale of the Marshall Plan. In the four years after the war, the United States invested $5 billion a year in the European Recovery Program—2 percent of its gross national product (GNP). Today the 2 percent figure applied to the GNPs of 7—not even 24—of the strongest industrialized nations (G-7) would amount to no less than $200 billion in aid a year. Of course, there is no need to spend that much on east central Europe, especially if one considers the enormous problems of poor countries in the Third World. Besides, fostering democracy is not necessarily a function of financial aid. Nevertheless, the comparison with the Marshall Plan indicates the modest level of Western readiness to bear sacrifices aimed at transforming the region that, after all, has been a source of its cold war obsession for several long decades.

Several factors explain the limited scale of Western commitment to the building of democracy in east central Europe. First, time and again the West has been confronted with other major problems erupting in various parts of Europe and the world. East central Europe is important, but Mikhail Gorbachev's perestroika is considered even more important, and the latter seems to have run into real trouble. Germany, which would be in a position to help the most, is overburdened by the costs of its own reunification. . . . When the United States was funding the Marshall Plan, there was little doubt that Western Europe represented America's greatest concern. Today the same cannot be said about east central Europe.

Confusion in the West

Second, the collapse of communism in East Germany, Czechoslovakia, Hungary, and Poland produced enormous confusion among Western policymakers. They are divided in assessing the impact of the change that has taken place and are unable to reach consensus about the future security and economic and political architecture of the old continent. In addition, some important institutional decision-making frameworks are being eroded (the North Atlantic Treaty Organization most notably), other frameworks are undergoing a profound change (the European Community and the Conference on Security and Cooperation in Europe in particular). In this situation, short-term considerations and national factionalism prevail, undermining the efforts toward a long-term collective strategy that would be needed for the creation of any major aid program.

Third, the policy of helping democracy in east central Europe is not a vote winner in Western states. Communities of ethnic Poles, Hungarians, Slovaks, and Czechs in Western Europe or the United States are small and unable to exert any significant pressure. Major lobby and interest groups are not directly concerned about the fate of east central Europe. In fact, the recent controversy about the ways of investing the expected peace dividend showed that the interests of some of these groups are in conflict with the policy of democratic aid. The idea of including east central Europe in the European Community, in particular, does not make Western trade unions and various groups of producers happy. In the past, anticommunism (on the Right) and disarmament rhetoric (on the Left) could appeal to some voters. But today the idea of aiding democracy building cannot count on the same constituency.

> "The cold war division of Europe was unjust, but it was fairly stable."

Failure to come up with a substantial aid package for democracy building in east central Europe may have serious negative implications for Western countries as well. Most important are the security implications of any instability resulting from an eventual collapse of democracy. The cold war division of Europe was unjust, but it was fairly stable to the extent that the successive explosions in east central Europe could easily be contained within the region. But today the European security system is in a state of flux and full of uncertainty about who threatens whom, who will oppose whom, and who will gain or lose from the actions of states involved in potential local conflicts. As a consequence, the possible eruption of chaos and violence in Poland, Czechoslovakia, or Hungary can have unpredictable consequences for the entire European continent. Collapse of democracy in east central Europe will also dash hopes for possible Western economic expansion in this region. This expansion has only just started, but, as the recent London report by the Centre for Economic Policy Research showed, for example, Eastern Europe could provide profitable use for between $1,350 and $2,910 billion in capital imports over the next decade.

Finally, a collapse of democracy in east central Europe will further weaken the democratic course within the former Soviet Union, and the West has an obvious interest in preserving the policy of perestroika. Reformers in various parts of the Soviet federation would be unable to legitimize their campaign if democratic efforts in Poland, Czechoslovakia, and Hungary were to produce anarchy, poverty, and ethnic violence.

In summary, the demise of communism in east central Europe does not guarantee the instant advent of democracy. We cannot rule out a revival of autocratic patterns in the face of rising nationalism, populist demagoguery, or economic mismanagement. East central Europe has always displayed a mixture of hope and despair, of democratic progress and autocratic temptation. Yet the trend toward freedom and democracy seems now to be crystallized, and it can hardly be reversed without a major political battle affecting the entire European continent. As Pierre Hassner put it: "Democratic legitimacy is both indispensable and implacable. [This constitutes] the message of hope that communism has left to us from beyond the grave."

> *"The trend toward freedom and democracy seems now to be crystallized."*

Capitalism Would Benefit Eastern Europe

by A.W. Clausen

About the author: *A.W. Clausen is the chairman of the executive committee of BankAmerica Corporation.*

Those of us who both observe and participate in current affairs are fortunate to be experiencing one of the most fundamentally pivotal moments in the history of the modern world. I refer to the monumental economic and political changes sweeping Central and Eastern Europe. These changes are coming with a suddenness and carry a portent that border on awesome. How fast and how substantive is illustrated by the fact that in 1989, Erich Honecker of East Germany predicted that the Berlin Wall would last another hundred years. Today, his prediction and the Wall itself are rubble.

The Price of a Market Economy

Precipitous and far-reaching as are these changes, they are, most important, irreversible. Which fact raises the fundamental questions: What will be the price for achieving successful market economies in Central and Eastern Europe? And who will pay the price?

I am afraid the playwright, George Bernard Shaw, may have pinpointed our dilemma when he said, "There are two great tragedies in life: One is to lose your heart's desire. The other is to gain it."

The "heart's desire" of supporters of democratic capitalism has been the triumph of the principles of the market system throughout the world. Now it appears that we are gaining our heart's desire. Can we handle it? Certainly, one would think so. But the real tragedy is the possibility that the fires of freedom in Central and Eastern Europe will flare and then die . . . suffocated under the burden of inadequate infrastructure, unproductive investment, and inflated and unmet expectations of the people.

Well, that need not happen.

The promise of economic growth in Central and Eastern Europe can be ful-

From A.W. Clausen, "Paying the Price," a speech given to the Swiss-American Chamber of Commerce, Zurich, Switzerland, May 3, 1990. Reprinted with permission.

filled. I invite you to consider with me the preconditions of a new economic order in this region; the fuel, if you will, that will keep the flame lit. Such a conceptual tour will uncover both worrisome uncertainties and boundless opportunities. Further, it will lead us to acknowledge our responsibilities to keep capital flowing into budding democracies at appropriate levels and to keep the gates of free trade among nations wide open.

Improving the Standard of Living

Recent history has supplied us with some highly pertinent lessons about the linkages between economics and politics. The common thread of social change in the world today . . . be it in China, in Czechoslovakia, in Poland, or in Nicaragua . . . is the popular recognition in countries run by inefficient, repressive governments that democratic capitalism holds out the achievable possibility of better lives . . . of enjoying a higher standard of living.

> *"Democratic capitalism holds out the achievable possibility of better lives."*

Prior to the Tiananmen Square massacre, for instance, the economy of the People's Republic of China was allowed to edge toward reform with a rapidly growing entrepreneurial class. Heightened economic expectations led to calls for democracy. But political reforms were not very forthcoming, or at least not forthcoming fast enough, and the result has been human suffering and severe economic deterioration.

Conversely, in some Latin American countries, we see political establishments imperiled as inefficient economies unravel. As standards of living worsen, people lose hope. And hopelessness is our worst enemy in every respect. It is the altar on which democratic capitalism is sacrificed.

The obvious lesson in these calamities is that democracy and market systems must develop in tandem. Where we see breakdown in Central and Eastern European economies today, it is perhaps because political developments have so far outpaced economic reforms.

Less obvious are two more lessons in current economic and political movements: First, economic reforms have to proceed a step at a time, but they must be decisive and coordinated. It is not feasible to overhaul a national economy in one fell swoop. Each economic change must be put in place with careful analysis of its impact on the whole system, yet the process must not be allowed to falter. It must be completed in a reasonable period of time—perhaps within five years. Second, reform in either the political or economic sector cannot occur without attention to the operational basics . . . the social processes and governmental institutions that allow democratic capitalism to function.

Hungary provides the most immediate example of what happens when the first lesson is ignored. Since the mid-1960s, Hungary has been attempting to implement an indecisive program of slow relaxation of state controls along with a gradual privatization of publicly owned enterprise. This, along with unproductive government interference, created a mire of inefficiency, inflation, and debt for Hungary in the 1980s.

Today, many new governments are grappling with the second lesson . . . the nuts-and-bolts mechanism of democratic capitalism. The successful marriage of democracy and the marketplace in industrial nations has been accomplished over time, and through deeply rooted institutions that extend their influence well beyond elections. If you will allow me to use a familiar example, in the United States elections are only the beginning of a circuitous, often frustratingly slow process that leads finally to legislation and regulation.

Nominal Democracies

In younger democracies that lack economic success, particularly in Latin America, presidents may be elected, but their administrations then proceed to promulgate rules with no accountability to the public. The crucial balance between those who make the rules and those who must live by the rules is upended. Instead, in these nominal democracies, rules result from bargaining between the executive branch of government and favored special interest groups. These bargains lead to laws that restrict access to markets, distort prices, and ultimately exacerbate societal disharmony as the economy becomes uncompetitive in the global marketplace.

"There is great danger . . . that public expectations of better economic times will exceed these nations' short-term ability to produce them."

The underlying mechanisms of democratic capitalism . . . fair and open elections, broad public disclosure of governmental actions, popular debate, legislative representation, freedom of the press, and separation of powers, to name a few . . . cannot be overlooked. These mechanisms are not particularly exciting or glamorous, and so the framers of policy have perhaps tended to give them short shrift. By way of example, consider the mechanisms for establishing checks and balances in the creation of tariffs in the United States. Tariff modifications must be authorized by Congress, published by the Government, independently analyzed and discussed at hearings, and able to survive judicial challenges.

Another important detail in building a market economy is an efficient, easily accessible, and legally secure way to obtain title to property. This mundane process is a critical factor in much of the credit that is extended to small businesses in America.

Such details of a newly formed political system need to be put in place right away, while enthusiasm for freedom runs high. These political mechanisms will be needed to support necessary economic reforms which are going to seem harsh and almost insupportable in the short run. Harsh they may be, but insupportable they are not.

The list of necessary economic reforms for most new democracies and developing nations is short. The policies needed to promote sustainable economic growth must focus on at least five areas.

— One, market economies live or die by the level of private sector participation in the economy. Setting up the institutions and clearly articulating the rules of the market game for the private sector involve establishing regulatory, labor, exchange rate, tariff, and tax policies that increase the productivity of capital and the efficiency of resource use.

— The second area of reform would allow the marketplace to reallocate scarce resources toward a nation's comparative advantages. This means doing away with most quotas, tariffs, and trade controls that discourage competition.

— The third policy mandate centers on raising and maintaining a high level of domestic savings. There are two roads to this policy end, and both really need to be travelled: the public sector route requires controlling expenditures, creating money market instruments, and increasing revenues through tax and state company pricing policies; the private sector route involves financial system reforms . . . particularly the establishment of a competitive banking system . . . allowing real interest rates to take effect.

— The fourth policy area for economic reform involves controlling consumption and increasing productive investment. This is a tough call for the goods-starved consumers of East European countries, particularly those that have been tantalized by Western advertising.

— And economic-reform imperative number five is establishing monetary and exchange rate policies that keep inflation in check and encourage investment and exports.

The Fight for Capitalism

I firmly believe that if a market economy is to survive and grow—if the living standards of a nation are to be raised—these economic reforms are inescapable. They are in essence . . . the "price" that must be paid. I also know . . . from more years than I care to count in international development matters . . . that these reform policies are very difficult to achieve. And there is great danger, as we are learning in Latin America, that public expectations of better economic times will exceed these nations' short-term ability to produce them.

"Freedom, and the openness that goes with it, does not simply happen. Mankind has to fight for it . . . time and time again."

The beneficiaries of democratic capitalism, by and large, must pay its price. Freedom exacts a high toll. As the Deutsche Bank's late chairman, Alfred Herrhausen, noted, "Freedom, and the openness that goes with it, does not simply happen. Mankind has to fight for it . . . time and time again." And the fight that the new democracies of Europe must wage, along with all of us who support their ambitions, is an economic fight.

A Demoralized Public

The first and most perfidious attacks on these struggling economies will come from inflation and high unemployment as market-based pricing and competition are unleashed on inefficient enterprises. From the average citizen's point of view, things could well get worse before they get better. After the euphoria of the revolutions, fear and uncertainty are settling in among much of the population. People are becoming demoralized, asking "What now?"

Compounding the uncertainties, Central and Eastern Europeans, although they have been deprived of many economic benefits for more than forty years now, have also been insulated from the rigors of competition, particularly from the fact that a free market economy implies that there will not only be winners in the daily challenges of commerce, but there will also be losers as well. In seeking democratic capitalism, these people are casting their lives into economic uncertainty, where once they knew only economic security, albeit highly impoverished security.

Difficult as it will be to implement the five basic areas of economic policy reform, these are only the beginnings of the challenges facing new democracies.

I was privileged to spend several weeks on the Continent, . . . mostly in Eastern Europe. I found the diversity among individual countries and among ethnic groups within those political borders striking. And, as a Norwegian son of America's melting pot, I found the ethnic diversity tremendously appealing. There is strength in diversity; but also, clearly, there is tension that can foment discord. As totalitarian regimes fall, nationalist and religious ambitions, long held in check by repressive policies, are unleashed.

The new democracies, and their Western supporters, must navigate a precarious course between the right of self-determination and the danger of aggressive chauvinism. As economic difficulties intensify in the course of structural change, so too will nationalist tensions. However, there is one overriding new hope to sustain Central and Eastern Europe through these extraordinary trials: the hope of better times ahead. The trick is to get over the difficult hump of transition as quickly as possible.

> *"Too much capital, too fast, can cause far more harm than good."*

If the peoples of Central and Eastern Europe screw up their courage to see the economic reforms through, to trade a life of centrally planned but stable economic deprivation for the uncertainties of the marketplace and the possibility of prosperity that it holds out, then they will find that they do not stand alone, that they have the support of international institutions, both public and private. In the process, counterproductive nationalism will be diffused. A well functioning market economy is unassailably unbiased . . . impervious to ethnicity unless it represents a competitive advantage. As economic decline is reversed, prosperity will become a reality for broad swaths of the population, regardless of the ethnic origins.

> *"Democratic capitalism, like a fire that offers warmth and light, must be coaxed, tended, and guarded."*

Western business leaders can help Central and Eastern Europe capitalize on their momentum for positive change. Part of the task we set for ourselves involves actively discouraging chauvinism.

Western Investment

The five economic reform measures I have outlined may sound like a stiff price to be paid by those they will most directly affect. But if these reforms are decisively implemented over a realistic time frame—say five years or so—they will serve as beacons for productive investment. Already, capitalists are swarming to Central and Eastern Europe to establish beachheads before their competitors.

The list of promising direct investments in Central and Eastern Europe is long and well diversified among industrial nations eager for ringside seats on what could eventually be a burgeoning market.

— General Motors will be making automobiles in East Germany.

— In Hungary alone, more than 750 joint ventures were set up with Western companies in 1989. And, I am impressed to note that the Budapest American Chamber of Commerce already has 75 members.

— The CGE of France (French Compagnie Generale d'Electricite) has a joint venture with a telecommunications company in East Germany to make digital switches and build one million phone lines a year. Close to half of the lines could be exported to Eastern Europe.

— And the Czech industrialist Thomas Bata, head of the world's largest shoe company, now based in Toronto, is talking to the Czech government about moving back into plants he abandoned when the Communists nationalized his family business in 1945.

— Mitsubishi signed an agreement with powerhouse Daimler-Benz of West Germany, and the joint venture is expected to capitalize on the benefits of German unification.

This sampling, of course, doesn't account for the already considerable investments by West Germany in East Germany. By early March 1990, 140 West German companies had already signed up for more than 1,100 joint ventures in East Germany. All of these investments represent only a small sliver of the action that will grow as economic policy reforms take hold.

A major attraction, albeit a temporary one, is the widespread availability of well educated workers with good skills: currently relatively low-priced labor. In fact, Digital Equipment Corp. attributes its deal with two Hungarian computer companies in part to the high number of Hungarian computer experts, some of whom were so skilled that they were already producing clones of DEC equipment. For now, the cost of Central and Eastern European labor is a comparative advantage that both industrialized and developing countries will have trouble matching, but as European integration proceeds and comes to encompass these countries, wage rate differentials will diminish rapidly.

A Huge Consumer Market

Even more alluring than the labor force are the market opportunities. When we include the U.S.S.R., reforming communist nations represent more than 420 million new consumers to Western businesses. The demand potential has everyone from entrepreneurs to major international corporations eager for a piece of the action. Newly liberated consumers want and need everything Western consumers do, starting with infrastructure. Demand for consumer goods should be soaring soon, too. Just ask PepsiCo, which has 70 bottling franchises in these countries, or McDonald's with its highly publicized and popular Moscow franchise. And services represent untold potential. They are the fastest-rising component of investment everywhere in the world. As investments in infrastructure and manufacturing capacity multiply, service investments should increase even faster. . . .

"There is one overriding new hope to sustain Central and Eastern Europe through these extraordinary trials: the hope of better times ahead."

Also favoring strong trade and investment flows are Central and Eastern Europe's proximity to the European Community, and the still-strong vestiges of shared cultural traditions among Europeans of various ethnicities. At this early point, Bank of America estimates that trade and investment with these countries will increase annual economic growth in the European Community by as much as one-half of one percent per year.

This vast potential is alluring to be sure . . . but it is still a very long way from realization. Too much capital, too fast, can cause far more harm than good. As Latin America taught us, it is counterproductive to direct capital to countries in amounts exceeding their ability to put it to productive use.

Despite recent, minor jitters in the financial markets, the near-term capital requirements of Central and Eastern European countries (excepting an East Germany unified with West Germany) are minor in the global scheme. Our economists forecast the capital demands of these nations over most of this decade to increase gradually, not exceeding an annual level of $25 billion dollars.

The European Bank for Reconstruction and Development, or "BERD" by its

French acronym, should have little trouble amassing sufficient capital for investments that will bootstrap post-communistic countries into the sphere of competitive market economies. While capital adequacy is not likely to be a problem for BERD, productive applications are another matter. After considerable controversy, it was decided that BERD financing should be available to both the tiny private sectors in Central and Eastern European countries and to the public sectors of those countries for infrastructure developments necessary to private sector development. This is appropriate, since the private sector cannot become competitive in world markets without world-class telecommunications, transportation networks, and other elements of infrastructure. Also critical to development, and requiring further investment, will be massive efforts to "clean up" an environment that has become noxious under inefficient communistic enterprises.

Bright as the future looks, shadows hover on the perimeter of Europe. An ominous shadow hangs not only over Europe, but over market economies throughout the world today as the prospect of an insular Europe looms larger, especially as its internal markets expand. Certainly, it is to be expected that intra-European trade should intensify and grow with the disintegration of the Iron Curtain. But at the same time regional protectionist tendencies must be held at bay.

I am convinced that the current trend in global trade toward the development of regional trading spheres is no more than a way station on the road to true globalization of markets. Eurocentrism is understandable, perhaps even laudable, if it serves as the lever to bring several economies out of a dark and stagnant political repression. After all, even in our high-tech world, geographic proximity and cultural affinity still matter. But the benefits of shared trade should not . . . and in a peaceful world cannot . . . be limited to any one locality on earth.

We stand at an exhilarating and perilous point in history. If the bounty of capitalism is to foster a lasting and healthy peace on earth, we must accept and meet certain responsibilities. It would be presumptuous to applaud the demise of communism and congratulate ourselves as capitalists. Rather, we have now to make sure that capitalism can work for the good of all market economies. Such good can come only through continued progress on multilateral trade . . . *global* multilateral trade. . . .

> *"Democratic capitalism distributes the most good among the most people."*

Success Must Be Earned

To conclude, history teaches us that, while imperfect, democratic capitalism distributes the most good among the most people. However, comfortable as we may be with the mechanisms of democratic capitalism and their outcomes, they cannot be taken for granted. They are not yet in place in Central and Eastern

Europe

Europe, and we cannot stand idly by, waiting for efficient functioning markets to spring Phoenix-like from the ashes of communism. Democratic capitalism, like a fire that offers warmth and light, must be coaxed, tended, and guarded. Even in Western economies, the market system is by no means guaranteed. Always there is a temptation to allow governments to intervene in the market, to follow leveling policies that penalize initiative and private sector industriousness.

We business executives, through our investment decisions and competitive expertise, inevitably will be drawn into a larger public role as the nations of Central and Eastern Europe struggle toward a market system.

We must actively and visibly offer guidance and technical assistance in helping budding market economies to implement the necessary, difficult reforms ahead of them . . . to bring the private sector to the fore, to allow comparative advantage to allocate resources, to sustain savings and increase productive investment, and to back these reforms with a financial system attuned to the global marketplace. And we must vigorously defend free trade.

That is the price *we* must pay.

U.S. Aid Would Benefit Eastern Europe

by Lawrence S. Eagleburger

About the author: *Lawrence S. Eagleburger is the deputy secretary of state for the Bush administration.*

In March 1990, I gave a speech on Eastern Europe before the Eximbank's last annual conference at a time when truly revolutionary events in that region had just taken place. There was, understandably, a good deal of euphoria then over the sudden collapse of the Iron Curtain and the triumph of freedom throughout Central and Eastern Europe. At one end of the spectrum, there was the curious assertion that history had come to an end, and at the other, a kind of complacent assumption that the conversion of Eastern Europe to democracy and free enterprise meant that we would no longer have to concern ourselves with developments in that region as we had for the previous half century.

More level-headed observers were, of course, aware of just how unusual and difficult would be the tasks facing our East European friends and how important their success is to American interests. But the drama of their struggle was no longer of a nature to capture newspaper headlines, particularly as they settled down to the humdrum business of democratic electioneering and economic policymaking with which we are all too familiar. . . .

The Post-Cold War Era

If there is one point which I would like to reassert, however, it is the strategic place which Central and Eastern Europe will continue to occupy in American foreign policy for the foreseeable future. In fact, I believe we ought to look at the revolutions in Eastern Europe as having ushered in a new era in international relations, one which, for lack of a better name, we are calling the post-Cold War era. This era will have two defining features:

First, it will be dominated by the worldwide transition from command to free market economies, a movement whose outcome will help determine the fate of the worldwide trend toward democracy, which is also underway; and

Lawrence S. Eagleburger, "Central and Eastern Europe: A Year Later," *U.S. Department of State Dispatch*, May 20, 1991.

Second, as we saw with Iraq's invasion of Kuwait, it will be characterized by a much greater fluidity in international relationships, as the historically unusual discipline imposed by the Cold War disappears.

Both of these features of the new era are apparent today in Central and Eastern Europe, where the struggle to consolidate democracy and the market economy has coincided with the waning of the Cold War security order. Clearly, our goal must be to see the successful integration of the former communist countries into the wider pattern of European and Western cooperation, which has fostered both peace and prosperity among nations which habitually were at each other's throats for the better part of a millennium. No one can say what failure would bring. We do know, however, that nature abhors a vacuum and that when Central and Eastern Europe was weak and unstable in the first half of this century, the great powers twice wound up colliding. And so we must succeed.

> *"Our goal must be to see the successful integration of the former communist countries into the wider pattern of European and Western cooperation."*

Achievements and Obstacles

So much for the stakes involved. What I would like to do is to describe the progress and the problems our European friends have encountered on the path of reform, and what the US government is doing to help.

There have been important successes, most notably in the political and security fields. The commitment to democracy is unequivocal in Poland, Hungary, Czechoslovakia, and even Bulgaria. It is being institutionalized in parliaments, in a free press, and in legal safeguards which protect individual liberties and human rights. . . .

You do not have to be a rocket scientist, however, to understand that the region is in tough shape economically and that its fledgling democratic institutions will face severe testing for some time to come. The year has seen deepening recession, a legacy of the outmoded and decaying economic infrastructure left by the communists, and, to a degree, a result of the very reform measures undertaken to restore economic health. There has been a series of unanticipated shocks: the cutoff of Iraqi and Kuwaiti oil; the collapse of trade with the USSR; the Soviet decision to force payment for goods in hard currency; and the loss of the East German market.

Fortunately, these events have not shaken the fundamental commitment of the governments in the region to navigate the transition to market economies, nor have they appreciably blunted their willingness to implement the painful reforms needed to reach the ultimate destination.

Poland continues to set the pace of reform. Its bold stabilization program—aided significantly by the United States and its Western partners—succeeded in

Chapter 3

driving down inflation, lowering interest rates, and making the zloty convertible. It is true that a serious drop in industrial output and a major increase in unemployment have resulted. But unemployment still does not reach West European levels, and for the first time in memory, store shelves are full, and queues have disappeared.

Poland's neighbors have demonstrated, to varying degrees, greater caution in implementing reforms. However, both Hungary and Czechoslovakia now have plans in place for macroeconomic stabilization and, over a several-year period, for removing the distortions of state intervention in the economy. And Bulgaria, after electing a multi-party parliament, has moved boldly down the path of economic reform.

To be frank we have encountered two sets of obstacles to fundamental reform in Central and Eastern Europe. First has been the slowness in moving from macro- to microeconomic reform; that is, from macroeconomic stabilization to the actual transformation of command economies into market economies. The second has been the emergence of potentially dangerous political phenomena, which coexist with the nascent democratic institutions in the area.

The fact of the matter is that history affords few, if any, examples of attempts to privatize an economy which was entirely run by the state. There are no precedents, and, thus, no guidelines. You will recall that we rejected proposals for a massive bailout of the East European economies on the lines of the 1947 Marshall Plan. It tended to be forgotten by some that a market economy was already in place in Western Europe after World War II, ready to absorb the infusion of capital needed to get the region back on its feet. That simply is not the case in Central and Eastern Europe today.

The Problems of Creating a Free Market

Instead, the first order of business in the region, following macroeconomic stabilization, was, and is, the creation, piece by piece, of a free market infrastructure. This has been a contentious and confusing process. Fundamental issues have to be decided. To whom does formerly state property belong? To whom should state enterprises be sold? How should those whose property was confiscated by the communists be compensated? Which industries should be salvaged and which sacrificed to the realities of the international marketplace?

"History affords few, if any, examples of attempts to privatize an economy which was entirely run by the state."

To the list of fundamental issues to be decided we must add a list of fundamental skills to be acquired—worker skills, management skills, information skills, and financial skills to name but a few.

And finally, the infrastructure of a modern and internationally competitive economy needs to be created—in banking, communications, transportation, housing, and other sectors.

Thus, it is not surprising that in Poland, for example, where macroeconomic stabilization has been most far-reaching, the desired supply-side response has been slow to follow. Privatization has lagged, and state enterprises have remained insulated from the market and competitive forces. Moreover, we cannot discount important psychological obstacles to microeconomic reform resulting from the communist era: the attachment to job security, and quite simply, fear of change and fear of the unknown.

New U.S. Strategy for Economic Reform

Let me assure you that the Administration has drawn a lesson from previous experiences and has shifted its assistance priorities accordingly. This is not to say we are abandoning macroeconomic support—witness the US-led Paris Club initiative which produced agreement on exceptional debt reduction for Poland. But we feel that the greatest needs in Central and Eastern Europe today are microeconomic in nature, particularly the need to stimulate private sector activity. We believe that the number one way to meet those needs is to promote enhanced trade and greater access to Western markets as well as larger flows of Western investment. Accordingly, our new approach will have the following three components.

> *"One thing we in the West should not do is sit in judgment on our East European friends or attempt to dictate choices which are theirs to make."*

First, emphasis on technical assistance to help train bankers and managers; to help draft tax, labor, and commercial laws which will make competition a reality; to help build financial intermediaries to assist in the privatization process; and to help with enterprise restructuring and with removing the bureaucracy's stranglehold over economic activities: Together with the Enterprise Funds for Poland, Hungary, and Czechoslovakia, technical assistance will receive the greatest commitment of US resources in the coming years.

Second, expansion of trade with the West. At a time when East European trade with the USSR and East Germany has collapsed, Western markets are more important than Western aid. Unless they can increase their exports, the new democracies of Central and Eastern Europe will lose more from the trade hemorrhage than they could possibly gain from any transfusion of Western aid. Therefore, the United States has launched a trade enhancement initiative, which includes:

• A significant expansion of duty-free benefits covering Central and East European exports under the Generalized System of Preferences;

• Technical assistance on US trade laws and regulations to help overcome informational barriers trade; and

• Development of a program through which the Commerce Department will match companies, especially small- and medium-sized firms, in complementary economic regions of the United States with those in Central and Eastern Europe.

We should not be taking these steps alone. The European Community, which represents the greatest market for Central and Eastern Europe, should also provide—and, indeed, has an obligation to provide—greater market access, and we are encouraging them to do so in the context of their association agreements. We emphasize, however, that these agreements should conform to GATT [General Agreement on Tariffs and Trade] rules by covering all areas of trade, including agriculture.

> *"The major obstacles to direct investment are to be found within the countries of the region themselves."*

Our third and final priority is to expand the region's productive capacity, and thus boost trade, by promoting increased levels of direct Western investment in the Central and East European economies. Frankly, this form of support has been disappointing to date. For example, [Polish] President [Lech] Walesa noted during his visit here that US private investment in Poland has totaled only $30 million thus far.

Promoting U.S. Involvement

The centerpiece of this effort is our recently launched American Business and Private Sector Development Initiative, which is designed to promote the growth of US investment in the region, increase participation by US firms in infrastructure development, and increase the involvement of small- and medium-sized US companies in bilateral trade. This is a $45 million 2-year project carried out by the US Agency for International Development (USAID), the Department of Commerce, the Overseas Private Investment Corporation (OPIC), and the US Trade and Development Program, in partnership with the private sector. Primary emphasis will be on five key sectors identified by the Central and East European countries, and which represent unique opportunities for American business—agriculture and agribusiness, energy, environment, telecommunications, and housing. The initiative includes, *inter alia*, the following elements.

• An American Business Center in Warsaw, which will make available office space and technical business services on a user-fee basis in cooperation with the private sector.

• Consortia of American Businesses in Eastern Europe, which will support small- and medium-sized US companies wishing to enter the East European market. Grants will assist US trade and business associations in selected sectors in establishing a presence in the region.

• A USAID Capital Development Initiative, which is designed to provide assistance to East European governments and private sector firms in designing infrastructure projects in ways that will encourage the involvement of US companies.

• We are seeking legislative authority to expand OPIC's pilot equity investment program to include Eastern Europe so that OPIC can make direct investments in promising joint ventures.

We fully recognize that the major obstacles to direct investment are to be found within the countries of the region themselves. They need to take more steps to lower their barriers to trade with each other, and to effect changes in laws, policies, and institutions to enable private enterprise truly to flourish. In particular, specific barriers to foreign investment must be removed, such as limitations on foreign ownership of real estate, ceilings on foreign equity holdings, and retroactive liability for past environmental damage. I might add that these impediments also hamper the development of domestic enterprise, since foreign capital can bring technology and management expertise and help restructure industry in a way that does not burden these economies with debt.

The Future of Democracy in the Region

I mentioned earlier that we have encountered a second set of challenges in the form of some disquieting political trends, particularly the emergence of ethnic strife within several Central and East European countries, and, to a lesser extent, nationalist tensions between and among them. Whereas after World War II, West European historical enmities were dealt with openly and attenuated by factors such as economic prosperity, common democratic institutions, and the construction of a Pan-European identity, in the East, such sentiments were merely repressed under communist rule. It ought, therefore, to have been no surprise when they suddenly reemerged following the revolutions of 1989.

Ethnic animosities are not the only negative political legacy of the totalitarian era. Communism accustomed its subjects to the politics of absolutism—that is, a belief in magic formulas and all-encompassing blueprints, and the tendency to view opponents as enemies and to see all issues in black and white terms.

Confronting this legacy forces us, I believe, to the sober conclusion that moving from macro- to micro-level reform may be just as challenging in the political sphere as we have discovered it to be in the economic sphere. The institutional structure of democracy is falling into place, but the habits and the everyday practice of democracy—the virtues of patience, tolerance, and respect for diversity—will have to be acquired over time.

"Western markets are more important than Western aid."

Unfortunately, these virtues are going to be needed not over the long run but in the present. The fact is that there is bound to be a collision between the nearly universal expectation that democracy will mean rapid attainment of Western standards of living and the harsh reality of adjustment to reform and the transition to a market economy. There is, thus, the danger that disillusionment could spawn impatience with the deliberate pace and essential give and take of democracy and lead to different kinds of instability.

What the West Can Do

One thing we in the West should not do is sit in judgment on our East European friends or attempt to dictate choices which are theirs to make. We should, after all, remember from our own historical experiences that democracy is perhaps the most challenging form of government under the best of circumstances.

However, there are certain things which the West, particularly we in the United States, can do to help ensure that the difficult economic transition underway does not destabilize either the fragile new democratic institutions or the peace of the region as a whole.

First, we must continue to provide advice and technical assistance in the field of democratic institution-build-

> *"We must concentrate on strengthening democracy at the grass-roots level."*

ing. Our friends in the region tell us that such help, to date, has been absolutely critical to the successes achieved thus far—the elections held, constitutions written, and the like. Henceforth, we must concentrate on strengthening democracy at the grass-roots level, namely, the institutions of local government plus those bodies which safeguard and mediate a healthy pluralist society—such as unions, press organs, and the judiciary. Our aim must be to help create a system from top to bottom in which debate and opposition are channeled constructively and democratically, a system which can absorb the inevitable shocks to come.

Second, we must make sure that the overall system of European security, transformed by the end of the Cold War, can itself withstand any potential shocks emanating from Central and Eastern Europe. On a concrete level, this effort will eventually mean the creation of a new European political, economic, and security architecture. But we must also endeavor to convince the Central and East Europeans that staying the course on democracy is the *sine qua non* of joining the family of Western nations. Merely hectoring them about their investment regimes or ethnic troubles is not the answer. They must understand for themselves that there is no alternative to Western political and economic practices if their goal is to enjoy Western prosperity and consolidated freedoms. And they must also learn to reconcile the perfectly legitimate right to ethnic self-determination and self-expression with the imperatives of economic and political development in a Europe which is fast moving not toward fragmentation but integration.

Finally, we must influence the psychological dynamic at work today in Central and Eastern Europe to ensure that euphoria is replaced with confidence, and not with despair. We can do this by convincing our friends that there is light at the end of the tunnel, and that we will walk with them through that tunnel until they achieve full-fledged membership in the Western community of nations.

This cannot, however, be the work of Western governments alone. The ultimate test of our commitment to democracy and free enterprise in Central and Eastern Europe may well be the willingness of our private sector to involve itself in this great experiment and, thereby, help the region to acquire the human skills and the capital which are urgently required.

Investment, Not Philanthropy

I fully realize that, for the American business community, this is not a matter of philanthropy. I have not pulled any punches in describing the obstacles to change and reform that we have encountered over the past year. But I am willing without any hesitation to renew my appeal to you to invest in the region. I am convinced that the payoff, though not immediate, will be great.

Yes, the status of private property is still unclear, but it will be clarified. Yes, the investment regimes do not yet meet all expectations, but soon they will. Yes, the pace of privatization has been slow, but there is simply no alternative to its going forward.

The fact of the matter is that Central and Eastern Europe are going to make it, and this consideration ought to be central to investment decisions. And by making it, I also mean that the region will surely join itself over time to the historic process of economic integration underway in Western Europe—a process from which American business cannot afford to be excluded. Central and Eastern Europe can be a profitable gateway to the Europe of tomorrow—but only if American business is willing to assume the risks, and to face the obstacles, which are present in the region today.

Western Policies Will Fail in Eastern Europe

by Thomas E. Weisskopf

About the author: *Thomas E. Weisskopf is an economics professor at the University of Michigan in Ann Arbor. He is co-author of* The Capitalist System.

As the waves of popular revolution swept across Eastern Europe in 1989, great hopes were aroused for the future of the East European nations. The prevailing view in the West was that, once liberated from the oppressive communist yoke, these countries could and would soon develop into economically dynamic democratic market-capitalist societies. Some doubts remained about Romania and Bulgaria; but surely East Germany, Poland, Czechoslovakia, and Hungary could be counted upon to join the international capitalist order.

On the left there was a quite different hope. It appeared to many of us that workers, students, and intellectuals, having played a prominent role in most of the revolutionary movements of the 1980s, might be able to combine a new democratic politics with the ideological legacy of socialist commitment to egalitarianism and economic security in constructing a democratic socialist order that would avoid the worst features of both bureaucratic collectivism and market capitalism.

Easterners Embrace Capitalism

One year later, the ground for optimism on the left has been severely undermined. The great majority of people in Eastern Europe want nothing more than to become part of the "common European home" as soon as possible. Tired of social and economic experiments, increasingly aware of the huge gap in standards of living between Western and Eastern Europe, they are eager to embrace the "tried and true" institutions of Western market capitalism. It is not only the old ruling communist parties and their hierarchical, bureaucratic economies that have been discredited: even much more benign forms of public enterprise are viewed with suspicion. Socialist and social democratic parties have fared poorly in elections in East Germany, Poland, Hungary, and Czechoslovakia.

Thomas E. Weisskopf, "Economic and Political Prospects in Eastern Europe," *Dissent*, Winter 1991. Reprinted with permission.

Poland, Czechoslovakia, and Hungary have elected governments committed to dismantling the old state-dominated structures and to promoting the spread of markets and the growth of private enterprise along explicitly capitalist lines. In these countries the left is divided and weak. There are numerous parties, as well as groups within Solidarity in Poland and Civic Forum in Czechoslovakia, that reflect currents all the way from the remnants of the old communist parties to reincarnated social democratic parties. The progressive left has only the most tenuous relations with the majority of workers, who are represented mainly by unions with close links to the previous regimes. These unions are now becoming more independent, but their demands are largely defensive in nature, seeking to protect workers from the effects of economic transformation without having much to say about an alternative path of reform.

> *"Rapid marketization and privatization ... will prove especially hard to turn into a success."*

Does all this mean that the countries of East Central Europe are launched irreversibly toward Western-style market capitalism? Does the success of the peaceful revolutions against communist rule and the holding of free elections mean that Poland, Czechoslovakia, and Hungary have indeed been transformed into durable Western-style political democracies?

Obstacles to Economic Success

One cannot study the economic situation of the East European countries without being overwhelmed by the difficulties they face in overcoming economic stagnation. It is partly a matter of becoming aware of how deep the crisis is. Quantitative indicators of economic stagnation are only a small part of the story, and have misled analysts into underestimating the extent of the crisis. Qualitative problems seem even more serious—the poor quality of many of the goods produced, the lack of maintenance and service facilities, generally poor working conditions, overstaffing (where there is not outright unemployment), neglect of public services, environmental deterioration, and so on.

In Poland and Hungary, the need to service huge international debts will continue indefinitely to reduce the resources available for economic development and to squeeze the average citizen's standard of living. Current international trends offer little hope for significant debt relief. The United States is itself a major debtor, Germany will devote most of its resources to the East German economy, Japan has no special interest in Eastern Europe, and the rest of the major capitalist countries do not have enough to spare. Moreover, the economic collapse of the Soviet Union—and the related decision by the Soviets to insist on a hard-currency basis for trade with Comecon countries—will reduce the quantities and (real) prices of Eastern European industrial-good exports to the USSR, which are important especially for Czechoslovakia and Hungary. And if this weren't enough, the Middle East crisis will make energy more costly for these oil-importing nations.

Such dismal conditions would make any kind of economic revitalization difficult. But there are additional reasons why the economic strategy underway now in East Central Europe—rapid marketization and privatization—will prove especially hard to turn into a success:

• Foreign investors—upon whom much reliance is placed—are very wary of making major commitments in Eastern Europe. The institutional infrastructure for a successful capitalist market economy is woefully weak: banking, accounting, and legal services remain very poorly developed, and there are few people with the kind of experience to make such services work. Record keeping and communications technologies are inadequate for a modern economy of the Western capitalist type, as the computer age is barely dawning in Eastern Europe. With many other countries that have much more hospitable business climates bidding for multinational corporate investment, it is hardly surprising that Western firms have yet to make substantial investments in Poland, Czechoslovakia, and Hungary.

> *"Proponents of a rapid transformation to capitalism assume that people will agree to accept economic sacrifice in exchange for political freedoms."*

An Open Door to Corruption

• There are very few potentially viable enterprises in any given line of production, with the result that the transition to a capitalist market economy will provide great scope for monopoly power and corruption. Relatively free trade could provide some competition for potential monopolists in the form of imports, but balance-of-payments problems—and the need to nurture domestic industries—are likely to limit such competition. Since there are also very few potential domestic purchasers of privatized state assets, a limited number of large holding companies—along with a few foreign capitalists—are likely to play the major role in taking over those public enterprises that are salvageable. A privatization process that leads to monopolistic or foreign control of many industries seems likely not only to limit efficiency gains but to generate serious social tensions.

• Whether or not it is successful in its own terms, the processes of marketization and privatization will lead to tremendous inequalities—between budding capitalists who strike it rich and workers whose wages and job security will decline, and between people with scarce skills in high demand and people whose skills become redundant as their former inefficient enterprises go broke. The new governments will simply not be able to mobilize enough financial and organizational resources to provide an adequate "social safety net" for all the workers who are expected to become unemployed. In Poland the government expects to be able to support at most 800,000 unemployed at the current modest rate of unemployment compensation; this level of unemployment had reportedly already been surpassed by the fall of 1990.

• The need to balance government budgets to maintain monetary stability and currency convertibility, and to raise domestic resources for investment without harming profit incentives, will require a squeeze on most people's private incomes and on public services—thus continuing the downward trend in living standards that began ten years ago. How long people will accept such a squeeze—in an environment in which some of their compatriots are becoming conspicuously wealthy—is a question.

Given such obstacles, the optimism exhibited by many market-oriented economists about the transformation process in East Central Europe seems naïve. Czechoslovakia is probably better placed than Hungary or Poland to achieve a successful transition to capitalism because it begins with the strongest of the three economies, it does not have a major debt problem, and its government is proceeding more cautiously—but even in this best case there is much doubt as to whether the economic transformation can survive the social and political tensions to which it is bound to give rise.

Threats to Political Democracy

Will the Oder-Neisse become the Rio Grande of Europe? This question was raised at a conference of left-leaning social scientists in Warsaw in the summer of 1990, and to many observers it does seem that the answer is yes.

Insofar as marketization and privatization proceed, with a gradual integration of the East Central European economies into the world capitalist system, these countries will enter as very weak players. They will be dependent on international financial institutions for management of chronic trade and debt problems, they will be dependent on foreign governments for economic and technical assistance, and they will be dependent on foreign capitalists for investment resources and managerial know-how. These countries will also be characterized by growing inequalities of income and wealth—though they are not likely to have as highly skewed a distribution of land ownership as most Latin American nations. And there will be high levels of unemployment and an extensive urban "lumpenproletariat" (which even Spain, the most recent European capitalist success story, has been unable to avoid).

> *"As the economic transformation begins to take its toll on a growing number of losers, there is bound to be mounting public disaffection."*

But there are real grounds for doubt that the processes of marketization and privatization will be able to proceed to the point where the East Central European economies become absorbed into the world capitalist order. Skepticism is warranted not only because of the economic obstacles but also because of the social and political tensions that are bound to accompany the economic transformation. Such tensions have already become visible in Poland, within the year that elapsed since the introduction of capitalist "shock therapy" treatment in January 1990, in the form of strikes by railway workers, vociferous protests by farmers, and other disturbances.

Big Losses, Big Gains

In Eastern Europe almost everything is up for grabs. There are tremendous opportunities for personal gain by those who, through political power, connections, or specialized knowledge of the institutional transformations, are able to position themselves well in the new economic arena. And there are corresponding opportunities for loss on the part of the majority of the people. Proponents of a rapid transformation to capitalism assume that people will agree to accept economic sacrifice in exchange for political freedoms and the prospect of greater prosperity sometime in the future. But there is every reason to doubt that they will continue to do so as and when the economic burden is perceived to be highly unequally distributed.

> *"The only safe bet is that political conditions are bound to change in dramatic ways in the coming years."*

The drive to transform the East Central European economies along market capitalist lines has been spearheaded largely by intellectuals, professionals, and politicians who are liberal (in both the political and economic senses) and secular and Western oriented in attitudes. In Poland and Czechoslovakia these people are currently in power; in Hungary their main party (the Federation of Free Democrats) is not in power, but they still represent the kind of people who will be most closely involved in the processes of marketization and privatization. These people are really very much of a minority in all three countries; they have managed nonetheless to have a very strong influence on the direction of the postcommunist societies because they were prominently associated with the popular revolutions against the old regimes and because the average person in the street has been quite prepared to believe that the best—if not the only—alternative is the capitalist economics that appears to have worked so much better in the West.

In all three countries—but especially in Poland and Hungary—there is also another group of prominent people, including some intellectuals as well as politicians and religious leaders, who are much less liberal and Western oriented. These people are much more nationalist and Catholic than the pro-Western professionals; and they are also somewhat less enamored of the market and of integration into an international capitalist system. They are to be found in the Christian Democratic and Peasant/Farmers' parties, as well as in the Hungarian

Democratic Forum; some are also in the right wings of Solidarity and Civic Forum. Their appeal is largely to rural areas and small towns, to peasants and the petty bourgeoisie, and of course to the more devout Catholics; they cultivate suspicion of "cosmopolitan" urban elites (often a euphemism for people of Jewish origin, who—although few in number after the Holocaust—are disproportionately represented among liberal and leftist intellectuals in each country).

As the economic transformation begins to take its toll on a growing number of losers, there is bound to be mounting public disaffection with the pro-Western liberal leadership that ushered in the changes. This will put great pressure on the liberal reformers (such as the Mazowiecki government has already been feeling in Poland), and it will generate a political climate in which opposition politicians can gain a great deal of support. Lech Walesa, who has become increasingly vocal in his criticism of both the Mazowiecki government and leading Polish liberal intellectuals (such as Adam Michnik), is discovering how well a populist/nationalist rhetoric plays in Eastern Europe. Other, less savory, characters have already emerged and will no doubt gain strength in Poland and Hungary, perhaps even in Czechoslovakia. Calls for a "strong man" to take over and protect the "little people" from economic adversity associated with the machinations of the Western-oriented leadership and their foreign capitalist allies may not be too far away.

It is hard to predict whether such trends would be more likely to lead to the emergence of a Peronist figure, with strong roots in an aggrieved and defiant labor movement, or a right-wing form of authoritarianism rooted in the peasantry and petty bourgeoisie. Yet another possibility is suggested by an alarm recently sounded by Soviet liberal reformer and Moscow mayor Gavriil Popov, who warns of the "dangers of democracy." Popov foresees increasing contradictions between the new democratic environment in the USSR and the economic policies of marketization and privatization that he favors. In particular, he is worried about the growth of a new populism that would feed on the growing economic inequality inevitably accompanying such a transformation, and he therefore advocates "new and different political mechanisms" as an alternative to the

> *"Authoritarianism of one kind or another—whether on the part of opponents or proponents of capitalist transformation—may be in the cards."*

"purely democratic model." In sum, authoritarianism of one kind or another—whether on the part of opponents or proponents of capitalist transformation—may be in the cards.

The Left Must Gain Power

Is there no more optimistic scenario for the nations of East Central Europe? It is clear that the left will not become a force to be reckoned with in any of these countries unless it can somehow unite its disparate elements, develop a stronger base among workers, and project a plausible vision of the society of the future. A theoretical possibility, at least, is the development of a new coalition of left-wing forces—grouping everyone from reform communists through socialists, social democrats, and left liberals—with a strong base of support among workers and their trade unions. Such a coalition could formulate and oversee a more gradual transition to a market economy, preserving multiple forms of enterprise ownership and control, limiting the pace and degree of integration into the world capitalist economy, and spreading the gains and the losses from economic change more evenly throughout the population.

At the moment this prospect appears to be exceedingly dim. The most critical factor is the direction that the great majority of workers will take. This remains the biggest unknown, for workers in East Central Europe have yet to articulate their interests in a politically coherent way. When they do, we may be in for a surprise. The only safe bet is that political conditions are bound to change in dramatic ways in the coming years.

U.S. Aid Could Harm Eastern Europe

by Nicholas Eberstadt

About the author: *Nicholas Eberstadt is a researcher at Harvard University's Center for Population and Development Studies at the American Enterprise Institute in Washington, D.C. He is the author of several books, including* The Poverty of Communism, Foreign Aid and American Purpose, *and* The Tyranny of Numbers.

As the West's long battle with Soviet Communism draws to a close, practical men in America and elsewhere ponder a novel question: how to bring forth a lawful, prosperous, and secure order from the rubble of the former Soviet Union. For many statesmen, diplomats, and captains of industry, the answer is already clear: we should rely upon foreign-aid policies, skillfully designed and massively financed. Through existing agencies or new ones, it is argued, such transfers will speed the transition from Communism to market democracies for hundreds of millions of people.

Yet the ongoing dramas in Moscow, and the attention these have commanded, have obscured the fact that America and other Western states are *already* experimenting with a series of aid programs for ex-Communist countries. The recipients in question are the societies of Central and Eastern Europe. The population of those five former members of the Warsaw pact—Hungary, Czechoslovakia, Poland, Romania, Bulgaria—totals nearly 100 million (and will be larger still if Yugoslavia and Albania are added to their ranks), and while the sums involved are not historic, neither are they trifling. The United States, for example, has already authorized over $1.5 billion in grants for Eastern Europe and has guaranteed several times that amount in subsidized loans through the International Monetary Fund (IMF) and the new European Bank.

Copying Previous Programs

There is every indication that the new U.S. programs for the ex-Communist countries will build upon the tradition and experience of American aid pro-

---

From Nicholas Eberstadt, "How Not to Aid Eastern Europe." Reprinted from *Commentary*, November 1991, by permission; all rights reserved.

Chapter 3

grams in other parts of the world. Thus, in Poland the U.S. Agency for International Development (USAID) is helping with "two model cooperative [housing] developments of 100 units total"; Bulgaria is receiving 300,000 metric tons of surplus feed grain for its livestock; and previously pro-natalist Romania is now the beneficiary of a "priority program" in the field of family planning. In light of these continuities, it may be appropriate not only to consider the prospects for aid for these post-Communist societies, but to reflect more generally on the performance of American "development assistance" to date.

> *"One strikingly unhealthy characteristic of the East European states is the inability to manage external debt."*

We can begin with a simple thought experiment. What would we have expected the economies, societies, and polities of Eastern Europe to look like in 1990 if those five countries had been recipients of American development assistance over the previous two decades?

Like all such experiments, this one is necessarily speculative. But we can pursue it by comparing various characteristics of the countries of Eastern Europe immediately after their revolutions of 1989 with those of the dozens of African, Asian, and Latin American countries that did in fact enjoy steady flows of bilateral American development assistance during the 1970's and 1980's.

One strikingly unhealthy characteristic of the East European states is the inability to manage external debt. Over the course of the 1980's, the governments of Poland and Romania (and also Yugoslavia) not only failed to repay their international creditors on the schedules to which they were contractually committed, but sought and obtained debt-relief agreements from them. At the time of its liquidation, the international finances of Hungary's Communist government had also become precarious. After the collapse of Communism in the German Democratic Republic, previously secret documents showed that the state's external hard-currency debts were nearly twice as great as officially acknowledged. And a few months after the demise of the Zhivkov regime, Bulgaria suspended its repayments of both interest and principal to its hard-currency creditors.

During the 1980's, such debt crises were also characteristic of the states that had been long-term recipients of bilateral American development assistance. During that decade alone, by the World Bank's count, 45 of the 74 countries in Africa, Asia, Latin America, and the Caribbean which were receiving direct economic assistance from USAID sought and obtained debt-relief agreements.

The Problem of Nonconvertible Currencies

Compounding the financial difficulties of Eastern Europe's Communist states was their determination to maintain nonconvertible currencies which would restrict the role of international trade in the local economy. This meant that before

1989, for all practical purposes, the currencies of Eastern Europe were nearly worthless in the open market.

Such nonconvertibility, or limited convertibility, is also characteristic of the currencies minted by the states that have been receiving economic assistance from the United States over the past two decades. According to the IMF, only ten of the more than 70 countries today receiving bilateral economic assistance from the United States are deemed to have "independently floating" (that is, spontaneously convertible) currencies—and there are reasons to believe this may be a generous estimate.

Scars from Socialism

In the late 1980's, the countries of Central and Eastern Europe bore the disfiguring scars of decades of socialist planning. The structures of their economies had been severely deformed. Their central governments, which had arrogated utterly dominant roles for themselves within the local economy, had amassed vast networks of state-owned enterprises. Without regard to consumers, these governments had directed forced-pace transitions out of agriculture and into state-owned heavy industries. They depressed private consumption and diverted funds into state investment, not on the basis of economic calculation but as a matter of political principle.

Parallel distortions are just as evident in the economies of long-term recipients of American aid. For example, the ratio of central-government spending to national output in Egypt—the principal U.S. aid recipient in Africa—was about the same as in Poland or Romania during the 1980's. The Comoro Islands, Jamaica, Jordan, Tunisia, Zambia, and Zimbabwe are some other long-term recipients whose ratios of central spending to output seem roughly to match Poland's and Romania's. By the same token, the war against agriculture, and against the consumer, looks to have been taken as far in some recipient countries as in Soviet-occupied Europe, or even farther. By the World Bank's reckoning, the share of agriculture in the economies of Zimbabwe, Jamaica, Peru, and Jordan was lower in the 1980's than in Hungary. And such long-term recipients as the People's Democratic Republic of the Congo and the Ivory Coast have evidently managed to achieve ratios of private consumption to national product nearly as low as in Jaruzelski's Poland.

"American development-assistance policies . . . have been more likely to lead a prospective beneficiary toward an Eastern Europe-style economic morass."

For obvious reasons, the Communist governments of Central and Eastern Europe did not attract significant quantities of foreign capital for direct private investment during the 1980's. Such inflows were also negligible for long-term recipients of American development assistance during those years. This systemic inability to attract voluntary investment from abroad speaks to the business climate of the countries in question. The factors affecting business climate, difficult to quantify, include such things as the state of civil order, the extent to which law presides, and the degree of hostility toward the rights of the individual (including the right to property)—in short, the quality of the civil and political liberties that the local population may be said to enjoy. In many recipient states, as in the Communist countries of Central and Eastern Europe, that quality was, to say the least, low.

One can, of course, identify a number of characteristic differences between the policies and practices of today's East European states and the group of states involved in long-term participation in U.S. development programs. But in many important areas, what seems most striking is precisely the *lack* of distinct differences.

Our thought experiment thus points to a fundamental question. If the conditions of the present states of Eastern Europe cannot be distinguished by such meaningful economic and political criteria from those of governments that have been obtaining American funds and development advice these last few decades, why should U.S. aid be expected to help Eastern Europe evolve *away* from its current characteristics—much less in the direction of self-sustaining economic growth or open, liberal polities?

Harmful Aid

The fact is that American development-assistance policies, for many years, have been more likely to lead a prospective beneficiary toward an Eastern Europe-style economic morass than to help it escape from one toward economic health and self-sufficiency. To understand why this should be so, we need a quick glance at the past.

In its early years, American development aid (or "technical assistance," as it was called at the time) was extended to governments in the free world to help them participate more fully in the liberal international economic order that had been created after World War II. To American policy-makers, the primacy of private and commercial effort was self-evident. So too, in their minds, was the link between government policies and local prospects for material advance.

> *"Only a handful of countries that started receiving U.S. assistance in the 1950's and 1960's has ever graduated from dependent status."*

American development-assistance programs were tested by many minor challenges in the 1950's and 1960's, but they were shaken to their foundations by the Vietnam war. A confusion between the political and economic objectives of foreign aid, already evident in the discussions that surrounded USAID's founding in 1961, was permanently impressed upon the agency by the Johnson administration's decision to harness it to the war-winning effort. The programs that emerged in the field in response to these pressures—refugee relief, relocation projects, "pacification" programs, and the like—were not, in fact, meant to be judged by economic criteria. Severing the link between the living standards of local populations and the productive capacities of their economies had previously been regarded as a matter of enormous practical and moral hazard; during the Vietnam war, U.S. aid programs embraced the principle of such a separation, and sought to enforce it widely in practice.

Ironically, the new approach was soon globalized by American *critics* of the war. By the early 1970's, the U.S. foreign-aid budget was the battlefield for a sort of guerrilla action against the President by a Congress discontented with the course and conduct of his Southeast Asian policy. After repeated failures to obtain its requested appropriations, the Nixon administration agreed to a congressional rewriting of the aid mandate in 1973. This was the so-called "New Directions" legislation, which remains in force today.

> *"The success stories of U.S. economic assistance do not seem to offer any immediate or obvious encouragement to . . . Eastern Europe."*

The "New Directions" language instructed USAID to focus its attention directly on the poorest of the poor: not only to reach them, but to "satisfy their basic needs and [enable them to] lead lives of decency, dignity, and hope." This "Basic Human Needs Mandate," as it came to be known, not only authorized but seemingly required development policy to involve itself in the uplifting of local living standards through direct provision of goods and services—much as had been done in Vietnam. Though theoretical arguments were advanced to explain the contributions such activities would make toward the goal of self-sustaining development, the practical result was to mandate not development but long-term relief programs. Significantly, the "New Directions" legislation did not require, or even urge, American agencies to monitor the impact of recipient governments' policies and practices on the economies they supervised.

No Graduates of Aid

With the "lessons of Vietnam" thus perversely codified into its new operating procedures, American development-aid programs, originally based on the premise of strict conditionality, became a vehicle for unconditional resource transfers. With the decline in conditionality, "graduations" out of the U.S. aid program also came to a virtual end—despite the fact that graduation, by its very nature, is one of the criteria by which the success of policies designed to promote self-sustaining economic development can be measured. In 1989, an unusually frank report by USAID acknowledged this and other problems:

> Somewhere between 1949 and the present, the original concept of development assistance as a transitional means of helping developing countries "meet

their own needs" has been lost. . . . All too often, dependency seems to have won out over development. . . . Only a handful of countries that started receiving U.S. assistance in the 1950's and 1960's has ever graduated from dependent status. . . . Where development has worked, and is working, the key has been economic growth. And this is largely the result of individual nations making the right policy choices. . . .

What about the role of American aid in fostering political liberalization in recipient countries? Long-term receipt of American development assistance has certainly not *prevented* a transition toward a more open and participatory political order, as happened in much of Latin America and the Caribbean in the 1980's. Yet similar transitions took place in Latin countries that did not enjoy bilateral American economic-aid programs at the time. Moreover, many long-term recipients in other regions during the same decade did not undergo liberalization. So the record in this regard is equivocal at best.

In sum, an East European government seeking assistance from America's existing aid apparatus would be engaged in a singular act of faith, for there is little in the record to suggest that these programs contribute to economic liberalization or development, while there is considerable evidence to the contrary.

Arguments for Aid

Is, then, the story of America's postwar international economic policy one of unremitting failure? Quite the contrary: the framework for trade and finance that the United States helped to fashion in the 1940's is surely one of the more extraordinary successes in the history of international relations; indeed, it is one of the few whose accomplishments may have exceeded the hopes of its creators.

Moreover, specific American interventions are widely thought to have succeeded as well. For example, American assistance is commonly considered instrumental to the postwar recoveries and expansions of Western Europe and Japan, and later to the dynamic growth of such newly industrializing economies as Taiwan and South Korea. Advocates of aid initiatives for Eastern Europe, indeed, sometimes make their case by broad analogy with these earlier experiences. Are they right to do so?

> *"All too often, dependency seems to have won out over development."*

Unimpressive Results

Reviewed as a group, the success stories of U.S. economic assistance do not seem to offer any immediate or obvious encouragement to the new initiatives now being contemplated for Eastern Europe. Few of the components that figured importantly in these earlier successes are likely to be replicable today. Other components are no longer necessary to replicate, since they already exist.

For example, although the several states of Eastern Europe may or may not ultimately choose to join the NATO alliance, they are unlikely to require the sorts of security guarantees and military aid that Western Europe, Japan, Taiwan, and South Korea variously enjoyed. It is also hard to imagine that these countries, long subjugated to a Soviet-style dictatorship, would now voluntarily invite the United States or other governments to exercise even temporary mastery over their arrangements to fashion new constitutional or civil orders. Finally, the international trade and finance markets so vitally important to the earlier success stories are already in place for East European countries to avail themselves of.

What about conditions in Eastern Europe itself? First and foremost, it may be misleading to think of the region as a region. "Eastern Europe" was defined, indeed created, by Soviet occupation. With the passing of that occupation, many of the differences that have historically characterized the area are again more easily perceived. The populations differ by language, religion, cultural heritage—even by alphabet. They also differ in their political and legal traditions. There is no reason to expect that those differences, which were not erased under the common experience of occupation, will disappear in the near future.

> *"The socialist rulers of Eastern Europe spent more than four decades destroying the institutional framework of a civil order."*

Second, political developments vary significantly from one state to the next. In Prague, the current Minister of Finance is an avowed disciple of Milton Friedman; in Romania, by contrast, both polity and personnel mark a continuity between the old regime and the new. As one observer has commented, "the age of uniformity is over." This is true of prospects for political liberalization as well as of prospects for economic development.

Third, conditions are still evolving, and retain at least a degree of fluidity. The volatility of the landscape at the moment not only makes it less useful to focus on current events (such as proposed or pending measures for policy reform), but also limits the ability to generalize about problems and opportunities.

Obstacles to Development

Yet the diversity and fluidity of conditions in Eastern Europe today are in a sense also a boon to analysis, for they serve to emphasize two problems that are central to these societies' prospects. Both derive from the region's Soviet "interlude."

The first and arguably most important obstacle to economic and political development is the pervasive institutional maladaptation wrought by Soviet rule. Such maladjustment, unfortunately, goes beyond even the irrational process of central economic planning and the cumbersome, expensive system of socialist management. For in the exercise of Communist power, the socialist rulers of

Eastern Europe spent more than four decades destroying the institutional framework of a civil order in these countries. It was not only the framework of property rights, and individual rights, that came under assault, but the very rule of law itself.

> *"Overcoming the legacy of the immediate past is likely to require bold and fundamental departures from existing practices."*

The political implications of this are clear enough. Scarcely less important, though, are its economic implications. Economic historians are in general agreement that the rise of the Western world was directly and inextricably linked to the new institutional arrangements it developed, and perhaps none of those arrangements was more important than the framework of legal protections for individuals that included the right of enforceable private contracts. The populations of Eastern Europe have been separated from that framework for more than four decades. The majority have no memory of firsthand exposure to it, to say nothing of personal familiarity.

Privatization Will Be Difficult

This suggests that the institutional obstacles to Eastern Europe's development are much greater than would seem to be implied by today's intense discussions about, and proposals for, privatization of state-owned enterprises. To be sure, disendowing the states of the assets they have taken for themselves will be an immense task. Over the course of Margaret Thatcher's eleven-year tenure as Prime Minister, the British government succeeded in transferring something less than 5 percent of the country's output from government ownership back to private hands; in Eastern Europe, the privatizations now contemplated are greater by far. These are ambitious undertakings. But how much more ambitious by comparison will be the task of establishing a permanent, legitimate arrangement for the protection of individual rights and the enforcement of private contracts.

Institutional maladjustment is not the only enormous obstacle to development in Eastern Europe. Poland, Romania, Czechoslovakia, Hungary, Bulgaria, and East Germany are also beset by what might be described as a crisis of human capital. Perhaps the most telling evidence of that crisis has been the long-term deterioration of health conditions in both the USSR and its former satellites. The deterioration is represented very clearly in the local patterns of mortality. Between the mid-1960's and the mid-1980's, age-standardized death rates in the USSR and Soviet-occupied Europe actually rose. No other region of the world reported such a trend, and, in fact, no other industrial country has *ever* experienced such a general and long-term peacetime decline in public health. By the late 1980's, Eastern Europe's *lowest* death rates (East Germany) were substantially higher than Western Europe's *highest* ones (Ireland), and also higher than those reported for such Latin American societies as Argentina, Chile, and even Mexico.

One need not posit a tight, mechanistic relationship between levels of health and levels of output to appreciate the significance of these facts. By its very nature, rising mortality imposes constraints upon the productive capacities of the societies affected. Moreover, because rising mortality trends are so anomalous in the modern era, they suggest the possibility that other, more poorly measured aspects of human capital may also have been affected.

Can American development assistance specifically assist in relieving these obstacles to development in Eastern Europe? It is very difficult to imagine how. AID has no comparative advantage in helping to build the foundations of a civil order. Nor was it designed for helping to arrest mortality increases in industrial societies, or even for contributing to the preservation and augmentation of human capital in such places.

What is true of AID's limitations applies more generally to the entire field of development policy. A conventionally trained development economist may offer advice to a policymaker on how to get prices right, or achieve balances in the macroeconomy, or devise realistic measures for stabilization. There is merit in such activities, but for societies that were forced to march down the perverted path of Soviet-style socialism, they are hardly central to the problems at hand.

A Discouraging Picture

Overcoming the legacy of the immediate past is likely to require bold and fundamental departures from existing practices and arrangements in each of the countries of Eastern Europe. Respected local voices—Vaclav Klaus in Czechoslovakia, Janos Kornai in Hungary, Jan Winiecki in Poland, Ognian Pishev in Bulgaria, and many others—recognize as much, and urge immediate and decisive action. Such voices, indeed, offer the one cheering note in an otherwise thoroughly discouraging picture, for a number of the officials who will be receiving our development assistance may turn out to be wiser and braver than those dispensing it. Thus, in an address to a September 1990 meeting of the World Bank and the International Monetary Fund, Vaclav Klaus announced, "We know that there have been cases where major financial assistance caused the deceleration, not the acceleration, of the necessary systematic changes that we consider of the utmost importance." Though these were simple words, they were telling—for the highest officials at the World Bank and the International Monetary Fund have been unable to utter them publicly....

It is a relief to turn to the wisdom which seems so obvious to East European exponents of fast, radical transformation; namely, that the longer the transition to an independent, liberal order is delayed, the lower the ultimate chances of its success.

Capitalism Will Harm Eastern Europe

by Cornelius Lehane

About the author: *Cornelius Lehane, an assistant professor of English at Rockland County Community College in Suffern, New York, is a labor activist.*

The chest-thumping, hooray-for-us reaction of the U.S. press and various other flag wavers of free enterprise to the phenomenal political and economic changes now taking place in Eastern Europe has been so one-dimensional as to be misleading, and so self-righteous as to be actually embarrassing. The overriding assumption seems to be that the people of Eastern Europe, so long oppressed by communism, finally have realized what the dumbest American knew all along: socialism means failure, oppression, and poverty; capitalism, on the other hand, means success, freedom, and economic well-being.

For my generation, growing up in the U.S. in the 1950s, communists were the epitome of cruelty and violence. They enslaved nations, murdered nuns, and built iron curtains. In short, they were the enemy of freedom and truth. All things were justified in the name of fighting communism, including suspending civil liberties, firing tenured professors, blacklisting actors and writers, demanding loyalty oaths from union leaders, and jailing people for practices heretofore protected under the Bill of Rights.

Western Perceptions of Communists

All that is over now. Communism is finished, we are told by the TV anchors. Not only that, it's beginning to look like we were wrong about the communists all along. Far from murderous marauders, they turn out to be a bunch of old softies afraid to make the tough economic decisions and unable to discipline a lazy labor force that has been sitting around all these years not doing any work and living off government handouts in the form of subsidies for factories, housing, and food; free health care, pensions, and education; as well as laws protecting them from being laid off.

The rulers of Eastern Europe lacked the courage of the wimpiest of American

---

Cornelius Lehane, "Eastern European Workers, Beware! Capitalism Isn't All It's Cracked Up to Be." Reprinted, with permission, from *USA Today* magazine, May 1991, © 1991 by the Society for the Advancement of Education.

bosses. Our economic rulers have closed factories, cut pay, and forced workers out on strike, then replaced them with scabs willing to do the job for less than half the going rate. They have destroyed entire cities with the flourish of a single pen (*i.e.*, Flint, Mich., and Gary, Ind.). They fight continuously for tax cuts for the rich and cutbacks in services for the poor and wage earners.

Lately, the rulers of Eastern Europe have smartened up and come to us for advice. Our recommendation is clear—a dose of good old capitalistic austerity. You have inflation?—just cure it with a depression. Already in Poland, thousands of formerly gainfully employed workers are out of a job. They believe their sacrifice will make Poland better for their children.

America's Poor Record

Eastern Europe wants to be more like America, where, in 1988, 20% of children under the age of 18 were living in poverty; where, according to the Washington, D.C.-based Economic Policy Institute, 31.5% of the population is working at poverty level wages; where, between 1979 and 1988, the top five percent of wage earners experienced a 9.6% gain in real income, while the bottom 20% suffered a 12.5% decline; where, between 1977 and 1987, the average family income of the poorest 10% of Americans fell 10.5%, while that of the wealthiest one percent rose 74.2%.

In addition to the entrepreneurial spirit, what the West exports is not freedom, but greed. In Rockland County, N.Y., where I work, no affordable housing has been built in recent years, nor is any on the horizon for the immediate future. Housing also has been a perennial problem in the socialist world. The reason there, however, is that they simply don't have the money. (Some theorists suggest that the entire rearrangement of socialist nations is taking place precisely because they don't have capital and need to make themselves more attractive to the West to borrow some.)

In suburban America, it's the what's-in-it-for-me phenomenon that creates the problem. "If I can build a house and make $100,000 off it, I'd be stupid to put the same time and energy into one that I'd only make $5,000 off of." In New York City, tenants are forced out so owners can convert their apartment buildings into luxury condos. (In my old Upper West Side neighborhood, decent housing is affordable only for families with an income in the $150,000-a-year range.) Tenants in East Berlin may experience the same sort of phenomenon when the West German landlords take over their buildings. That's the other side of the profit motive everyone is so excited about exporting. In contrast, the old socialist morality of the U.S.S.R. was perhaps unrealistic, but certainly kinder and gentler, requiring that no one pay more than 10% of their income for housing.

> *"What the West exports is not freedom, but greed."*

The arrogant, I-told-you-so American economists now dancing on the grave of the Soviet communism they knew all along wouldn't succeed have yet to explain the growth of the U.S.S.R. into a world economic superpower during the first three-quarters of the 20th century. This occurred despite the absence of any economic base as late as 1920 and the destruction of their economic base during World War II. They fail to explain why the Soviet economy grew at *twice* the rate of the U.S.'s during the 1950s and continued to increase at a healthy pace into the 1970s, before beginning to decline.

It is obvious to all, it seems, that communism doesn't work, and that's the only explanation we need. Every band plays the same tune: stick to capitalism; capitalism won. It may not be the ideal system, but it's the only one that works. So what if we've created a drug epidemic we can't solve and a crime wave which does not abate, no matter how many prisons we build. So what if reliance on the market brought us face to face with a war over oil in the deserts of the Middle East.

By following in our footsteps, the people of Eastern Europe will be able to buy 400 different kinds of candy, but not find affordable day care. They will purchase new automobiles on time and subscribe to credit cards, then lose them when the steel mills shut down. They'll be able to live in luxurious suburbs with swimming pools until their version of Wall Street goes bust. They may eat prepackaged dinners cooked in a microwave and watch color television, but won't be able to provide care for their elderly parents or afford to send them to a private nursing home. Their kids will drink juice from convenient throw-away cartons, then run out of landfill space in which to discard them.

> "Even when there is food on the shelves, the prices are so high that most people can't afford to buy it."

I'm no economist and certainly not an expert on how one should structure an economy. I do have my own sense of priorities, though. A society requires good schools, adequate health care, clean air and water, enough housing for everyone, safe streets, and a myriad of other social needs that should be taken care of before we lose any sleep over Ivana Trump's divorce settlement. These necessities aren't being taken care of very well in the U.S.

Exporting Ideas

Before we pat ourselves on the back for having beaten the communists, we ought to take a good look at the kind of ideas we are exporting: housing for the rich before schools for the poor; luxury cars before clean air and adequate mass transit; expensive medication and medical procedures for the elderly rich before preventive medicine; and corporate profits before job security or retraining.

In New York, 83% of the schools are in need of major repair, and it has a higher infant mortality rate than many underdeveloped countries. The streets of Manhattan are filled with more beggars than Bombay. Drugs are infecting an entire generation. Bridges, on the brink of collapse, have to be closed. Water mains explode weekly. Seymour Melman, a Columbia University industrial engineering professor, estimates that the cost of repairing the U.S. infrastructure could reach five trillion dollars. Instead of spending money to fix any of this, we build luxury apartment buildings, open trendy restaurants, and pour billions into the defense industry as we continue to act as the world's policeman.

> *"Socialism resulted from the abuses, oppression, and exploitation of capitalism."*

The National Commission on Children reports that nearly 500,000 American youngsters are affected by malnutrition and 100,000 are homeless. Yet, this does not suggest to us that we have systemic poverty and a housing shortage of epic proportions. That almost 50% of African-American children live below the poverty level does not tell us that our society has failed dismally in its attempts to provide equal opportunity for all. Our steel mills have closed, our cars are produced overseas, and manufacturing jobs in the hundreds of thousands have disappeared. Obviously, something is wrong with the U.S.'s sagging economy and declining morality.

Is this the plan the workers of Eastern Europe want to embrace—the poor get poorer and the rich get richer? I suggest the steelworkers of Krakow consider the former steelworkers of western Pennsylvania, 61% of whom, according to a Gallup Poll, are making an average of $7.18 an hour less than they earned in 1980. Most of them also are without health insurance and pension benefits.

The realization is dawning on the Polish people that a system which throws them out of work and deprives their children of food to enable "entrepreneurs" in Warsaw to wear imported jeans, drive BMWs, and build luxury apartment buildings may require a second look. The railroad workers struck in the summer of 1989 and others are chomping at the bit. The Paris Club (17 Western nations to whom Poland owes money) have insisted on strict austerity measures if that nation is to postpone making payments on a $40,000,000,000 debt it cannot possibly afford. The economic measures taken in Poland, under the auspices of Solidarity, have lowered the inflation rate significantly, stabilized the zloty against foreign currency, and created a trade surplus with the West.

Low Wages, High Prices

When the other shoe dropped, however, they found a 40% drop in real wages for Polish workers and an unemployment rate zooming from one to eight percent in less than a year and heading higher. In the old days, bread cost the equivalent of a penny a loaf. When it arrived in the stores, it immediately was bought up and the shelves often were empty. Shortages were the bane of socialism. Now, even when there is food on the shelves, the prices are so high that most people can't afford to buy it.

An American capitalist's investment plan for the Gdansk shipyard is a case in point. Saving the birthplace of Solidarity required losing the patient. The plan called for slashing the workforce in half, freezing wages (this at a time of rapidly rising prices), and a no-strike guarantee for five years. The shipyard workers rejected this particular capitalist poison pill. Consequently, the Solidarity government, still preaching capitalism, continues it as a state-run operation.

The pre-revolution Solidarity membership of 10,000,000 has plummeted to around 2,000,000. Its approval rating in the polls has dropped from 78% to 47%. This is not surprising, considering that unions are supposed to protect its members from those attempting to balance economies on the backs of workers.

Soviet Union Workers Protest

The Soviet Union furiously is debating how quickly it should rush into the market economy. Not surprisingly, the workers there have been skeptical, given the Polish experience, and actually put up a fuss at the 1990 May Day celebration in Moscow, demanding safeguards and job security. They immediately were taken to task by William F. Buckley, Jr., who, in his syndicated column, championed unemployment and poverty as an important and necessary part of the capitalist package.

We cannot deny that the economies of Eastern Europe are in dismal shape, brought down, at least in part, by the weight of their own bureaucracies. Central planning overwhelmingly has been rejected in democratic elections by the workers of Poland, Hungary, and Czechoslovakia. Those of East Germany have surrendered to the prosperous capitalism of West Germany.

This does not mean that socialism is dead, however, or that it even is the primary cause of all the economic difficulties of Eastern Europe. It certainly does not signify that the economic failures of socialism prove that capitalism has succeeded.

One of the biggest problems for the Soviet Union is the amount of money that country squandered on military expenditures, especially the ill-advised war in Afghanistan. All this expenditure on the military was money not available for upgrading the economic infrastructure.

When the smoke clears and the mirrors are removed, it's obvious that the U.S. has similar problems to the Soviet Union. Basically, America too must recover from the insanity of the arms race. The U.S. military-industrial complex employs 6,500,000 civilian and military personnel. What will happen to them if peace breaks out permanently? The unexpectedly brief war in the Persian Gulf did nothing to improve our economy or solve our long-range problems. We have 135,000 factories, laboratories, and bases that, sooner or later, we'll have to begin dismantling. Many are wards of the Pentagon and

> *"The people of Eastern Europe should look at their own traditions, . . . rather than get too caught up in the Western cult of selfishness."*

function outside of the marketplace under a system of planning and pricing not all that dissimilar to the one they're trying to junk in Eastern Europe.

So much of our productive energy has gone into military research and development and production, particularly under the Reagan Administration, when military spending increased by as much as 50% in some years, that we seriously have weakened our industrial base. From 1894 until 1971, the U.S. annually produced a trade surplus. The concept of a trade deficit was unheard of. Now, it is heard of to the tune of $110,000,000,000 in 1989, and if we deducted military related exports, the sound would be deafening.

> *"The hated communists had the humility to admit when they were wrong and the courage to try new approaches."*

The economic recovery and expansion of the 1980s is illusory when debt is factored in. The U.S. was the world's largest creditor nation in 1980, with a surplus of $106,000,000,000. By 1989, as the world's largest debtor nation, America owed $620,000,000,000. Which means the nation is doing just fine until someone calls in the notes.

What we have as the legacy of our years of economic expansion is a large debt on top of a badly eroded industrial base. Does this sound familiar? Just ask a Pole.

Socialism resulted from the abuses, oppression, and exploitation of capitalism. People who have forgotten that—whether in the East or the West—must remember. Capitalism put little children to work in factories and fields (and still does), provided no relief from unemployment or poverty, and allocated health care only for those who could pay for it. (In the U.S., there still is qualitatively different health care for people with money and those without.) It provided no relief for old age and often did not provide food and shelter.

The Fruits of Socialism

To those East Europeans who argue that capitalism has redressed these grievances, I suggest that the relative well-being of their West European fellow-workers did not arrive in a gift package from the capitalists. Rather, it is the fruit of decades of struggle by workers' parties and militant trade unions, most of them led by communists and socialists.

Another phenomenon that the American press seems not to have noticed is that the profound changes taking place in Eastern Europe are occurring because the hated communists had the humility to admit when they were wrong and the courage to try new approaches. The people of Eastern Europe—communist and non-communist—are hashing out their differences and creating new societies.

The horn-blowers of democracy refuse to acknowledge the flowering of real democracy, a true people's movement in Eastern Europe. Why has so little been made of this? Have the "enslaved" ever thrown off the yoke so easily?

Chapter 3

If capitalism returns to Eastern Europe, the workers will find that, if they ever want to convert back to socialism, it will not be accomplished with demonstrations and negotiations, but by the same brutal and bloody process we've seen in Latin America, Asia, and Africa. I remember the guns and dogs and tear gas that greeted those in America who had the temerity to disagree with the established order during the 1960s and I wonder why we don't stand back watching this European process of social change with hushed reverence. Instead, we holler from the rooftops, "We told you so," gloat over our own tenuous prosperity, and continue in our fathomless arrogance to think that we have the handle on everything.

An interesting piece of news from Hungary told how the democratization of the society was to include the dismantling of the Communist Party cells in the factories. Typically, the article did not explain why this was done, only suggested that these groups were seen as a threat to the new order. As someone who has spent a good part of his life as a union organizer and who knows how hard it is to get organizations set up in the workplace to begin with, I wonder why these groups need to be dismantled. The army certainly, even perhaps the militia, could prove a threat, but why the workers' organizations?

They would do it, it seems to me, for the same reasons bosses keep trying to break up unions here. The workers then would be less able to resist layoffs and speed-ups or complain about unsafe conditions and unfair treatment. Are the workers of Eastern Europe now the enemies of the new progress? If so, they must wonder about the nature of this progress.

Walking the Middle Road

Some of the less talked-about proposals being considered in the socialist world include the zero hours plan in East Germany whereby laid-off employees or those on short hours receive full pay until they find other jobs. The assumption of this kind of thinking is that workers need to eat and have a place to live, even if they do get laid off. It's something that, in kinder times, has been proposed in the U.S., though I'm sure no politician would dare mention the idea now. Mikhail Gorbachev walked a middle road, trying to pacify the working people by promising no meteoric price increases or massive layoffs, while offering retraining and job placement for those displaced by the closing of factories. The Soviet Union has taken measures to involve more people in decision-making at all economic and political levels. Gorbachev promised democracy on the shop floor. He suggested that workers elect their managers and take part in the decision-making of the plants. He even proposed a referendum on the most important economic question of the day—ownership of private property.

> *"Subsidized food is better than some eating well and others going hungry."*

Europe

Our political pundits now claim the Soviet Union is going too far toward democracy. The American press backs the *privilegentsia*, the Soviet Union's counterpart to our MBAs, professionals, stock manipulators, and junk bond salesmen. These people have seen a chance to make a buck—an opportunity for a plush condo and a BMW. They want the free market immediately. Like their counterparts in the U.S., they care nothing about the health of society as a whole. They just want to get theirs first. That mentality is dangerous to the process of change taking place in Eastern Europe. It also has dominated the American belief system for too long and has become dangerous here as well.

That seems to be the kind of political and economic change for which we are cheering. Perhaps the people of Eastern Europe should look to their own traditions in developing new economies, rather than get too caught up in the Western cult of selfishness. At the same time, perhaps we might look to the East and discover that job retraining is better than layoffs; that subsidized food is better than some eating well and others going hungry; and that society has a responsibility for the lame as well as the fleet-of-foot.

Chapter 4

What Measures Would Strengthen Eastern European Economies?

Eastern European Economies: An Overview

by Carol J. Williams

About the author: *Carol J. Williams is a staff writer for the* Los Angeles Times *newspaper.*

It is known in Brussels and Washington as "adjustment fatigue," though millions of Eastern Europeans suffering the debilitating and dangerous malady could not put a name to what ails them.

They know only that they are exhausted by the runaway pace of change in the post-Communist era. They have been incessantly clobbered with unemployment, inflation, rising crime rates, divisive nationalism, revolving-door leadership and a gnawing fear that the West has abandoned them in turmoil.

They are tired of living in a whirlwind that has swept away every familiar structure, from free day care and health services to modest but secure pensions.

They are helpless to undo the damage industry has inflicted on the environment and disappointed to discover that the first fruits of capitalism have enriched the few, not the masses.

They are also fearful that the worldwide recession and demands for aid to the former Soviet Union are depleting foreign assistance and investment funds that might have come their way.

In short, they are angry at the disorder they have brought on themselves, that they have lost control of their revolutions and that there is no relief in sight.

A Desire to Slow Reform

Most troubling among the symptoms afflicting the determined anti-Communist warriors of 1989 is a tendency to put the brakes on reform in an attempt to relieve the hardships.

Opinion surveys suggest Eastern Europeans are deeply resentful of the current difficulties, and economists warn of growing sentiment for slowing down the process to ease the pain.

"We were lacking a lot of luxuries under communism, but at least we had se-

---

Carol J. Williams, "Tough Times," *Los Angeles Times*, April 14, 1992. Copyright, 1992, Los Angeles Times. Reprinted with permission.

curity. We didn't have to worry about how we would buy food to feed our children," lamented Maria Popova, a 40-year-old Bulgarian laid off from a factory job who now sells yarn and cheap cosmetics on the streets of Sofia.

"Now I have to work twice as many hours to make the same living," she complained, voicing doubts shared by millions in the region about capitalism. "It's the same for all honest people. The only ones benefiting from our so-called democracy are bandits and tricksters."

Although the burdened peoples lament the agony and disruption of the transition, the majority seem to have concluded there is no choice but to plod on.

A study of 8,000 Eastern European households concluded that most people in the region want to slow the transition, not stop it. The five-nation survey by Britain's Center for the Study of Public Policy indicated that Eastern Europeans are unhappy with their lives but remain hopeful that time will correct the chaos.

> *"The only ones benefiting from our so-called democracy are bandits and tricksters."*

"Support for democracy is still strong among at least two-thirds of the populations, but the other third seems to be reconsidering whether it is worth the price to be paid," said Richard Rose, director of the research center in Glasgow, Scotland.

Poles and Hungarians gave the lowest approval ratings for their political systems, although they are regarded as the most successful in breaking with the past. A third of the Poles questioned said they would welcome an authoritarian takeover.

Among the respondents in Bulgaria, Czechoslovakia, Hungary, Poland and Romania, 62% claimed that their wages are too little to make ends meet. But in an indication of faith in their nascent capitalist systems, 73% said they expected more favorable conditions within five years.

Economists with expertise in the region say the public's ambivalent attitude toward reform is due to "adjustment fatigue."

They warn that reform is at risk if the battered societies are not provided with some midterm rewards, but they, too, tend to believe that the majority remains committed to the goals of a market economy and democratic society.

"The liberalization is irreversible, both politically and economically," said Eugenio Lari, a senior adviser at the World Bank who has been tracking Eastern European economies for more than a decade.

Competition from the Soviets

What appears to be backsliding in some countries is more an effort at addressing immediate needs of the public, he said, noting that lenders and investors may have to accept a slower transition than idealistic leaders initially forecast.

Many in Eastern Europe also worry that Western attention has shifted from their plight to that of the former Soviet Union.

"This concern [of the West] is natural, as the stakes in the ex-Soviet Union are enormous," Lari said. "Success there, or failure, would have broad, worldwide implications."

But he described the region's fears as exaggerated, as foreign investment in Eastern Europe continues to outpace that in the former Soviet republics. He also noted that Third World countries have more reason than the former Communist states to worry about unfair diversion of development funds.

The dramatic nature of the 1989 anti-Communist revolutions put Eastern Europe in the investment limelight, spurring private and government campaigns to draw money and expertise to the region.

Political Stability Is Essential

One such effort is being spearheaded by the U.S. ambassador to Austria, Roy Huffington, who is trying to pair off private American investors with promising entrepreneurs in the East. A successful Texas oilman before his appointment to Vienna in 1990, Huffington argued that Eastern Europe has the advantage over the former Soviet republics because most of the countries threw off communism two years earlier and have laid down at least a secure political foundation.

"The No. 1 thing the business community needs is political stability. If you don't have that, no one is going to put money in there," said the ambassador, one of the Bush Administration's point men in drawing the private sector into the process of redeveloping Eastern Europe.

> *"While all of Eastern Europe is embarked on the same process, . . . the pace and success of the transition vary widely."*

While all of Eastern Europe is embarked on the same process of changing from centrally planned to market-driven economies, the pace and success of the transition vary widely from country to country.

Here is a brief assessment of the progress and pitfalls in each country:

Poland. The disastrous effects of sacrifice without immediate reward are most visible in Poland, where the nation's 38 million people are largely abandoning economic "shock therapy."

Public impatience with 2 million jobless and falling industrial output prompted President Lech Walesa and the Polish Parliament to reject a government austerity program. Despite warnings from Western lenders, Polish politicians are now trying to protect bankrupt state industries from closure to stave off social unrest that could be spawned by further rises in the numbers of unemployed.

Hungary. Although Hungary is the regional leader in disentangling its economy from the mire of socialism, Hungarians bemoan the erosion of living standards caused by inflation still over 30% and unemployment that has idled about one in 15 workers.

"What is very much irritating public opinion is that certain people are accumulating a lot of capital, while the majority of the population is not as well off as it was before," said Alajos Dornbach, a prominent Budapest lawyer and vice president of the Hungarian Parliament.

A Strong Private Sector

Despite persistent complaints, Hungarians have seen a stellar rise of their private sector, which now accounts for more than one-third of the economy.

The country's stable if uncharismatic leadership has created an atmosphere of confidence for Western investors, drawing more than half of all new foreign business development in the region. The resulting export boom has allowed Budapest to keep up payments on the $20 billion it owes foreign creditors—the largest per capita debt in the region.

Czechoslovakia. Czechoslovakia's steadily adjusting economy could be viewed in the same hopeful light as Hungary's, if not for the divisive issue of Slovak separatism threatening the federation's future.

Opinion polls show most voters in the poorer eastern region of Slovakia prefer continued unity with the Czech lands to going it alone. But Slovak nationalists are pushing for broader autonomy from Prague, vowing to declare independence if their demands are not met.

Meanwhile, the country is engrossed in an ambitious mass privatization program that seeks to restore individual property seized by the Communists more than 40 years ago and to parcel out ownership of state enterprises through sale of shares to the federation's 15.6 million people. Western investors have largely had to wait for the property transfers to be completed before delving into new joint ventures. . . .

Bulgaria. Bulgaria has lately won praise for ousting Communist rulers, writing a new constitution and enacting laws that will encourage foreign investment. U.S. Undersecretary of State Lawrence S. Eagleburger claimed Bulgaria had joined Hungary, Poland and Czechoslovakia in the newly democratic vanguard.

The country labors under a $12-billion foreign debt on which it hasn't made a payment since 1990. That has discouraged new investment and undermined Bulgaria's fiscal credibility—facts that some lenders, like Germany's Deutsche Bank, are unwilling to ignore despite Sofia's recent moves toward reform.

> *"Nowhere is the post-Communist vista as bleak as in the remnants of the Yugoslav federation."*

Romania. Romania, although still politically volatile, has recently shown signs of a turnaround. Local elections in February 1992 ceded control of most major cities to opposition forces, although the National Salvation Front that emerged from Romania's revolutionary confusion still dominates in the countryside and the national Parliament.

The front, which has split into neo-Communist and reform factions, could see its grip on power loosened or removed. But it remains unclear whether opposition rule will provide a stabilizing influence. The Democratic Convention, uniting more than a dozen anti-Communist forces, is an alliance with little government experience.

Romania suffers inflation of over 300%, and voters are deeply divided over how to transform their beleaguered economy. Little Western investment has come Romania's way because of political turmoil, even though the country is a good credit risk by virtue of having no foreign debt.

Yugoslavia. Nowhere is the post-Communist vista as bleak as in the remnants of the Yugoslav federation. Feverish nationalism has spawned recurring waves of violence, which have scuttled an economy that in 1990 was the region's most developed and promising.

Economic Problems in New States

The dominant Serbian republic has repeatedly printed money to finance the federal army's war against secessionist republics, producing hyperinflation expected to reach an unprecedented annual rate of 100,000%.

Croatia suffered an estimated 65% loss of its gross national product during nine months of a war that has claimed 10,000 lives. Slovenia, which turned back a federal onslaught in a matter of days after declaring independence in June 1991, is slowly recovering but suffered more than $2 billion in war damage and saw its economy shrink last year by about 10%.

The Serbian-backed federal army's wrath has now been turned against Bosnia-Herzegovina, the third former Yugoslav republic to be recognized by the West as independent.

With no end to the conflict in sight, the future of Serbia, Montenegro and Macedonia remains uncertain as they teeter on the brink of economic collapse.

Albania. A predominantly agrarian country of 3 million, Albania is now entirely dependent on foreign aid for its food and survival.

But elections in March 1992 ended 48 years of repressive Communist rule and saw a charismatic, pro-Western politician—Democratic Party leader Sali Berisha—installed as president. The country appears set on a long path toward reform and recovery.

Western aid and investment may be forthcoming now that the Communists have been displaced. But Albania's new leadership will be running against the clock to relieve widespread hunger and hardship in Europe's poorest country, where 70% are unemployed and antiquated industry has ground to a halt.

Socialism Would Strengthen Eastern European Economies

by Tim Wohlforth

About the author: *Tim Wohlforth is a writer in Oakland, California.*

Revolutionary change has swept through Eastern Europe and the Soviet Union with such remarkable speed that it has clearly outpaced thinking. Democracy has replaced one-party dictatorships almost everywhere, and the process appears to be irreversible. An upsurge of popular hatred for the previous dictatorships and their command-state economies have placed in power non-Communist intellectuals dedicated to establishing what they call "free markets." For 40 years the Soviet Union imposed its system upon Eastern Europe. Today Eastern Europe has taken the lead, and the Soviet Union, its republics in tow, is rushing to follow the East European model.

Nowhere has thinking lagged further behind these events than among socialist intellectuals. In Eastern Europe, "socialism" has become the new name for the remnants of the old Communist parties seeking to hold onto what they can from the past. Missing from the political scene in any of these countries is a sizable democratic-socialist trend posing an alternative to the old bureaucratic command economies or to a return to capitalism.

The Disappointing Behavior of Socialists

Western socialists have not fared much better. The most "revolutionary" among them have shown themselves to be the most conservative thinkers. Some of these revolutionaries have become gloom-and-doom merchants, confidently predicting the triumph of "capitalist restoration" and "counterrevolution." This certainly suggests that in their minds the old system—while perhaps distorted or deformed—was preferable to the present democratic movement for change.

Others, while welcoming change and supporting the spread of democracy, have reacted to the new situation by tossing old formulas at it. Ferenc Feher, the

---

Tim Wohlforth, "What Role for Socialism in a New Eastern Europe?" *In These Times*, February 6-12, 1991. Reprinted with permission.

Hungarian dissident and former student of George Lukacs, makes the obvious point that "for the average intelligent citizen of Soviet-type societies, the slogan 'return to Leninism' stands for courting [Tiananmen-like] disaster." Our Western revolutionary may argue that a second time around for Leninism would avoid Stalinist degeneration. Perhaps, but the point is that few who have suffered the consequences of the last leap of faith are prepared today for a new leap.

Just as important, such talk lacks concreteness because it avoids relating one's proposals to what is actually happening in Eastern Europe and the Soviet Union. A revolution to uproot the capitalist mode of production is not needed because capitalism, even in a country like Poland, has very weak roots. A revolution to destroy the political power of the Stalinist bureaucracy has already taken place. The Hungarian sociologist Ivan Szelenyl, another Lukacsian, describes the current situation well. "The social formation that exists at present in Eastern Europe is unquestionably not capitalist. Eastern Europe today is a socialist mixed economy with a dominant statist sector, or state mode of production—which still employs full time probably up to 85 to 90 percent of the labor force—combined with a rapidly growing private sector." The *New York Times* recently noted that Hungary has targeted only 20 of 2,000 major enterprises for immediate privatization, while the Poles have chosen only 12 out of 7,000.

> *"In a socialist society, the economy and the government are both subordinated to the will of the people."*

Marketing Socialism

Much of the confusion both in the East and the West is caused by the notion of "free markets." Western socialist ideologues oppose markets as inherently sinful and capitalist, while the liberal intellectual ideologues running most East European societies have embraced markets with uncritical abandon.

The market system has two great strengths. It permits members of a society to choose among competing products to meet their needs. This is imminently democratic and is being warmly embraced by Eastern European citizens. Second, the competition between producers of different products tends to be won by the producer of the least costly product of comparable quality. This encourages the productivity of labor and, therefore, the wealth of society as a whole.

Market economies have met the needs of people better than statist command economies. A system that seeks to plan the totality of a complex modern economy by establishing input and output goals for each productive unit of that society requires an immense bureaucratic structure to administer it. It needs the whip of a single-party political dictatorship to drive it. Whatever its original purposes or the idealism of its advocates, such a system ends up serving the interests of those who control it and denying the needs of those it claims to serve.

Chapter 4

Ernest Mandel, among the most intelligent of the visionary revolutionary school, has suggested as an alternative to both market mechanisms and bureaucratic directives that "the simplest and most democratic way of adapting material resources to social wants is not to interpose the medium of money between the two but to find out people's needs just by asking them what they are." The idea would be to hold meetings in neighborhoods at which people would vote on whether they want shoes of low quality and low price or high quality and high price, what colors they would like, etc. Considering the low voter turnout not only in the U.S. but in the recent Polish presidential races, it is doubtful if many people would show up for frequent meetings to discuss the thousands of different consumer products a modern society produces. I would think the average worker would prefer a trip to the local department store or shopping mall to vote with his or her pocketbook.

The truth of the matter is that there is no practical alternative to the market system and money. Dreams of a marketless, moneyless society are just that, dreams that Marx borrowed from his utopian socialist contemporaries. These utopians in turn developed their notions from romanticized versions of the earliest, and therefore necessarily the most primitive, societies. Markets and money existed prior to capitalism and markets and money will exist in any realizable socialist society.

Role Slaying

What role is there for socialists and socialist ideas in Eastern Europe today? This is no minor question, because if we are incapable of articulating a socialist vision for these societies today we will have no such vision for our own society tomorrow. Are we only to raise our fists in anger and shout impotently at what is presently happening? Or are we to simply accept it all uncritically, cheering alongside the opponents of socialism we oppose so vigorously at home?

The best place to begin is with the dilemma the liberal free-market leaders of these countries now face: how to privatize the 90 percent or so of industry that remains in state hands? The world has never faced a problem quite like this one. Here in the West, the large corporations justify their existence—and their profits—by referring to the efforts and risks we are told the original owners undertook. In Eastern Europe, these factories are the direct creation of the state and the product of the labor of those who work in the factories. Is government now simply to hand these factories over to any passersby on the street, to those who have risked nothing and displayed no special talents of entrepreneurship? Are they to be given to foreign interests and, in this fashion, the nation transformed into an economic colony of the West?

"The time is ripe to articulate a feasible socialist alternative."

Rejecting such notions, some Eastern European leaders are suggesting that the ownership be transferred to the public by distributing stocks to all citizens. This proposal is really an admission that the factories actually do belong to all the people and should not be placed in the hands of a few who can become wealthy and powerful at the expense of the many. In practice, the wide distribution of stocks would mean that actual control of the factories would revert to the existing management. In most cases, this management has changed little since Communist days; the old Communist managers remain the most competent. I fail to see how this process would be beneficial to the people of these countries or in any way increase efficiency in these factories. It suggests that the liberal rulers of these countries are also ideologues and believe that private ownership is a magic bullet.

> "We can understand why the people in Eastern Europe ... are temporarily blind to the weaknesses of the capitalist system."

Socialists do have something to propose concretely in these countries. Why not turn over the ownership of many of these factories to the workers employed in these factories? The workers, in turn, would be able to choose competent management, and all would benefit to the extent that the factory efficiently produces products that fill people's needs. This kind of employee ownership has been tried successfully in limited ways in the U.S. and has worked.

Cross-Purposes

The distinction between socialist and capitalist societies lies not in the existence or non-existence of markets, money, competition, individuality or even some degree of inequality. It does lie in the purpose of that society and its economy. In a capitalist society, government and civil society are subordinated to the need to accumulate capital and enrich those who possess it. In a socialist society, the economy and the government are both subordinated to the will of the people with the objective of the free and full development of humankind. The experience of the past 70 years proves that human beings will not and cannot march toward such a goal under the sting of the bureaucratic lash. The experience over the past 300 years proves that the enrichment of the few neither necessarily betters the lives of the many nor brings human beings closer to a more socially humane existence.

We can understand why the people in Eastern Europe, in rejecting their recent experience, are temporarily blind to the weaknesses of the capitalist system. However, each week of crisis in those countries is teaching people about the vicissitudes of an unchecked free-market economy. The time is ripe to articulate a feasible socialist alternative.

Privatization Would Strengthen Eastern European Economies

by Anne Applebaum

About the author: *Anne Applebaum is the Warsaw, Poland, correspondent for the* Economist, *a weekly magazine.*

After the revolutions, street demonstrations, political changes, and flag wavings of 1989, a few things in Central Europe remain comfortably constant. In Warsaw, the telephones still refuse to work, no matter how often you throw them to the ground. In Budapest, thick, brown clouds of smoke continue to billow gently from the exhaust pipes of buses, leaving the scent of burning diesel fuel in the air. In Prague, it is still possible to waste entire days looking for a single, perfect, accurate statistic, lost somewhere in the mountains of paper hoarded by jealous Czech bureaucrats.

State Sector Devours Resources

Among these endearing mementos of Communist rule, state property ownership stands out as one of the hardiest. Many other things have disappeared: Communist parties, censorship, secret police, Russian soldiers, price controls and subsidies. Poland has even dispensed with the erstwhile budget deficit and the unconvertible zloty. Yet state enterprises still account for eighty to ninety percent of industrial production in all three countries. The state remains the primary landlord and the most important taxpayer, the greatest debtor and the biggest drain on the budget. So long as the state sector continues to devour (and waste) people, money, and resources, no economic reform will succeed.

Nevertheless, when someone mentions mass privatization—the most fundamental part of economic reform in post-Communist society—politicians everywhere stall, mumble something about "not rushing things," and change the subject. This nervousness is not due to a lack of debate. The press, the parliaments, and the cabinet meetings of Central Europe are full of new words: share, bond,

---

Anne Applebaum, "Who Owns Central Europe?" *The American Spectator*, February 1991. Reprinted with permission.

ESOP (Employee Stock Ownership Program), limited company, holding company, mutual fund, pension fund, public offering, active and passive investor. Nor is the failure to privatize due to lack of knowledge. Most Central Europeans know that private property is part of "how things are done in the West," and understand, at least intellectually, that private owners make things work better. No, the tendency of otherwise pro-free market governments to stall and hedge on privatization has its roots in two very basic human emotions: fear and envy.

New Classes Will Emerge

Fear arises because privatization—far more than democratic elections or a free press—promises to change the social and class structure of Central Europe in unknown ways. Communist ideology taught an entire generation that society consists of workers, peasants, and intellectuals. Communist economies, which prevented anyone from owning anything, produced these three classes. Once privatization begins, this will change. When workers begin to own their shops and offices, when peasants begin to own their land, and when intellectuals join the service industries, the result will be entrepreneurs, farmers, and a new middle class.

> "So long as the state sector continues to devour (and waste) people, money, and resources, no economic reform will succeed."

So far, the only experiences most Central Europeans have with these new entrepreneurial social classes are their encounters with the ubiquitous black marketeers, mostly Polish, who crowd the train stations, the medieval market squares, and lately the airports of the region, furtively displaying their packages of cigarettes, chewing gum, and matchsticks on small tables. Usually selling imports from the West, sometimes reselling cheaper products from their own bloc, they are unmoved by snow, rain, and police.

Some find the sight of this budding business sector upsetting. "Will we all look like that?" wondered a distressed Hungarian friend of mine. I tried to answer no, but thought twice. Perhaps he was right to worry. Soon, people may find themselves doing things they never imagined, as jobs open up that never existed before. No one would have predicted that so many people would make a living from selling so much junk; no one can tell what new opportunities or disasters the sale of state enterprises—and the accompanying transformation of the working habits, incomes, lifestyles of millions of people—will bring to a given individual. This is where fear comes from: to be completely unable to envision one's future is a terrifying prospect, the equivalent of jumping into a muddy lake without knowing whether there are sharp rocks just below the surface.

Envy—an even stronger sensation than fear—arises because privatization will make some people, but not everybody, very rich. Envy is what makes it impossible for privatization to occur in the fastest and most logical manner: selling enterprises to people who have money. In post-Communist society, the only people who have money are foreigners, returning expatriates, and ex-Communists and their ilk, still known by the ugly Russian word *nomenklatura*. But no one wants to see ex-Communists benefit from democracy, nor do the much-invaded nations of Central Europe particularly care to be reconquered by their old enemies (the Germans) in a new guise.

Corrupt Privatization

While perfectly understandable, these emotions do make efficient privatization hard to carry out. Only Hungary has experimented with both sales to foreigners and sales to the *nomenklatura*, which is perhaps why Hungary has sold off more of its state property than any other country. Since the mid-1980s, managers of Hungarian state enterprises have been able to sell shares in their own companies both to foreigners and to other Hungarians. Although not owners, they were allowed to dispense with property as if they were; this resulted in speedy and often corrupt privatization, with managers naturally cutting deals for their own benefit. The process ground to a halt in 1990, after a series of scandals turned public opinion against this so-called "spontaneous" privatization. In one famous case, the managers of Hungar-hotels, a company which controlled over thirty prime hotel and restaurant properties, sold a controlling stake in the entire concern to a tiny Swedish company for the estimated price of a single hotel. Bribery was suspected, and the Hungarian courts threw the deal out on a technicality. Because, even if the deal had been a good one for the state company, the thought of *nomenklatura* managers and foreigners greedily enriching themselves at the expense of the general public was unpopular.

> *"Politicians want to move from socialism to capitalism, while at the same time insuring that no one emerges much better off than anyone else."*

Because of these early policies, Hungary is now afflicted with what amounts to a national schizophrenia on the subject of state company sales. Within the same month, the Hungarian government called for a mass acceleration of privatization, while at the same time blocking a lucrative deal between Hungaroton, the respectable Hungarian state recording concern, and EMI. The government didn't like the old Communist connections of Hungaroton's manager; they didn't like the idea of his getting anything out of the deal, and in general they didn't like the thought of anyone, even EMI, making a profit out of one of the nation's "crown jewels." Official policy may encourage privatization, but envy prevented it from happening in this particular case.

In Poland, envy has also been responsible for the catastrophic overvaluation of state assets, which in turn prevents sales to foreigners. A classic case is that of the famous Gdansk shipyard: "birthplace of Solidarity," and also home to a lot of rotting hulls, mountains of rusty scrap metal, turn-of-the-century brick warehouses, and obsolete machinery. An American millionairess, Barbara Piasecka-Johnson, offered to take a percentage of it off the government's hands for a few million dollars, in return for the right to run it as she pleased. Horrified at the "low" price, and fearing that Mrs. Johnson might make a profit off their labor, the workers refused to approve the deal. (Their confusion was deepened by Mrs. Johnson's phraseology: "I will save the shipyard," she said, not "I will buy it and run it for profit.")

> "The idea of giving away free shares ... is an acceptably populist, perfectly reasonable way to conduct some—if not all—privatization."

It is not a nostalgia for socialism that is causing governments and companies to hesitate. Even in Vaclav Havel's entourage of ex-hippies and skateboarding rock stars, it is hard to find anyone anywhere who will say, in public, that he believes in an "alternative" to capitalism or a so-called "third way." The stumbling blocks are not ideological, but technical: how to do it, how to do it fairly, how to do it quickly, and how to control it. Some have described the task of mass privatization as the political equivalent of squaring the circle: politicians want to move from socialism to capitalism, while at the same time insuring that no one emerges much better off than anyone else. The transition period—the period of privatization—will be plagued by this dilemma.

Poland's Problems

The slow progress towards private ownership may have disastrous political and economic consequences. Poland—the nation which leads Central Europe in fiscal, monetary, and currency reform—has already run into most of them. While Hungary and Czechoslovakia have had their difficulties, Poland provides a spectacular example of what can go wrong in the absence of ownership reform.

Poland's economic reform program began bravely enough on January 1, 1990, when Prime Minister Tadeusz Mazowiecki's economic team, lead by Finance Minister Leszek Balcerowicz, carried out what has become known as either the "Big Bang" reform or simply "The Balcerowicz Plan." The program slashed subsidies, freed prices, liberalized import/export laws, froze wages, hardened the currency and ultimately cut inflation. The novelty of the reform plan came with Balcerowicz's decision to take several of these steps all at once, whereas in the past, the benefits of one type of reform could be lost due to the absence of another. While the world applauded this plan, which had many immediate positive effects (including Poland's first trade surplus in decades), the Balcerowicz team nevertheless began stalling in mid-1990, and became stuck on the issue of privatization. Rather than going ahead as fast as possible, rather than experimenting with different ways to execute changes in ownership, ministers and deputy ministers squabbled among themselves, each trying to retain as much regulatory control as possible. Although Poland's parliament finally did pass a privatization law, the first companies did not go up for public subscription until November 30, 1990. Even now, there is debate about whether public subscription (used to great effect in Britain in the 1980s) is an appropriate way to sell large state companies in a country where few people have any money for investment at all. Faster, but admittedly more haphazard privatization techniques remain untested: worker/management buyouts, direct purchase, company liquidation. . . .

The economic consequences of failing to privatize quickly can already be seen in Poland. When prices were freed and demand dropped in response to the monetary squeeze on January 1, 1990, state companies failed to react the way private companies would react in the West. Because most are monopolies, and because managers have a greater interest in keeping their jobs than in making profits, state companies generally preferred to raise prices and cut production in the face of tighter monetary controls and lowered demand. With no competition, and therefore no incentive to sell goods in greater quantities, production simply dropped.

A Slow Death

Because of this reaction, natural restructuring has not occurred. Companies have not gone bankrupt, and real unemployment is still astonishingly low. Many companies which should be out of business are still treading water. Without privatization, this process could go on indefinitely; the under-invested economy and infrastructure may be slowly run into the ground. Without privatization, the otherwise excellent Balcerowicz Plan will fail.

But the political consequences of failing to privatize are even more dire. The absence of ownership change was the cause of the Polish malaise: the popular complaint that "nothing is happening," that the Communists had disappeared but "nothing is changing." Whereas intellectuals felt the effect of Communism's collapse right away, with the disappearance of censorship and travel restrictions, ordinary people still found themselves living the same lives, doing the same work for the same people, earning the same pay. Poles wanted to feel a real break with the past, and wanted changes in management and work practices to happen faster.

> *"The economic consequences of failing to privatize quickly can already be seen in Poland."*

Just when these complaints were reaching a crescendo, Lech Walesa stepped into the fray and announced he would "speed up" the process of change, "with an axe" if need be. His blunt rhetoric frightened Warsaw intellectuals, but the general direction of his thinking was pro-privatization, rather than anti-reform (as it was sometimes portrayed). At one point during the election, he mumbled something about "giving every Pole ten million zlotys to buy shares." For this he was ridiculed. Yet the idea of giving away free shares, of allowing Poles to buy back Poland, is an acceptably populist, perfectly reasonable way to conduct some—if not all—privatization, particularly in a country where people lack the capital to buy anything, let alone shares. Giveaway plans can make privatization popular, effectively bribing people to accept economic change. But although there were people in Mazowiecki's Finance Ministry already working on such a project, Mazowiecki himself was unable to grasp the potential appeal of such programs.

> *"The focus of reform has to be on privatization and the creation of good conditions for private business, or reform will fail."*

This failure is part of why voters knocked the former prime minister out of the presidential elections in the first round. It also partly explains the success of the mysterious Peruvian-Canadian-Polish émigré businessman, Stanislaw Tyminski, who came literally from nowhere to cause his defeat. Although Tyminski went on to lose the second-round ballot to Walesa, the Tyminski phenomenon finally brought to Poland's attention the real dangers posed by failure to communicate the goals of economic reform, and in particular the failure to explain and carry out fast privatization. Setting aside the more bizarre aspects of Tyminski's biography (his obsession with Peruvian mysticism, his alleged links to former secret police), the success of his economic rhetoric among 25 percent of the Polish population is reason enough for Polish reformers to worry that the transition period will not be easy.

Appealing to Fear

For Tyminski's message focused on privatization; his words, repeated in a hypnotic monotone, seemed explicitly designed to appeal to the natural emotions—fear and envy again—surrounding ownership change. "Foreigners are buying up your best factories," he hissed at his electoral audience. "The government is betraying you, the government is selling you out, the government is selling factories to foreigners on the cheap," he said, despite the fact that foreign investment in Poland accounts for less than 2 percent of yearly production, and despite the small number of joint venture deals completed in 1990.

"The Balcerowicz Plan is a disaster, the Balcerowicz Plan is destroying Poland," was another of Tyminski's campaign mantras. This he told to uneducated miners, small town dwellers, and farmers, people who have little understanding of monetary reform, and no idea whether Tyminski, in his Western suit and Western tie, might not indeed know better. Perhaps without forethought, Tyminski brought alive their hidden anxieties about capitalism, and especially about privatization; their fear that any change might well be for the worse, their envy of those they believed were already profiting.

Playing on xenophobia and ignorance, Tyminski gathered around himself the closest thing to a counter-revolutionary force that has so far appeared in Central Europe: people who are afraid of reform, afraid of capitalism, and most of all afraid of privatization.

Yet something besides simple ignorance united Tyminski's supporters. Most (like most Poles) own nothing, let alone stocks, companies, shops, or even apartments. Without owning anything, they have no stake in the country's economic progress. Had privatization already been underway, had people already felt the beneficial effects surrounding the shift to capitalism, Tyminski's success would not have been possible. Poland's electoral debacle need never have occurred.

But I repeat: I am writing about Poland only because Poland's case is the clearest and most dramatic. Hungary, where privatization remains stalled after the first failed experiments, and Czechoslovakia, where the government is afraid to begin, will run into similar difficulties sooner or later. In the Soviet Union, fear of privatization has helped block reform altogether. In Yugoslavia, disastrous experiments with odd forms of worker ownership have led to virtual economic and political collapse.

In the West, the significance of privatization and the debate over privatization techniques in Central and Eastern Europe are often given short shrift. Living in economies dominated by private business, we are used to thinking of economic reform in terms of monetary policy or taxes. In Central Europe, these are secondary issues. The focus of reform has to be on privatization and the creation of good conditions for private business, or reform will fail, economically and politically.

Capitalism is a tough system to live in; people, fearful and envious, have to be bribed to accept it. Conducted with intelligence and political skill, privatization can become such a bribe, whether through the distribution of shares, by allowing peasants to buy their land and workers to buy their warehouse, whether through auctions, public subscriptions, and a few sales to foreigners. The mass sale of state industry represents an unprecedented political and economic opportunity for Central European governments. They must be encouraged to use it, before demagogy fills the gap where ownership should be.

> *"Capitalism is a tough system to live in; people, fearful and envious, have to be bribed to accept it."*

© The American Spectator

Stable Currencies Would Improve Eastern European Economies

by Steve H. Hanke and Kurt Schuler

About the authors: *Steve H. Hanke is a professor of applied economics at The Johns Hopkins University in Baltimore and chief economist at Friedberg Commodity Management, Inc., an investment firm in Toronto. He has advised senior government officials in Albania and Yugoslavia. Kurt Schuler is a graduate student in economics at George Mason University in Fairfax, Virginia.*

Eastern Europe and the former Soviet Union (which we shall simply call the USSR) are struggling to throw off the shackles of socialism and to embrace capitalism. To do so successfully, they must rid themselves of their unsound currencies and establish stable, convertible currencies. The "new" currencies should be convertible into one of the major international hard currencies.

The Functions of a Sound Currency

A sound currency, which is vital for a well-functioning market economy, serves as a satisfactory store of value, medium of exchange, and unit of account. An unsound currency does not fulfill any of those functions. An unsound currency is not a reliable store of value because inflation makes its value highly unpredictable. As a result, people save by hoarding bricks, timbers, food, and other commodities, which retain value better than money and other financial assets. Although commodity hoarding slows economic growth, it is rational for people in nations with unstable currencies. U.S. dollars and other stable currencies also serve as substitute stores of value in nations with unstable currencies. For example, individuals and enterprises in the USSR probably hold over $10 billion of foreign currency, which is more than the real value of the ruble money supply. "Dollarization" is costly. It requires Soviet citizens to give up real goods and services to obtain bits of paper that Western central banks print at almost no cost, generating a perverse form of foreign aid that flows from the

---

From Steve H. Hanke and Kurt Schuler, "Currency Boards for Eastern Europe," The Heritage Lectures series, no. 355. Copyright 1991 by The Heritage Foundation. Reprinted with permission.

USSR to Western central banks.

An unsound currency is not a good medium of exchange. The outside world refuses to accept it. It impedes foreign investment and trade, and hence competition and economic growth. Nor is an unsound currency a good unit of account. Inflation distorts prices and makes business calculation more difficult. Without a good unit of account, it is impossible to make meaningful accounting calculations or to write contracts. In sum, then, an unsound currency prevents important elements of a market economy from working.

> *"As long as Eastern Europe and the USSR have unsound currencies, they will be unable to transform themselves into market economies."*

Eastern Europe and the USSR have primitive financial systems that cannot intermediate efficiently between savers and investors because their currencies are unstable and inconvertible. The status of their currencies also explains why they have limited trade with the outside world. As long as Eastern Europe and the USSR have unsound currencies, they will be unable to transform themselves into market economies.

A sound, convertible currency allows people to carry out decentralized planning, which is more efficient than central planning. In nations with so-called internally convertible currencies, all that is usually required to buy goods domestically is to have currency to pay a domestic seller. Internal convertibility implies that it is not necessary to obtain authorization from any central planner to buy or sell goods that are available inside the country. The exchange of goods is much more extensive, rapid, and efficient where internal convertibility exists, as in the United States, Germany, and Poland, than where it does not, as in Albania and the USSR.

Convertibility Attracts Investment

The foreign trade counterpart of internal convertibility is external convertibility—the ability to convert as much domestic currency into foreign currency as one wishes, at market rates rather than at much higher or lower official rates. External convertibility can be unlimited, as in the major Western countries, or it can be limited, as in Czechoslovakia and Poland at present. Czechoslovakia and Poland allow most current account purchases, in which people buy foreign goods for import, but they prohibit many capital account transactions, in which people buy foreign financial assets. Current account convertibility exposes domestic producers to foreign competition and helps introduce the structure of prices that prevails in world markets. That induces a nation to specialize in making the goods it is best at producing and then trade abroad for other goods, which increases wealth all around. Capital account convertibility helps attract foreign investment, because unless foreigners can repatriate profits they will be reluctant to invest. Foreign capital investment can offset a large current account deficit and speed the introduction of urgently needed foreign goods to modernize the economy.

The ability to purchase both domestic and foreign goods readily is what makes Western currencies fully convertible "hard" currencies, and what makes them so highly prized in Eastern Europe and the USSR. To reap the full benefits of participating in world markets, Eastern Europe and the USSR themselves need to establish fully convertible currencies. Their present monetary systems are obstacles to a market economy. Inflation is in mid-double digits or higher throughout the region. In the USSR, inflation is projected to surpass 200 percent. Even in Poland, which has allowed most formerly subsidized prices to rise to market levels and has linked the zloty to the U.S. dollar, inflation remains above 40 percent per year.

Banks Lack Credibility

Inflation will remain high, even in nations that follow Poland's course, because central banks in the region have no credibility. They have long histories of bowing to political pressures for inflation. For instance, the USSR has had government currency issue since 1768, and a central bank since 1860. In all that time it has had a fully convertible currency for only 35 years, the last year being 1914. All East European central banks, except in the Baltic nations and Albania, caused hyperinflations in the 1920s, and some caused hyperinflations again in the late 1940s. The new central banks established in various former Soviet republics do not have the handicap of bad past performance to undermine their credibility, but they face other problems. So far, none has announced any definite plan for keeping its currency stable. Also, the general experience of central banks in developing nations suggests that both the established central banks and the new central banks will face ferocious political pressures for inflation. For the 99 nations that the World Bank classifies as low- and middle-income, average annual inflation was 16.7 percent from 1965 to 1980 and 53.7 percent from 1980 to 1989.

> *"To gain credibility, central banks in Eastern Europe and the USSR must painstakingly establish good track records."*

This poor performance explains why Paul Volcker, the former chairman of the U.S. Federal Reserve System, has indicated that he has little faith that central banks in Eastern Europe and the USSR can achieve full convertibility. Addressing central bankers in Jackson Hole, Wyoming, Mr. Volcker noted that markets developed long before central banks, and stressed that Eastern Europe and the USSR might actually retard their transition to markets by relying on central banks. Central banks are essentially not market institutions, which is why Marx and Engels said in the *Communist Manifesto* that one of the steps for achieving communism was "Centralization of credit in the hands of the state, by means of a national bank with state capital and an exclusive monopoly."

Chapter 4

To gain credibility, central banks in Eastern Europe and the USSR must painstakingly establish good track records. The lack of credibility of official promises has already led people throughout the region to conduct their own unofficial monetary reform. They have dollarized local economies. To the extent that dollars and other hard currencies are unavailable, some transactions are even taking place in barter, because barter is the only way for people to prevent domestic currency inflation from robbing them of their savings. The shift to barter is particularly disruptive in the USSR, where it is choking trade among republics. Making national currencies stable and convertible would revive trade among republics and among East European nations.

> *"With a stable monetary environment, Eastern Europe and the USSR would be able to successfully take the next steps towards a market economy."*

The problem of credibility has locked central banks and the public into a game that has no winners. Central bank promises to maintain currency stability, even by means of fixed exchange rates, are not credible. Prices will continue to rise quickly because workers will base their wage demands on established central banks' dismal past performance, or on well-founded skepticism of new central banks' promises of good behavior. State-owned enterprises and government ministries will likewise continue their free-spending ways, because they will correctly expect that the government will rescue them by forcing the central bank to print money, as has so often happened before. Workers and enterprises will anticipate that this "soft budget constraint" will continue, and they will behave accordingly.

Banks Must Gain Trust

If central banks in Eastern Europe and the USSR miraculously do maintain currency stability, the consequences could almost be worse than under continued inflation. Because the central banks lack credibility, people will remain skeptical of them for years. To gain credibility, the central banks will have to keep their currencies overvalued and keep real (inflation-adjusted) interest rates high. That may plunge national economies even deeper into depression. In such depressions, the export sector will suffer more than other sectors. That is what has happened in Yugoslavia, whose December 1989 currency reform was not completely credible. People correctly anticipated that the National Bank of Yugoslavia would not maintain the original fixed exchange rate, so real interest rates have exceeded 30 percent per year because the rates contained a large devaluation risk premium. A credible monetary reform that has *no* devaluation risk can keep real interest rates in single digits (for the least risky loans), as it is in the Western industrial nations, and hence can save Eastern Europe and the USSR much pain.

Eastern Europe and the USSR could make their currencies convertible by maintaining floating exchange rates rather than fixed rates. But though floating exchange rates balance supply and demand for domestic currency against foreign currency, they do not restrain central banks' powers to create credit. Instead, they are likely to lead to South American-style hyperinflations. Domestic political pressure groups representing the old order favor renewed inflation rather than stable money and prices. As inflation mounts, prices become increasingly unreliable indicators for guiding economic activity and the transition to a market economy becomes even more difficult because a market economy needs fairly stable prices to work well.

To have stable currencies, Eastern Europe and the USSR need to remove monetary policy from political influence. They need to give their monetary reforms instant credibility, to avoid the dangers of continuing inflation on the one hand and depression on the other hand. The best way to do so is to strip their central banks of currency issuing functions, and to establish *currency boards*, whose only job will be to issue convertible currencies according to strictly defined rules. Currency boards are explicitly designed to maintain a fixed exchange rate. Currency boards are easy to establish and operate, and they have *always* been able to maintain fixed-rate currency convertibility, even during the most trying times.

Currency boards would quickly establish hard domestic currencies and instill monetary confidence. As a result, economic agents would alter their expectations. If the U.S. dollar or the German mark were used as a currency board's reserve currency, workers could not raise wages and enterprises could not increase prices much beyond their rates of increase in the United States or Germany unless they achieved corresponding gains in productivity or quality. If governments in Eastern Europe and the USSR established secure property rights and removed barriers to foreign investment, interest rates would also be close to American or German levels. Under the currency board system, East European governments would have to finance themselves exclusively by taxation and borrowing, not by inflation, because a currency board cannot be an agent of government finance.

> *"Currency boards would quickly establish hard domestic currencies and instill monetary confidence."*

Restoring National Dignity

Linking domestic currencies to foreign currencies in Eastern Europe and the USSR would not subject the region to foreign political domination, as some people think. Rather, it would restore an element of national dignity by giving the region the sound currencies it now lacks. By establishing domestic currencies that are as sound as the foreign currencies to which they are linked, currency boards offer a way for domestic currency to become attractive as a store of value and to displace foreign currency from circulation. That would stop the perverse form of foreign aid that now flows from the region to Western central banks.

The cost of establishing 100 percent reserves against domestic currency and sufficient fractional reserves against deposits is surprisingly low in Eastern Europe and the USSR. At present market exchange rates, the real value of domestic currency and deposits throughout the region is small. The hard-currency reserves necessary to establish currency boards range from about $70 million for Albania to perhaps $6 billion for Poland and the USSR. Alternative estimates that claim currency boards would cost many times more are based on flawed assumptions.

Currency boards are essential to wider fiscal and economic reforms. With a stable monetary environment, Eastern Europe and the USSR would be able to successfully take the next steps towards a market economy.

Joint Ventures with Western Businesses Would Improve Eastern Europe's Economies

by Eberhard von Koerber

About the author: *Eberhard von Koerber is the executive vice president of Asea Brown Boveri Group, a German industrial firm.*

What are the incentives for Western European industry to invest in Central and Eastern Europe? Why should business take risks in countries where the unfolding of political, social and economic reform will assure instability for several years? Why not concentrate on more stable markets in the Western world?

I see three groups of opportunities for Western business in Central and Eastern Europe, and one obligation. The opportunities are:
- markets with a large potential,
- the establishment of low-cost manufacturing bases, and
- the re-establishment of links within Europe.

The obligation is:
- creating jobs in order to avoid large-scale migration from East to West.

Market Opportunities

Close to 100 million people live in Central and Eastern Europe, and another 200 million people in the European parts of the Soviet Union. Some 300 million people then, whose standard of living is far lower than that of Western Europeans. These people, who have freed themselves from the inefficiencies of the centrally planned system, want to see their standard of living increase, and increase fast.

In spite of a well-educated scientific and engineering workforce, Central and Eastern Europe spend huge amounts of resources on an aggregate Gross Domestic Product that is quite small. Look at electricity: Central and Eastern Europe generate and consume roughly the same amount of electricity that Western Europe does, but Eastern productivity is far behind Western standards. In addition, the output is produced with little concern for the environment.

Western European business can find many opportunities to help boost productivity in Central and Eastern Europe, mainly by cooperating with local industries serving domestic markets and the former COMECON region.

> *"Western European business can find many opportunities to help boost productivity in Central and Eastern Europe."*

In many parts of Central and Eastern Europe, scientists, engineers and skilled labor are all available. Compared with Western Europe, the cost of production is considerably lower and will, at least for some time, remain lower. This holds true even after considering the lower productivity of labor and capital. The establishment of manufacturing bases in the Eastern part of the continent, run according to Western standards of efficiency, will help Western European business improve its global competitiveness and is, therefore, a necessity.

New Links Needed

For more than four decades, Europe has been divided between East and West and between market economies and centrally planned economies. The opening of Central and Eastern Europe makes it possible—and the growth potential makes it mandatory—to re-establish links from East to West and vice versa. Better infrastructure is a necessary condition for spurring economic growth. Linking electricity grids between East and West, improving transportation links, in particular with modern public transport, providing satisfactory telecommunications, introducing services like banking, insurance and accounting—all are crucial pillars of the European house to be built.

But the Central and Eastern European countries are unable to simply import products and systems from the West because of their considerable foreign debt and the consequent scarcity of foreign exchange. Western companies can, however, counteract the lack of imports by mounting cooperative industrial ventures with local manufacturers.

Though Western business needs a medium-to-long-term outlook when planning the development of markets in Central and Eastern Europe, cooperation with local industry must be established now, because those Western businesses that move fastest will likely find the best partners for a long-term industrial commitment.

East-West industrial cooperation can provide employment and income in Central and Eastern Europe. Hundreds of millions of people are expecting quick and tangible results from economic reform; expectations are probably unrealistically high in many areas. To avoid increasing disappointment, Western business has a responsibility to provide jobs and income. If jobs are not provided where people live, millions might want to move West, looking for what they cannot obtain at home. The potential threat of a large-scale migration to Western Europe can, at least to a large extent, be avoided by Western business' determined move East.

The West's Role

Cooperation between Western European business and partners in the East brings together mutually supportive industrial advantages. Western business can contribute three main assets necessary to develop efficient industrial cooperation in Central and Eastern Europe:
- technology,
- management skills and training facilities, and
- finance.

Electric power generation is a good example of how the West can make a technological contribution. I have mentioned the waste of electric power in Central and Eastern Europe. There are a number of ways to reduce it.

First, saving electricity offers a large potential. Studies in Czechoslovakia estimate that between 10% and over 30% of electricity can be saved, using a number of methods well-known from Western European experience gained during the seventies and eighties.

Secondly, the modernization of existing production facilities will increase output. Repair, overhaul and better maintenance of power-generation equipment increase both yield and lifetimes of existing capacities. The combination of gas and steam turbines increases the efficiency of power stations by up to 15%, as examples in Western Europe demonstrate. Modern control systems can make power plants more efficient. District heating systems, already widely used in Central and Eastern Europe, can be expanded for both industrial and private heating.

The addition of new power-generation capacity will have second priority because with higher productivity, present capacity will suffice by and large, and even allow for exports.

Transportation is another field ripe for technological improvement. It is a key to the development of infrastructure. People want to travel in all directions; goods must be moved efficiently. It is estimated that traffic between Germany and Eastern Europe will increase fivefold until the year 2010, admittedly from a relatively low base. In order to avoid the mistakes made in Western Europe, where road and air links are close to collapse, a resolute push for public transport is necessary.

"Industrial cooperation is one of the key factors contributing to economic growth in Central and Eastern Europe."

Electric traction is clean, safe and efficient. For example, the proposed high-speed passenger train link between Vienna and Budapest would decrease traveling time to roughly one hour for the 250-kilometer distance; today, by motor car, it takes more than three hours. The distance between Berlin and Warsaw, some 550 kilometers, could be covered in something like three hours for passengers; for cargo, perhaps eight hours. The new rails necessary would use only a fraction, say 10%, of the land necessary for a motorway.

> "*Underwriting economic growth in Central and Eastern Europe requires large funds.*"

Urban transportation by electric traction, both on and under ground, could control the present congestion of capitals and other large cities in Central and Eastern Europe. In order to be an alternative to motor cars, public transport requires not only modern technologies and speed but also comfortable coaches, efficient stations and modern dispatch systems. Therefore, up-to-date products and systems must be introduced with standards comparable to the latest developments in Western Europe.

Management Training

The transfer of modern technologies to industrial partners in Central and Eastern Europe requires an environment in which new techniques are readily absorbed, disseminated and applied. Capital and human resources are available. What is required? Organization, training and Western systems.

My company runs a number of industrial joint ventures in Poland, Hungary and the Soviet Union with a staff of some 10,000 people. They are managed by local staff who are successfully trained in programs developed and run in cooperation with a European management institute.

In addition, the Asea Brown Boveri Group (ABB) has completed a training program in Germany, Switzerland and Sweden for 250 technical managers from Poland, Hungary, Czechoslovakia, Romania and Bulgaria that covered such topics as principles of the market economy, business administration and modern technologies. Another contingent of some 250 Soviet technical managers will travel to ABB operations in the same countries (plus Finland) in the Spring of 1991 for an analogue program.

Also, with the Soviet Union, we have started an exchange program for research-and-development experts. Such initiatives respond to the large program launched by former President Gorbachev to educate millions of Soviet managers, the brightest of whom will be educated in the West.

Finance

Underwriting economic growth in Central and Eastern Europe requires large funds. This has been recognized in the Western world—finance facilities amounting to more than $100 billion from official sources have been earmarked for that purpose. In addition, private markets, institutional investors and Western business will contribute to financing projects and industrial cooperation.

In order to put financing to its most efficient use, a number of conditions must be met:

• The release of various sources of finance must be coordinated, linking official, market and business funds according to established priorities.

• Finance should be directed to a maximum extent toward investment, not consumption.

• Local finance must contribute; industrial cooperation makes use of local resources and decreases the need for foreign exchange.

• Products available from industrial cooperative activities, which must be competitive on world markets, can be exported against foreign exchange.

• Requirements for foreign exchange can be further decreased by barter and offset agreements. For example, additional electricity generated by modernized power stations and fed into the European grid is a hard-currency-creating export for which there is demand in Western Europe; the links between Western and Eastern power grids can be established within one-to-two years.

• Governments in Central and Eastern Europe will have to contribute a legislative environment that is favorable for Western investment. Non-bureaucratic handling of applications for cooperation, tax incentives, investment protection, and double-taxation agreements are all necessary for both domestic and foreign partners.

Industrial cooperation is one of the key factors contributing to economic growth in Central and Eastern Europe. Joining supportive industrial potential strengths is consistent with Western and Eastern ambitions. Western business sees opportunities, has the instruments for exploiting them, and finds partners in Central and Eastern Europe who can and are willing to contribute.

Helping Eastern Europeans Adopt Free Market Policies Would Improve Their Economies

by John Brademas

About the author: *John Brademas is the president of New York University in New York City.*

In the journal *Foreign Affairs*, author William Pfaff writes:

> The radiance of Western justice and success is the power that caused the east European nations and the Soviet Union to abandon what they were and attempt to become what we, the democracies, have made of ourselves. . . . It is a moment to seize.

It is, indeed, this "moment" that brings us together—from both sides of the Atlantic; from the public and private sectors; from the worlds of business, academia, foundations and government—the moment to consider how best to encourage democracy and market reform in the newly liberated nations of Eastern and Central Europe. . . .

America's Problems

We Americans face a burgeoning array of problems of our own, from combating crime and drugs to cleaning up the environment, from fighting AIDS to dealing with homelessness, from reinvigorating a listless school system to reigniting a stalled economy.

Worse, our ability to finance the immense efforts necessary to address these troubles has progressively deteriorated. The cost of the Mid-East war, soaring toward $1 billion a day, has sharpened the contours of a deepening recession and poured kerosene on the fires of a $300 billion deficit in a Federal budget already strained by the cost of the savings and loan bailout.

From a paper given by John Brademas at a conference titled The White House on Economies in Transition: Management Training and Market Economics Education in Central and Eastern Europe, Washington, D.C., February 26, 1991. Reprinted with permission.

Europe

Despite our domestic dilemmas, we cannot ignore our obligations abroad, particularly when they embrace goals so long sought and so eminently desirable as assisting the nations of Central and Eastern Europe in setting up market-based economies and free political institutions.

What Should Be U.S. Role?

Our task, it seems to me, is to determine, in this respect, the appropriate role of the United States. Given the nature of the challenge and the limits of our financial means, I want to assert, as clearly as I can, two fundamental principles.

First, if Americans are to be effective in contributing to democratic practices and market economies in Central and Eastern Europe, we must forge in this country a creative, innovative, broad-scale partnership that will command the talents and energies of American business and industry, private foundations, colleges and universities, and the Federal government.

> *"The development of competitive economies in Central and Eastern Europe will depend . . . on how rapidly and effectively new managers can be trained."*

Second, some of the resources of that partnership must be targeted squarely on management training and education in market economics. Without knowledgeable practitioners, market economies and democratic regimes in Eastern and Central Europe can neither be successfully introduced nor developed.

The reasons we in the United States should forge such a partnership, among ourselves and with our European colleagues, must be obvious. Not the least is that at our best, Americans are champions of free peoples and open markets. Clearly, such a policy of partnership is in our national interest as a world power. And finally, a politically and economically vibrant Central and Eastern Europe affords opportunities for American business and industry. Whether trade, investment or multinational ventures, promising new fields ought not to be left solely to other industrialized countries.

We recognize, of course, that the European Community can be expected to play a major role in the transformation going on within its neighboring nations. This is natural, given proximity and history. EC involvement is also a financial imperative as the United States can provide only limited aid.

We welcome initiatives on the part of Western Europe, Japan and others. But I reiterate that I would not wish to see a resurgent Central and Eastern Europe in which the major contributions came only from Germany and Japan. The United States must be a partner, too, and a continuing presence, in the economic revival of that vital heartland.

Our contribution need not come only from the government, which is why I have urged the creation of a broad-based partnership. Nor must our participation always take the form of cash. We have much else of value to offer.

Chapter 4

As fundamental to economic development as roads, bridges, tunnels, power and communications is the indispensable element of brainpower—trained minds, skilled managers, educated leaders.

The development of competitive economies in Central and Eastern Europe will depend in no small part on how rapidly and effectively new managers can be trained and new knowledge imparted. You and I know the conceptual problems in these countries. What is a free market? How does it work? We know, too, the lack of basic skills required to operate in a market economy. How to set up a business, calculate profit and loss, perform basic accounting, establish production and marketing goals—all these functions require education and training.

Education Is Vital

In an article in *The Atlantic*, entitled, "The REAL Economy," Robert B. Reich of Harvard celebrates the crucial role of education in society. He writes:

> Increasingly, educated brainpower—along with roads, airports, computers, and fiber-optic cables connecting it up—determines a nation's standard of living. . . . In the emerging economy of the twenty-first century only one asset is growing more valuable as it is used: the problem-solving, problem-identifying, and strategic-brokering skills of a nation's citizens. . . . [I]ntellectual capital has become a uniquely important national asset.

Certainly one source of education and training in Central and Eastern Europe will be American business and industry as American firms become more actively involved there.

I note, for example, the purchase by General Electric of a half-interest in Tungsram of Budapest, a tentative agreement by General Motors to buy a plant in Slovakia, the purchase by Sara Lee of a controlling interest in Compack, third largest food company in Hungary.

> *"One source of education and training in Central and Eastern Europe will be American business and industry."*

Such acquisitions in Central and Eastern Europe bring with them both an infusion of American business management skills and education in market economics. These capabilities may be imparted either by on-the-job example or in formal training sessions set up by the companies.

Even as each corporation will tailor in-house instruction to fit its own needs, broad-gauged programs of education remain the province of colleges and universities. In the United States there are some thirty-five hundred institutions of higher learning with an enormous diversity of academic strengths. At New York University, for example, we offer courses and carry out research in subjects ranging from business to law, from the humanities to medicine, from the performing arts to computer science. And we are particularly strong in European area studies.

Here I must return to the concept of partnership, for although institutions of higher learning can supply the expertise, they are unable, as non-profit organizations, to subsidize assistance projects. Universities must depend on support from such sources as the SEED program of the Federal government.

SEED is, of course, the acronym for the Support for Eastern European Democracy Act, first passed in 1989, an initiative in which Congress had a strong role.

SEED essentially represents the commitment of the American people to helping the democracies emerging in the former Communist-controlled countries develop free political institutions and market-oriented economies. The legislation is an umbrella for a variety of assistance programs directed at housing, agriculture, environment, medicine and trade as well as private sector activities.

To carry out the purposes of SEED, Congress appropriated $370 million for fiscal 1991, an increase of $90 million from the year before. SEED projects have benefited Poland, Hungary, Czechoslovakia, Romania, Bulgaria, Yugoslavia and East Germany. This support has provided food, children's relief, humanitarian aid, parliamentary orientation, trade and business connections, water pollution control training and student exchange.

Here I note that in both the House and Senate reports accompanying the appropriations for SEED for fiscal 1991, Congress emphasized several specific uses of the funds. Among these uses was a program to provide practical business management training to the nations of Eastern Europe. Activities in both the United States and the home countries were encouraged.

The Agency for International Development—AID—and the United States Information Agency—USIA—are leading the efforts to implement SEED.

I believe colleges and universities in the United States can play a major role here.

Indeed, my own institution, New York University, through our School of Continuing Education, has launched two programs. . . .

Specifics of NYU's Program

Both our projects would be coordinated through the office of Polish Deputy Foreign Minister Antoni Kuklinski and undertaken in cooperation with the University of Poznan and the Institute of East-West Business Dynamics, an American organization formed by business, academic and public sector leaders seeking to encourage U.S. trade with the Soviet Union and Central and Eastern Europe. The Institute is chaired by a distinguished former United States Ambassador, Angier Biddle Duke.

"The race which does not value trained intelligence is doomed."

Let me describe these projects briefly.

Chapter 4

Under the first, designated "Management Training and Economics Education Program in Eastern Europe," 250 people a year, in groups of 50 each, would be brought to the United States for intensive seven-week courses on our campus. These persons would include executives, managers, union leaders, entrepreneurs, government officials, university faculty and technical school instructors. Attendees would be expected, on their return to Poland, to pass their freshly acquired know-how on to others.

This "teach the teacher" aspect makes the program not only a renewable resource but an expandable one. It can exert a tremendous multiplier effect.

Classroom lectures and workshops would cover managing, marketing, finance, law, data management and analysis. To see consumer choice functioning in the marketplace, our guests would go on field trips to retail stores, industrial suppliers, the New York Stock Exchange and a wholesale food distribution facility, among other examples of the free market system.

> *"There are massive obstacles to the establishment of parliamentary democracies and market-based economies."*

Finally, each participant would be placed in an internship with a business firm where he or she can observe a manager, owner or business professional responding to the daily demands of a competitive market.

NYU faculty members would visit Poland annually to provide follow-up instruction to those who completed the New York phase and to conduct seminars for new groups of trainees.

A permanent international computer link would be set up, making our faculty and staff available on-line to consult on market transition problems in Poland. The network could also spur the development of an electronic learning community among Polish business managers.

How-To Business Courses

Our other project would take the form of a six-week, intensive training program at the University of Poznan taught by NYU faculty. How-to-do-it techniques and modern business practices would be emphasized. The instruction would be targeted on thirty-five business school faculty and entrepreneurs in undergraduate and graduate programs, technical schools and institutes in Poland.

Here I applaud the efforts of other universities in the United States which have developed, or are developing, their own plans to offer management and marketing education in the countries of Central and Eastern Europe, and I would encourage other institutions of higher learning to do so.

Let me conclude with an observation on the public-private partnership I have so vigorously advocated and the great significance I assign to it. We all realize that after nearly three generations of command economies and authoritarian governments in Central and Eastern Europe, there are massive obstacles to the establishment of parliamentary democracies and market-based economies. To achieve these goals will be neither simple nor easy. But to do so is essential.

Surely the task of consolidating free and democratic governments in the nations of Central and Eastern Europe and transforming their economies demands the efforts of us all in this country—business and industry, foundations and universities and the Federal government—a genuine partnership.

And indispensable to the success of this partnership is . . . education.

That is why I recall the solemn words of the philosopher Alfred North Whitehead:

> In the conditions of modern life, the rule is absolute. The race which does not value trained intelligence is doomed.

Well, I do not believe our race, the human race, is doomed . . . so long as we recognize the value—indeed, the necessity—of trained intelligence and insist on the resources to support it.

Free Trade Unions Would Strengthen Eastern Europe's Economies

by Adrian Karatnycky

About the author: *Adrian Karatnycky is a special assistant to the president of the American Federation of Labor-Congress of Industrial Organizations (AFL-CIO). He is the coauthor of* The Hidden Nations: The People Challenge the Soviet Union, *and has written on Eastern European and Soviet affairs for the* Washington Post, *the* Los Angeles Times, *the* Wall Street Journal, *the* New Republic, *and other publications.*

Workers' movements have played key roles both in the establishment of communism and in its downfall. They are now also likely to play a crucial part in determining whether the postcommunist countries of Eastern Europe and the former Soviet Union can successfully establish stable democratic regimes and modern market economies.

Under communism, trade unions throughout Central and Eastern Europe and the Soviet Union were pliant institutions that served as "transmission belts" between the ruling communist party and the workers. Although they had millions of members and vast resources, such unions did not engage in strikes or collective bargaining, and did not hold democratic elections. Their leaders were often party functionaries or recruits from the ranks of management; their aims were to mobilize workers to fulfill the state plan and to enforce labor discipline. Before the upsurge in democratic worker activism that began in Poland in the summer of 1980, unions as we conceive of them in the democratic world simply did not exist in the Soviet bloc.

Worker Activism Is Essential

In most of the postcommunist countries of Europe, worker activism has been decisive in bringing about both democratic revolution and subsequent moves toward multiparty democracy and a market-based economy. The achievements of

From Adrian Karatnycky, "The Battle of the Trade Unions," *Journal of Democracy*, April 1992. Reprinted with permission.

Poland's Solidarity, the first independent mass movement to emerge and persist in what was then the Soviet bloc, have rightly been lionized. First rising to prominence under the leadership of Lech Walesa during the Gdansk shipyard strike of 1980, it survived eight years of official suppression beginning in 1981 to take part in the 1989 Roundtable negotiations that led to the demise of communist rule in Poland and touched off the stunning revolutionary events of later that year in the rest of Eastern Europe. Also worthy of mention is the Bulgarian trade union movement Podkrepa, which began in February 1989 as a tiny group of dissident workers and intellectuals, helped to bring down communist strongman Todor Zhivkov later that year, and now has over half a million members. In Czechoslovakia, a massive one-day general strike on 28 November 1989 attracted the participation of most of that country's workers and struck the crucial blow against the communist regime and in favor of Václav Havel's Velvet Revolution.

Old Unions Will Not Die

Despite the success of democratic revolutions and the collapse of communism, the new independent unions in most of Eastern and Central Europe must coexist with erstwhile "official" unions that still linger on as unwelcome legacies of communist rule. Only in Czechoslovakia, where free workers' committees leaped to preeminence on the basis of the nationwide general strike of November 1989 and seized control of the old trade union structures, is there no mass-based communist labor movement. In Bulgaria, Hungary, and Poland, the old communist unions are still larger than their democratic rivals.

Several circumstances explain this odd state of affairs. The old official unions are still in possession of vast financial and material holdings accumulated under communism; in many cases, much of their old membership sticks with them because they administer a broad range of health, vacation, and social benefits. Moreover, for many workers and democratic leaders, the very idea of trade unions has been badly tainted by association with the communist *apparat*. Finally, despite the crucial role that workers played in toppling communism, democratic leaders have all too often placed worker concerns near the bottom of their agenda as they grapple with the immense challenges of economic and political reform.

"Trade unions are once again taking center stage in the emerging democracies of the East."

Democratic governments and legislators have simply not assigned union reform a high priority, meaning that the sort of free elections which led to a thorough cleansing of national and local governments has not yet been reproduced on the postcommunist trade union scene. The delay, of course, has given the old communist union bosses some breathing space.

Today, trade unions are once again taking center stage in the emerging democracies of the East. Amid conditions of rising unemployment, declining industrial production, high inflation, and general economic depression, the way in which workers respond to change will be crucial to the stability of democratic governance. The rapid shift to markets has proved far more difficult than many free-market enthusiasts imagined. Two years after communism's fall in Central and Eastern Europe, blue-collar workers and their allies in the intelligentsia—the shock troops of the anticommunist opposition—are the big economic losers of the democratic revolution. The very workers' movements that led the way to democratic change are now often sharing blame for the economic policies of the governments that they helped put into place, but whose policies they do not control.

The new democratic unions must now gird themselves to face concerted attacks from the old communist unions. Democratic unions must balance their deep commitment to the stability of free popular government with their duty to represent the interests of their members, many of whom are paying a heavy price for reforms made necessary by decades of communist economic misrule. The rival communist unions have no such inhibitions. They can freely attack established democratic governments, attempt to incite strikes and protests, and seek to exploit popular economic discontent for the purpose of undermining democracy itself.

> *"The new democratic unions must now gird themselves to face concerted attacks from the old communist unions."*

Developments in Eastern Europe

The postcommunist trade union scene varies widely from country to country. In Poland, Solidarity has been home to the political leaders of the country's first three postcommunist democratic governments. As 1992 began, the union was abandoning its initial stance in favor of wage restraint and radical free-market reform, and several of its industrial branches had launched strikes. On January 13, the union held a one-hour warning strike that was supported by some 80 percent of Solidarity locals. This action came in response to electricity and heating-oil price hikes that were imposed without legally mandated consultations with the trade unions. Public opinion in general has also shifted in a direction similar to Solidarity's on the questions of rapid privatization and free trade. Both policies are now supported by only a quarter of the Polish people, while fully half support government subsidies to protect endangered state industries.

Surprisingly, Solidarity's defense of worker interests evoked sympathy from Prime Minister Jan Olszewski, a lawyer who defended many union activists during martial law and the underground period. Olszewski has suggested that if Solidarity had shown less self-restraint in defending the economic interests of its members in recent years, his government's task of negotiating with the union would now be easier. Arrayed against Solidarity's 2.5 million members is the All-Polish Trade Union Alliance (OPZZ), a trade union grouping established by communist authorities after the declaration of martial law in December 1981. OPZZ claims over 4 million members and remains firmly in the hands of ex-communist leaders. A third player is the radical Solidarity 80 trade union, a splinter group that broke with Lech Walesa in 1989. Solidarity 80 has a strong base in the port city of Szczecin and claims around 100,000 members. Both of these groups have led vocal protests against government economic policies since the autumn of 1991.

> *"Free trade unions clearly are important actors in the transition to democracy in virtually all postcommunist countries."*

In Bulgaria, the main rival of Podkrepa is the Confederation of Independent Trade Unions of Bulgaria (CITUB), an ex-communist movement boasting between one and two million members that has sought to distance itself from the communists (who now call themselves the Bulgarian Socialist Party). In the parliamentary elections of October 1991, CITUB worked closely with the Bulgarian Social Democratic Party, which won less than 5 percent of the vote. The strike that CITUB launched in January 1992 to protest the confiscation of much of its property fizzled and came under strong criticism from Podkrepa, which supported the confiscation of all union property retained from the period of communist rule. In January 1992, Podkrepa's chairman Konstantin Trenchev demanded the resignation of Bulgaria's ministers of finance and industry, who he claimed were guilty of pursuing ill-considered economic reforms and refusing to consult with the democratic labor movement. Originally highly supportive of economic "shock therapy," Trenchev and Podkrepa have gradually moved to a more nuanced position that supports state intervention to save potentially profitable industries and to provide a social safety net for the most vulnerable. Significantly, because of the union's longstanding defense of the rights of all ethnic groups, Podkrepa enjoys a close relationship with Bulgaria's large Turkish minority. Candidates endorsed by the union represent at least one-third of the governing United Democratic Front's parliamentary bloc.

Czech Unions

In March 1990, the Czechoslovak free labor leadership that had orchestrated the general strike of the preceding November succeeded in wresting control of the trade union movement away from the communists and established the Czech and Slovak Confederation of Trade Unions (CSKOS). Since its inception, CSKOS has shown social democratic leanings: its founding congress reserved its warmest applause for a speech by Valtr Komarek, then a government minister and now a social democratic opponent of Finance Minister Václav Klaus's free-market approach. The union movement's criticism of Klaus has been very sharp. In November 1991 the metalworkers' union KOVO held a one-day strike by 380,000 members, who were joined by additional hundreds of thousands of workers in education, machine building, metallurgy, mining, and retailing. Today, the Czech trade unions of CSKOS enjoy a close, albeit informal, working relationship with the Social Democratic party. In Slovakia, the unions appear to be closest to the Movement for a Democratic Slovakia, led by former Slovak prime minister Vladimir Meciar. A small communist trade union exists in Slovakia, but has almost no influence on political life. On 26 December 1991, a new labor organization called the Christian Trade Unions of Slovakia was formed. It is independent, but enjoys strong encouragement from the republic's ruling Christian Democratic Movement.

Unions Popular in Hungary

In Hungary, where workers were less active in the struggle for democracy, communist or ex-communist dominance of the trade union scene persists. The postcommunist National Council of Hungarian Trade Unions (MSzOSz) claims a membership of over 1.5 million. The chief free trade unions are grouped under the Democratic League of Independent Trade Unions (LIGA), with a membership of over 275,000, and the Workers' Council, with 100,000 members. In July 1991, after a long campaign by LIGA and the Workers' Council, the Hungarian parliament passed the most wide-ranging trade union reform legislation yet seen in the former Soviet bloc. The new law froze the assets of the old official unions and ordered free union elections within one year. Public-opinion research done in late 1991 suggests that the democratic unions will win the support of over 50 percent of Hungary's workers in these elections, which are designed to determine the reallocation of trade union assets. If these poll results prove correct, the LIGA David will have scored a remarkable victory over the MSzOSz Goliath, with its huge professional staff, deep coffers, and extensive trade union press.

In Albania, where the old communist *apparat* remains in firm control, the free trade unions are the largest mass movement pressing for democratic change. Since its founding in February 1991, the Democratic Alliance of Independent Trade Unions of Albania (BSPSh), with a membership of

> *"Communist or ex-communist dominance of the trade union scene persists."*

300,000, has become an active and visible presence in the campaign for democratic reform. In January 1992, a BSPSh rally voiced strong criticisms of the communist-dominated government. Tens of thousands of trade unionists gathered to call for the indexation of wages to rising food prices, the implementation of a social assistance law, and the removal from power of the communist old guard. The rally was addressed by several former political prisoners. Within weeks of the protest, the leaders of the Albanian Democratic Party left the Socialist Party-dominated government.

In Romania, the trade union scene mirrors the complexity and factionalization of national politics. There is a multiplicity of unions, the largest of which is the formerly official Confederation of Independent Romanian Trade Unions (CNSLR), which claims over two million members. Trade unions that emerged after the collapse of the Ceausescu regime include FRATIA (500,000-800,000 members); the ALFA Cartel, a union confederation representing industrial workers (up to one million members); FIDES, a union of teachers, doctors, and other white-collar workers (several hundred thousand members); and the Fifteenth of November Confederation, a democratic group launched in Brasov (250,000 members). In recent months, most of the new trade unions have expressed sharp criticism of the ruling National Salvation Front and of President Ion Iliescu. Several of the unions backed a democratic opposition coalition during municipal elections in February 1992.

A Rare Source of Democracy

Today, free trade unions clearly are important actors in the transition to democracy in virtually all postcommunist countries. Because East European societies have little recent tradition of democratic participation and because the security *apparat* long hampered the development of civil society, free trade unions are among the few ready sources of new leaders for emerging democracies.

> *"Democratic unions have been at the forefront of the fight to strip the old communist nomenklatura of its privileged position in the emerging market system."*

On the economic front, democratic trade unions in Central and Eastern Europe have displayed diverse responses to the problems posed by economic transformation. Initially, unions like Poland's Solidarity and Bulgaria's Podkrepa were strong advocates of rapid and radical moves toward markets and privatization. More recently, in the midst of prolonged economic depression, these unions have begun to urge increased state intervention. In Albania, the BSPSh is pressing for the rapid privatization of agriculture and attacking the holdover Socialist Party's sabotaging of land reform. In the Czech and Slovak Federative Republic, free trade unions generally favor a gradual move toward the market, but have strenuously rejected what they regard as extreme free-market policies. In Hungary, democratic unions have adopted a similarly moderate position.

The transition to markets and democracies in Eastern and Central Europe would prove a far more daunting project without these mass-based anticommunist forces to help it along. Democratic unions have been at the forefront of the fight to strip the old communist *nomenklatura* of its privileged position in the emerging market system. They have pressed for the confiscation and privatization of communist property and have been vocal proponents of worker participation as shareholders in privatization efforts. . . .

The active intervention of free trade unions will be essential in ensuring that the burdens of the transition from statism to the market will be equitably distributed within the emerging democracies of the old Soviet bloc. Because they took part in the struggle for democratic change, free trade unions are likely to be strong mass-based guarantors of the strength and endurance of the new democracies. Trade unions, a once neglected outpost of the democratic struggle, are likely to remain at center stage as the democratic transition unfolds in Eastern Europe.

Tax Reform Would Strengthen Eastern Europe's Economies

by William D. Eggers

About the author: *William D. Eggers is a policy analyst at The Heritage Foundation, a conservative think tank in Washington, D.C.*

In the wake of their successful revolutions, Eastern Europe's new democracies now face fundamental decisions that will decide their economic destinies. One of the most important is the choice of new tax systems to replace those inherited from communist regimes. Under communism, East European governments supported themselves mainly by raking off revenues from state-owned industries. Today, as these countries make the transition from communist to market economies, they need new tax policies designed to promote economic growth through the expansion of private enterprise.

So far, East Europeans have been inclined to follow the example of West European states which, by and large, tax their citizens at some of the world's highest rates. These systems are designed to fund social welfare states rather than to spur economic growth. This approach has not worked particularly well in Western Europe—where it has failed to deliver on its promise of social justice and has ensured sluggish economies—and it would be disastrous in Eastern Europe.

If East European governments impose a heavy tax burden on struggling businesses and suffering consumers, the growth of these countries' nascent free market economies will slow down, perhaps leading to further social and political upheaval. This would not be in the interests of East Europeans, or of Americans, who have a strong interest in the stability of the region's new democratic governments.

Asian Nations Set Example

In contrast to the high tax systems, there are pro-growth tax models for East Europeans to follow. Examples are the dynamic "tigers" of East Asia. These are

From William D. Eggers, "A Pro-Growth Tax Reform Agenda for Eastern Europe," The Heritage Foundation *Backgrounder*, May 23, 1991. Reprinted with permission.

Hong Kong, Singapore, South Korea and the Republic of China on Taiwan. They can attribute much of their economic success to low tax policies, which encourage investment, improved goods and services and hard work. Further, these countries have much higher rates of job creation and lower rates of unemployment than countries with high taxes. These tigers also have some of the most equitable income distributions in the developing world. The message is clear: low-tax economies grow faster than high-tax economies.

> *"Taxes on business are now so high throughout Eastern Europe that businesses are driven underground to operate in the informal, or gray, economy."*

In Eastern Europe, overall tax levels, tax rates, and the tax mix among business, personal income and other levies will play a major role in deciding whether these countries quickly catch up to the industrialized world, or further impoverish themselves. Right now, East Europeans are getting advice on tax reform from many quarters, including the International Monetary Fund (IMF) and other financial institutions. These institutions can have tremendous sway in Czechoslovakia, Poland and other countries since they impose certain policy requirements on recipient countries in exchange for loans. But the advice offered by international financial organizations may be wrong. The IMF, for instance, has pressured Argentina, Brazil, Chile and the Philippines to increase rather than to decrease taxes.

The United States can help East Europeans resist pressures to impose burdensome high-tax policies. Washington should use its influence with the IMF and other international financial institutions to encourage them to back low-tax/high-growth policies in Eastern Europe. Mostly, however, the U.S. can offer expertise and advice in helping East Europeans to restructure their tax systems. . . .

Taxes and Revenues

Government officials in Eastern Europe are rightly concerned about raising enough money to balance their budgets and run the government. They worry that cutting the high tax rates will cause budget deficits and insufficient revenues to provide essential government services.

These concerns are ill founded; only by cutting taxes will East European countries be able to generate steady increases in government revenues. There are two reasons for this. The first reason is that taxes on business are now so high throughout Eastern Europe that businesses are driven underground to operate in the informal, or gray, economy where they pay no taxes. This deprives the government of substantial revenues. Only by significantly cutting taxes on businesses can the governments induce private businesses to enter the formal, legal economy and pay taxes.

The second reason why lower tax rates ultimately can mean higher government revenues in Eastern Europe is that tax cuts stimulate economic growth.

This means that there are more incomes and production to tax. This, after all, is what happened in America in the 1980s. The Reagan tax cuts, inspired in part by the economic studies of economists such as Arthur Laffer, ignited economic growth and increased federal revenues. (The federal deficit grew only because federal spending increases outpaced the revenue gains.) The result: the longest peacetime economic expansion in U.S. history, a 31 percent increase in the tax base, and significant growth in real tax revenues.

The Evidence Mounts

Substantial evidence collected over the past decade supports the proposition of Laffer, Gerald Scully and others that high taxes stifle economic growth and low taxes encourage growth. A seminal 1983 study for the World Bank by economist Keith Marsden examines the relationship between economic growth and taxation in twenty countries during the 1970s. Ten of these countries imposed high tax burdens on their citizens, and ten had low tax levels. Without exception the countries with lower tax burdens had faster growth in employment, investment and productivity, and even in government services. All had higher rates of overall economic growth.

> *"It may be possible for the countries of Eastern Europe either to avoid income taxes altogether, or to impose very low, simple income taxes."*

Among the more interesting of Marsden's findings: investment grew at nearly 9 percent in low-tax countries, but declined by 0.8 percent in high-tax countries. Strong private sector investment is critical to economic growth because it finances factory modernization, technological breakthroughs, entrepreneurial firms and other important elements of a dynamic economy. Marsden found that high taxes imposed directly on business income were particularly destructive to investment. According to his study, every 1 percent increase in corporate income tax relative to Gross Domestic Product (GDP) led to a 2 percent decrease in the growth rate of investment. . . .

Low Taxes, Low Pay

East Europeans cannot make the transition from poverty-stricken command economies to prosperous, free market economies unless they dismantle the tax systems inherited from four decades of communism and replace them with new systems conducive to economic growth. The systems of taxation employed in communist economies simply do not work in market economies. In communist countries, virtually all business enterprises are owned by the government. Taxation mostly is a matter of the government transferring money from the accounts of its own enterprises to other accounts earmarked for government expenditures. In effect, most taxes are paid by the state to the state.

Taxes in communist countries can take various forms. One is the payroll tax.

Chapter 4

This often is levied on the payrolls of state enterprises and private companies in lieu of taxing workers' incomes directly. This method is meant to give the illusion that workers pay no taxes. Of course, all it really means is that taxes are taken out in the form of lower salaries. Another ploy is the profits tax. State-owned enterprises or private businesses typically pay tax rates between 40 and 85 percent on profits.

A third major revenue source is the turnover tax, which is like a sales tax except that it is levied at thousands of different rates depending on the product. In communist countries, the turnover tax really is just the difference between the price consumers pay for goods and the one retail outlets pay to wholesalers. It functions in raising revenue and in assisting the state in setting prices.

The one advantage to communist taxation is that without a history of high income taxes, it may be possible for the countries of Eastern Europe either to avoid income taxes altogether, or to impose very low, simple income taxes.

Low Grades on Tax Reform

The need for fundamental tax reform in Eastern Europe is urgent. As state enterprises are allowed to fail or to become private companies, tax revenues from the state-owned sector, the main source of revenue under communist tax systems, will tumble. Moreover, if newly privatized firms continue to be taxed at the astronomically high rates now imposed on state enterprises, they will not be able to accumulate the profits needed to invest in new plant and machinery, pay higher wages and compete on world markets.

Despite the widespread recognition that fundamental change is in order, there is no consensus on whether Eastern Europe's new tax systems will follow a low-tax/high-growth model, or a high-tax/low-growth model. Based on the reforms instituted so far, East European governments seem to be heading toward high-tax disaster....

If East Europeans are to jump start their moribund economies, they need a major overhaul of their tax systems. Old communist tax systems should be dismantled. An aggressive, pro-growth tax agenda is needed to eliminate excessive taxes on business, simplify tax codes and minimize government interference with the workings of Eastern Europe's nascent free markets.

There will be opposition to this program. The foremost impediment is likely to be a strong redistributionist impulse left over from decades of communism. There will be enormous pressure on legislators to adopt heavily progressive income taxes, wealth taxes and high corporate income taxes.

> *"Income taxes are the most anti-growth of all taxes."*

These pressures must be resisted and the arguments strongly rebutted. Many governments worldwide have gone the high-tax route, often trying to soak the rich in the hope of helping the poor. They have succeeded only in keeping everyone poor. Economic growth is the best way for East European countries to raise themselves out of poverty. The tax systems of Eastern Europe should be structured to promote growth.

America can help, mostly by offering expertise and advice. America also can use its influence with the IMF and World Bank to prevent these institutions from luring Eastern Europe down the high-tax path. George Bush should offer as an alternative America's own Pro-Growth Tax Reform agenda for Eastern Europe. The agenda:

> *"The emerging market economies in Eastern Europe cannot afford to punish people for making the economy stronger by saving and investing."*

Point No. 1: Avoid steeply rising so-called "progressive" income taxes; impose a low flat-rate personal income tax.

Income taxes are the most anti-growth of all taxes. They reduce savings, cut the incentive to work, and thereby lower economic output and growth. If possible, income taxes should be avoided altogether and government revenues should be financed by such other means as user fees for government services and taxes on consumption. The development of tax systems without, or with very low, income taxes on individuals may be politically feasible in Eastern Europe, since income taxes were not a major component of the communist tax systems these countries are trying to replace. Rising marginal tax rates, which tax higher earnings at progressively higher rates, are the most damaging of all income taxes.

Benefits of a Flat Tax

There is an alternative to rising, marginal tax rates on individuals: a low flat income tax. It could be levied at a rate of 15 percent or under. Only wages and salaries would be taxed. To minimize the tax's impact on economic growth, no taxes would be paid on any personal income earned as interest from savings or capital gains from investments. There would be no exceptions or deductions. A flat tax has numerous advantages over rising marginal taxes. Among them:

• *Simplicity.*

Progressive income taxes tend to be complicated, typically including many deductions, exemptions and depreciations. The governments of Eastern Europe have neither the money, the qualified accountants or the administrative structure to process millions of complicated individual income tax returns. As a result, most income taxes will go uncollected. The flat tax avoids these problems. Employers would withhold the flat tax from the worker's income; each individual would fill out only a few lines on a postcard-size form once a year confirming the amount of withholding. Taxpayers could claim personal exemptions for themselves and their dependents.

• *Higher incentive to work.*

Chapter 4

Increasing marginal tax rates discourage people from earning that extra dollar since they know that less of it will be theirs and more will belong to the government. A flat tax does not penalize added income, and therefore encourages work. More work ultimately means more and improved goods and services.

Boosting the Economy

• *Increased savings and investment.*

The emerging market economies in Eastern Europe cannot afford to punish people for making the economy stronger by saving and investing. By exempting savings from taxation, the flat tax on income will encourage investment and stimulate economic growth. It also will keep capital in Eastern Europe, to be invested at home, instead of flowing to other parts of the world where it might be taxed at lower rates.

• *No "bracket creep."*

In inflationary environments—temporarily unavoidable in post-communist countries because prices, controlled for decades, must rise to their market levels—progressive tax rates cause a phenomenon termed "bracket creep." Bracket creep occurs when people are forced into higher tax brackets owing to inflation, rather than to income increases. Bracket creep was a major cause of America's "stagflation" in the 1970s, when there were high levels of unemployment and high inflation. The flat-rate tax eliminates bracket creep since there only is one tax bracket.

> *"The flat-rate tax eliminates bracket creep since there only is one tax bracket."*

• *Fairness.*

Flat taxes strictly limit the tax burden on poor families. By taxing everyone at the same rate, the rich still pay more because their incomes are higher. Further, wealthier individuals may in some cases pay a higher percentage of their incomes to taxes once personal and family allowances are considered. Example: A family of four with an annual income of $8,000 claims a $1,000 personal allowance for each family member; this family pays taxes on $4,000, which at a 15 percent flat rate equals $600, or 7.5 percent of total family income. A family of four with an income of $16,000, however, pays $1,800 after allowances, or 11.3 percent of family income.

Point No. 2: Cut tax burdens on business; adopt a flat business tax that exempts capital investment.

Without exception, East European countries impose very high tax burdens on private businesses. Examples: Czechoslovakia has a 60 percent tax rate on profits; private businesses in Hungary are forced to pay social security taxes at five times the rate of state-owned enterprises. These taxes—higher than in America, Western Europe or among the Asian tigers—put East European countries at a strong competitive disadvantage. Business taxes in Eastern Europe must be lower than those in the West if technologically backward and inefficient East European businesses are to compete with the West.

Most business expansion and job creation takes place in small- and medium-sized companies. High business taxes rob these firms especially of the capacity to expand. Reason: Most smaller businesses finance expansion through their own savings and by reinvesting their profits. High taxes on savings and profits mean businesses can hire fewer workers, purchase fewer raw materials and tools, and thus produce fewer goods and services....

Point No. 3: Be wary of the Value Added Tax.

Most East European countries are planning to adopt the VAT [value added tax] in part because they wish eventually to join the European Community (EC), and the VAT is an important part of the EC's harmonized tax system. East Europeans should approach the VAT gingerly. The VAT should be considered only in lieu of an income tax on individuals and corporations, not in addition to these taxes. As Hungary's experience already shows, the imposition of a VAT on top of new income taxes imposes a tremendous tax burden on a country's citizens. The result is predictable: economic growth is lowered and tax evasion increases.

Political Measures Also Necessary

Political safeguards, meanwhile, are needed to ensure that the VAT does not become an ever expanding government money machine. One safeguard would be to require a two-thirds majority of parliament to approve any VAT rate increase. Or, governments could require any increases in the VAT rate to be approved by public referendum.

To reduce the VAT's administrative burdens, the same rate should be levied on all goods. In Western Europe different VAT rates apply to different products. This can create bookkeeping nightmares for small businesses. A uniform VAT rate applied to all items would eliminate these problems....

Point No. 4: Do not impose high tariffs to discourage imports.

The eternal rationale of protectionists is that high tariffs protect local industries and jobs from foreign competition. In fact, tariffs are very destructive to local economies. High tariffs hurt consumers because they have to pay more for foreign goods, which are taxed at a higher rate. They also pay more for domestic goods because competition to local industries from foreign producers is reduced, allowing the local industries to charge higher prices and become sluggish and inefficient. Domestic businesses, too, are hurt by high tariffs; they are forced to pay higher prices for imported supplies and raw materials to produce goods. This, in turn, makes them less competitive on international markets, decreasing exports.

> *"Protectionist measures designed to keep out foreign goods ultimately keep out investment, too."*

Chapter 4

The domestic economy as a whole is hurt by protection because capital and labor are diverted away from their most efficient uses, and move instead toward the production of goods needed to replace lost imports. This process, known as "import substitution," damages local economies because it drains resources from the industries and services in which a country is most competitive. Result: Prices go up; locally produced goods become less competitive on international markets; unemployment increases; and economic growth suffers.

Protectionist measures designed to keep out foreign goods ultimately keep out investment, too, since declining growth rates induced by protectionism mean decreased opportunities for profitable investments from abroad. Import quotas and other non-tariff trade barriers should be eliminated; tariffs should be eliminated, or at least kept at the lowest possible levels.

Point No. 5: Where possible, finance government operations with user fees.

User fees can finance a wide range of government operations. A common user fee in America and Western Europe is the toll charged to motorists for the use of some highways. People are not forced to pay for roads they may never use. Fees also can be charged for the use of libraries and public parks, for garbage collection, or to land on airport runways. By increasing the use of user fees in lieu of taxes, countries can increase the probability that only those government projects and services that are economically justified will be undertaken. Reason: If there are not enough users to finance the operating costs of the government service, then the operation will not be provided.

After years in the economic shackles of communism, Eastern Europe is struggling to free itself from state control and to build strong, free market economies. Eastern Europe has tremendous economic potential. Its greatest asset is a highly educated, skilled and energetic population; but for decades this tremendous human resource was locked up under tight state control. With these controls lifted, East Europeans can in time raise themselves to the economic levels of the West.

The success of this effort in part will depend on whether old, communist tax systems are redesigned in a way that spurs economic growth. For this, East European countries should tax individuals and corporations at very low rates, leaving them with more time and money to devote to creating wealth and raising themselves out of poverty. Time and again around the world—from Hong Kong to America—experience demonstrates that lower taxes equal economic growth. Eastern Europe would do well to heed the message.

> *"Experience demonstrates that lower taxes equal economic growth."*

Chapter 5

What Role Will International Organizations Play in Europe's Future?

Chapter Preface

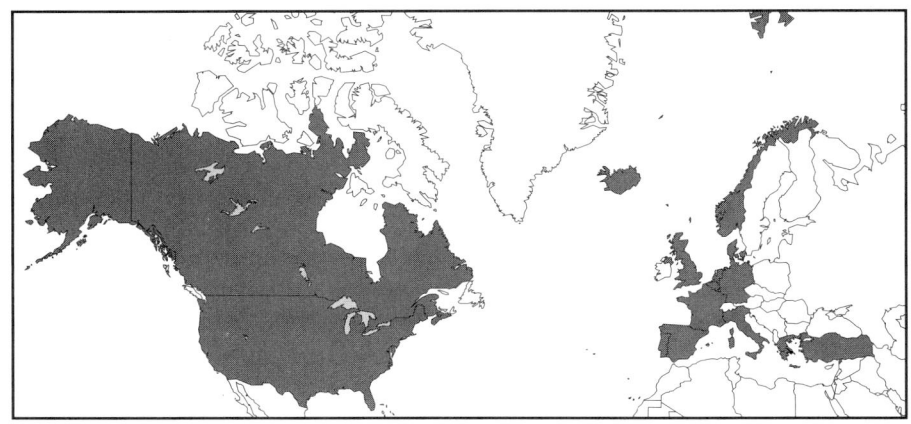

NATO Member Countries

Belgium	Germany	Luxembourg	Spain
Canada	Greece	the Netherlands	Turkey
Denmark	Iceland	Norway	United Kingdom
France	Italy	Portugal	United States

Many international organizations and alliances are active in Europe today. Some of these organizations were founded after World War II, before the demise of the USSR and the unification of Germany. Others have formed relatively recently in response to economic changes in Europe. What role these organizations will play in the new Europe or whether they should continue to remain active at all has become an issue of debate.

For example, NATO, the North Atlantic Treaty Organization, was created in 1949 as a collective defense alliance linking Canada and the United States with fourteen European countries. Its primary goal was to counter and abolish Communist aggression. Today, many experts argue that NATO is obsolete. B.J. Cutler, a foreign affairs columnist, agrees, arguing that NATO has come to the end of its useful life and that Europe's security should be Europe's responsibility. Doug Bandow, a scholar and writer on foreign affairs, states that NATO's cost

Europe

to American taxpayers of $130 million a year is excessive and wasteful. He believes NATO should be phased out of existence by the end of the century.

Supporters of NATO, however, argue that it is still viable. NATO supplies Europe with a united defense strategy that continues to benefit the world. According to former U.S. secretary of defense Caspar Weinberger, NATO enabled the United States to "field a unified highly effective military force in a matter of days" during the Persian Gulf crisis.

Europe is in the midst of change. NATO is only one of many international organizations that have shown an interest in participating in Europe's continuing efforts toward unification. The following articles debate whether or not international organizations benefit Europe in its struggle toward peace and cooperation.

International Organizations Can Help Maintain Peace in Europe

by Uffe Ellemann-Jensen

About the author: *Uffe Ellemann-Jensen is the minister of foreign affairs for Denmark.*

Europe—and the world—is presently undergoing tremendous changes. The Communist dictatorships in Eastern and Central Europe have been replaced by new states based on core values which, three years ago, could only have been described as Western—democracy, respect for human rights and the rule of law.

The challenges facing us after the upheavals in Eastern Europe are immense. At times, the situation may even seem so confused and the future so incalculable that we catch ourselves longing for the order and predictability of Europe of not so long ago, at least until we remember on what principles this order was based.

Integration and Cohesion

As a small country situated adjacent to the young democracies of Eastern Europe, Denmark is particularly sensitive to the potential security consequences emanating from the new situation. These fragile democracies may not be sufficiently firmly grounded to resist the threat of instability posed by the sudden unleashing of forces that were suppressed under Communist rule.

However, though the future may be incalculable, the state of things is anything but lamentable. For the first time since the second world war, Europe is free of the constraints of fixed action patterns resulting from ideological rivalries. What we are faced with, then, are the opportunities of a lifetime that we simply cannot afford to miss, and responsibilities to the peoples of Europe and their future generations that oblige us to act and to do so now.

How, then, do we handle this precarious situation that, on the one hand, holds out promises of a new and better-cooperating Europe but, on the other, might

---

Uffe Ellemann-Jensen, "The New Europe—A Danish View," *NATO Review*, vol. 40, no. 1, February 1992. Reprinted with permission.

apparently just as well degenerate into a chaos of uncontrollable ethnic and national conflicts? In my opinion there is only one answer: we must summon all our collective energy and make every possible effort to establish close and mutually committing ties between the *old* Europe, where democracy and political stability are deeply ingrained, and the countries that are only just setting out along this perilous road. Integration and cohesion will be the catchwords in the years to come.

> *"We must summon all our collective energy and make every possible effort to establish close and mutually committing ties."*

No single nation—European or otherwise—is capable of shouldering this responsibility by itself. We in Europe cannot merely assume a passive stance, confidently expecting that our American allies will eventually pull our chestnuts out of the fire as they have done so many times before. Most Europeans, I am sure, acknowledge that the reconstruction of our continent is a task mainly to be performed by the Europeans themselves.

On the other hand, it would be fatally wrong to perceive the European predicament as only a regional matter. European and global security are two sides of the same coin. A Europe fraught with national and ethnic conflicts but without integrating institutions and frameworks to deal with matters peacefully, is simultaneously a potential hotbed of totalitarianism and armed confrontations that might well escalate to pose a threat to world peace.

Redefining Functions

In these circumstances, the adaptability and sense of responsibility of organizations in Europe's institutional landscape like NATO, the European Community, and the CSCE (the Conference on Security and Cooperation in Europe) become matters of vital importance. These institutions were all instrumental in maintaining the kind of peace and stability that reigned on our continent before the Iron Curtain started rusting away. And they still do. However, as the environment of these organizations changes, so do their assignments and role in the European security architecture.

It has been particularly gratifying to note how swiftly NATO has proved itself capable of reacting in this respect. The NATO Summit in Rome in November 1991 was in itself a milestone—not only in the history of the Alliance but also on the arduous road towards comprehending and adjusting to the requirements of the new age.

The new strategic concept of our Alliance is a case in point. While reaffirming its indispensable military dimension, NATO broadened its approach by fully taking into account the fact that stability and security include a wide range of political, economic, social and environmental aspects. Thus in the future, purely political means to enhance the security of Europe will acquire a more conspicuous role as a supplement to the Alliance's military capability.

Recognizing that we no longer face the threat of a massive, possibly nuclear, attack on our territory, such adjustments may seem only natural. However, to my knowledge no military alliance has ever before voluntarily accepted such a drastic reformulation of its core functions. Indeed, NATO deserves to be commended for its open-mindedness and determination in this respect. Likewise, the decision to intensify relations with the countries of Central and Eastern Europe, not so long ago the likely adversaries of the Alliance, can rightly be characterized as a qualitative leap forward in our way of thinking about security.

Statements from a large number of political leaders of countries that formerly belonged to the Warsaw Pact, testify to the fact that these countries look to NATO to safeguard Europe from disintegration and armed conflicts. At the moment, it is still premature to extend formal security guarantees to these countries and include them in the Alliance itself. What we can do, however, is demonstrate that as far as we are concerned, Europe is a whole in terms of security policy. It is the fate of all of Europe that concerns us—not only the short-term safety of the allied countries.

Framework for All of Europe

I believe that our decision to form a North Atlantic Cooperation Council (NACC), that serves as a framework for consultations between the foreign ministers of the Alliance and their colleagues from the former Communist countries in Eastern Europe, is particularly useful in this respect. This institution is certain to endow the latter with a sense of belonging.

Equally, we should stress that the reason for our preoccupation with the plight of these newly democratized countries is not an obligation that we would rather shirk. Our initiative to found the NACC was not a mere act of grace designed to stave off more committing relations with these countries. Instead, an institutional relationship of consultation and cooperation in political and security issues is an absolute necessity to us all. The boat may seem to be leaking at their end but since we are all on board the same vessel it is a matter of no less concern and gravity to us than to them.

NATO's role and assignments, however, are not exclusively of a political nature. In a Europe where peace and stability for many years to come will be fragile, the military dimension of the Alliance cannot be left to languish. However, in the light of the qualitatively different threat to the Alliance posed by the disintegration

> *"The reconstruction of our continent is a task mainly to be performed by the Europeans themselves."*

tendencies in Europe, adaptations are necessary to allow for more rapid deployment of forces in reaction to a wider range of contingencies than before. The transformation towards smaller but more flexible force structures, also decided at the Rome Summit, goes a long way towards meeting these requirements.

Fortunately, we need not expect NATO alone to meet the challenges facing Europe. The European Community and the CSCE in various ways complement the role of the Alliance, thus contributing to a structure of interlocking security institutions. The European Community is a vital ingredient in the recipe for a safer new Europe. Shortly before Christmas 1991, the 12 member states reached agreement on our hitherto most ambitious project: a European Union entailing concerted action in fields as diverse as economic policy and foreign and security policy.

Assisting Eastern Europe

However advantageous the new Union may be expected to prove to be for each of its member states individually, its primary asset is its contribution to stability and peace in Europe. To put it bluntly: without a politically and economically strong Union as the anchor of Europe, there is every reason to fear that the young democracies of the continent will be left to drift before the wind, thereby being exposed to a degree of instability eventually affecting the security interests of Europe as a whole.

The European Community is acutely aware of what might happen if poverty comes in through the door of its neighbours to the East. History has shown us that frail democracies combined with material want may pave the way for totalitarianism and jingoism. These countries to a large extent depend on the EC as purchasers of their products—and occasional benefactors when all else goes amiss. Recently, association agreements were concluded with Hungary, Poland and Czechoslovakia. The EC has provided aid to help the inhabitants of St. Petersburg and Moscow. And the policy of the new Union will reflect this awareness to an even greater extent. More and more countries in Eastern Europe will obtain association agreements with the European Union in the years to come. And I would not be surprised if the Union by the year 2000 numbers a few of these countries as full members.

"It is the fate of all of Europe that concerns us—not only the short-term safety of the allied countries."

This is but one dimension of the Union's contribution to the security of the new Europe. Equally interesting is the potential for close cooperation and joint action envisaged in the field of security policy, designed to develop gradually towards the inclusion of a common Union defence policy. The Western European Union (WEU), with its links also to NATO, will be the vehicle for this cooperation in the first instance. No doubt this constellation will be well-adapted to a situation whereby a considerable scaling down of the US military presence in Europe has become a fact. In this sense—and in its capacity as the European pillar within the Alliance—the WEU will supplement NATO as Europe's security anchor.

Last but not least there is the CSCE. The CSCE has potentials in several respects, first and foremost because it encompasses *all* European countries. For one thing, it holds every prospect of gradually evolving into an efficient mechanism for managing and solving crises before they escalate to armed conflicts. In time, the institution may even develop into a sort of European security council. Though of course the negotiated peaceful settlements of conflicts would be the primary goal of such an institution, I can easily imagine the CSCE being provided with multilateral peace-keeping forces of its own, to be deployed in the European region where resolutions and agreements prove insufficient to contain violent conflicts.

> "The European Community is a vital ingredient in the recipe for a safer new Europe."

Evaluating the CSCE

The strengths and weaknesses of the CSCE in its present shape are currently being evaluated against the background of the tasks which face it. Among the issues that ministers and their representatives at the senior official level might do well to re-examine in detail in this context, is the requirement of unanimity for any CSCE decision to be reached. The extended role for the CSCE outlined above is hardly feasible as long as an aggressor member state is capable of effectively vetoing any joint CSCE reaction, however much the other member states may agree in condemning an act of aggression.

Arms control and disarmament is another important CSCE jurisdiction. The breakdown of central power structures in what used to be the Soviet Union underlines the relevance of such issues. The ratification and implementation of the CFE Treaty on reductions in the field of conventional arms, negotiated within the framework of the CSCE, is threatened by the abolition of the Soviet state—as are other arms control agreements. Due to the cooperation and acute sense of responsibility of most political leaders in the newly independent republics, we have reason to hope for a happy outcome. However, it is doubtful that prospects would have been equally favourable had there been no formally concluded treaty but merely unilateral proclamations on disarmament. One lesson to be learnt, then, is that without a formalized framework for disarmament there is, in the present unstable phase of history, reason to doubt that commitments will be felt to be sufficiently binding. That is why the coming new permanent security forum in the CSCE will be so important.

Europe is preparing itself for a decisive battle—a battle for stability and peace against instability and armed conflicts led on by the battlecries *integration* and *cohesion*. The instruments we are endowed with, namely institutions like NATO, the CSCE and the European Community, however familiar and time-honoured they may appear, have so far demonstrated remarkable adaptability to the reality of Europe's new security environment i.e. that the battle ahead of us can only be won by political and economic means applied in the hope of creating a well-integrated European entity to replace the present threat of disintegration. However, even more flexibility will be needed in the future if we are to carry the day.

If we win—and I am confident that we shall—it will be yet further proof that "Peace hath her victories no less renowned than war" as John Milton observed 340 years ago following the Treaty of Westphalia.

NATO Will Play an Essential Role in European Peace

by Richard Nixon

About the author: *Richard Nixon was the thirty-seventh president of the United States and the only one to resign from office. He has written many books on U.S. foreign policy and other issues including* No More Vietnams, 1999: Victory Without War, In the Arena, *and* Seize the Moment, *from which this viewpoint is excerpted.*

With the collapse of the Soviet Union, the traditional rationale for the U.S. role in Europe has been dealt a fatal blow. In 1971, the Mansfield amendment—which would have halved the U.S. military presence in Europe—was defeated by only one vote in the Senate. It is only a matter of time before a modern-day Mansfield amendment calling for a total withdrawal is introduced in Congress. Some on the American left argue that our new emphasis should be on domestic issues and that our victory in the cold war allows us to shake off old commitments. Others on the American right argue that a Europe fully recovered from World War II should not need the assistance of the United States and should pay the bills for its own defense. Many Europeans, tired of NATO low-altitude training flights and exhausted by forty years of brinkmanship, simply want the Americans to pack up and go home.

U.S. Role in Europe

All of these arguments are flawed. First, two world wars have proved that the United States ignores events in Europe at its own peril. Had we been engaged in Europe, rather than sulking in isolation after World War I, we could have tipped the balance of power against the aggressors, possibly deterring rather than fighting World War II. Despite the waning of the cold war, the United States has major political and economic interests in Europe. Our commitment to Europe is based not on philanthropy but on interests. The U.S. role in NATO

From Richard Nixon, *Seize the Moment*. New York: Simon & Schuster, 1992. Copyright 1992 by East-West Research, Inc. Reprinted with permission.

is not only needed on its merits but also gives us significant indirect leverage in addressing such issues as the Persian Gulf crisis and trade disputes. Without a military presence in Europe, we will have no voice in Europe.

In a historical perspective, Europe has been an even less stable place than the Middle East. The rigid stability of a Europe divided into two cold war camps has been the exception for a continent buffeted by centuries of war and instability. With the end of the cold war, Europe will not descend into fratricidal war, but the possibility for conflict and armed clashes will persist and even increase. Yugoslavia's civil war is a case in point. It is astonishing that the return of open warfare in Europe has not set off alarm bells in every European capital. The intermingling of scores of ethnic groups and the myriad competing territorial claims throughout the continent create endless possibilities for conflict and particularly as the relationships among the newly independent Soviet republics are sorted out. We have a profound stake in preventing the return of armed conflict to Europe. If we abandon our major role in Europe, we will relegate ourselves to the position of supporting cast, effectively writing ourselves out of any significant part in Europe's new geopolitical script.

> *"Two world wars have proved that the United States ignores events in Europe at its own peril."*

Second, though more self-reliant, Europeans still need a security relationship with the United States. The two major reasons for the creation of NATO forty-four years ago were to deter Soviet aggression and to provide a secure home for the Germans. Those reasons are still valid today. While the threat of aggression by an increasingly democratic Soviet Union is now minimal, the idea that four centuries of Russian and Soviet expansionist tradition will instantly evaporate might be comforting but cannot be counted upon. Moscow still has thousands of strategic nuclear warheads targeted on the United States, the most powerful conventional army in Europe, and a modern blue-water navy. Mikhail Gorbachev and Boris Yeltsin have already made some welcome changes in Moscow's foreign policy. But Russia is a major world power, and the Russians are a proud people. We should not automatically assume that a democratic Russia will be an international pussycat.

NATO's Role

Europe needs a security structure. A NATO with a major U.S. leadership role has played an indispensable role not only in shielding Western Europe during the cold war but also as an example to the nations of Eastern Europe and the Soviet Union. Today, no alternative security structure exists. Until a viable substitute evolves and proves itself, we would be making an irrevocable error in dismantling NATO or disengaging from NATO. In a period of massive instability in Eastern Europe and the Soviet Union, we should be exploring ways to preserve NATO rather than looking for ways to eliminate it.

Some observers argue that a post-1992 superstate can unify the cacophony of European views and speak with one voice in addressing all these concerns. But that vision has become a pipe dream. Concrete national differences over policy, not petty parochial disputes over procedure, have kept Europeans divided. And they will continue to do so. In the Persian Gulf crisis, our European allies scattered like a flock of quail. A few, particularly Britain and France, fought side by side with our troops in the Kuwaiti deserts. But most, especially Germany, stuck their heads in the sand. In Yugoslavia's internal crisis, mediators from the European Community responded like Keystone Kops. During the initial phases of the crisis, European powers split over whether to support the Communist Serbian and central government or the democratic secessionist republics of Slovenia and Croatia. The community sent teams to act as ceasefire observers but did not marshal its massive political and economic leverage to demand a nonviolent resolution based on democratic self-determination. In its first major political play in the post-cold-war period, Europe fumbled the ball.

No single locus of decision-making exists among our European allies. Aristotle was profoundly perceptive when he wrote that government by the many or government by the few cannot act as efficiently as government by one. In foreign policy, a single point of executive authority is indispensable for decisive action. The premise of those who foresaw the emergence of a European superstate was that Germany would become its natural leader. But the Germans, hamstrung by pacifist tendencies during the Gulf crisis and preoccupied with the costs of unification, forfeited the role. In the meantime, the rest of Europe no longer views German leadership as the answer. Britain and France—who performed decisively in the Gulf—do not wish to defer to Berlin. And the rise of a unified Germany, which dwarfs all other European countries in size, has prompted fears that German leadership will inevitably mean German domination.

> *"The myriad competing territorial claims throughout the continent create endless possibilities for conflict."*

Accepting Eastern Europe

The question is not whether but how the United States should maintain its presence in Europe. If we seek to build a common transatlantic home, we must find ways to include those nations in Eastern Europe and among the newly independent republics of the Soviet Union who accept our democratic values. We must also define common purposes and missions with our traditional allies that will give direction to our partnership. While much will depend on the direction of change in the former Soviet republics, a common transatlantic home should be built on five pillars:

1. NATO guarantees for Eastern Europe. Soon after their liberation, the East

European democracies began casting about for new security arrangements. At first, they sought to elevate the Conference on Security and Cooperation in Europe (CSCE) into a new all-European collective security arrangement. Then, Poland, Czechoslovakia, and Hungary discussed the formation of a trilateral partnership of their own. Later, all three began floating the idea of creating some kind of "associate status" with the NATO alliance. While NATO has welcomed observers from the new democracies at its headquarters, no concrete security commitment has been expressed or implied. A common transatlantic home requires us to be more responsive to East European security needs. . . .

NATO should develop formal security links with the East European democracies. Our goal should be their full integration into NATO. In the interim we should take concrete steps in that direction. Historically, almost no previous alliance comes close to matching the level of cooperation inherent in NATO. Its integrated military command stands as the exception, not the rule. Much can therefore be done to build a security relationship with Eastern Europe without bestowing the full rights of NATO membership. For example, formal ties could be developed between NATO and a new trilateral pact between Poland, Czechoslovakia, and Hungary. In a treaty, the two organizations could agree to respond to threats and attacks on the other, though leaving the choice of specific counteractions to each side's constitutional and alliance procedures. At the same time, cooperative programs could train the new East European officer corps at NATO institutions, as well as seek eventually to achieve a degree of interoperability in military equipment. . . .

Encouraging Economic Growth

2. U.S. activism in Eastern Europe. Interests, not altruism, lead states to cooperate. We must recognize that in the coming decades the thrust of our policy in Europe should center on those states that most need the U.S. connection: the new democracies in Eastern Europe. The United States should make its new relationship with Eastern Europe as important as its traditional ties with Western Europe. . . .

We should open Western markets to East European exports. Trade represents the major hope for rapid economic development. With Moscow demanding hard-currency payment for its exports, East European energy costs soared by $20 billion in 1991. Foreign debts limit their credit. Because of the current uncompetitive quality of East European goods, the 30 percent of Polish, Czechoslovak, and Hungarian exports that went to the Soviet Union or East Germany—markets now closed or vanished—have few buyers. It is imperative that the European Community grant them associate status

> *"Until a viable substitute evolves and proves itself, we would be making an irrevocable error in dismantling NATO."*

as soon as possible and that the United States immediately liberalize trade by increasing the list of imports given duty-free entry. Since sustained economic growth depends not on aid but on trade, the West must lift these counterproductive obstacles. . . .

We should encourage Europe's leaders—from both west and east—to develop a formal charter of national minority rights. The international community has articulated individual human rights in the U.N. Charter, the Helsinki Final Act, and other documents. But apart from the Genocide Convention of 1948, it has not stipulated the legitimate rights of national minorities. While the issue arises also outside of Europe—the Kurds and the Tibetans, for example—Europe's democratic consensus might enable its leaders to address the question forthrightly. A new European charter must not shift the basis of law from individual to group rights. But it could set guidelines for guaranteeing legitimate national rights in such areas as language use in education and respect for religious freedom, thereby helping to reduce the danger of civil strife or even war resulting from Eastern Europe's and the former Soviet Union's potentially explosive national mosaic. . . .

> *"In the Persian Gulf crisis, our European allies scattered like a flock of quail."*

Cooperation with Germany and Russia

3. Close U.S.-German partnership. . . .

A U.S.-German partnership does not mean that our interests will always coincide. But our profound stake in such mutual cooperation will override our differences. Working together, President Bush and Chancellor Helmut Kohl achieved something Moscow repeatedly vowed it would never accept: a united Germany fully integrated into NATO. While Germany may not be fully comfortable with its growing world role, it is still the undisputed economic heavyweight of Europe. In the future, our partnership should become ever-more pivotal in advancing our common interests and values.

This partnership will take time to develop and will only work if Germany remains a responsible Western power rather than a country jockeying for position between East and West. At the same time, a special relationship with Germany does not imply the United States putting greater distance between itself and Britain, France, Italy, and other NATO nations. Not only will close relations with our traditional European allies check Germany's drift to the East, but they also make strategic sense. Britain's and France's support, both political and economic, represented a linchpin of success in the Persian Gulf War. Moreover, together they represent a major economic counterweight to Germany within the European Community, as evidenced by the fact that France's advances in integrating communications and computer technologies lead the world.

4. An open-door policy vis-à-vis the newly independent republics of the Soviet

Union....

For most of its history, Russia has been pulled by two traditions—one to withdraw into an insular existence and the other to join the Western world. The defeat of communism following the August 1991 coup signaled a decisive move away from the tradition of Asiatic despotism that dominated Russian foreign policy for over four hundred years and particularly since the Bolshevik Revolution in 1917. Much remains to be done to undo the legacies of the Russian imperial tradition. But under Boris Yeltsin, Russia has placed its relations with the non-Russian peoples of the former Soviet Union on a new and just footing. If he succeeds in creating a nonimperial, noncommunist Russia, the West should roll out the red carpet of freedom in welcoming his Russia into the common transatlantic home.

The Challenge NATO Faces

5. Restructuring NATO for new missions. Alliances are held together by fear, not by love. When fear of a common threat fades, allies tend to drift apart. To paraphrase General Douglas MacArthur, old alliances never die, they just fade away. Today, NATO must adapt or risk irrelevance. To survive, the alliance must redefine its missions and sense of purpose....

> *"NATO should develop formal security links with the East European democracies."*

As NATO finds its footing in the new Europe, it should also expand its mission. In Europe, it should focus not just on common defense but also on pressing for just solutions to such conflicts as the Yugoslav civil war. It must also look beyond Europe. Its creators did not envision that by specifying that the NATO commitment applied to Europe and North America, the alliance would operate only within a strict boundary. Instead, they simply sought to exclude Europe's colonies from security guarantees requiring an automatic response from other members. Today, as demonstrated in the Persian Gulf, challenges to Western interests can arise half a world away. If NATO adheres mindlessly to artificial geographical restrictions, we will simply be shooting ourselves in the foot, compromising our interests to legalism. For example, an effort to cut the oil lifeline of Western Europe is as great a threat to the security of NATO nations as a military attack against a NATO member. While European defense must remain NATO's core mission, so-called "out of area" security cooperation must become its cutting edge. Unless we adopt such a policy, the American people—whose commitment to NATO has depended on the perception of a Soviet threat—will inevitably seek to disengage from Europe as the alliance increasingly speaks of Moscow not as an adversary but as a "partner in security."

While we already cooperate in distant crises, our solutions tend to be ad hoc. To improve NATO's capabilities to cope with out-of-area conflicts, we need to move forward in three areas. First, the European members of NATO should develop a joint rapid deployment force that would function, depending on circumstances, independently or under an integrated command with similar U.S. forces. Second, the United States should welcome European activism in parts of the underdeveloped world where their historical experience exceeds our own. For too long, Americans have assumed that our superior military power gave us superior political wisdom. In addition, because the next crisis will likely take place in the underdeveloped world, the United States should open its overseas bases outside Europe to our NATO allies. Our current policy restricts foreign military powers from using our bases, but we should be more flexible in order to facilitate greater European activism in critical parts of the underdeveloped world. Third, NATO should develop better mechanisms for more coordinated crisis management. Working together, the members of the Atlantic alliance—which control over half of the world economy—wield power that no potential adversary can afford to ignore. In addition, if the Western allies back a common course of action in the U.N. Security Council, potential aggressors will have to take notice.

Revitalizing NATO

NATO must loosen, not tighten, its structure. To grow, it needs greater flexibility to be able to respond not only to military but also to political contingencies. This does not mean that either the United States or Western Europe should have a strict veto over the other's actions. Each will have interests that the other will not share. But they must develop ways to arrive at common policies to out-of-area conflicts when possible, as well as equipping the alliance with the needed military, economic, and political instruments to carry them out. Unlike other alliances, which have dissolved as the threat of a common enemy wanes, a renewed NATO can survive the test of victory.

The Western European Union (WEU) Could Provide European Security

by Hugh De Santis

About the author: *Hugh De Santis is a professor of international security affairs at the National War College in Washington, D.C.*

A little more than two decades ago, inspired by the climate of détente, the members of the Atlantic Alliance set out upon the task of making the North Atlantic Treaty Organization (NATO) more relevant to the times. The product of their deliberations, the Harmel Report of 1967, shifted NATO's traditional emphasis on defense to one that combined military security and progress toward East-West political reconciliation. In the wake of the revolutionary upheavals that have taken place in Europe since the summer of 1989, members of the Alliance are once again reexamining the relevance of NATO. In contrast to the 1960s, however, the changes that they are currently experiencing are likely to transform the European political system. Rather than bend, spindle, mutilate, and fold NATO into a political-security institution that barely resembles itself and is scarcely relevant to the conditions of a reunified Europe, this viewpoint contends that allied policymakers ought to be planning for its eventual dissolution.

New Security Framework

This is not to say that NATO should be disbanded tomorrow. The precipitous dismantling of an institution that has successfully underwritten European security for four decades would be in neither allied nor U.S. interests. But NATO will not endure indefinitely. The bipolar world order that spawned the Atlantic Alliance and the defunct Warsaw Pact is gradually being replaced by a looser, more dynamic multilateralism reminiscent of the pre-World War II period. NATO belongs to the period that now may be more appropriately called the "aftermath of war," the period of global reconstruction and realignment that ex-

Reprinted from Hugh De Santis, "The Graying of NATO," *The Washington Quarterly* 14 (4) by permission of The MIT Press and The Center for Strategic and International Studies, © 1991 by The Center for Strategic and International Studies and The Massachusetts Institute of Technology.

tended from 1945 to the removal of wartime controls on Germany in May 1990. The real postwar era of national rediscovery and self-assertiveness is just beginning.

It is, therefore, curious that the United States and its allies, at the very moment that the division of Europe has ended, are seeking ways to sustain the utility of NATO. In fact, efforts to shore up NATO may actually serve to retard European unity. What is needed to promote integration and reduce instability in the postwar era is a new security framework built on the Western European Union (WEU) and a network of mutual assistance agreements linked to that organization and, indirectly, to NATO that would ultimately form the basis of a Europeanized collective defense organization. . . .

Alternatives to NATO

If NATO's days are numbered, which institution is likely to replace it? Until recently, many European officials believed that the new security order should be built on the foundations of the Conference on Security and Cooperation in Europe (CSCE), a Soviet-inspired forum that ironically became the catalyst for détente during the Cold War. Buoyed by the collapse of the Soviet empire and the sweeping public repudiation of communism from Berlin to Bucharest, Germany's foreign minister, Hans-Dietrich Genscher, and Václav Havel, president of the Czech and Slovak Federal Republic, trumpeted the CSCE as the harbinger of the millennium of peace in Europe.

In contrast to NATO, the CSCE contains all the European countries, including the states of the former Soviet Union, thereby enhancing the prospect of European integration. Unlike NATO and, to a lesser degree, the WEU or the Council of Europe, the CSCE is not freighted with the cultural baggage of the Cold War. As the child of détente, the CSCE shares with the Harmel Report a vision of a reunited Europe committed to progress on political, security, economic, and human rights activities. Finally, the membership of the United States and Canada in the CSCE gives it a Euratlantic character. More important, it enables it to address European aspirations without sacrificing the stabilizing presence of the United States.

Convinced that the democratic paroxysms of 1989 prefigured the emergence of a peaceful and prosperous Europe, the leaders of the CSCE states convened in Paris in November 1990 to celebrate their new world order. Officials and pundits alike compared the gathering to the Congress of Vienna in 1815.

"The precipitous dismantling of an institution that has successfully underwritten European security for four decades would be in neither allied nor U.S. interests."

As a result of Gorbachev's retreat from reform and growing nationalistic tensions in Eastern Europe, however, the ebullient faith in the CSCE has waned.

Even the philosopher-prince of Czechoslovakia seems to have questioned his earlier faith in the power of the CSCE. In light of the polyethnic confusion that reigns in Yugoslavia, Havel may have concluded that a European-wide body was too cumbersome to transact business efficiently. It has been difficult enough to sustain cohesion in NATO, the ultimate purpose of which its signatories unequivocally endorse. To expect the now 52 nations to agree on a common security program when many of them have mutual grudges to settle is pure fantasy.

No Military Force

The recent establishment by the CSCE of an executive secretariat, a conflict prevention center, and a mechanism to monitor national elections eases the problem of managing a large and diverse membership. But even if such bodies facilitated common security policies, there would be no way to enforce their implementation without the threat of military sanctions. The peaceful revolutions of 1989 and 1990 seem to have mesmerized too many people into believing that collective security would be the rationally ordained outcome of democratic reform. Unfortunately, the end of the Cold War has not transformed human nature. The CSCE might succeed in damping down regional quarrels between its member states, but it would be no more capable of preventing armed conflicts among revisionist states than was the League of Nations unless it were prepared to use military force to enforce its collective decision-making authority.

> *"Efforts to shore up NATO may actually serve to retard European unity."*

To compound the security problem, a CSCE-centered Europe, whether it nurtures peace or not, is not likely to sustain an active U.S. commitment. The U.S. public has never been interested in the CSCE. Given that public's chronic complaint about having to defend rich and ungrateful allies and its new worries about an emerging European economic fortress, the emphasis on a CSCE "architecture" for postwar Europe may accelerate the process of U.S. military retrenchment at the expense of continental stability.

Disillusioned with the CSCE, Euro-optimists seem to be gravitating toward the European Community. Although West Europeans continue to believe that NATO and the U.S. military presence are necessary for their near-term security, a majority of them would prefer to see the Community form a common defense organization to protect their interests in the future, according to a recent EC poll. Similarly, a U.S. Information Agency (USIA) opinion survey conducted in June 1990 found that over 70 percent of French society and more than 40 percent of Britons and Germans sampled favored a security structure that revolved around the EC.

It is only natural that Europeans would hope that the considerable progress the EC has made toward economic integration might eventually extend to political and security matters. For the French and others who suspect that the U.S. presence in Europe may soon be coming to an end, the EC represents the only institutionally viable way of providing for European security and ensuring that Germany remains institutionally tethered to the West.

At its present state of development, however, the EC is just as ill-suited as the CSCE to assume the security trusteeship of a reunited Europe. Efforts to establish an adjunct defense role in a body that includes neutral or security-phobic members such as Ireland, Denmark, and (Turkey aside) Greece are bound to founder. The key to the development of a peaceful Europe is economic integration. To divert the EC from its single-minded pursuit of this crucial objective by burdening it with a security function that it is unprepared to accommodate is to retard and possibly undermine European unity.

> *"70 percent of French society and more than 40 percent of Britons and Germans sampled favored a security structure that revolved around the EC."*

Besides, economic unity in the West is not a foregone conclusion. Neither the vaunted monetary union nor the social charter that is intended to give economic progress a human face is yet a reality. Still chafing over Bonn's precipitate decision to establish a currency union with East Germany, the former president of the West German Central Bank, Karl Otto Pohl, recently cautioned against a premature move toward EC monetary union. Meanwhile, Bonn's preoccupation with German unification and Mitteleuropa apart, Italy, France, Spain, and Portugal are advocating closer regional ties with the North African members of the Arab Maghreb Union. Adding a complicating security issue to the EC's agenda at this critical moment in postwar Europe would only widen these divisions.

If neither the EC nor the CSCE is capable of replacing NATO, one could always opt for a new security organization. But one might wait forever for a new security structure to emerge. Membership, the role of nuclear weapons, and burden-sharing arrangements would provoke disagreements far more intense than anything the allies have encountered in the past. While the allies tiresomely debated the future, Europe might enter a dangerous period of drift. In the process, Germany might eventually opt for neutrality or a policy of military unilateralism. And the United States would sooner or later be pressed by Congress and public opinion to remove its forces from the continent.

A Better Alternative

Besides, there is no need to create a new edifice when there may already exist a better alternative to NATO than either the CSCE or the EC or some hybrid of these and other organizations: the Western European Union. The WEU is the only European institution whose members have pledged to defend one another. Moreover, given its explicit commitment to European integration, it is the security analogue of the EC and the CSCE in their respective economic and political domains.

True, the WEU has not had a distinguished history as a collective defense organization. Established in 1955 as a successor to the Brussels Treaty Organization to monitor German rearmament, its security functions were preempted by NATO after the Federal Republic's entry into the Alliance. Except in Paris, where it still excited *troisième voie* fantasies of a French-led European defense organization, the WEU served thereafter mainly as a souvenir of security cooperation immediately after the war, a sort of monument to good intentions. In the United States, it was all but forgotten until its resuscitation during the intermediate-range nuclear forces (INF) crisis, when the overly sensitive administration of President Ronald Reagan publicly renounced its deliberations and gave it more attention and status than it deserved.

Since then, however, the WEU has taken on new life. At the end of 1987, as the outlines of change in the Soviet Union became more sharply etched, it adopted a "Platform on European Security Interests," which called for more active cooperation among its signatories in support of rather than in opposition to NATO in the areas of arms procurement and arms-control verification. Free of legal constraints on its activity outside Europe, the WEU authorized European participation in the 1987 reflagging of Kuwaiti tankers and in the U.S.-led coalition against Iraq in the Gulf War.

> *"The WEU is the only European institution whose members have pledged to defend one another."*

Quietly, interest in the WEU is intensifying in allied capitals. On December 6, 1990, the German chancellor, Helmut Kohl, and President François Mitterrand of France sent a letter to the heads of the European Council expressing the hope that the WEU would become the centerpiece of European security. Rumors are also circulating that the WEU may move its headquarters from Paris to Brussels, which would allow the member states to accredit their ambassadors simultaneously to NATO.

Still, the European allies are treading softly on the issue. The Kohl-Mitterrand letter reportedly triggered a stern demarche from the United States to allied capitals. In response, Genscher and the French foreign minister, Roland Dumas, issued a bland statement on European unity that subordinated the WEU to NATO. Fearful of alienating Washington and thus precipitating a U.S. withdrawal from the continent, the allies, led by the British and the Dutch, have resumed referring to the WEU as a "European pillar" within NATO.

Taking Charge

But this transatlantic dance cannot continue indefinitely. The tune is already changing, and the partners risk getting uncomfortably out of step. Whether the United States likes it or not, Europe is Europeanizing. Consequently, U.S. influence will inevitably decline. But a reunited Europe must also accept the responsibility for its own defense. It cannot, therefore, expect the United States to maintain an indefinite military presence on the continent.

To be sure, U.S. leadership will be needed in the short term to provide stability and reassurance to an unsettled continent. But the role of the United States as well as NATO in the unfolding postwar Europe can only be transitional. In the long term, the Western European Union, or whatever it may then be called, is the most likely steward of a united Europe's security.

Europeanizing European Defense

The most vexing security problem facing the Euratlantic policy community is the issue of integrating the former members of the Warsaw Pact in a collective defense framework without alienating either the United States or Russia. There are two dimensions to the problem: political-military and military-strategic.

At the political-military level, too rapid an attempt to incorporate the East European states into a Western security structure such as NATO could worry Moscow and invite Russian political interference, possibly even intervention, in the region. Too dilatory a response to the former Pact states would produce a power vacuum that would sooner or later result in military clashes and possibly a regional war.

At the military-strategic level, a precipitate embrace of the former Pact allies would probably inhibit Russia and Ukraine from further reducing their nuclear arsenal, including their stock of tactical weapons. Moscow's unwillingness to make further strategic arms reductions, assuming that a strategic arms reduction (START) treaty is signed, could also lower the nuclear threshold in Europe.

A cautious, deliberate response to the changing security environment, on the other hand, would help to achieve a third zero, that is, the withdrawal of all nuclear artillery and short-range ballistic missiles from Europe. Germany will surely demand their removal to ensure the departure of all Red Army troops from its eastern states by 1994. But the elimination of all ground-based nuclear weapons is likely to erode the military utility of the Atlantic Alliance. It would accelerate U.S. military retrenchment, thereby leaving the British and French nuclear forces as the sole theater deterrent to Russia. Both the U.S. departure and the continued presence of British and French nuclear forces, in turn, are likely to provoke anxiety in Bonn, and they could lead Germany to develop its own nuclear deterrent or, at least, to insist on participation in joint nuclear planning, targeting, and use.

> *"Whether the United States likes it or not, Europe is Europeanizing. Consequently, U.S. influence will inevitably decline."*

Neither London, Paris, nor Moscow would find such a situation tolerable. Nor would they feel much more comfortable if a third zero led to European denuclearization. The removal of nuclear weapons may simply transfer anxieties to the conventional sphere, where the Germans, their agreement with Moscow to reduce the size of the Bundeswehr notwithstanding, could again become a dominant military force in Europe.

> *"Western European Union, or whatever it may then be called, is the most likely steward of a united Europe's security."*

The risk in the ad hockery of the decision making in which the United States, the former Soviet states, and the European states have engaged since the summer of 1989 is that no one will have the foresight to think beyond the exigencies of the present and devise a new concept from which a set of security relationships for postwar Europe can evolve. What is urgently needed is an integrated approach that includes, at the multinational level, a U.S.-led NATO as a support structure for a new security system and, at the national level, a panoply of mutual assistance agreements in the East that would be incorporated first into the WEU and eventually into a European collective defense organization. . . .

Like the regional associations and the Warsaw Pact, NATO will gradually wither away. The skeletized force of two U.S. divisions and three air wings in the mid-1990s, say, will be phased out by the end of the decade. To allay allied anxieties about the return to neo-isolationism in the United States, however, U.S. officials would be well advised to underscore their continuing commitment to European security. At a minimum, this would require the United States to leave prepositioned equipment in Europe for the foreseeable future, maintain adequate airlift and sealift capability to respond to crises, if necessary, and foster a consultative relationship with the WEU Council on a broad range of defense topics, especially nuclear weapons policy. . . .

A Viable Solution

Conflict cannot be prevented in the emerging postwar Europe. It can be contained, however. In order to do so, the United States and the European allies must first part with their illusions. Efforts to superimpose prefabricated architectures on the new Europe without examining and shoring up, if necessary, its existing foundations are bound to fail. Viewing the future through the lens of 1949 gives an equally distorted picture of reality. Neither approach is rooted in the present.

At the same time, political leaders in the United States and Europe must have some vision of the future that they would like to see emerge from the present. The EC should figure prominently in their thinking—it has the quintessential role to play in the new Europe as the engine of economic unity. So should the CSCE. Just as the CSCE provided a process of interaction that sustained détente in Europe during the superpower chill of the 1980s, it can perform an equally valuable service as a conciliator and mediator in the ethnic, religious, and territorial disputes that lie ahead. But Western leaders also need to develop a new concept of security to replace the alliance structure that has served peace so well for the past four decades. The WEU appears to be the only viable institutional base on which a new structure can be built.

The WEU is no panacea for the problems that await the new Europe; it may struggle to manage the process of integration. Unlike NATO, however, it points the Euratlantic community in the direction of tomorrow rather than yesterday. That alone is a hopeful sign. For its part, the United States should assist rather than resist the development of the WEU. After all, no country has made a greater contribution on behalf of European unity. Besides, the security and stability that a collective defense organization will provide to a continent that is about to resume responsibility for its own affairs can only enhance the long-term geostrategic interests of the United States.

International Monetary Fund Policies Harm Eastern Europe

by Paul Hockenos

About the author: *Paul Hockenos is the Eastern European correspondent for the Chicago-based, socialist periodical* In These Times.

Every third month, an International Monetary Fund (IMF) delegation calls on Hungary's economic policymakers. It is a day of reckoning for the National Bank and Finance Ministry chiefs in Budapest. They know well that their progress on the IMF's economic stipulations holds the key to the country's financial solvency.

For Hungary, as for all of the former communist countries, IMF approval of its free market transition policies is critical to its short-term survival. Should the IMF deem the policymakers too lenient in the application of the austerity programs, loans would be halted, and the financially strapped countries would be forced to default on their looming debts.

Austerity Policies

Such a cutoff of loans, government economists claim, would extinguish any hopes of economic recovery. The IMF's word not only determines countries' access to its own reserves, but functions as a seal of approval, esteemed by all major private and government creditors, as well as investors. The fragile Eastern European economies could plunge into chaos if foreign loans were cut off.

Facing massive debts and politically committed to the free market principles of the IMF, Eastern Europe's new heads of state have not resisted the hard terms of the IMF's tight monetary packages. All of the post-communist governments, whether IMF members or not, have dutifully implemented the general conditions of the IMF recipe: monetary restriction, price liberalization, deregulation and privatization. Top among the demands of the prescribed "shock therapy" are massive cuts in domestic expenditures—from investment to food sub-

Paul Hockenos, "Capital Goes East—The Role of the IMF in Eastern Europe." This article first appeared in the June 1991 issue of *Multinational Monitor*, PO Box 19405, Washington, DC 20036; subscriptions, $22/year. Reprinted with permission.

sidies—in order to meet balance-of-payment (the level of imports versus exports) targets.

While every government in the former East bloc ascribes to the ultimate goal of a free market transition, the issue is how radically to proceed. The unspoken question is how great a burden the people will bear without rebelling. The austerity policies combined with the demise of the East bloc market have sparked falls in living standards, sharp drops in output and rising inflation and unemployment. The net domestic product in 1990 dropped in every East European country, from 3.1 percent in Czechoslovakia to 13 percent in Bulgaria and 19.2 percent in East Germany. The tight domestic budget targets allow no funds for programs to address soaring homelessness, crime and drug use.

> *"For Hungary, . . . IMF approval of its free market transition policies is critical to its short-term survival."*

The IMF's role has been to discipline governments which waver in their commitment to push forward with the transition. When, for example, Hungary's 1989 budget, under the reform communist government, showed an unexpectedly large negative balance of payments and budget deficit, the IMF halted stand-by loans. The government quickly drafted an emergency mid-year budget and loan access was restored.

While the exact terms of IMF contracts are secret, the influence of the Fund's money managers is plain to see. "When one reads between the lines," says economist Laszlo Andor of the Hungarian Trade Unions' Institute for Economic Research, "it's clear that the IMF is practically dictating Hungarian monetary policy." When politicians are challenged about the cuts in education or medical subsidies, for example, they openly admit that the IMF has tied their hands. "The IMF policies embody the full logic of Reaganomics, and one hears that in politicians' language," says Andor.

The Power of Debt

The IMF's influence in Eastern Europe stems largely, although not exclusively, from the region's massive indebtedness. Eastern European countries desire IMF contracts which guarantee annual loans they need to help service their debts. Even the less indebted countries, in part because of their desire to be in the IMF's good graces and receive loans from the Fund, generally adhere to the IMF's policy prescriptions. Romania, for example, with almost no debt, has eagerly applied a radical version of the IMF calculus to its ailing economy. Along with Poland, Hungary, Czechoslovakia and Bulgaria, Romania as of April 1991 can negotiate credit and reform packages with the IMF. The country's first reward: a $295 million loan from the Export Deficit and Crisis Fund to soften the fallout resulting from cutbacks in Soviet aid and oil shortages caused by the Persian Gulf War.

With the exception of Romania, where the government pushed the people to starvation in the 1980s to cover the country's debts, all of the former East bloc countries suffer heavy indebtedness. Poland boasts the largest Central European debt at $47 billion and Hungary the highest per capita debt at $21 billion total. Bulgaria, whose foreign debt has more than doubled from $4.7 in 1986 to $10.8 billion, defaulted in spring 1990. Czechoslovakia stands in somewhat better shape with $8 billion outstanding. Yugoslavia and the Soviet Union owe foreign creditors $17 and $52 billion respectively.

While each country's case varies, the pattern of Eastern bloc indebtedness has its roots in the early 1970s. The East Europeans, along with the Third World countries, borrowed heavily, taking advantage of the rock-bottom interest rates which lasted until the mid-seventies. The plan was to use the borrowed funds to switch to import-led growth strategies, fueling domestic growth through technology and capital imports from the West. In theory, the export of the derivative manufactured goods back to the West would cover the accrued debts.

The expected export payoff on the world market never materialized, however. Industrial goods were peddled instead to the Soviet Union for rubles, leaving balance-of-payment deficits in internationally traded currencies. When the oil-price shocks hit, followed by the 1979-1982 world recession, the Eastern Europeans, Africans and South Americans plunged together into an abyss of debt. As interest rates skyrocketed, debtors' foreign deficits, of which only a fraction had ever been invested, soared. Hungary, for one, had invested only $3.5 billion of the $12 billion that it owed by 1981.

Trapped in Debt

When the debt crisis came to a head in the early 1980s, Hungary and others sought out the IMF for help. The structural adjustments and debt-financing schedules began a vicious circle of borrowing that would double and triple the East Europeans' debts during the decade. Hungary continued to borrow, paying off its early 1980s principle three times over, while the total amount of its debt doubled. Poland also paid back its initial debt at least once, as its total indebtedness increased dramatically.

"Eastern Europe's new heads of state have not resisted the hard terms of the IMF's tight monetary packages."

Hungarian sociologist Andrea Szego sees the dilemmas of the East European countries as classic examples of the "international debt trap." Governments take out new credits simply to finance old ones, and countries' entire economies then become geared toward exports. "Once a country is stuck in the debt trap, it is forced to export at any cost for foreign currency. The forced growth of exports leads to domestic losses that are taken out at home," she says.

The credit provided directly or indirectly by the IMF failed to translate into any significant growth in the debt countries, Szego explains. "After the first period of borrowing, the vast majority of funds went directly to financing debt payment. The debt-servicing plans were simply implemented to protect the international monetary system from collapse." She notes as well that the Hungarian Communist Party's attempt to sell the conservative IMF adjustment policy as a Marxist-Leninist program of renewal precipitated its fall. "This caused not only their own defeat, but the crisis of Marxism as well."

> "While the exact terms of IMF contracts are secret, the influence of the Fund's money managers is plain to see."

Today, the nationalist-conservative Hungarian Democratic Forum (HDF) government grapples with the same tight conditions as the communists. Hungary's pact with the IMF stipulates that the country's export surplus and tourism revenue must cover $1.6 billion in interest payments if it is to receive $2.35 billion in loans to pay off part of the principle on its debt.

The president of the Hungarian National Bank optimistically points out that the country's debt service ratio (servicing costs as a percent of total export earnings) has fallen to "only" 40 percent from 70 percent. But the collapse of the COMECON trade bloc and conversion to dollar-based trade with the Soviet Union (particularly for oil) has the government predicting a 14 percent drop in the terms of trade for 1991. Hungary's trade with the Soviet Union accounted for 30 percent of its total trade in 1980 but only 20 percent in 1990. The 10 percent increase in the volume of 1990 hard-currency exports to the West helped offset a 26 percent decline in ruble trade. But with the East now competing with the West on an equal basis for Soviet markets, the boom in westward exports will not cover Hungary's losses this year.

Human Costs

According to IMF rationale, the only recourse is harsher austerity at home. Last year, the additional 5 percent of gross domestic product extracted from the Hungarian economy to bolster the balance of payments came in large part from workers' pockets. With over a third of the population living at or below the poverty line, the government cut real wages through a calculated inflationary policy. The closure of "inefficient, centralized" industries—the same targets of investment cuts in the 1980s—is another means to trim the domestic budget. The much-heralded privatization of the industrial sector, which government economists hoped would bring in foreign currency, has fallen catastrophically short of expectations. Western investment is only a trickle, leaving the countries in the lurch, falling more than $10 billion short of anticipated totals.

"The economy is expected to [shoulder the] burden [of] higher and higher financing costs from a stagnating GDP," says Andor. "In the long run, the chances of repayment could only be improved if the economy developed competitive, productive industries. But, with these restrictive monetary policies, there's no chance for development. Internal investment is almost nonexistent because everything is going to the debt."

The human costs of austerity are daily more visible on the streets of every East European city. Domestic consumption fell in Czechoslovakia, Hungary, Poland, the Soviet Union and Bulgaria. The drops have forced even mid-level wage earners to take second or third jobs. Inflation jumped high above estimates in every country, with the exception of Hungary and East Germany. In Budapest, the train and subway stations are filling with homeless people and families. Slowly, economists and citizens alike are recognizing that the "belt-tightening" that politicians in 1989 promised would last only three to five years will be a fact of life for much longer.

Alternatives to Austerity

Despite these consequences, opposition to the IMF's policies is almost nowhere to be seen. In Hungary, the entire spectrum of parliamentary parties backs prompt debt servicing and adherence to the general terms of the IMF contract. Politicians feel that "there's no alternative." The ruling HDF-led coalition has resisted the all-out "shock therapy" that IMF bankers pushed through in Poland. Yet, their somewhat more "gradual" approach is only a revised version of the same economic program that all of the parties endorse.

The major opposition party, the former dissident-led Free Democrats, supports even more draconian policies. The party's top economist, Attila Soos, sees the IMF role in Hungary as positive. In contrast to Andor and Szego, he charges that mismanagement and waste, not the debt cycle, are at the heart of the country's economic woes. "The IMF has been essential in pushing the government toward a capitalist market economy," he says. "Much of the HDF program is accepted only under IMF pressure." He notes, the HDF advocated a "third way between capitalism and socialism. It was the IMF that pressured them to abandon this idea."

But André Gunder Frank, of the University of Amsterdam, recently in Prague to discuss the debt crisis, and others dispute the contention that there is "no other alternative" than to suffer from austerity measures implemented under the yoke of debt. "Debts have come and gone for ages," says the expert on debt issues. He sees three ways in which Third World and East European debts could be reduced or eliminated. The first is to pay them back, the path taken by Romania's dictator, Nicolas Ceausescu, with its well-known consequences. The second avenue is to default, which many countries did in the 1920s and 1930s. Another alternative is for creditors to write debts down or forgive them entirely. This option is not without precedent. The Allies wrote off

"The former East bloc countries suffer heavy indebtedness."

Chapter 5

West Germany's remaining war debt at the 1948 London Conference. East Germany's domestic debt was simply taken over by West Germany.

The most dramatic breakthrough in this regard came in spring 1991, when the Paris Club, an informal grouping of the world's 17 leading industrial countries, announced that it would halve Poland's enormous debt and reduce accumulated interest by 80 percent. The creditor governments agreed that economic recovery for Poland was inconceivable without substantial debt reduction. Unlike Hungary and the other East European countries, an unusually high proportion of Poland's debt was owed directly to foreign governments rather than banks or multilateral agencies.

Setting a Precedent

The decision, however, was no act of charity. The Western countries knew well that Poland had no prospect for full repayment. The wave of strikes and strike threats against the government's "shock therapy" dangerously jeopardized the reform process. The finance ministry finally convinced the IMF and member states that the population would not endure the crisis without greater support. As the London-based *Economist* warned, "Debt relief is a reward and an incentive, not a right. . . . When a company nears bankruptcy, creditors will reduce its debts only if they think doing so stands a chance of making the firm able to survive in the longish term and this to repay or service those debts that remain. It is the same with countries. . . . Debt relief could be—and was—made conditional on those reforms staying in place during the next four years."

> *"According to IMF rationale, the only recourse is harsher austerity at home."*

The mechanism for that control is the gradual lifting of debt burdens. In the first phase of three years, 30 percent of the agreed sum of $33 billion will be dropped. A further 20 percent will go in 1994 if Poland's recently sealed pact with the IMF is deemed "successful," states the Paris Club communiqué.

Until then, Poland must haggle with the individual governments as well as private banks over the exact terms of reduction. Germany and Japan have put up the fiercest resistance. The "Polish precedent" piqued no one more than the German banks, which hold the lion's share of Poland's debt as well as that of many other East European countries. The United States' elimination of 70 percent of Poland's debt to U.S. banks upon President Lech Walesa's March 1991 visit raised a furor in Vienna and Frankfurt. "The whole $3.8 billion that Poland owes the USA is only a fifth of what the country owes little Austria," complained the Vienna daily *Die Presse*. "It will be difficult now to prevent a chain reaction [across Eastern Europe]."

Already, the "Polish precedent" has triggered the feared murmurs of dissent in Hungary. A leading politician's claim that the government was "split over asking for a debt reduction" unleashed a storm in the Budapest financial community. Politicians, bankers and experts rushed to deny the charge. "The government," a spokesperson reassured the press, "is fully united on the question of debt repayment."

Closing the Third Way

In the immediate aftermath of the 1989 revolutions, proponents of neo-classical free market reform were just one voice among many. From Berlin to Sofia, somewhat vague but nevertheless different ideas of "third ways," "social market systems" and "social ecological economies" were bandied about by the parties now in office. But the IMF moved fast to see that these alternatives never saw the light of day. In a spring 1990 brief on Eastern Europe policy, the IMF managing director wrote that "any attempts to find a third way between central planning and a market economy" must be ruled out. The debt trap ensured the IMF the leverage that it needed to encourage countries to follow a free-market trajectory. The results may please Western governments, bankers and industrialists, but the consequences have been devastating for the people of Eastern Europe, who, having earned a measure of political freedom, are finding themselves under the thumb of a new tyrant.

The World Bank Encourages Regressive Socialist Economic Policies

by Melanie S. Tammen

About the author: *Melanie S. Tammen is a free-lance journalist living in Winter Park, Florida. She is a scholar with the Cato Institute, a research foundation that promotes the idea of limiting government involvement in business. She has written policy papers and articles on organizations such as the International Monetary Fund and the World Bank.*

Central planning brought ruin to Eastern Europe, a $450-billion foreign-debt burden to Latin America, and even greater poverty to sub-Saharan Africa, where per capita incomes are lower today than they were in 1970. Yet the United States continues to support the institutions that counsel and finance still more central planning—the World Bank, the related regional development banks, and the International Monetary Fund.

Socialist Planning Efforts

Now Washington is poised to sidetrack Eastern Europe's opportunity for a true free market by joining the World Bank and related organizations in promoting a variety of rear-guard socialist planning efforts.

In Eastern Europe, the World Bank and the IMF are extending unprecedented levels of loans to governments. Since February 1990, the IMF has committed about $2 billion to Poland, Yugoslavia, and Hungary. The World Bank plans to lend $7 billion to $8 billion in the region over three years. Furthermore, the Bush administration has pledged $1.2 billion in U.S. funds to support a new multilateral bank for Eastern Europe.

And in 1989, Congress approved the $938-million Support for East European Democracy Act, which provides $300 million for "private enterprise" loans in Poland and Hungary. Government-appointed boards of directors will dole out $240 million in Poland and $60 million in Hungary. As former Assistant Treasury Secretary Paul Craig Roberts told a congressional panel in 1990, "Contracts and financing will be awarded based on political connections.... The economic process will be taken over by 'rent-seekers' competing for a share of the largess. Real private enterprise will languish as entrepreneurial skills are directed into the political arena."

In May 1990, the Bush administration formally pledged U.S. participation in the European Bank for Reconstruction and Development. Designed to lend to governments in Eastern Europe and the Soviet Union, this new multilateral bank will have $12 billion in initial capital.

Funding Rehabilitation

During international negotiations over the creation of the European Bank in early 1990, U.S. Treasury officials portrayed the institution as a new-and-improved development bank. They suggested that the bank will play an important role in Eastern Europe's privatization efforts. Yet multilateral development banks have never linked significant amounts of assistance to privatization of bloated, money-losing state enterprises. The World Bank's emphasis remains rehabilitation, not privatization. Despite its market-oriented rhetoric, it continues to tinker with socialism and central planning.

Advocates of the European Bank emphasize that many of its loans will go directly to firms that are already private. But the World Bank provides the principal model for channeling multilateral bank money to private borrowers. Its "directed-credit" system funnels money through "development finance institutions," (DFIs) generally state-run banks.

The World Bank lends DFIs hundreds of millions of dollars, which they in turn are supposed to lend to small and medium-sized private enterprises. Government bureaucrats run most World Bank-supported DFIs, allocating credit by "picking winners"—or, in reality, picking anyone. Since the mid-1970s, the World Bank has lent some $30 billion to DFIs throughout the developing world.

> *"Washington is ... joining the World Bank and related organizations in promoting a variety of rear-guard socialist planning efforts."*

In 1985, an internal World Bank review looked at a sample of these banks and found that many borrowers had failed to repay their loans. In almost half of the cases, more than 25 percent of loans were delinquent; at nearly one-quarter of the DFIs, more than 50 percent of loans were delinquent. "Many governments used credits from DFIs for low interest rate lending to public and quasi-public institutions," the report said. "On loans made at the behest of government, financial discipline was often poor, and for political reasons the DFIs were not able to foreclose on delinquent loans." The review concluded that "few DFIs have become financially viable, autonomous institutions capable of mobilizing resources from commercial markets at home and abroad."

But the World Bank continued to extend about $2 billion in new loans to DFIs each year. In 1989, the bank's annual *World Development Report* issued another damning verdict. Among a sample of 18 DFIs, 50 percent of loans, on average, were overdue. "It is clear [directed-credit programs] have damaged financial systems," the report concluded, noting that cheap DFI loans had encouraged unproductive investments, promoted both unintentional and willful defaults, impeded development of capital markets, and fostered bank borrowing where equity financing would have been more appropriate.

An Unlikely Leader

Nevertheless, in February 1990 the World Bank approved two directed-credit loans for Poland. The National Bank of Poland, the country's central bank and monopoly lender, will disburse the money, which includes $245 million for export-oriented industrial projects and $100 million for agricultural processing industries. Funneling loans through the central bank will enhance its power and retard the development of a private banking system.

The track record for similar loans elsewhere isn't encouraging. In Yugoslavia in the 1980s, the World Bank channeled at least $700 million in loans through seven of the government's nine regional lending groups. The bank knew that these institutions were lending money at rates that were negative in real terms, ranging from minus 10 percent to minus 20 percent. In 1989, a confidential World Bank study disclosed that all the banks were in the red. In 1983, the World Bank provided a $275-million "structural adjustment loan" to Yugoslavia's state-owned Udruzena Beogradska Banka; four years later, the bank was $1.2 billion in the red. Yet the World Bank continues to bankroll Yugoslavia's socialist experiment; In April 1990 it approved a second structural adjustment loan, this time for $400 million.

> *"The World Bank plans to lend $7 billion to $8 billion [to Eastern Europe] over three years."*

The World Bank's credulous attitude toward Eastern Europe's self-destructive economic policies makes it an unlikely leader on the path of market-oriented reform. Consider this excerpt from a 1979 World Bank study of Romania: "Between 1950 and 1975 the economy grew rapidly within the framework of comprehensive economic planning made possible by the state's control of the major productive resources and its monopoly over foreign trade.... According to official statistics, Social Product and National Income grew by 9.8 percent per annum for 25 years.... Picture for 1981-90: National income should grow at 8 to 8.9 percent per annum."

This is sheer nonsense. As Sir Alan Walters, former top economic advisor to

Margaret Thatcher, explained in a 1990 *Forbes* interview: "In 1975 Romania's per capita income was $800 or $700. If they grew at 10 percent per annum for the previous 25 years, then in 1950, they must all have been dead from starvation!"

More recently, a 1989 report by the World Bank's Economic Development Institute, *Financial Reform in Socialist Economies*, outlined how Yugoslavia can introduce a stock market without private property. (The state would own and trade the shares.) One chapter concludes: "The issue is not one of returning to capitalism, but of using its financial instruments by adapting them to socialism . . . not that of introducing private property rights, but defining alternative incentive mechanisms that could play the role they play in capitalist economies."

Loans Strengthen State Control

As Hungarian economist János Kornai and Polish economist Jan Winiecki argue, the nations of Eastern Europe need flesh-and-blood entrepreneurs more than anything else. Their point is simple: You can't have capitalism without capitalists. The countries of Eastern Europe must cultivate true capitalists—both domestic and foreign—on their own, through a functioning convertible currency, viable legal accounting systems, modest levels of taxation and regulation, and full, constitutionally-guaranteed property rights.

The World Bank's record throughout the developing world and in Eastern Europe demonstrates that it cannot be a catalyst for radical economic liberalization. Following in its path, the new East European Development Bank is fundamentally a socialist undertaking. Loans from multilateral development banks will only serve to further politicize economies already burdened by state control. The new political structures in Eastern Europe are weak, and the inflow of subsidized credit can easily forestall the necessary transition to market prices and private investment. With the verdict on socialism so clear, the United States and other Western Governments should abandon the oxymoronic idea of planning for capitalism.

NATO Is Unnecessary

by Doug Bandow

About the author: *Doug Bandow is a senior fellow at the Cato Institute. A former special assistant to President Ronald Reagan, he is the author of* Human Resources and Defense Manpower, *a national defense university textbook.*

In the eyes of President George Bush, NATO is forever, or almost so. The alliance's job may be over one day, says Bush, but he won't "project out over 100 years" toward that utopian time. While the American president feels NATO is still in the security business, some supporters say mission accomplished. They're looking to find new work for the alliance. Still other members of the NATO family take their cue from political scientists: The first order of business of any bureaucracy is to entrench itself and justify its existence. They say of NATO, job well done, it's time to call it a day.

Doubt About NATO's Future

NATO's struggle, it seems, is no longer East-West but internecine. No one expects the Warsaw Pact, if it can be said to exist any longer, to roll westward, and even such mainstream hard-liners as Richard Perle acknowledge that the Soviet threat has been transformed. Similarly, the Pentagon's *Soviet Military Power 1990* not only admitted significant reductions in Soviet weapons production but concluded that "the likelihood of a conflict stemming from U.S.-Soviet confrontation is lower than it has ever been in the post-war era." Whatever the resolution of the USSR's political and economic problems, the chance of Soviet aggression has fallen from unlikely to inconceivable.

Which means that NATO's future, at least as an *Atlantic* alliance, is in doubt.

NATO was created four decades ago to protect war-ravaged Europe from Soviet domination, but the geopolitical dynamic today could not be more different. The Western nations are populous and prosperous, capable of enormous exertion should a Soviet threat reemerge; the East Europeans have gone from formal allies to de facto adversaries of the USSR, likely to fight any Red Army attempt to march across them to the Atlantic; and the Soviet Union is in a state of near collapse, with the economy imploding and the "Union" of Soviet Socialist

Doug Bandow, "NATO: Who Needs It?" *Defense and Displomacy*, August/September 1991. Reprinted with permission.

Republics exploding.

Regardless of what happens to the USSR's unsteady move toward capitalism and democracy, West Europeans have more to fear from a flood of starving refugees than of tanks.

> *"The Western nations are populous and prosperous, capable of enormous exertion should a Soviet threat reemerge."*

"The purpose of NATO is achieved," says Alan Clark, the British Minister for Defense Procurement.

Is there some other reason, then, for the U.S. to maintain troops in Europe—whether the official 195,000 floor or the 80,000 to 100,000 figure tossed around informally by administration officials until the "utopian day" in the next century when President Bush thinks they just might go home?

Justifying NATO

Hard-liners may reverse the course of reforms, but the resulting regime would face objectively overwhelming constraints: A military racked by desertion and dissension, an economy that cannot feed its people, a burgeoning democratic movement, a dozen major ethnic, nationalist and religious groups demanding independence, and the end of friendly communist regimes in Eastern Europe. Whatever new threat that might arise in such circumstances could easily be countered by a reunified Germany, which is now helping to feed the USSR, and the other European states, east as well as west. Indeed, the Western European Union (WEU) provides the perfect framework, or "nucleus," in Alan Clark's words, for a new European security system manned and funded by the Europeans.

Lots of alternative tasks remain to be done. Robert Zoellick, Secretary of State James Baker's counselor, acknowledges that the Department's Policy Planning staff has been looking "at how you transform established institutions, such as NATO, to serve new missions that will fit the new era." But what should the quintessential anti-Soviet military alliance now do? The creativity of the NATO-forever crowd is boundless.

For instance, Robert Hormats, vice-chairman of Goldman Sachs International, argued in *Foreign Affairs* that Western leaders must "expand the range of issues on which NATO engages the common efforts of the European and North American democracies—from student exchanges, to fighting the drug trade, to resisting terrorism, to countering threats to the environment." Similarly, former U.S. NATO Ambassador David Abshire has suggested NATO "coordinate the transfer of environmental-control and energy-conservation technology to the East, thereby benefiting the global ecology." A proposal to turn American tanks into bookmobiles is probably only a matter of time. Other, more serious tasks have been proposed. Before the Persian Gulf crisis, for instance, *The Economist* magazine suggested NATO respond to security threats elsewhere in the world. NATO commander Gen. John Galvin similarly proposed turning alliance troops into a mobile "fire brigade" for use around the world, with the Persian Gulf its first test.

Taking Responsibility

But the U.S., not NATO, orchestrated the response to Iraq; among NATO members only Great Britain made a meaningful contribution, and that was a result of former Prime Minister Margaret Thatcher's determination rather than NATO's policies. Indeed, cooperation in the past on "out-of-area" activities, such as Libya and Nicaragua, has been nil.

Some alliance officials have spoken of NATO "managing" change in Eastern Europe. The ongoing struggles in Bulgaria, Romania and Yugoslavia hardly seem manageable by anyone. And exactly what American tank divisions in Germany would do has never been explained. Regional consultation would, of course, be a good thing, but a military alliance is not the best forum for talking.

As tragic as would be the spilling of blood if Hungary and Romania fought over Transylvania, it would be more tragic for the U.S. to intervene and spill American blood. And unless troops are stationed directly in the Balkans, NATO is unlikely to have much impact on Serbian nationalism or any other force of instability. In any case, the U.S. has spent four decades ensuring the security of Western Europe. The countries that have benefited so long from American military protection should now take on the responsibility for assisting Eastern Europe.

A Necessary Enemy?

Of course, many Americans and Europeans who worry about "instability" are really only concerned about Germany. Christopher Smart of the Hudson Institute explains that "the presence of U.S. troops on the continent not only reassures Germany's neighbors that they are not alone, but it can also help protect Germany from an anti-German coalition." Retired Army Chief of Staff E.C. Meyer is blunter, opining that with the changes in the USSR, the "reunification of Germany, and what that really might mean," is one of the biggest threats remaining. The belief that the prosperous, freedom-loving burghers who, until recently, were complimented as the mainstay of the Western alliance are ready to revert to rapacious Huns determined to conquer their nuclear-armed neighbors can come only from

> *"The purpose of NATO is achieved."*

a desperate search for a "necessary enemy" to justify NATO's continued existence. While history should never be forgotten, it should not be twisted to justify obsolescent alliances.

The changes in Eastern Europe and the Soviet Union have made it difficult for NATO officials to keep a straight face while explaining the vital American interest in continuing to station hundreds of thousands of troops in Europe. The Persian Gulf crisis has made their task impossible. If Washington can strip Europe of combat units while sending one-fifth of its military to confront a third-rate dictator in the Mideast, it sees no realistic threat to Europe's security. And the lack of such a threat ends any pretense that NATO has a role in the future. It's time to send the American-led alliance into early retirement.

Glossary of Acronyms

ABB   Asea Brown Boveri. A German industrial firm.

CDU   Christian Democratic Union. A conservative German political party.

CFE   Conventional (armed) Forces in Europe. An agreement made during the Cold War by the NATO nations and the former Warsaw Pact nations to supply each other with information on the number of weapons made and on the location of their armed forces.

CFSP   Common Foreign and Security Policy. A common defense plan proposed by members of the EC in December 1991.

CIS   Commonwealth of Independent States. An alliance of some of the nations that were a part of the former USSR.

DDR   German Democratic Republic. The official name of the former East Germany.

DGB   German Trade Union Federation. The umbrella organization for a number of trade unions that includes skilled workers and public servants, based in Dusseldorf, Germany.

ECU   European Currency Unit. Proposed currency that would be used by the European Community if the twelve nations combine their monetary systems.

EMU   Economic and Monetary Union. The EC committee proposals to unite Europe economically and monetarily.

EPC   European Political Cooperation. EC nations' efforts to coordinate their separate foreign policies.

FDP   Free Democratic Party. A liberal German political party.

FRG   Federal Republic of Germany. The official name of the former West Germany.

ICL   International Communist League. An international communist organization that promotes the ideals of Vladimir Lenin, Karl Marx, and Leon Trotsky.

Europe

OECD Organization for Economic Cooperation and Development. Established in 1961, this organization gives economic advice, coordinates economic policies, and encourages economic growth and world trade. Nineteen of the twenty-four nations in the OECD are in Europe.

OPIC Overseas Private Investment Corporation. A U.S. government agency that provides loans, loan guarantees, and political risk insurance to developing countries that encourage free market principles and espouse democratic ideals.

OPZZ All-Polish Trade Union Alliance. A trade union made up of seven million factory workers. Its objective is to legally represent and protect its members against job discrimination, unemployment, and mismanagement.

PDS Party of Democratic Socialism. The New German democratic party that replaced the former East German Communist Party, *SED*.

SED Socialist Unity Party of Germany. The name of the former East German Communist Party.

SpAD The German Spartacist Worker's Party. The German affiliate of the International Communist League.

WEU Western European Union. A defense alliance established in 1954. Composed of all EC members except Greece, Ireland, and Denmark. It is closely tied to NATO and is concerned primarily with developing a security policy for Europe.

Bibliography

Books

Paul E. Barfield and Mark Perlman, eds.	*Industry, Services and Agriculture in the 1990s: The United States Faces a United Europe.* Lanham, MD: University Press of America, 1991.
Eric Bjornland and Larry Garber, eds.	*The New Democratic Frontier: A Country by Country Report on Elections in Central and Eastern Europe.* Arlington, VA: Public Interest Publications, 1991.
Jan Bossak, Vittorio Corbo, and Fabrizio Coricelli, eds.	*Reforming Central and Eastern European Economies.* New York: The World Bank, 1991.
Henry Brandon, ed.	*In Search of a New World Order.* Washington: The Brookings Institution, 1992.
Roland Calori and Peter Lawrence, eds.	*The Business of Europe: Managing Change.* Newbury Park, CA: Sage, 1991.
Patrick J. Clawson and Vladimir Tismaneanu	*Uprooting Leninism, Cultivating Liberty.* Philadelphia: Foreign Policy Research Institute, 1992.
Carol Cool, Damien J. Neven, and Ingo Walter, eds.	*European Industrial Restructuring in the 1990s.* New York: New York University Press, 1992.
Christopher Cviic	*Remaking the Balkans.* London: Pinter, 1991.
Ralf Dahrendorf	*Reflections on the Revolution in Europe.* New York: Random House, 1990.
Jacques Derrida	*The Other Heading: Reflections on Today's Europe.* Bloomington: Indiana University Press, 1992.
Michael Emerson and Christopher Huhne	*The ECU Report: The Single European Currency—and What It Means to You.* London: Pan, 1992.
John Feffer	*Shock Waves: Eastern Europe After the Revolutions.* Boston: South End Press, 1992.
A. Giovannini and C. Mayer, eds.	*European Financial Integration.* Cambridge: Cambridge University Press, 1991.
Paul Godt, ed.	*Policy-Making in France: From DeGaulle to Mitterand.* London: Pinter, 1989.
Jeffrey C. Goldfarb	*After the Fall.* New York: Basic Books, 1992.
Peter Hall et al., eds.	*Developments in French Politics.* London: Macmillan, 1990.
Leah A. Haus	*Globalizing the GATT.* Washington: The Brookings Institution, 1992.
Institute of Economic Affairs	*Europe's Constitutional Future.* New York: New York University Press, 1991.

Europe

Mary Kaldor, ed.	*Europe from Below: An East-West Dialogue.* London: Verso, 1991.
Michael Kaser and Aleksandar M. Vacic, eds.	*Reforms in Foreign Economic Relations for Eastern Europe and the Soviet Union.* New York: United Nations, 1991.
Bennett M. Kovrig	*Of Walls and Bridges: The United States and Eastern Europe.* New York: New York University Press, 1991.
Jacques Riboud	*A Stable External Currency for Europe.* London: Macmillan, 1991.
J.M.C. Rollo, et al.	*The New Eastern Europe.* London: Pinter, 1990.
Jane O. Sharp, ed.	*Europe After an American Withdrawal.* New York: Oxford University Press, 1990.
Paul B. Stares	*Command Performance: The Neglected Dimension of European Security.* Washington: The Brookings Institution, 1991.
Gregory F. Treverton	*America, Germany, and the Future of Europe.* Princeton, NJ: Princeton University Press, 1992.
Richard H. Ullman	*Securing Europe.* Princeton, NJ: Princeton University Press, 1991.
Jozef M. van Brabant	*Economic Integration in Eastern Europe.* Hemel Hempstead, England: Harvester/Wheatsheaf, 1989.
Nils H. Wessell	*The New Europe: Revolution in East-West Relations.* New York: Academy of Political Science, 1991.

Periodicals

Anders Aslund	"Four Key Reforms," *American Enterprise*, July/August 1991.
James Baker and Hans-Dietrich Genscher	"U.S.-German Views on the New European and Trans-Atlantic Architecture," *U.S. Department of State Dispatch*, May 13, 1991.
Daniel Bell	"Socialism and Planning," *Dissent*, Winter 1991.
Henrik Bering-Jensen	"Common Defense and Foreign Policy Elude Continent," *Insight*, February 18, 1991. Available from 3600 New York Ave. NE, Washington, DC 20002.
Henrik Bering-Jensen	"Unification of Europe Hits Snags," *Insight*, December 16, 1991.
John Brademas	"A Moment to Seize," *Vital Speeches of the Day*, May 1, 1991.
Silviu Brucan	"An Austro-Korean Model for Eastern Europe," *New Perspectives Quarterly*, Fall 1990.
Zbigniew Brzezinski	"The Road to Strasbourg? Or to Sarajevo?" *Vital Speeches of the Day*, June 15, 1991.
James M. Buchanan	"An American Perspective on Europe's Constitutional Opportunity," *Cato Journal*, Winter 1991. Available from the Cato Institute, 224 Second St. SE, Washington, DC 20003.
Roger Cohen	"Smaller Companies Grease the Wheels in Hungary," *The New York Times*, May 3, 1992.

Bibliography

John Diebold	"New Elements in Determining Strategy for the 1990s: A European/American Perspective," *Vital Speeches of the Day*, January 1, 1992.
Robert J. Dowling and Gail E. Schares	"Lessons from Prague's Full-Tilt Rush to Capitalism," *Business Week*, June 1, 1992.
William Drozdiak	"Suddenly, Cold Feet over the Urge to Merge," *The Washington Post National Weekly Edition*, June 22-28, 1992.
Gertrude Schaffner Goldberg	"Women on the Verge: Winners and Losers in German Unification," *Social Policy*, Fall 1991.
Adam Gwiazda	"Eastern Europe Is Ripe for Joint Ventures," *European Affairs*, Winter 1990. Available from Elsevier, PO Box 470, 1000 AL Amsterdam, The Netherlands.
Anthony Hartley	"The Once and Future Europe," *National Interest*, Winter 1991. Available from Department NI, PO Box 3000, Denville, NJ 07834.
Bill Javetski, et al.	"48,000 Votes That Shook a Continent," *Business Week*, June 15, 1992.
Journal of International Affairs	Entire issue on Eastern Europe, Summer 1991.
Tony Killick and Christopher Stevens	"Lessons from the South," *International Affairs*, October 4, 1991.
Pablo Liebl	"The Illusions of 'Euro-Optimism,' " *American Enterprise*, March/April 1991.
Thomas Molnar	"Europe Is Not What It Seems," *Chronicles*, April 1991. Available from PO Box 800, Mt. Morris, IL 61054.
Bruce W. Nelan	"Which Way to Maastricht, Mijnheer?" *Time*, December 9, 1991.
Daniel N. Nelson	"Will Property and Profit Set Eastern Europe Free?" *In These Times*, November 21-December 4, 1990.
Richard Rose	"Toward a Civil Economy," *Journal of Democracy*, April 1992. Available from the Johns Hopkins University Press, Journals Division, 101 15th St. NW, Suite 200, Washington, DC 20005.
George Ross	"Confronting the New Europe," *New Left Review*, January/February 1992.
Jerry Schmidt	" 'Invisible Hand' Shakes East's Free-Market Faith," *In These Times*, May 27-June 9, 1992.
Dieter Senghaas	"Peace Theory and the Restructuring of Europe," *Alternatives*, Summer 1991.
Anthony D. Smith	"National Identity and the Idea of European Unity," *International Affairs*, January 1992.
William R. Smyser	"The EC: Powerhouse in 1992," *The World & I*, May 1991. Available from 2800 New York Ave. NE, Washington, DC 20002.
Melanie S. Tammen	"Will Western Socialism Conquer Eastern Europe?" *USA Today*, March 1991.
Jack Trumpbour	"1992 and the Europe Without Frontiers," *Z Magazine*, November 1990.
Caspar W. Weinberger	"The European Community's New Army," *Forbes*, November 25, 1991.

Organizations to Contact

The editors have compiled the following list of organizations that are concerned with the issues debated in this book. All of them have publications or information available for interested readers. The descriptions are derived from materials provided by the organizations. This list was compiled at the date of publication. Names, addresses, and phone numbers of organizations are subject to change.

American Defense Institute (ADI)
1055 N. Fairfax St., 2d Floor
Alexandria, VA 22314
(703) 519-7000

The goal of ADI is to educate young Americans about foreign threats to freedom and the need for a strong defense program. The institute sponsors internships, fellowships, and programs that emphasize the preparation of young people for leadership in defense policy-making. It believes that NATO is still vital for the security of Europe and the United States. ADI publishes the quarterly *ADI Newsletter*.

Amnesty International (AI)
322 Eighth Ave.
New York, NY 10001-4808
(212) 807-8400

Amnesty International monitors human rights throughout the world. It is unaffiliated with any government, political faction, ideology, economic interest, or religious creed. It publishes an annual report on worldwide human rights conditions and monitors the changes going on in Europe. AI publishes the bimonthly newsletter *Amnesty International*.

The Brookings Institution
1775 Massachusetts Ave. NW
Washington, DC 20036-2188
(202) 797-6000

The institution, founded in 1927, is a liberal think tank that conducts research and education in economics, government, foreign policy, and the social sciences. It publishes the quarterly *Brookings Review*, the biannual *Brookings Papers on Economic Activity*, and various books, including *In Search of a New World Order: The Future of U.S.-European Relations*, *Euro-Politics*, and *Europe 1992: An American Perspective*.

Cato Institute
244 Second St. SE
Washington, DC 20003
(202) 546-0200

Organizations to Contact

The institute is a libertarian public policy research foundation dedicated to stimulating foreign policy debate. Several of its publications have addressed economic and security changes taking place in Europe. It publishes the triannual *Cato Journal*, the periodic *Cato Policy Analysis*, and a bimonthly newsletter, *Cato Policy Review*.

The Council on Foreign Relations
58 E. 68th St.
New York, NY 10021
(212) 734-0400

The council is a group of individuals with specialized knowledge of foreign affairs. It was formed to study the international aspects of American political and economic policies and problems. It publishes the renowned journal *Foreign Affairs* five times a year.

Delegation of the Commission of the European Communities
2100 M St. NW, 7th Floor
Washington, DC 20036

The delegation serves as the European Community's representative in the United States. It is part of the administrative, policy-making branch of the European Community and provides free brochures and other information on the official activities and policies of the European Community.

Foreign Policy Association
729 Seventh Ave.
New York, NY 10019
(212) 764-4050

The association is an educational organization that provides nonpartisan information to help citizens participate in foreign policy decisions. It publishes the monthly *Foreign Policy Preview* and a free catalog of other publications.

The Foundation for Economic Education Inc.
30 S. Broadway
Irvington, NY 10533
(914) 591-7230

The foundation sponsors research in the areas of economic policy, open markets, and limited government. It publishes the monthly journal *The Freeman: Ideas on Liberty* and a bimonthly newsletter. Both are free.

The Heritage Foundation
214 Massachusetts Ave. NE
Washington, DC 20002
(202) 546-4400

The Heritage Foundation is a public policy research institute dedicated to the principles of free, competitive enterprise, limited government, and individual liberty. Its publications include the periodic *Backgrounder*, the monthly *Policy Review*, and other materials.

Hudson Institute
PO Box 26919
Indianapolis, IN 46226
(317) 545-1000

The institute studies public policy aspects of national and international economics. It supports the view that the United States must continue to lead international policy-making. Publications include the quarterly *Hudson Institute Report,* research papers, and books.

National Committee on American Foreign Policy
232 Madison Ave.
New York, NY 10016
(212) 685-3411

The committee is composed of Americans from varied backgrounds who are interested in foreign policy and want to encourage citizen participation in foreign policy decisions. It also organizes fact-finding missions that meet with top political and economic leaders. Publications include the bimonthly *American Foreign Policy Newsletter,* monographs, and books.

The Spartacist League
PO Box 1377 GPO
New York, NY 10116
(212) 732-7860 or 267-1025

The Spartacist League is an international organization that advocates revolutionary, socialist political theories. It publishes the periodic journal *Spartacist,* the biweekly tabloid *Workers Vanguard,* and monographs.

Index

abortion, 115-117, 121
Act of European Union (Maastricht Treaty, 1991), 49, 50, 52
Adenauer, Konrad, 52, 77, 81
Africa
  European Community and, 25-26
  foreign debt of, 168, 259, 264
  socialism in, 182
  U.S. aid to, 168, 169
Agnelli, Giovanni, 24
agriculture
  Eastern European, 169
  EC subsidies for, 23, 54, 65, 79
  German, 100
Albania, 167, 203
  communism overthrown, 126, 189
  hard-currency needs, 206
  trade unions, 222-223
All-Polish Trade Union Alliance (OPZZ), 221
American Business and Private Sector Development Initiative, 156
American Telephone & Telegraph Company (AT&T), 40-41
Andor, Laszlo, 258, 260-261
Andreotti, Giulio, 58-59
Andriessen, Frans H. J. J., 47
Applebaum, Anne, 194
Ash, Timothy Garton, 140
Asia, 169, 182
Astramowicz, Jarek, 123-124
Austria, 57, 139
  EC membership application, 80, 86
  Polish debt to, 262
authoritarianism, 137-138, 139-140, 165, 186

Bahr, Egon, 103, 106
Bainbridge, Michelle, 17
Baker, James A., III, 33, 49, 50, 67, 269
Balcerowicz Plan, 197-198, 199
Bandow, Doug, 268
Belgium, 64, 79, 118
Bergner, Jeffrey T., 96
Bering-Jensen, Henrik, 69
Berlin Wall, 24, 80, 92, 107, 112, 143
biotechnology, 17-18
Bismarck, Otto von, 75, 102, 105
Brademas, John, 212
Brandt, Willy, 83, 103

Brentano, Heinrich von, 77
Brezhnev, Leonid I., 103
Brock, William, 65-66
Brzezinski, Zbigniew, 131
Buckley, William F., Jr., 180
Bulgaria, 167, 174
  communism overthrown, 126
  democracy in, 153, 154, 188
  economic reform, 154, 160, 186
  EC trade provisions, 48
  foreign debt, 129, 188, 259
  IMF policies and, 258, 261
  NATO and, 270
  parliament, women in, 118
  trade unions, 219, 221, 223
  U.S. aid to, 168, 215
  Western business investment in, 129-130, 188
Burstein, Daniel, 37
Bush, George
  Eastern European economies and, 50, 229
  EC policies and, 50, 56, 65, 67, 92
  German unification and, 90, 91, 246
  NATO and, 268, 269
businesses
  European union benefits, 21, 37-45, 66
  in Eastern Europe
    education for, 214
    joint ventures benefit, 207-211
    tax policies, 230-231

Canada, 18, 38, 250
capitalism
  Eastern European adoption of, 123-124, 201
    benefits economies, 143-151
    con, 130, 160-164, 176-183, 190, 191, 193
    free market education in, 212-217
  Bulgaria and, 188
  difficulties of, 130, 134, 185-186, 197, 220
  IMF policies harm, 257, 258, 263
  suspicion of, 199-200
  threatens women, 116, 119, 121
Cecchini reports, 21-22
Chandra, Dilip, 129-130
Churchill, Sir Winston S., 24, 56
Civic Forum, 136, 161, 165
Clausen, A. W., 143
Codevilla, Angelo, 52
Commonwealth of Independent States (CIS), 47,

Europe

48, 49-50
communism
 central banks in, 203
 Eastern European, 103, 174
  collapse of, 131-132, 135, 141, 142, 198, 247, 250
  economic problems of, 106, 155, 176
  economic successes of, 177-178, 185-186
  ethnic tensions and, 157
  tax policies, 225, 227-228
  trade unions in, 218-219
  transition to capitalism, 123, 134, 150-151, 160, 195
  unemployment and, 139
 European Community and, 52-53
 German unification and, 109, 114
Conference on Security and Cooperation in Europe (CSCE)
 Eastern European revolutions and, 141, 250-251
 European union role, 31, 33, 34-35, 64
 military security role, 237, 240, 255-256
  insufficiency of, 250-251, 252
 NATO and, 239, 245
 Yugoslav civil war and, 29, 48
Conventional Forces in Europe (CFE) Treaty (1988), 34, 240
Croatia
 civil war in, 87, 189, 244
 German influence on, 84
 German recognition of, 70, 72, 82, 83, 87, 90
currency stabilization, 201-206
Czechoslovakia, 167, 174
 capitalist development, 125, 160, 161, 163, 186, 188
  currency stabilization, 202
  economic reforms, 154, 164, 165, 261
  privatization in, 67, 127-128, 188, 197, 200
  Western business investment in, 74, 129, 162, 188, 209
 Civic Forum, 136, 161, 165
 communism in
  industries under, 126-127, 129
  overthrow of, 141, 144, 180, 219
 democracy in, 132, 135, 139, 142, 153, 161
 economic recession in, 123, 258
 European Community and
  association agreement, 46, 47, 48, 239
  membership aspiration, 80, 85, 86, 87, 140
  trade relations, 22
 German influence on, 84, 85, 86
 IMF policies and, 226, 258, 261
 Slovak separatism, 84, 133, 136, 188
 Soviet trade with, 161-162, 245
 trade unions, 219, 221-222, 223
 U.S. aid to, 155, 215

Dahrendorf, Ralf, 137
Daimler-Benz A.G., 41, 148
de Gaulle, Charles, 52, 56, 75
Delors, Jacques, 50, 58-59, 60, 76, 79
democracy

Eastern European
 capitalism and, 145, 152, 190
 dangers of, 165, 182-183
 difficulties of transition to, 134, 136, 157-158, 186
 ethnic tensions and, 133
 in trade unions, 182, 218, 220, 223-224
 tradition of, 139-140, 181
 Western policies can assist, 135-142, 153, 159, 236
Democratic League of Independent Trade Unions (LIGA), 222
Denmark, 63, 79, 236, 252
De Santis, Hugh, 249
détente, 249, 250, 255-256
development finance institutions (DFI), 265-266
Dijmarescu, Eugen, 124, 125, 127
Dinan, Desmond, 46

Eagleburger, Lawrence S., 152, 188
Eastern Europe
 economies of, 185-189
 harmed by
  capitalism, 179-181
  foreign debts, 133, 161, 168
  IMF policies, 175, 257-263, 264
  U.S. aid, 168-172, 264-265
  World Bank loans, 265-267
 strengthened by
  capitalism, 143-151
  con, 162, 163-164, 177-178
  currency stabilization, 201-206
  debt relief, 133-134
  con, 161
  democracy, 138-139, 145
  con, 165
  free market education, 212-217
  free trade, 245-246
  joint business ventures, 148-149, 207-211
  privatization, 194-200
  con, 162-163, 165, 192
  socialism, 178, 190-193
  con, 264-267
  tax reform, 225-232
  trade unions, 218-224
 ethnic conflicts in, 60, 133, 134, 250
 European union and
  economic development in, 29, 32, 33, 92
  is beneficial to, 31, 32, 35,
  con, 59, 60, 61, 62
  military security in, 34, 49, 237-240, 251-252
   NATO enhances, 243, 244-245, 254
   con, 268, 269, 270-271
  U.S. business investment in, 44-45, 66-67, 75, 123
 revolutions of 1989, 28, 131, 219, 236
 Soviet trade with, 133, 153, 155, 161-162, 245, 260
 U.S. trade with, 155-156, 157, 245-246
 Western policies toward, 123-130
  are beneficial, 131-134

281

Index

con, 160-166
capitalism benefits, 143-151
  con, 176-183
strengthen democracy, 135-142
U.S. aid, 49-50, 130, 215
  is beneficial to, 140, 152-159
  con, 167-175, 264, 267
women in, 118
East European Development Bank, 267
East Germany (German Democratic Republic), 70, 103-104
  IMF policies and, 258, 261
  social policies, 117-118
  Soviet trade with, 153, 155, 245
  see also Germany
Eberstadt, Nicholas, 167
Economic Policy Institute, 177
economies. *See* Eastern Europe, economies of; Europe, economies of; Germany, economy of
Eggers, William D., 225
electric power generation, 207-208, 209, 211
Ellemann-Jensen, Uffe, 236
Engel, Wolfgang, 108-109, 114
English language, 41-42, 71
Estonia, 93
Europe
  cultural institutions of, 17, 24-25
  economies of, 19-20
    recession in, 19-20
  German unification benefits, 75-76, 82-89, 90-91
    con, 101, 102, 104-105
  military security, 33-34, 158, 236-241, 251-252
    best provided by
      CSCE, 33, 34-35, 64, 239, 240
        con, 250-251
      NATO, 93, 237-239, 242-248
        con, 249-250, 268-271
      WEU, 34, 239-240, 249-256, 269
  nationality conflicts in, 29, 58, 134
  unification of, 17-23
    benefits American businesses, 37-45
    harms U.S. relations, 63-67
    helps unify the world, 24-27
    is a model for Soviet states, 46-51
    opposition to, 53, 58, 59
    strengthens Europe, 28-36
      con, 52-56
    economically, 20-22, 77, 149
      con, 53-54
    will increase regional conflict, 57-62
  U.S. troops in, 64-65, 93, 269, 270-271
  see also Eastern Europe; European Community; Western Europe
European Bank for Reconstruction and Development, 46, 134, 149-150, 167, 265
European Community (EC)
  Council of Ministers, 34, 50, 78, 250
  Eastern Europe and
    association agreements with, 31, 47, 239, 245-246

encouragement of democracy in, 141
financial assistance to, 33, 46, 50, 130, 213
membership in, 80, 85, 86
recognition of new states in, 48-49
trade relations, 22, 47-48, 149, 156, 245
economic union, 17-20, 29-30, 77, 252, 255
benefits European economies, 19-21, 22-23, 77, 149
  con, 53-54
international competitiveness, 19, 20, 22-23
policy goals of, 20-21
tax policy, 21, 53, 231
federal model of, 30
financial budget, 23, 78
foreign policy, 31, 36, 49, 80
German unification and, 32-33, 69-71
membership requirements, 31, 55
monetary union, 30, 55, 91, 252
political union, 18, 20, 25, 30, 55, 81
Soviet relations, 31, 46-47, 48, 49-50
trade relations
  protectionist policies, 19, 47-48, 53, 65
  with Eastern Europe, 22, 47-48, 149, 156, 245
  with Germany, 85
  with the United States, 38, 63, 65-66
U.S. business investment in, 37-38, 44, 63, 66
U.S. political relations, 31, 50, 88, 91-92
European Economic Community (Common Market), 19
European Energy Charter, 46, 50
European Free Trade Agreement (EFTA), 31
European Parliament, 59
  Germany and, 78, 79, 81
  membership in, 71
  role in European union, 30

Federal Republic of Germany. *See* West Germany
Feher, Ferenc, 190-191
Ford Motor Company, 37, 41
France
  European union and, 48, 54, 91
    Arab relations and, 26, 36, 55, 252
    German relations and, 30, 58, 59, 60, 86
    German unification and, 70, 72, 75, 80, 82-83
    leadership in, 69-70, 75-76, 85
    role in NATO, 93
    U.S. relations and, 64, 65, 246
  in Persian Gulf War, 73, 244
free markets. *See* capitalism; trade
Friberg, Eric, 39-40

Gaus, Guenter, 109, 112
Gdansk shipyard, 179-180, 196-197, 219
General Agreement on Tariffs and Trade (GATT), 65-66, 156
General Motors Corporation, 38, 42, 148, 214
Genscher, Hans-Dietrich, 28
  CSCE and, 87, 250
  European union and, 70, 76, 78, 79, 253
  German unification and, 83, 102-103, 105

282

Europe

Yugoslav civil war and, 104
German Democratic Republic. *See* East Germany
Germany
  Bundesbank, 71, 78 81
  Bundestag, 110-111
  currency, 205, 252
  debt relief and, 262
  Eastern Europe and, 26
    business investment in, 74-75, 83
    economic domination of, 58, 67, 74-75
    fears of immigration from, 73-74
    financial assistance to, 67, 93
    political domination of, 73, 84, 93-94, 213
    recognition of Croatia and Slovenia, 70-71, 72, 82, 87, 90, 104
    trade with, 44, 74, 133
    transportation between, 209
  economy of
    Marshall Plan and, 107, 140
    unification strengthens, 85, 93, 96-101
      con, 53, 104-105, 108
  in European Community, 32-33
    budgetary contribution, 23, 78
    economic damage from, 54, 58, 59
    French relations and, 30, 69-70, 75-76, 91
    leadership role in, 70-71, 77-78, 79-81, 85-86, 93
      resented by other nations, 71-72, 74-76, 80, 82, 244
    military security role, 65, 75, 88, 91, 252
      European fears of, 63, 270
      in CSCE, 64
      in NATO, 69, 87, 88-89, 91, 92-93, 243, 246
      in WEU, 254-255, 269
    Soviet relations and, 47, 74
    trade with, 85
    U.S. relations and, 65, 75, 86, 91, 246
  Persian Gulf War and, 72-73, 87, 88, 244
  Soviet troops in, 47, 74, 84-85, 254
  unification of, 69-76
    beneficial to
      Eastern Europe, 61-62, 73-74, 83, 84, 85, 86, 93-94
      European Community, 77-81, 84, 85-86, 88, 94, 95
        con, 53, 58, 59, 60
      Europe and the U.S., 82-89
      German economy, 85, 93, 96-101
        con, 53, 104-105, 108
      United States, 90-95
    costs of, 98-99, 100, 104, 141
    harmful to
      Eastern Europe, 109-110, 133, 161
      East-West relations, 103, 106-114
      Germany, 102-105
      women's rights, 115-121
    incorporation of East Germany, 60, 80, 96, 103-104
      East German revolution and, 28, 82, 119
      increases East-West tension, 103, 106-114

    Western business investment, 148, 177
  NATO and, 69, 87, 88-89, 91, 92-93, 243, 246
  see also East Germany; West Germany
Goethe Institute, 74, 94
Gorbachev, Mikhail S., 132, 141
  European union and, 16, 46, 47, 64
  German unification and, 92
  Soviet reform policies, 182, 210, 243, 250
Goytisolo, Juan, 59
Great Britain
  European union and
    German unification and, 70, 75, 80, 82-83
    resistance to, 55, 58, 91
    U.S. relations and, 26, 64, 246
  in Persian Gulf War, 73, 244, 270
Greece, 23, 54, 140, 252
Groeben, Hans von der, 77
Group of Seven (G-7), 87, 95, 140
Group of 24 (G-24), 50, 140

Hallstein, Walter, 77
Hanke, Steve H., 201
Harmel Report (1967), 249, 250
Havel, Václav, 48, 136, 197, 219, 250, 251
Havemann, Joel, 123
Helsinki Final Act (1975), 48, 246
Herrhausen, Alfred, 146-147
Hitler, Adolf, 84, 88, 115
Hockenos, Paul, 257
Honecker, Erich, 103-104, 143
Hort, Peter, 77
human rights, 236, 246
Hungary, 167
  capitalist development in, 125-126, 160, 161, 163, 187-188, 257
    resistance to, 164-165
  communism in
    industries under, 126-127
    overthrow of, 141, 260
  democracy in, 80, 132, 135, 139-140, 142, 153
  economy of
    agriculture in, 169
    IMF policies and, 256, 257, 260, 261, 264
    obstacles to development, 174
    privatization in, 127, 128, 144-145, 191, 196, 197, 200, 260
    recession in, 123, 187-188
    reform policies, 154, 186
    Western business investment in, 58, 129, 148, 149, 162, 188, 210
  European Community and, 31
    association agreement, 46, 47, 48, 239
    membership aspiration, 80, 85, 86, 87, 140
    trade relations, 22
  foreign debt, 133, 161, 168, 259, 262-263
  German influence on, 84, 93
  German unification and, 133
  NATO affiliation, 245, 270
  Soviet trade with, 161-162, 260
  tax policies, 230, 231
  trade unions, 182, 219, 222, 223

Index

U.S. aid to, 155, 215
Hurd, Douglas, 71

Iliescu, Ion, 129, 223
Independent Trade Unions of Albania (BSPSh), 222, 223
International Business Machines Corporation (IBM), 37, 40-41, 42, 44
International Monetary Fund (IMF)
  Eastern Europe and, 169
    harms economies of, 175, 257-263, 264
    loans to, 167, 260, 264
    tax policies and, 226, 229
Iraq, 72-73, 153, 253, 270
Ireland, 23, 54, 175, 252
Islam, 25-26
Italtel, 40-41
Italy
  economic development, 53
  European union and
    Arab relations and, 26, 36, 252
    in establishment of EC, 52, 78-79
    U.S. relations and, 64, 246
  politics in, 54

Japan
  CSCE involvement, 87
  Eastern Europe and, 32, 161, 213
  economic success of, 16-17, 25, 83, 134, 172
  European competition with, 19, 20, 22, 53
  Polish debt and, 262
  United States and
    business competition with, 38, 44, 66, 82
    investment in, 17, 37
Johnson, Lyndon B., 170-171

Karatnycky, Adrian, 218
Kielinger, Thomas, 72, 73, 74
Kimmit, Robert, 67, 75
Klaus, Václav, 125, 175, 221-222
Knight, Robin, 63
Koerber, Eberhard von, 207
Kohl, Helmut
  Eastern Europe and, 84
  European union and, 58-59, 79
    German role in, 71-72, 86, 91
    military security in, 246, 253
  German unification and, 104
    abortion policies, 116
    on eastern Germany, 110
    on foreign fears of Germany, 72
    role in accomplishing, 69, 102, 103
    tax policies, 96
  military forces and, 75, 83
  Poland and, 74
  visit with Waldheim, 82
Komarek, Valtr, 221
Kopinski, Thaddeus, 125-126
Kornai, János, 175, 267
Krauthammer, Charles, 50
Kruse, Michael, 111-112
Kuklinski, Antoni, 215

Kuwait, 153, 253

Laffer, Arthur, 227
Lamers, Karl, 111
Lari, Eugenio, 186, 187
Latin America
  dictatorship in, 136, 182
  economic difficulties, 144, 146
  foreign debt, 168, 264
  U.S. aid to, 168, 172
Lehane, Cornelius, 176
Livingston, Robert Gerald, 82
Lukacs, George, 190-191
Lukasiewicz, Thomasz, 128-129

Maastricht Summit (1991), 49, 71-72
Maastricht Treaty (1991), 49, 50, 52
Major, John, 58-59, 71
Makridakis, Spyros G., 17
manufacturing, 17, 38, 41, 43, 208
Marshall, Tyler, 106
Marshall Plan, 107, 140-141, 154
Marx, Karl, 192, 203
Mazowiecki, Tadeusz, 74, 165, 197, 199
Michnik, Adam, 60, 136, 138, 165
Mielke, Erich, 103-104
Mitterand, François, 36, 49-50, 58, 253
Molnar, Thomas, 57

Napier, Andrew, 37-38
nationalism
  European union and, 18, 29
  in Eastern Europe, 134, 147-148, 165, 185, 250
  in Soviet Union, 94
  Yugoslav separatism, 189
Nazism, 88, 103-104
New York University, 214, 215, 216
Nixon, Richard, 171, 242
nomenklatura, 137-138, 196, 223
North Atlantic Cooperation Council (NACC), 87, 238
North Atlantic Treaty Organization (NATO)
  Eastern Europe and, 141, 268
    inclusion of, 87, 173, 245
    security of, 173, 238, 244-245, 270
  European Community and, 49, 64, 65, 239
  European security and, 237-240
    insufficiency of, 249-250, 251, 254
    is necessary, 242-248
    con, 255, 256, 268-271
    U.S. role in, 93, 242-243, 248, 255, 269
  Germany and, 103
    original mission of, 69, 83, 87, 243, 253
    unification and, 86, 92, 94, 270
    U.S. partnership with, 88-89, 91, 93, 246
nuclear weapons, 84, 90, 243, 254-255

Olszewski, Jan, 220-221
Overseas Private Investment Corporation (OPIC), 45, 156, 157

Paris, Charter of (1991), 29, 33, 35, 48

Europe

Paris, Club of, 133-134, 155, 179, 262
PepsiCo, Inc., 44-45, 149
Perlmutter, Amos, 102
Persian Gulf War
   Eastern Europe and, 134, 136, 180, 258
   European Community and, 35, 36, 244, 246
   Germany and, 72, 87, 88
   NATO and, 247, 270, 271
   U.S. role in, 50, 253
Philip Morris Company, 45, 75
Pinder, John, 46-47
Podkrepa union, 219, 221, 223
Pohl, Karl Otto, 252
Poland, 167
   capitalist development in, 125, 126, 144, 160, 161, 186, 187, 191
      education for, 216
      resistance to, 164, 165, 199-200
   communism in
      industries under, 126-127
      overthrow of, 141, 219
   economy of
      currency stabilization, 202, 203, 206
      IMF policies and, 261, 262, 264
      privatization in, 128, 191, 196-200
      recession in, 123, 177, 187
      reform policies, 153-154, 155, 194, 197-198
      Western business investment in, 74-75, 129, 162, 179-180, 210
   European Community and, 31
      association agreement, 46, 47, 48, 239
      membership aspiration, 80, 85, 86, 87, 140
   foreign debt, 133, 161, 168, 179, 259, 262
   German unification and, 70, 133
   politics
      democracy in, 80, 132, 135-136, 139-140, 142, 153
      elections, 74, 180, 192
      populism in, 165
   trade unions, 218-219, 220-221, 223
   unemployment rates, 163, 177, 179
   U.S. aid to, 155, 168, 169, 215
   World Bank loans to, 266
Pond, Elizabeth, 90
populism, 138, 139, 140, 165, 199
Portugal
   democracy in, 134
   European Community and, 30, 32, 36, 252
   financial subsidies to, 22, 54, 140
poverty
   Eastern Europe, 180, 260
   United States, 177, 179
Pracz, Krystyna, 128
privatization, 57, 127-128, 223-224
   strengthens Eastern European economies, 194-200
      con, 162-163, 165, 192
   U.S. businesses and, 67
   World Bank and, 265
protectionism, 18, 47-48, 53, 65, 231-232

Quayle, Dan, 64, 65

railroads, 209-210
Reagan, Ronald, 181, 227, 253
Reich, Jens, 109-110, 114
Reich, Robert B., 214
Roche, David C., 125, 130
Roman Catholic church, 61, 93, 116-117
Romania, 167, 174
   capitalist development in, 127, 129-130, 186, 188-189
   economy of, 266
      IMF policies and, 258-259
      privatization in, 124, 129
      Western business investment in, 123, 189
   ethnic tensions, 133, 160, 270
   foreign debt, 168, 189
   political instability, 125, 173, 188-189
   U.S. aid to, 168, 169, 215
Rome, Treaty of (1958), 18
Ros, Carl Wilhelm, 66
Roth, Wolfgang, 108, 110-111
Russia
   German unification and, 61-62, 84
   nationalist conflict in, 60, 247

Schorlemmer, Friedrich, 113-114
Schuler, Kurt, 201
Serbia, 55-56, 189, 244, 270
Servan-Schreiber, Jean-Jacques, 39, 63
Siemens Corporation, 40-41, 44
Singapore, 225-226
Single European Act (1986), 20, 55, 78-79
Siwicki, Janusz, 124, 128
Slovakia, 84, 188, 222
   see also Czechoslovakia
Slovenia
   German recognition of, 70, 72, 82, 87, 90
   independence, 189, 244
socialism
   strengthens Eastern European economies, 178, 190-193
      con, 264-267
   see also communism
Solidarity movement
   as labor union, 196-197, 218-219, 220-221, 223
   in Polish government, 117, 179, 180
   political split in, 135-136, 161, 165
South America, 205, 259
South Korea, 172, 173, 225-226
Soviet Union
   Afghanistan war, 180
   arms control agreements, 240
   capitalist development in, 33, 132, 167
      dangers of, 177-178, 180
      education and, 212
   coup of 1991, 74
   demise of, 64, 70, 91, 131
   democracy in, 142, 182-183
      authoritarian reactions to, 136, 137-138, 165
      dangers of, 190, 191
   Eastern Europe and

Index

former domination of, 61, 173, 190
trade relations, 133, 153, 155, 161-162, 245, 260
Western development assistance and, 125, 126, 185, 187
economy of
currency stabilization, 201-202, 203, 204-205, 206
Western business investment in, 44-45, 207, 210
European union and, 29, 31, 32, 34, 35
as model for Soviet states, 46-51
in CSCE, 33, 240, 250
German aid to, 67, 93
German unification and, 70, 83, 84
NATO and, 92, 242, 243-244, 246-247, 268-269
troops in Germany, 47, 74, 84-85, 254
U.S. aid to, 64, 67, 265
Spain
economic success, 125, 163
European Community and, 32, 48, 54-55, 140
Arab relations and, 26, 36, 252
financial subsidies to, 54
Germany and, 58, 74
Support for Eastern European Democracy Act (1989), 215, 264
Szego, Andrea, 259-260, 261

Taiwan, 172, 173, 225-226
Tammen, Melanie S., 264
tariffs, 18, 53, 145, 231, 232
tax reform, 225-232
Thatcher, Margaret, 58, 71, 79, 174, 270
Theissen, Horst, 116, 117
Thies, Jochen, 74, 75
Third World, 138, 140, 187, 259, 261
trade
Eastern European, 150
currency reform and, 202, 204
with European Community, 22, 47-48, 149, 156, 245
with Soviet Union, 133, 153, 155, 161-162, 245, 260
with United States, 155-156, 157, 245-246
European Community, 20, 36, 53
protectionism, 18, 47-48, 53, 65
with United States, 38, 63, 65-66
tariffs, 19, 53, 145, 231-232
trade unions, 218-224
transportation, 209-210
Treverton, Gregory F., 70, 73
Turkey, 72-73, 82, 88
Tyminski, Stanislaw, 74, 135-136, 199-200

Ulbricht, Walter, 103-104
unemployment, 19
capitalist reforms and, 125, 139, 147, 162-163, 180, 185, 258
German unification and, 96, 119
in Poland, 154, 163, 179, 198
tax policies and, 226, 232

United Nations, 88
Charter, 35, 246
Genocide Convention (1948), 246
Security Council, 70, 71, 248
United States
Agency for International Development (AID), 156, 168, 170-171, 175, 215
Commerce Department, 92, 155-156
Congress
Eastern European aid and, 215, 264
European troop levels and, 65, 242, 252
tariffs and, 145
Vietnam War and, 171
Eastern Europe and
business investment in, 44-45, 66-67, 75, 123
democracy in, 138, 141, 145, 215
financial aid to, 49-50, 130, 215
benefits economies of, 140, 152-159
con, 167-175, 264, 267
free market education in, 213, 214-216
economic recession, 180-181, 212
European Community and, 31
business investment in, 37-45, 66
military security role
cutbacks in, 64-65, 239, 242, 249, 252, 253-255
is necessary, 242-243, 244, 248
con, 250, 251, 268, 269, 270-271
WEU and, 253, 255, 256
trade with, 38, 63, 65-66
unification threatens relations with, 63-67
Germany and
military security of, 69, 86, 246
unification of
is beneficial to, 82, 85, 88-89, 90-95
Information Agency (USIA), 215, 251
Marshall Plan investment, 140, 141
poverty in, 177, 178-179

value-added tax (VAT), 21, 231
Vietnam War, 170-171

Walesa, Lech, 60, 165
as labor leader, 219, 221
elected president of Poland, 74, 136, 199
Polish economy and, 156, 187, 198-199, 262
Wallace, William, 64, 66
Warsaw Pact
dissolution of, 34, 249, 255, 268
former members of, 167
inclusion in NATO, 87, 238, 254
Weisskopf, Thomas E., 160
Western Europe
Eastern Europe and, 61
economic development of, 138, 181
business ventures will help, 207-211
European union and, 24, 46
opposition to, 58
U.S. relations and, 64, 67
German unification and, 69, 85, 102
Marshall Plan and, 141, 154, 172
NATO and, 173, 243, 247, 248, 270

286

tax policies, 225, 231
U.S. business investment in, 45, 245
Western European Union (WEU), 34, 239-240, 269
    can best provide European security, 249-256
West Germany (Federal Republic of Germany), 84, 87
    economy of, 96, 97, 98, 101
    European Community and, 23, 58, 69-70, 86
    in NATO, 253
    United States and, 89, 93
    war debt, 261-262
    see also Germany
Williams, Carol J., 185
Williams, Donald, 42-43
Winiecki, Jan, 175, 267
Wohlforth, Tim, 190
Women and Revolution, 115
women's rights, 115-121
World Bank, 168, 169, 203
    Eastern Europe and
        harms economies of, 175, 264-267

    tax reform and, 227, 229
World War II, 61, 131, 134, 178, 242

Yeltsin, Boris N., 47, 243, 247
Yugoslavia, 21, 167
    capitalist development in, 126, 189, 267
    civil war in, 29, 64, 126
        EC response to, 48, 70-71, 244
        German response to, 70-71, 73
        international criticism of, 72, 87
        will help end the fighting, 90, 91
        worsened the fighting, 104
    NATO and, 247, 270
    U.S. response to, 92, 243
    economic conditions in, 189, 200
    currency stabilization, 204
    ethnic tensions in, 133, 189, 251
    loans to, 264, 266
    U.S. aid to, 215

Zhivkov, Todor, 168, 219
Zielonka, Jan, 135

DATE DUE

GAYLORD   PRINTED IN U.S.A.

Frontiers of
Fundamental Physics 4